About tl

James grew up in Yorkshire and believes his earliest foray into the world of fiction was listening to his father's long and very entertaining bedtime stories. A love of the arts was nurtured in his school days and continued through university and beyond. Despite a deep set passion for film and theatre, history and fiction, such pleasures became gradually buried under other obligations – namely work and bills.

Things often change on chance, and a battlefield tour to France rekindled his love of history, but more importantly the stories of the ordinary people in war and conflict. Much travelled, books were never far away from James' economy seat back, and the desire to write refused to be supressed under the landslip of debt. So another trip, this time to the magical Moniack Mhor in Scotland proved to be life changing. In fact James was so far up the wrong mountain looking over the edge of nothingness that he claims it truly saved his life and reminded him who he set out to be.

Since then he has begun a steady descent to happiness. While he may find himself at the bottom of the right mountain, he is proud and humble to now call himself a writer. And very happy. If you have taken the time to read this far, then please buy the book as the staff will be wanting to lock up. James brings compassion and humour into everything he creates, and a very experienced eye for detail. Above all he loves to write. He hopes you feel that, as you read his work. Thank you. JS

Praise for The Whistle

"I have just finished reading 'The Whistle' - it is amazing! I have read a LOT of WWI, WWII and War books in general and this sits up there with the best of them. Also, I know absolutely nothing about football and farming... but I thought the scenes were beautifully described."

Andrew Mackay - Author of *the Young Lions* series (www.amazon.co.uk/Young-Lions-Andrew-Mackay/ dp/1456774379)

"James transports us seamlessly from the fertile fields of Sussex to the hell of the trenches of France through the eyes and heart of a young farm boy - captivating and emotionally compelling to the end. [As a farmer and a mother] I laughed, I cried, I wore their boots - beautifully written in every respect."

Anne Rae - Farmer & Women In Agriculture member

"Be in no doubt - the passion with which Sowerby portrays the trials and torments of his protagonists shines through in every scene. His belief that love and fear play out through the smallest of details, and the most human of dreams, is present on every page. A wonderfully poignant, unsentimental and understated story of people coping with events beyond their control."

Graham Bullen - Historical fiction writer

"Master story teller James Sowerby weaves a captivating tale of enduring themes of love and loss against the backdrop of the Great War. It is impossible for the reader not to be drawn in to the lives of the characters, engagingly and beautifully drawn in this powerful and fresh take on a familiar historical setting."

Bridget Mackinnon, Writer and Editorial Consultant

The Whistle

James Owen Sowerby

James Sowerby Publications

For my father

First published in the UK in 2018 by James Sowerby Publications

Content copyright @ James Owen Sowerby, 2018
Cover illustration copyright @ Lilly Louise Allen, 2018
Design and format copyright @ Kumiko Chesworth, 2018

For historical accuracy to underpin this novel, key events from the First World War are referred to. The majority of names and characters in this book however are entirely fictitious and any similarity to people, events and places past or present is entirely coincidental. Where certain names or locations have been used from 1914/15 these have been done by kind permission as per the acknowledgements, or due to the fact that the towns in particular remain today, but with that, most of the buildings named are again entirely fictitious.

A CIP catalogue record for this title is available from the British Library

ISBN 978-1-5272-3004-0

Cover design by Lilly Louise Allen, https://lillylouiseallen.com
Typeset by Kumiko Chesworth, www.amadori.design

Printed and bound in Great Britain by Biddles Books

WWI GERMAN RANKS

German Army Officers		
Generalfeldmarshall	GFM	General of the armies
Generaloberst	GenObst	General
Generalleutnant	Genltn	Lieutenant general
Generalmajor	Genmaj	Major general
Oberst	Obst	Colonel
Oberstleutnant	Obstltn	Lieutenant colonel
Major	Maj	Major
Hauptmann	Hptm	Captain
Oberleutnant	Obltn	First lieutenant
Leutnant	Ltn	Second lieutenant
Fähnrich	Fhn	Ensign/cadet
Kadett	Kdt	Cadet
German Army Enlisted Men		
Feldwebel-Leutnant	Fwltn	Sergeant Major Lieutenant (Warrant Officer)
Offizierstellvertreter	Offstv	(acting or deputy officer)
Feldwebel	Fw	Sergeant major
Wachtmeister	Wtm	Sergeant major (cavalry, artillery)
Vizefeldwebel	Vzfw	Sergeant 1st class (sergeant major)
Sergeant	Sgt	Sergeant
Unteroffizer	Uffz	Corporal
Oberjäger	Objäg	Corporal (Jäger only)
Obergefreiter	ObGefr	Acting corporal (artillery only)
Gefreiter	Gefr	Private 1st Class

WWI BRITISH RANKS

British Army Officers		
Field Marshal	FM	
General	Gen.	
Lieutenant General	Lt.Gen	
Major General	Maj.Gen	
Brigadier General	Brig.Gen	
Colonel	Col	
Brigadier	Brig	commander of a brigade
Major	Maj	
Captain	Capt	
Lieutenant	Lt	
Second Lieutenant	2/Lt	
British Army Enlisted Men		
Warrant Officer 1st Class	1/WO	
Warrant Officer 2nd Class	2/WO	
Sergeant Major	Sgt.Maj	
Sergeant	Sgt	
Corporal	Cpl	
Lance Corporal	L.Cpl	
Private	Pvt	

The Whistle

Prelude

The heat was stifling. Will awoke to a loud rattling noise and the sound of buzzing flies close to his ear. As his senses came to life, he felt a steady bumping every few seconds that must have jolted him awake. He was lying down, but his body seemed to be trembling uncontrollably. The constant shaking made him cough, and a nauseating pain spread agonisingly across his chest. He looked around, fearful in that moment, and found himself in a dark box that clattered about him. But it hurt to open his eyes, and now the memory of the gas returned and he could feel the panic rise within him.

Will became aware of the sound of groaning and realised there were other men lying near him. He turned to look the other way and hit his head on something hard. He felt at it in the gloom; it was wooden, like a coffin. Was he dead? Now there was a smell of smoke that enveloped and choked his senses and made him cough again. The pain was unbearable and he cried out involuntarily.

The box shook and the noise grew louder – cries in the dark mingling with rattles and bangs. His eyes were running from the smoke, and as he tried to sit he found himself strapped down. He began to feel claustrophobic. Panic gripped his limbs as he believed the box to be on fire. *Oh, God, he was being cremated alive!*

"I'm not dead," he shouted. "I'm alive!"

There was a loud whistle from somewhere outside. Will flinched at the sound. A man yelled out. No, not cremated. Was he in a trench still? An attack on its way? He recalled the explosion in the communications trench and wondered if he had in fact been buried there and his spirit had run away. His mind struggled to make sense of the nightmare, trying to remember.

Then a face appeared by him, and he screamed.

Chapter 1 – Sudden Death. 1914

Three long blasts on the whistle triggered a myriad of emotions. Some of the men took the moment to move among their nearest friends, cajoling them and trying to raise their spirits to fresh endeavours. Others stood, heads bowed, silently reflecting on what was to come. Their laboured breaths carried across the broken ground in front of them as they tried to gulp in as much precious oxygen as time allowed for the next action ahead. Along the line where previously people had stood in nervous silence, now the whistle awoke them and they were like school children released at last from the strict confines of their studies. Everywhere people broke out in shouts and challenges; arguments and debates; encouragements and praise as the noise levels grew. Then finally news filtered through that a decision had been made. The game would be decided with penalty kicks.

Will Davison stood towards the centre of the muddy pitch, hands on hips, with his blond hair plastered in sweat and mud. As if playing in a cup final had not been nerve-wracking enough, now he had to suffer this. The match had finished 0-0, despite his team's best efforts. Although he took pride in stopping Shoreham FC from scoring, Will felt suddenly sick and his head began to pound. He looked over to where his parents were watching.

Despite giving him the thumbs-up, Will could tell his dad was just as nervous as he was, and was probably too hoarse for any words of encouragement, having yelled his way through the match. His mum was nowhere to be seen, which was never a good sign. He recalled her saying, "I can't stand near your Dad at times like this, he makes me feel worse," and knew she was probably off with their dog somewhere. Will was giddy and sat down, his head between his knees. Unable to go to his parents for support, he suddenly felt very much alone.

Steyning FC had not made a final since the Sussex Youth Cup in the 1901/02 season, when they had emerged triumphant. In recent years, however, with the development of larger clubs such as Brighton and Horsham, they had struggled to reach the same heights as before. But here today against Shoreham, after a strong season in 1913/14 when they finished a respectable fourth in their league, they had a chance for glory.

It had been a funny old year for weather, hotter than expected but with sustained periods of torrential rain. This had played havoc with the usual timings of the crops, some of which should have been in the ground a month earlier. With half the players and spectators unavailable before today, the final had been delayed by two weeks while the farms round about caught up; and so now, here, unusually in the middle of June, the match had finally gone ahead.

But there was no way they could schedule a replay; and the respective managers agreed that to decide such a big game on the toss of a coin would be unfair. So they decided to have penalty kicks instead and each team would, in turn, take five penalties. Whoever scored the most would win the match. In 1914 this was quite a novel way to decide a game, but it added to the drama. Shoreham would go first and, as Will struggled not to throw up, the referee blew long and hard on the whistle to get the shoot-out underway.

The wind was relentless. The weather on the original date at the end of May had been glorious, but today of course it was blowing a gale, and the ball had to be constantly replaced on the penalty spot, which didn't help anyone's nerves. Despite that no one had missed with Shoreham leading 4-3, when Danny stepped forward to take the fourth kick for Steyning.

Danny Boyd had been with the team for five years and was a calming influence on the rest of them – a joker and a friend to the new lads, always the loudest voice in the changing room, despite being one of the smallest. He looked up at Will now with those deep-set dark eyes and said, "Now or never," which, in truth, he seemed to say about anything. Then he jogged confidently forward. Without hesitating he took the shot.

The ball was saved!

A voice in Will's head cried *Oh no…* Now the pressure really was on and the Steyning boys' hearts sank. Will was standing with his arms around his teammates, huddled together in the centre circle. He felt his friends sag, and despite not being the captain he knew he had to do something.

"This isn't over!" he shouted, and in that moment noticed his sickness recede, the leadership instincts that served him so well in matches reigniting within him. As the strength returned to his legs once more, Will smiled to himself, and hugged the lads either side of him to gee them up.

But it was still 4-3 to Shoreham, and now their fifth player stepped forward with a chance to win it. He walloped the ball hard and low towards the corner… and for a moment even the rain and wind seemed to pause as the ball flew towards its intended target. But Owen was equal to it, and with an incredible leap pushed it one-handed onto the post and out of danger. Time seemed to stop.

Owen Entwhistle roughly brushed the mop of ginger hair away from his babyish face with his gloves, those wild curls just as much a reminder of his mum's Welsh heritage as the name she had insisted on. He looked back across the field to where his teammates stood bunched together, and gave a small punch of satisfaction. It was as if that gesture broke the spell. The Steyning boys and their supporters erupted, punching the air and slapping each other on the back, as if they had already won the cup.

All the boys but one.

Will had taken a few steps forward. He was yet to take a penalty and knew he must score to keep them in the match. For him the shouts were merely a distraction. As he took the long, lonely walk forward he shut them out of his mind. He placed the ball carefully on the spot and looked up. The keeper seemed to fill the frame of the goal. Tall, slim, his legs were strong and his gaze hard; piercing blue eyes betrayed no sign of nerves. He had already saved one penalty, and several other good shots in the match. *Keep focused,* Will told himself; *Pick a spot and go for it.*

His heart was pounding now, so loud he felt that it must surely be heard by everyone nearby. He touched the team badge on his shirt for luck, as he always did to calm himself at the start of a game, and he looked at the referee as he put the whistle to his lips. It was raining hard again now. Heavy drops, like falling stones, splashed and stung in equal measure, but Will wiped them from his face, knowing he must ignore everything and just focus on the ball and where he was going to shoot. He saw a drop explode in a puddle near the penalty spot, sending wet dark splashes onto the mud-caked ball. Will registered the place in his mind so he didn't step there and slip.

He took a deep breath, and in the profound silence that followed he heard Danny shout, "Now or never, Will!" The voice seemed a mile away, as if in a dream. Then the whistle blew and he took a stride forward, eyes fixed firmly on the ball.

There was a huge roar, as if a thousand voices were unleashed at once, and everywhere the whistle seemed to echo on and on. Will looked up, and just for a moment had a premonition of soldiers massing around him and the goalkeeper, rifle in hand, urging him forward. He shook his head, confused at the ridiculous image, and then shivered unexpectedly despite the cold. "Someone's walked over your grave William," his grandma would have said.

The whistle blew again and he saw the referee give a firm wave of the hand, beckoning him to take the kick. He looked up through the pelting rain and there were no soldiers, only the man-mountain of a keeper standing guard between the posts. Will's eyes narrowed and he strode forward. Now or never indeed, he thought, and struck the ball hard and true. It flew like a rocket with unerring accuracy towards its intended point. Before the keeper even twitched, it had thumped into the back of the net with a deep thud. Will punched the air with delight and jogged back to his waiting teammates.

"Never doubted you for a second," Danny grinned, and several of the boys patted Will on the back before they linked arms again. Now it was sudden-death time.

The momentum had swung back their way. Without doubt playing the final in their home town now came into its own – the right having been won on the toss of a coin. Sure enough the next Shoreham player looked anything but confident as he trudged forward in the rain for their sixth kick, running a gauntlet of jeers from the side line. Will realised it was John Banstead, the fishmonger's assistant, who had been sent off in their last league game for making a late lunging tackle on Tommy. John was a pleasant lad with a very red complexion, and on the odd occasion Will's family had a trip to the beach, he always had a cheery smile for his dad when they bought fish. For some reason the people John worked with, including his younger brother Herbert, called him Bod; but Will never knew why.

Despite being nearly twenty, 'Bod' was shy, and not the best footballer in the world; and Will noticed now he also had an unusual gait and walked as if limping. *Funny the things you observe in times like this*, he mused.

Owen didn't move. He just stared at him. And he kept staring as Bod ran up for his kick. In fact Will's heart was in his mouth, because Owen didn't flinch as the kick was taken. *Dive Owen for god's sake!* But by not moving Owen caused Bod to pause, and in doing so stumble into the kick and drive it wide. The Steyning boys cheered. Will let out a deep sigh of relief and punched the air once more.

Archie Bunden – at six feet four, and half as wide – was every bit the archetypal centre half. An amateur boxer in his youth, he had come late into the game, but excelled in the role amid the mud and madness of amateur football. His bearded features and imposing bulk made him look far older, anyway. Within a couple of years he had been made captain of the Steyning boys. If anyone else had nurtured claims to the captaincy, they had probably thought better of it. Now, at almost nineteen years old, it was his last season before he would go into the first team, for whom he had already made guest appearances for them several times over the last year.

"Go on, Bunny," Danny shouted, and the boys broke into a collective roar. After taking one look at Archie when he had first arrived in training, Danny had given him the nickname 'Bunny'. The hefty defender was anything but a small, timid rabbit, but the name had stuck and he liked it now. Archie picked up the ball. As he placed it on the spot he turned to his teammates, half hidden in the rain behind him, and roared "Steyning!" at the top of his voice.

Will felt a surge of pride. As the ref blew his whistle, he was already running forward. Archie blasted the ball so hard into the back of the net that it flew back out, hitting the Shoreham keeper on the back of the head and knocking him to the floor again.

Afterwards, Will could never recall what he did for the next few minutes in the pandemonium of success. Players were running, jumping, bellowing and hugging everyone in their sheer delight. Amid shouts of "Bunny!" Archie was bundled to the ground, (which took about six of them, led by Danny), and then it was all arms and legs in a tangle of wild celebrations. Will remembered belatedly to shake the hands of some of the devastated Shoreham lads. He called "Thanks, Ref," as he saw the man with the whistle walking quietly back to his bike, lit cigarette in hand. Will watched the bald official stroll off humming a tune he had heard his dad singing more than once during milking time, though the name of it now escaped him.

The rain paused and a liquid sun risked a look from behind the darkening clouds. The parents and supporters joined in the celebrations, coming over to mingle with the players and lifting one or two aloft on their shoulders. A lone figure caught Will's eye and he saw his dad standing, hands in pockets, a little way back from the line, appearing to take no interest. His broad frame was unmistakeable even though he was standing apart from the others. Will knew his dad was looking at him though, and nodded. He gave Will a thumbs-up in salute. He thought he heard his father shout something too, but it was lost in the noise and wind, and so Will just gave the same signal back. There would be time for congratulations later.

He knew his dad was crying with pride. He didn't have to be close to see it, nor would Harold Davison want Will to see him cry, the tears falling into the rain to be washed away without trace. So Will flashed a smile, as he knew that was all his father needed, and then turned and ran off, jumping on his friend Tommy's back with a cry of "Yes!" In seconds the whole team was bundling on them instead, laughing and shouting in the mud.

*

"Congratulations, Archie," the league chairman said, warmly shaking the young man's hand, as he had already done with the other Steyning boys. They now stood in anticipation to the left of the trophy table hastily brought out from the Star Inn nearby. "A fine win for you and your team."

"Thank you, sir,'" Archie replied, in as formal a tone as he could muster for a factory lad. He then shook his manager's hand, before joining the other boys.

"Well done, Bunny, bloody brilliant," his manager Tony said, slapping him on his broad shoulders with as much impact as a fly biting a bull. Archie smiled, and closed his eyes for a moment, letting the pale sun tease his square-jawed face. Then he walked the few strides to his teammates and without a pause raised the trophy high into the damp air. The noise was deafening.

Chapter 2 - Teammates

It was Sunday 28th June, and two weeks had passed since the glorious events of the cup final. Will was lying in bed reading about a cowboy shoot-out in the Wild West, in a book that his grandma had given him – but he wasn't concentrating. He was looking over at the table in the corner where his latest football trophy was standing in pride of place among the pack. He had twenty-six prizes now and he was still only seventeen.

Fred stirred in the bunk below and sat up, hitting his head as he did and moaning incoherently. He often banged his head. Will just smiled and sighed, merely annoyed that the thump under his mattress had disturbed his daydream of once again striding up to crack his penalty home. It got better every time he imagined it, and today he was scoring the winning goal...

At thirteen, Fred was the youngest of four brothers, with wild, unkempt brown hair that he made no attempt to control. He had his mother's soulful brown eyes and they made him even more special to her, more than just being the 'baby' of the family. Fred shared the attic room with Will.

A piece of torn paper, tossed on a sudden draught, caught Will's eye and stopped his day dreaming. He realised it was part of the wrapping from the chocolate his dad had given him as a special treat for winning. Will loved chocolate more than anything in the world, but he tried to savour it as his mum asked, one piece at a time. Though of course the pleadings of his brothers had soon led to him sharing it out, and it hadn't lasted an hour.

"Come on Will," David had said with an impish grin, "who plays with you in the yard and makes you so good?"

"Yeh," agreed Fred, "we are your proper teammates!"

"We'd share our chocolate with you," David continued with his sweetest face.

Will knew they would have said anything to get the chocolate, but he did enjoy kicking around with them as the evenings grew longer, if only to delay bedtime, and he succumbed.

The pleasant memory was disrupted by Fred's usual morning grumblings. He was looking forward to having the blue room all to himself if David also left home; but sadly David seemed bent on farming and wanted to stay. *God knows why*, Will thought. He hated farming, and only did the bare minimum of chores before sneaking off to kick a ball against a barn wall here or a stone wall there.

David was nineteen, and the second of the four boys, still occupying the blue room on the first floor that he had shared with their eldest brother James. That was before James had gone up to London two years ago to work for the Vinter's Company as an apprentice. His excellent school results had brought him to the attention of the chair of governors Charles Sanderson, who had significant property around Steyning. Charles had recommended James to a business colleague in London.

A shout from downstairs triggered a long-established alarm bell in Will's subconscious – and sure enough there was a responsive cry and a thump from downstairs as David launched himself out of bed. *It was too early for church, and none of them ran for that*, Will pondered.

Bacon! Of course! Sunday morning! What was he thinking?

His mother's shout created the usual stampede. Will leapt off the top bunk, pushing Fred out of the way with a laugh and a shout.

"Not fair!" Fred wailed, as he set off in pursuit.

The stairs echoed with the sound of three pairs of feet. The noise made Harold think of the shooters out in Picket Woods when the season was open. Repetitive muffled thumps carried on the wind then too, mixed with the occasional excited bark from the retrievers as Squire Goodman and his family enjoyed the fruits of their estate; game-shooting with their landed neighbours.

Sally added her bark to this sudden commotion that had disturbed her rest by the fire. She was smart enough to understand routine, and she knew that this smell and sound combined meant 'leftovers'. She wagged her tail with renewed energy to ensure they noticed she was there. The boys charged into the room in a tangle, David holding

Will back, and Fred hanging on to David's nightshirt.

"That's quite enough of that racket for a Sunday morning, you three," Agnes stated in a stern voice that stopped them all in their tracks. "And on the Sabbath too! Too much of your father in you, that's the trouble," she added, expecting some support from the top of the table. None came of course. Agnes sighed and went back to sorting the eggs out on the stove. She hummed contentedly though relishing Sunday mornings when all her 'boys' were about her.

Looking out of the back window for a moment to where the sheets strained on the line, Agnes thought of James and hoped he was all right and being properly fed in his new lodgings. She had been anxious about letting her first-born go up to 'town', but along with her husband shared understandable pride in his success. It certainly gave her bragging rights in the ladies' circle. Outside, a pillow case managed to shake off one of its wooden pegs and swung triumphantly about, but Agnes just smiled, lost in a memory of the first church meeting after James had moved to London…

"He's working for one of the twelve great Livery Houses you know," she had announced while serving teas for the parish committee. "And James a farmer's son. Who would have thought it?" Her twinkling brown eyes lit up her still-youthful face as she pushed long dark curls away from her forehead. It was the same endearing gesture that had made her future husband's heart skip a beat some twenty-odd years ago, leading him to spill beer down his shirt on their first date.

She was among friends in the committee, so although she endured gentle teasing she was also regaled with praise and smiles, no matter how many times she mentioned it. In truth they were proud that one of their little community had been given such an opportunity, even if that pride mingled with the odd twinge of jealousy regarding their own offspring.

Only one person was an exception. Celia Goodman, the chairwoman and choir mistress, and sister-in-law of Beeding Manor's estate-owner, made no secret of her disapproval that a working boy had made good.

"Law of averages I suppose," she announced in that clipped

choral tone she adopted for formal meetings, on hearing the news. Celia sniffed disdainfully over a cheese scone and continued. "I mean, if enough of them take the exams, one or two are bound to squeak through and get these chances, aren't they?" A couple of her weaker peers, who always agreed with whoever was speaking, nodded politely. Encouraged by that she added, "I just hope they don't fall flat on their face and embarrass us all!" Celia ensured her comments were just loud enough to be overheard.

Agnes didn't care. James was there and that's all that mattered. But whenever she was on tea duty she made sure to mention how well he was doing, just as she was pouring Celia's tea; letting the sugar drop from high enough to splash into the saucer. This was an unforgivable sin in life's upper circles.

"Oh, I am sorry, Celia," she said with a smile sweeter than any sugar. And she moved on, humming to herself, knowing the choir mistress' eyes were burning into the back of her neck.

*

Will attacked the bacon and eggs ravenously, squashing them into a large chunk of locally made bread.

"Slow down Will," Harold said, looking up from the harness he was working on, before reaching for a piece of bacon too and chewing it absent-mindedly. Her husband's stern tone broke Agnes' smiling reverie and she switched back into her mothering role rounding on the chaotic scene.

"And you shouldn't have that thing at the table either," Agnes admonished, putting more eggs onto the serving plate in the middle of the table, and cuffing her husband on the shoulder. "Put it away while you eat."

Harold exhaled with a shrug of his broad shoulders and laid the harness down, while Will took the opportunity to stuff more bacon into his mouth unchallenged.

"Old Gettings from the smithy reckons that in Brighton there's talk of war," he began, now his mind was off the repair, as the table rattled to the sound of his children's frenzied eating. "Told us in the Star Inn last night he had someone from down that way stop by when his horse threw a shoe, and this chap said the town was full of it. European treaties or something..." He brought a serious tone to the breakfast, continuing to talk about what had been said and what it meant for England. For a moment the boys listened without focusing on the words, before looking at their mum for silent permission to get down.

Agnes knew the time with her boys was already over and she interrupted her husband. "The breakfast table is not the time to talk of war," she announced. "And you know as well as I do that old Gettings always says there's something happening over the water when he's had half a dozen ales. All of you away and get ready for church. And don't make me have to call you twice when it's time to go."

"Yes, true enough," Harold replied with a laugh, picking up the harness again as the boys left more quietly than they had entered, with warm grateful smiles to their mum.

Fred turned back to give his mother a hug, smelling the flour on her apron as she pressed him close and kissed the top of his head. "Make sure you eat too, Mum," he said, noticing there was barely anything left on the table.

"Oh, I've picked as I went along," she replied, the lie coming easily in order to stop her son from worrying. She stooped to kiss her husband on the cheek, and Fred knew it was time to make himself scarce. He followed his brothers upstairs.

*

Later, as the Davisons left the church and turned into Steyning high street for their lunchtime walk, Will asked if he could go over to Tommy's and kick a ball. "No," Agnes had replied, as she did every Sunday. "Not today, it's a day of rest. Besides, I have jobs for you to do."

"How is that a day of rest then?" he muttered indignantly, his dad instantly cuffing him around the shoulders.

"Don't answer back to your Mum, William. You know today is a family day. You play enough football as it is, and those cows won't milk themselves."

"Sorry," Will muttered sulkily, reaching back to rub his shoulders, though it had hardly been a heavy slap.

Fred noticed his mum was now chatting to one of the committee about next week's cake rota.

"Daphne has a heavy cold and might not be up to it," Gladys Nightingale could be heard to fret.

So Fred piped up, emboldened. "Why do we have to do the same thing every week?"

Will noticed not for the first time, that as the youngest, Fred was given considerably more slack than the rest of them, and no admonishment came his way. But their father still replied sternly.

"Because we do. It's good to have routine. It's what keeps this country ticking over. Everyone knowing what's happening, and when. Like the seasons on the farm. We can't change when we sow and harvest, can we, Freddie, eh? Nor when the lambs are born. It would cause chaos."

Harold softened, hugging Fred in close. He ruffled his youngest son's hair. Will, wondered if his dad was right. *He liked routine, and the comfort of it. And life was good, so why worry?*

*

At the very moment the Davisons turned off towards Mill Road, past the bakery, an event of immense consequence took place far away in the city of Sarajevo. Archduke Franz Ferdinand of Austria, visiting the city with his wife, Sophie, was fatally shot by an assassin. The murdered man was someone Will had never heard of, and if he had heard the word 'Sarajevo' it was only because it was one of those obscure sort of places that Gettings was always talking about in the pub; conversations that Harold would duly repeat at the farmhouse table. Yet this one violent action would unravel all the order and routine in Europe for the next four years and change the lives of Will, his family, and millions more for ever.

Chapter 3 – The Kick-Off

Emmie snorted, and her warm breath coated Will's face with a stench of half-chewed grass and God-knows-what else that made him recoil. "Oh, Dad, she stinks," Will shouted. He looked along the fattened flank of the cow to where his dad half sat, half knelt, milking the last of the herd.

"You should try being at this end young William," Harold replied with a raise of his eyes. "The more she squirts, the more she farts, I'm sure of it!" In acknowledgement of being the centre of attention, Emmie let out another large blast of wind that echoed round the three-sided barn in the early hours, and then she licked Will's chest contentedly before reaching down to take another mouthful of hay from the byre.

"Cor, Will what did you have for breakfast?" Fred shouted, as he passed the open door, laden with a bag of eggs, still warm despite the unusually chilly start to the day. He put his hand to his nose to emphasise the point, screwing up his face and giggling – until the eggs unbalanced in his other hand, and he lurched forward with a startled expression, knowing that to drop them would mean a severe chiding.

Harold, somewhat unusually, laughed for a moment at his son's jibes before shouting after Fred, "You just mind what you're doing, boy, or you'll be the one going without."

Agnes called "Freddie" from the old side door. That meant *hurry up,* and he scurried off under this double assault from his parents, one hand gripping the bag tightly and the other underneath weaving about in case any dropped, as his dad watched him go with a shake of his head.

"Right, you smelly old sod, that's us done," he said, arching his back as he stood up. And with a wink to his son added, "I was talking to Emmie of course!"

16

"Oh, ha ha," Will replied, wiping his face on the rag hanging over the stall nearby.

"Walk her down with the others, lad," his dad said, and he gave a rare affectionate squeeze on Will's shoulder, pushing Emmie forwards towards the open side of the barn as he did. "I'm away up to the top field to help David with the sheep before breakfast."

They both paused at the entrance, as Emmie started to aimlessly clop across the yard. The sound of David's shouts and whistles working the flock with Sally carried to them over the misty morning air. Further away the old grain-barn door clanged in the wind behind them, its hinges overdue for repair.

"How's David doing?' Will asked, hoping to delay this rare moment when he had his dad's full attention.

"Not too bad," Harold replied, "though he hasn't the natural talent of James. Born leader that one. But wasted among all them city folk. Should be working a herd, not a pen."

Then, aware he was speaking private thoughts out loud, Harold shook his head and put his old cloth cap back on, stretching to get his cigarettes from the wall where he'd put them an hour ago. "You better use that famous speed of yours to get after the cows, Will, or they'll be out of the front gate and up Mill Road!" Will saw Emmie had no intention of wandering too far from the nearest grassy bank, but he made a show of running after her for his father's sake.

Harold watched him go, annoyed he had voiced his views to Will. He did miss James. His blond locks and rosy face still held much of the little lad who'd sat on the wall as a young boy and watched with wide-eyed wonder as his father milked the cows. He'd always thought that James would stay, but it was David who quietly grew to love the place under his older brother's shadow, while James yearned for adventure. In truth, Harold Davison was proud beyond measure that his lad had turned out so clever. *God knows how! It's his mother's brains, that's for sure,* he thought, as he puffed on the cigarette once more before discarding it a few yards in front of him. It was dispatched under his milk-coated wellies, as he began the well-trodden path up to the top field where Sally's barks signalled things were not under control.

He began to sing quietly to himself, but, in the still of the new dawn, the voice carried to Will.

"Oh Mary, this London's a wonderful sight,
There's people here working by day and by night..."

"What's that you're singing, Dad?" Will shouted up. His father paused for a moment and looked back.

"Mountains of Mourne," Will. A favourite of your Mum's." And then he turned on his heels and carried on without waiting for any further comment from his son. He didn't know all the words so he hummed the parts in between before breaking into the main chorus:

"...But for all that I've found there I might as well be,
Where the Mountains of Mourne sweep down to the sea."

Will suddenly realised it was the tune the referee had been humming as he walked away after their cup final match. *That's the one,* he thought, with a satisfied smile.

It was six a.m. and a starling trumpeted dawn's arrival. The summer sun was already up and awake, as the farm began its daily life all over again. But to Will the days were just a millstone of routine, grinding him down every day. He lived for the precious moments when he got out onto the village green for impromptu kickabouts with his mates. And so the days passed with farming and football, without too much excitement except perhaps once when Will scored a last-minute winner against Archie's team and got chased all the way home!

But nothing would break the monotony in a way this August morning would, as more birds joined the starling's cry.

*

Later that morning after Emmie and her own 'ladies' circle' had been safely restored to their pasture, the kitchen was rocking under a bombardment of noise once more. Clattering plates and lively voices competed with each other to create the din – the Davisons being no different from most families in the village. A brief respite in the chatter and scraping of knives on plates allowed the school bell's clang to penetrate.

"Oh, it only seems like yesterday you were all off up the road to school," Agnes said, ruffling Fred's hair, which did little to alter its chaotic appearance.

"Don't start, Mum," David replied, snatching the last of the bread from the table near his father, before Fred could get it, and smearing homemade gooseberry jam across the bread's jagged surface. He bit into it with a triumphant smirk at Fred, chewing noisily.

"Mouth closed, David," Agnes chided, and Fred mouthed the words silently at him again across the table, regaining some small triumph.

It was a year since Fred had finished school. Sometimes Agnes wished they could keep studying beyond the age of twelve, but she loved having them home and around to help. David had left at twelve too, more suited to farm life than books. Will should have stayed on like James did, but his heart wasn't in it. They managed to keep him there until he was fourteen, but he longed for the open fields. Whatever sport the school provided, it was not enough to compensate for the hours imprisoned in that draughty, dank classroom, lined up on benches well worn by generations of occupancy.

Will looked up from the remnants of his egg. "What's the date today?" he asked generally to the table.

"Fourth of August," his dad replied without breaking his gaze from the Farmer's Union leaflet he had acquired at the Star Inn last night. He was struggling to recall how he came to have it in his possession, though the dull ache reverberating around his head reminded him of an unusually rowdy Monday night's drinking. *Bloody Bill Yates and his ale nights,* he mused. *He's probably still in bed while the rest of the world's been up three hours.*

Will spoke again: "There's no school in August. Why's the bell ringing?"

The Davisons stopped.

Harold put the leaflet down carefully and stood up to walk to the old side door. He opened it and paused to listen to the bell tolling away more clearly now, as if in doing so it would answer his son's question. At that moment the church bell struck up in answer and Harold looked at his wife and frowned. He reached for his fading

19

brown boots, feeling the familiar twinge in his right side as he did.

"I'll go take a look over the cows, love," he said to his wife, who had joined him at the door, "and then have a wander down the street and see what the noise is all about."

"All right" she said with a concerned smile, drying a dish from the cluttered sink as she did so. She turned to go back inside to the boys when a shout from the gate made them both start. It was Bill Yates.

"Davison, Davison!" he was shouting, waving a spotted handkerchief above his head for some strange reason, as he pushed the main gate open with some effort.

At fifty eight, Bill Yates was every bit the local landlord. As round as a ball with a head to match in smaller proportions, he had a wide red nose that betrayed years of profit drunk away in the early hours. He was bald save for two small patches of hair on either side of his head behind his ears, and could barely muster a walk without gasping for breath most days. Normally he would stay wedged behind the main bar, entertaining his customers with embellished tales of his youth.

As he approached the house, his faded checked waistcoat flapped around an old white shirt, the two sides having given up years ago trying to meet anywhere near the middle of his huge stomach. It gave him the look of those circus masters that sometimes came to Horsham Park, or so it seemed to the boys, who had seen the circus once or twice when they were young. All that was missing was a top hat and tails. Despite his girth he was actually attempting to run up the yard, causing Will's parents to look at each other in bemusement.

"Davison! It's all kicking off!"

His shouting caused the boys to join their father outside. Will was excited by the possibility that there was a match somewhere being played that was 'kicking off'. Sally woke from her slumber and shot forward in the kitchen, barking as she did. David managed to grab her in time, closing the bottom part of the door to keep her in.

Alerted by the continued warning shouts from Sally, Bill stopped just short of the amused group and took a wheezing breath for a moment to regain himself. He held a hand in the air to silently ask for a moment.

"It's war" he said, and without waiting for a reaction went on: "Germany's declared war on France and Belgium, and Britain's declared war on Germany as a result. The vicar's got the news from the big house and now he's ringing the bell like a madman. Headmaster's at it too. Apparently the whole of Europe is involved." He paused to let his words sink in, but also to try and fill his tar-stained lungs with air, mopping his brow as he did. "Russia too," he added after a short, raking cough made him pause for a moment while it passed.

"Russia too…" Agnes murmured, as if coming to from a dream. "You'd better come in, Bill."

Agnes ushered the boys inside and made a space for him at the table. Harold propped himself against the door frame, cigarette resting in his left fingers, and in a quiet voice simply said, "Is it true?"

Bill looked at him. For once his wheezing had stopped, and he replied almost formally: "Yes, Harold. We are at war."

Chapter 4 – The Big Crowd

The Davisons were all out at the fete. In fact the whole town seemed to have turned out this year, as if in mutual understanding that this might be the last summer fair of its kind. The weather certainly added to that, the deep blue sky devoid of cloud as far as the eye could see.

The town band was in full flow, resplendent in their smart red uniforms with gold braid trimmings. With precious little shade for them in the bandstand, the afternoon sun offered no mercy to the uniformed group whose faces began to resemble their uniforms. Despite the heat they played on enthusiastically, and the nearby crowd clapped and cheered.

Children roared about in all directions, some trailing newly bought kites with multi-coloured ribbons. Others watched the various sideshows or begged their parents for a go on one of the many stalls. Jugglers, clowns and kite-sellers all vied for attention on this glorious Saturday afternoon in August. Without doubt the weather also contributed to a much bigger crowd than normal. The vicar was especially pleased with what this would mean to the contributions to the church roof fund, and allowed himself to sample a large slice of chocolate cake in his official capacity as 'Head Judge.'

Fred dragged his parents over to where a Punch and Judy show was just about to start, and David took the chance to go and watch some burly man daring people to smash a hammer on a bag and make a bell ring at the top. Young men queued to impress sweethearts, no doubt emboldened by the local ale flowing freely in the nearby beer tent, where men old and young were discussing the German threat with rising patriotism.

Will noticed that a group of lads had a football over on the green. He could see Tommy and Owen and a few others he didn't recognise, and he tugged at his father's arm with a pleading look. Harold was distracted. The news from Bill still forefront in his mind.

"Yes, go on," he said snapping out of his thoughts, "but no wandering off!"

"And try and stay clean for once," Agnes added, before glancing back to check that David was all right.

David joined the queue with the other would-be strongmen. It was clearly harder than it looked; as so far no one had managed to hit the bell. Every time someone failed, the burly stallholder had stepped forward and clobbered it casually himself, making the clanger shoot to the top with a loud 'dong' that brought more and more people over to try their luck. David decided there must be a catch. But he was determined to have a go.

With a shout of "Hard luck, feller," the muscular showman looked round. "Who's next, then?"

Now he was much closer, David saw that the stallholder's best years were behind him. He had obviously been a bare-knuckle fighter or something similar previously, as was attested to by the reshaped nose and missing teeth. There was also a worrying scar behind his right ear. The man bared his remaining yellow teeth and said loudly, "Here's a strapping feller. Fancy a go?"

"Yes, please," David replied nervously, wishing for once his dad was nearby, and noting from the accent that the man was plainly from East London.

"Two farthings then, me old china."

"I thought it was one?" David replied, regretting having asked as soon as the words left his mouth.

Lowering his voice, the man replied, "No, them was me beginner's rates to get the punters interested." He leaned in even closer so as not to be overheard, his gin-soaked breath caressing David's cheek. "It's two now all right, but you win a sixpence." Then, raising his voice he said, "So, you in, or having second thoughts in front of the ladies?" People jeered, and David handed over the money, his confidence draining. He saw the man reach round behind the pole and clearly do something. Undeterred he got ready to swing. As he raised the hammer, a voice stopped him.

"Straight and true like the posts back home, lad."

He looked around and his dad was there, the commotion round the stall having drawn him away from the shrieks of Mr Punch. Harold nodded and stepped forward to offer his hand to the ex-boxer by the bell pole. The man spontaneously moved his hand to shake, and David took his moment to whack the pad, sending the clanger right up to the top.

'Dong!'

David shouted and his father smiled. The man frowned, but as Harold fixed him with a firm stare he re-adopted his showman's persona and shouted, "Cor blimey, we have a winner, ladies and gentlemen! It's that easy. There's your two pennies, mate."

David started to protest, but Harold stepped in and looking the man directly in the eye said calmly, "Sixpence, I think, was the prize."

His fixed stare unnerved the stallholder. "Gawd, of course guv'nor. It's this heat you know, frazzles me brain." And with a penitent gap-toothed smile he added, "There you go, son, go and treat your Mum."

The crowd's cheering distracted Will for a moment from watching the impromptu football game. He smiled as he saw his father and David triumphantly walking away. The stallholder was shouting, "Right then, nothing too it. Who's next? Two farthings a hit gentlemen." He was tempted to go over and celebrate with them, but the pull of a 'kickabout' was too strong and he span back to the game.

It was then that he noticed a slim, brown-haired girl watching him from the corner of the nearby cake tent. Will wondered how long she had been there. He looked behind him to see if she could be watching anyone else, but there was no one behind him. As he turned back to face her again, she smiled. He blushed, and regretted not seeking the sanctuary of his parents' company. He pretended to focus on the game, but from the corner of his eye he was aware of her walking over.

The melee of the game came his way and, as the girl approached, a tackle close by span the ball out of play. Will effortlessly trapped the ball dead under his foot before flicking it back to one of the players.

"Oh, hey, Davison," said a slightly older-looking lad who clearly wasn't from the town. "You play for Steyning, right? Won the cup?"

"Yes, that's right," he replied.

"Eddie," the boy said, nodding. "I'm from Storrington. Over visiting my cousins. We saw your game when we were here last. June wasn't it?"

Will nodded, realising the girl was still standing next to him.

"This your sister?" Eddie enquired with a smirk.

"What? Oh, no," said Will, blushing once more. "I don't know her," he stuttered.

Eddie looked at the girl for a moment and then back at Will. "Oh, is that right?" he remarked, with a wide grin that made his whole face light up. Probably a couple of years older than Will, Eddie was aware that something unusual was occurring, and he backed off. "Well, when you've finished talking to strangers, come and have a kick." He booted the ball back into play and jogged after it, shouting "We've got Davison when he joins in."

"Hello, Davison." The girl's voice was soft and with a hint of tease about it. She offered her hand. "I'm Alice." Her smile was as disarming as her voice. She spoke with a beautiful rounded accent, and Will knew for sure that she must go to a private school somewhere.

"Hello," he said, his voice hoarse and unforgiving. He cleared his throat and, taking her hand, said "My name's Will."

"Hello, Will," she replied once more, smiling even brighter than the first time. "Do you want to go and play?"

He noted the teasing slant to her question again. "Er, well, in a minute."

She giggled, and he smiled awkwardly. They stood there for a moment before she said, "Would you like some chocolate cake?"

His head spun round at the mention of the one thing that might tear him away from his beloved football, and he nodded enthusiastically.

"Right, the church tent it is," she announced loudly and boldly taking his arm without asking, marched him over to the pastel-shaded tent she had just come from. Inside the committee ladies were serving all manner of goodies. Will's head was a mess of panicked thoughts, but the lure of chocolate kept him focused.

They sat at a table inside, where the cool shade brought instant relief from the heat, although Will could still feel his face burning up. Gladys Nightingale, the organist from Mouse Lane, approached demurely to take an order. Her voice resembled a squeaking mouse, and Will thought it was highly appropriate where she lived, her being diminutive in stature too.

"Two glasses of lemonade and a large slice of your best chocolate cake please Mrs Nightingale," Alice said, before adding, "and two forks if you wouldn't mind."

"Of course, Alice, nice to see you looking after our young sportsmen," Gladys replied pleasantly. "Do give my regards to Lady Pevensey, won't you?" she said, before walking off to the tables at the rear, where the ladies were busying themselves with the teas. Will frowned at the reference but decided not to ask.

Smiling, Alice turned back to look at Will. "The homemade chocolate cakes are delicious, but the slices are enormous. So one is more than sufficient, especially with you in training, and me watching my figure!" Will was aware he had been staring at her while she ordered. He started to say something about her not needing to worry about her figure, but then got embarrassed and mumbled a thanks, glancing away.

Alice touched his hand lightly and he jumped, looking back at her with renewed courage. "Thank you, Will, that is so kind of you to say."

In the months ahead Will would remember these soft touches, and how at ease she was with herself and others – mature beyond her years. Alice's light brown hair shone like the freshly dewed wallflowers in the early morning sun that transformed the old farm buildings everywhere they touched. Her pale blue eyes and light complexion only enhanced her bewitching demeanour. She wore a white summer dress that fell to her ankles in waves, deftly designed to accentuate her perfectly proportioned body. Will guessed she was a few inches shorter than him, but wore heeled boots that heightened her poise. His mind recalled how she had walked towards him with a grace unseen among the local farming girls. She was quite simply a vision of beauty.

She studied him for a moment. "How old are you Will?"

"Seventeen, eighteen in January."

"Oh that's ages away. Though you are older than you look. My brother is seventeen too, isn't that a coincidence? I am nineteen, although I can pass for twenty one at a ball. You probably thought that anyway," she stated, and without waiting for an answer continued to chat confidently. "I was at boarding school in Farlington, near Haywards Heath until the summer. Have you heard of it? I'm back at the family home in Pevensey now and enjoying my freedom once more..."

Alice smiled at her little joke and paused to ensure he was listening. Will was aware she was speaking and that occasionally he answered, but in truth the rest seemed to pass as if in a dream. He clung to the succulent tone of her words like a bee attached to nectar.

"Come on, tuck in, I thought you wanted it."

"Hmmm?" Will said dreamily, and then realised Alice had stopped speaking. She was gesturing with a fork at the large slice of cake that had magically appeared between them. "Oh, sorry," he mumbled, and took a swig of the lemonade while he composed himself. He self-consciously cut into the cake from his side, noticing the three-layered texture of sponge and chocolate icing with some kind of pink-iced decoration and cream on top. It crumbled as he did so, but he managed to get some into his mouth and it melted on his tongue.

Alice seemed to eat with the same grace and poise she carried with her in all her movements, and maintained a smile as she did so.

"Nice?"

"Delicious" he replied enthusiastically, taking a larger chunk than the first time as he relaxed. "How come you're at the fete today, then?" he asked her, feeling more confident.

"Would you rather I wasn't?" she replied with a gently mocking smile. Will was instantly disconcerted, and he shook his head. She laughed. "Sorry, I'm teasing you. My brother is at Lancing College. He's been a boarder there in the sixth form and we came to collect him as he's with the CCF, and was on exercise for a week, running around in the woods or something silly during the school holidays.

27

He wants to be an officer, I think. He's very dashing in his uniform, but I'm not sure if he's cut out for it. Mother is worried." She lost her smile momentarily.

"CCF?" he offered, to break the moment.

"Oh, sorry, Combined Cadet Force. All the big schools have them these days. Army, Navy, you know," Alice explained with a wave of her napkin, her smile returning to its rightful place.

"Ah, yes," said Will, although he didn't know, having left school at fourteen, and never having been in anything, not even the local church boys club.

"Anyway, Father wanted to speak to some people here while we were in the area," Alice continued. "Business matters. He thought the fete might be a little distraction for us while he did."

"So this is where you are hiding, William. I thought I told you to stay close."

The sound of his dad's voice made Will jump up, and he knocked his lemonade glass over. He looked round to see his whole family standing there as he tried to dab the lemonade up unsuccessfully while mumbling "sorry." His mother stepped in with a handkerchief and instantly began to regain control.

Ignoring the table scene Harold continued. "We've been looking for you for a while, lad. The boys at the football said you'd gone here with…a girl." He let his voice linger on the last point and switched his gaze to Alice, who had remained sitting opposite. She rose with a smile and curtsied.

"You must be William's parents. I'm Alice Pevensey. I'm very pleased to meet you." She offered her hand. Will saw his dad hesitate and almost stutter, and was amazed at the reaction. He noted she used his full name too, picking up on the formal tone of his dad. It bothered him and he wished it didn't.

Harold recovered and took the delicate hand before asking "Pevensey? Any relation to John Pevensey, the MP?"

"Yes, he's my father," Alice replied sweetly, "he's here today with my mother, and brother Philip."

Harold glanced at his wife, who smiled appreciatively and nodded almost imperceptibly. "Well, I hope he's been minding his manners,

Miss Pevensey," Harold continued, putting a hand on Will's shoulder, and softening his tone noticeably. "You must let me pay for this."

"That's very kind of you sir but..."

"Davison. Harold Davison from Mill Farm."

"Well that's very kind of you Mr Davison, but the ladies allowed us this for nothing because of my father's influence here, I think. It's a little embarrassing, but the cake is too good, isn't it William?" Will blushed and nodded.

"Well, we must be off," Harold said, "thank you for your kindness."

"A pleasure to meet you, Alice," Agnes added, before whispering, "Sorry about the table."

"Oh, don't worry, the ladies will sort it. Lovely to meet you all too. Goodbye, William. I hope we can meet again sometime."

David nudged him in the back. "Say something, then!"

"Er, yes, me too, thank you. See you later." He managed a smile and walked after with his family, glancing back once at the still-smiling angel standing by the wooden table.

Fred appeared by his side, eating a piece of chocolate cake he had silently stolen from Will's unfinished plate while everyone was chatting. "Lovely," he mumbled, spitting a mouthful of crumbs.

The band were playing 'Over the Fields and Far Away', a popular army song, as the Davisons walked back across the green.

"We will have to watch this one, Mother," Harold said in mock formal tones. "Wins a few football trophies and next thing he's dining with royalty!"

"Oh Hal," Agnes replied, "he was just enjoying himself."

"Maybe we can marry 'em all off to the daughters of Lords. Then we can retire happy!" Harold continued, as his wife linked arms with him and they strolled away.

"Far too pretty for you, anyway, Will," David chided. "Stick to football. That's what you're good at."

Harold nodded. "All women are trouble, boys. Especially rich ones."

Agnes frowned and was about to reply when they all became aware that the music from the band seemed to be disjointed, as if they were playing two different tunes at once. They paused as children began running towards the main road, and some people started cheering.

Will had been oblivious to the chatter. He looked at the bandstand now and saw several members of the band stop playing and stand up, looking to where the children were scrambling forward. They all heard it then, at the same time: pipes and drums playing in splendid unison. In moments soldiers appeared, marching smartly onto the green. It was the Royal Sussex Regimental recruiting party, and they were here for men.

Will noticed his mum and dad exchange a glance. For once he recognised a tune they were playing from the musical nights they sometimes had to sit through in the village hall. It was called 'The girl I've left behind me'.

Oh, thanks a bloody lot, he thought.

Chapter 5 –Time Running Out

Several days had passed since the Steyning fete. Will's mind was full of Alice. He had glimpsed her briefly once more at the fair, walking off to a waiting car with what he assumed to be her mother, and a tall boy in uniform. David was probably right. She might be out of his class after all, and he doubted he could ever afford a car like the one she was being driven away in. Yet despite that, he felt sure there was a strong connection between them and refused to give it up. *He hadn't imagined it had he?*

The Davisons had watched the soldiers for a while and listened to the tall Sergeant give a passionate speech about the war, and how the men of Sussex needed to do their bit. They wanted men between eighteen and thirty five and that evening there had been raised voices in the kitchen with David saying he should go. Being too young anyway, Will was sent to his room but lay awake late into the night unable to settle. Bill Yates had said men doing certain tasks crucial to the running of the country like farmers, miners and railway workers, could be exempt from the draft. Harold hung to this point for the next few days.

Then Walter Miller appeared and everything changed.

Walter Miller was the Station Master at Steyning, and also managed the telegram office. He had a different hat for each role. He had lost his wife to fever some three years previously but had two handsome sons, neither of whom were married. They were very close since their mother's passing, and both sons had made an unspoken bond to stay working locally in the Mills without complaint. Despite the loss of his childhood sweetheart, Walter remained cheerful in his work, and always had a friendly smile or word for the Davison boys.

Will was washing down the barn floor after evening milking with Fred when Walter appeared at their gate. Fred was doing his best to throw more water at Will than the floor, and laughed and dodged at his brother's half-hearted kicks in return. Walter popped his head through the opening and asked if their parents were home.

"Mum's in the kitchen sir," Will said, abruptly stopping his chase of Fred, who had launched the empty bucket over his shoulder just at that moment. The bucket clattered across the floor and hit Walter on the leg and the boys held their breath for the backlash. Instead Walter just burst out laughing and tossed the bucket back to Will who caught it with a sigh of relief.

With a hearty "Cheerio," Walter walked on up to the old side door. Harold had seen him from the hen run, where he was adding additional wire to the fencing. He knew the foxes would have given birth to their next young by now, and would be looking for easy meals for the extra mouths. As Walter knocked on the door, Harold appeared round the side of the house and ushered him in.

It was rare for them to receive any formal messages, and Walter waited patiently in case the Davisons wanted to reply, as was customary in the case of telegrams. He declined tea but took a glass of water from Agnes as she also waited while her husband read the note first. He frowned and read it again before passing it to his wife.

"We won't reply today Walter," he said, "not sure how much good it will do anyway." Walter had deciphered the message at the station so knew the content, but discreetly pretended otherwise and let himself out.

Curiosity got the better of the boys and they walked past the retiring Walter back up to the house. As Will pushed the door open they were halted by the sight of Agnes sobbing at the kitchen table. Their dad was stroking her head telling her it would be alright. Will noticed his dad's usual calm demeanour was gone and he was clearly struggling with whatever news Mr Miller had brought. The two boys paused by the table, and Will saw the telegram lying by the side of the teapot where it had floated down. He turned his head sideways and read the abridged note:

'Mum/Dad don't be angry (Stop) Felt moved to join the army owing to European situation (Stop) Great many of us joining up terribly exciting (Stop) Promise to return to London role when Germans sent packing! (Stop) Very proud to *be part of this grand adventure will write soon (Stop) Please understand Your James (Stop)'*

Will looked up and caught his dad's tear-filled eyes. Harold nodded struggling to speak. "Go and clean up for supper lads. I think we will go and visit your grandparents tomorrow."

*

The Davisons took the train up to Henfield to visit Harold's parents who lived in a small railway cottage near the station. His father had been a signalman for many years and they could often still cadge a ride with one of them as the trains passed through Steyning, without having to pay.

Arthur and Joan Davison lived in the end terrace of a row of six dark stone cottages. 'Two up, Two down' as they were known, owing to the tiny layout of kitchen and lounge downstairs and two bedrooms upstairs, and normally with an outside loo. Over time Arthur had expanded the side of his house to incorporate a scullery for Joan, and had brought the toilet inside by adding a door from the kitchen to both rooms; with a small bath and sink that made them feel very grand indeed. Even so Will thought it was a very small house and could not believe they had lived there with three children of which his dad had been the eldest.

Despite his grandad having retired some five years ago, it seemed like he'd never left the railways as he stood in the little back yard now speaking to Will and Fred. He was still able to name every train in order by time and driver and freight as they passed by a few hundred yards away.

"The next one is the ten past two from Shoreham boys, with the Downs sheep on for auction in Horsham," their grandad announced between strong puffs on his pipe. Then gesturing to the line, as the whistle could be heard at Halt end incline, added, "It should be Herbert Starling driving with young Ernie Barnes as fireman. He's just learning still."

As the small green steam train huffed and puffed into view with a number of carriages clearly carrying sheep, their curious black faces pressing through the side slits, he smiled and waved his pipe triumphantly. Herbert waved back from the driver's plate, knowing that more often than not, Arthur would be 'out back' watching them pass.

Arthur was also out here to reflect on the war that was now upon them, and the news that it may well soon affect all his family directly. He had brought Will and Fred out with him as he knew Harold wanted to chat to his mum about what to do, and Joan was quite down to earth in these matters. David was also inside as it concerned him directly, having been swayed by the marching bands and rousing speech of the recruiting sergeant at the fete.

Agnes called "Supper's ready" from inside the terrace house. The boys went inside as Arthur knocked his pipe against the wall with a sigh.

"Are you okay David?" Agnes asked as they all sat down.

"He's fine," Harold answered before David could speak. "He's thrown by all this talk of war and patriotism like the rest of us. They should never have come to the fete, it wasn't right. Bound to fire up the young lads, especially after a few beers. You stay on the farm where you belong."

David nodded, head bowed.

They squashed around the little table in the kitchen, eating vegetable soup and homemade bread. The conversation flew back and forth with the dramatic events of the last couple of weeks - the outbreak of war; the requests for men; James' telegram. Fred was complaining about the soup to his mum, while his grandma was telling him it was good for him. Harold was in a heated discussion with his own father about the farm.

"Surely someone should ask my consent before stealing my lads off to this damned war?"

Will looked about him and felt detached from the scene. The voices merged as his mind was absorbed with the shimmering image of Alice in her linen dress. Would he ever see her again? All that mattered to him now was to find Alice and impress her, and the war might be his chance to do just that.

*

August dragged on. With getting the lambs weaned, the silage made, and the harvest begun, there was more than enough to keep Will busy on the farm. His mind was never fully on his work though and his frustration grew. David had resolved to stay and although their dad was clearly more pensive, Will thought this news made his parents seem less anxious.

The unexpected visit of James at the beginning of September changed everything. The family reacted joyfully to see him. His appearance as a 2nd Lieutenant in the Coldstream Guards, brought a lump to his dad's throat. After the initial uproar, however, his return in uniform brought the whole reality crashing down on their sheltered farm life. The news from France that James brought with him hadn't helped either. It was clearly more accurate than old Gettings' gossip in the pub.

"We were told the British Expeditionary Force equipped itself well in its initial encounters with the German army. Our excellent training and marksmanship caused large casualties to the 'Hun' despite being vastly outnumbered," James said.

"Here, Here," Harold replied, "Teach those imposters to mess with the best army in the world."

"Sadly dad the Germans had superior numbers and firepower, and apparently we were defeated and pushed back repeatedly with heavy losses."

"What? Are you sure lad? They have been telling us here that it's all going well."

"I'm afraid not Dad. The reality is much worse."

"Bastards," Harold said angrily.

"Harold!"

The boys sat avidly around the kitchen table. They had heard their father swear many times before and were oblivious to it in the excitement of the tales of the war.

"Sorry love. Just makes my blood boil. Where did this take place?"

"All started at a place called Mons in Belgium."

"And what about the Belgium army and the damned Frenchies?

Where were they while we were fighting to the last man on their behalf? Sat about drinking wine no doubt."

"They have been hit pretty hard too Dad."

James saw that his mum was quite anxious. The mood had darkened as quickly as it had in Mons, and there was no changing that scenario. The first battle of Mons was now a fact in history and would always be known as a British defeat. Harold moved to stand by the side door and lit a cigarette. James knew he had to change the subject, and luckily Fred came to the rescue.

"So are you in charge of the whole army now then?"

James smiled and gave Fred a hug. "Not quite titch," he replied affectionately.

"But you are an officer?"

"Yes that's right."

"And can boss people about?"

"Something like that."

"No change there then," David interjected and the brothers laughed, and a small skirmish broke out. Agnes' heart heaved with a wave of memories of times past as the boys fought.

"So how did you get to be an officer then lad?" Harold asked keen to hear more.

"I joined the Artists Rifles originally, local outfit in London. It wasn't easy. A lot of the other men were from more privileged backgrounds than me despite the regiment's territorial status."

Harold frowned. "Nothing wrong with farming lad. Hope you stood up for yourself."

"Of course, they didn't bother me" he lied, reflecting on the strong prejudices he had initially encountered. Harold saw it on his son's face and wondered if that was why he joined the Guards. He was about to ask when James smiled suddenly and continued. "I signed up with a friend I met from the Vintners Company. His father was a Brigadier in the Guards. He's been a friend to me since my first days in London."

"Oh that's lovely, what's his name?" Agnes asked.

"Jonners...I mean Harry...Harry Johnson."

Harry Johnson was six feet four and very athletic. Educated

at Eton, he played Cricket for Surrey, and was considered a great England star for the future. His manicured moustache gave him an older look and twinkling eyes suggested danger to the ladies that followed him around. Harry was fed up with studying and wanted to get into business straight away, so joined his uncle's company in London for a year rather than following the family footsteps to Oxford University. The year had grown into five.

Despite being twenty three and the owner's nephew, Harry took a shine to the young farmer's lad from Sussex on their first meeting in 1912, when James arrived in London as the latest apprentice to join his uncle's business. He was clearly overwhelmed at first by the sights and sounds of the Capital, so far removed from Mill Farm. However, as the new men waited to start work, one of the other apprentices made sheep noises at James from across the yard. Without hesitating James threw his lunch apple with unerring accuracy and knocked the astonished boy off his feet. In that moment, watching the drama unfold, Harry knew they would be friends for life.

"How's that?" Harry had shouted with a great roar of laughter, before clapping James on the back. "Serves you right Preston, you should have caught it." He turned to James and shaking his hand warmly said, "Harry Johnson, Eton, at your service. Call me *Jonners*. Ever played cricket?"

They were inseparable thereafter and when war broke out, and the cry for men came, they joined within the hour. After only a fortnight of training with the 'Rifles' however, Harry's connections and James' clear aptitude for learning and keen mind had seen them dispatched to the Guards for assessment.

"Was it hard?" David asked, his own mind working overtime listening to his brother.

"Not compared to working the livestock here in winter," James replied with a nod to his dad. "Harry and I were selected for the Coldstream regiment of the Guards battalions, and in no time at all we were told to report for officer training. Apparently I had the right aptitude for it."

"Well of course you do," Agnes interjected. "All that hard work at school was bound to pay off."

"Quite right mother," Harold added, although he was still torn inside about his son's absence from the farm.

"We were placed in a new reserve battalion, the 4th, being formed in Windsor. There was talk among the men that this battalion might be kept in England in a support role, so Harry made use of the locality to tap into his Eton contacts and his dad of course. We were soon given permission to go overseas to join the 2nd battalion instead. It's all been a whirlwind really, and with barely three weeks training under our belts we are being deployed to France. That's why I've been given weekend leave."

There was a pause then, and Agnes had hoped for a moment that he would stay in England or indeed that the war would be over before James went to France. Harold moved in and placed his hand on her shoulder and she reached up and put her own hand on it. Will and David smiled awkwardly, admiring their brother but understanding what the news meant. It was Fred who broke the silence once more.

"Cold streams? We've got a couple of them here so you will be right at home! I'm surprised you didn't opt for the cowpat regiment."

James jumped up and chased Fred round the table and soon the kitchen was in uproar once more. As the four boys bundled out into the yard, Harold and Agnes hugged. Pride filled tears swirled between them.

"Well Aggie lass, he's all grown up now that's for sure. We can't keep 'em home for ever I guess."

"No Hal," she whispered and wiping a tear on her apron, turned back to the stove. "I better get the meat sorted. I hear soldiers have big appetites."

*

It was an emotional roller coaster of a weekend with lots more tears and laughter, as James regaled them with his stories. Despite the underlying anxiety the family enjoyed being whole once again. It passed too quickly for Harold and Agnes though, and soon they were all standing at Steyning station waiting for his train back to London. Agnes was crying but James' reassured her once more it would be over by Christmas, and he probably wouldn't even have to fight.

"There's a huge recruitment drive Mum and once the troops get over there the Germans will sue for peace. Everyone says. They don't want a war with England."

"Not just England, the whole of Britain's on the march," Harold replied.

The train came into view with a burst of smoke and noise. They all hugged, even David and James who didn't normally even shake hands. Will looked away and his heart lurched. Standing no more than twenty feet away was Alice. He wasn't sure at first if she had seen him but as he looked, she turned and smiled.

She was standing with the tall boy in uniform he had seen at a distance at the fete, whom Will assumed was her brother. The train pulled in with a loud whistle covering them all in clouds of billowing smoke. He turned to see his dad helping James on the train and smiled and waved trying to focus. He glanced sideways and was mortified to see that both Alice and her brother had vanished in the steam. With racing emotions, he joined in the waving with his family as the train pulled away.

The Davisons moved slowly down the platform, Harold with his arms round his wife and Fred. Will started behind them and came face to face with Alice who appeared almost magically at his side.

"Hello William," she said in a voice as warm as summer, her sumptuous smile disarming as ever.

"Hello" he replied startled. The Davisons paused, and as before, Alice's bold approach broke the silence.

"Hello Mr and Mrs Davison, was that your son you were seeing off in his smart uniform? Is he an officer?"

"Yes it was our eldest boy James," Mrs Davison replied. "He's a lieutenant with the Guards."

"How wonderful for you. My brother is going up to Horsham to try and get into the Territorials, as they are talking to all the Cadets. They will probably make him finish his final year at school first. I think all the young men want to be involved though don't you? It's such a great adventure." She was looking directly at Will.

"I'm not sure war is ever as glamorous as the politicians and papers would have us believe," Harold replied soberly, "they never get their hands dirty themselves."

"Have you been in the army then Mr Davison?" Alice asked.

"No, I've been a farmer all my life, but I know enough about life to wonder what these overseas adventures ever do to benefit us."

"Oh, I see," she replied. "I don't think we can have the Germans invading where they want and telling us what to do though, do you Mr Davison? We have to defend our empire."

Harold was not used to being spoken to like this, and Will noticed his dad bristle at a young girl talking to him about politics. Before anyone could reply there was a call of "Alice," and they all turned to see an immaculately dressed lady standing on the platform near the station office with her driver.

"Ah mother is waiting for me I see," Alice said with a raise of her eyes. Then to break the tension smiled, and added, "I didn't mean to be outspoken Mr Davison. I am sorry. I just get passionate about these things and I am a little emotional about my brother going off to do his bit. We all have to do our bit in different ways don't we, and we certainly need the farms now more than ever."

It sounded a little condescending but Will saw no reaction in his parents who both smiled graciously and told her not to worry at all. Taking her leave Alice walked away with little more than a brief glance at Will, leaving him nonplussed. They saw her speak briefly to her mother, and Lady Pevensey glance at them before nodding and walking off. Alice returned, her heels resounding confidently off the platform with every stride.

"I wonder if William would like to walk with me for an hour to pick some flowers in the meadow while my mother calls at the vicarage?"

Harold was caught completely off guard. " Er...maybe you'd like to come to the farm with us?"

"Harold," Agnes stated reproachfully, "in that dress? Good heavens above!"

"Well perhaps Fred could go with them?" he continued trying to regain control.

It was Agnes' turn to raise her eyes now and she turned to Will.

40

"An hour and no more William, and only the meadow mind so Alice's Mum knows where to find you. And then straight home for chores before supper understand?"

"Yes Mum, of course," Will replied bashfully, feeling like a little boy again.

"And mind them manners," Harold called after them as they hurried away along the platform to the wicker gate, which made them both laugh.

They walked for a while; her arm slipped easily in his as if they did it all the time. She stopped them near a small grass mound, bedecked with a colourful mantle of wild flowers. One of the smaller streams chattered along happily near their feet as they sat down to talk. Will waited for Alice to say something as she gazed at the natural scene about her. In that moment he thought there couldn't possibly be anyone as lovely as her, anywhere in the world.

"This is a pretty little town isn't it? I can see why you like it here."

"Yes I suppose it is. I haven't known anywhere else. My family's been on the farm for a long time now. It was my Great Grandad's they said."

"How big is it?"

"About 20 acres I think."

"Oh that's lovely."

"How big is your house then?"

"The Hall? Oh I don't know really. Around 300 acres father said when he bought it. Plus various woods and scrubland on the edges. I don't really worry about things like that. How many brothers and sisters do you have William?"

Will was aware his mouth was probably open from Alice's last comment and stuttered. "Three brothers, no sisters. What about you?"

"Oh just one younger brother. I don't think I'd care for sisters mind you," Alice replied. "Do you like it on the farm?"

"It's okay I guess," Will said unsure how honest to be. "It can be boring at times."

"Ah so you seek adventure like me!" She smiled then once more and the sun seemed a little brighter.

"Don't you like where you live then Alice? It sounds incredible."

"It's very nice of course. We have some wonderful parties there. And I love to ride across the grounds. Do you ride William?"

"No. I never have. Though James and David do. My older brothers. We used to have a big shire horse for ploughing. My Grandad's. They rode that. I'd like to, I guess." He tried to sound interesting, to impress her, but could sense in her smile she was just being polite.

"I love to ride, especially alone. I love the freedom. But I long for something more. After all that time cooped up in a girls' school. I need excitement William."

Will blushed at her directness. He wasn't quite sure where this conversation was leading. He felt relaxed in her company, but also a little in awe as she seemed so clever and confident compared to him.

"I do prefer Will you know," was all he could say.

"Of course, silly of me. Will it is."

There was an awkward pause then, and Will wished he had not corrected her, but Alice soon recovered.

"You know if you're bored you could join up like your brother has. I know farms are necessary but there's more than one way to do your bit before it's all over." Will knew it was inevitable that the war would come into their conversation, but it just seemed to heighten his discomfort. It seemed absurd to be talking of war in such a beautiful place, with this wonderful girl, and he didn't answer immediately. He stared at the multicoloured waves rippling along below the bank, their carefree shapes dancing in the sunlight.

Alice could sense Will was torn between home and country, and tried a different tack. "You would look wonderful in uniform you know Will," she threw out suddenly, "you are even more handsome than your brother."

He blushed now and smiled awkwardly and she moved in close to him and hugged his arm. He could feel the warmth from her face next to his, enticing him in, and his heart beat faster.

"Don't you want to fight?" she murmured.

"It's not that I don't. I do," he heard himself say, "but with James gone, Dad needs me on the farm. I'm only seventeen."

"You may miss it altogether if you wait too long," she teased, and pushed him away playfully. "Come on then *farm boy,* help me pick some flowers for mother."

The words had been thrown in jest but there was an edge to them and bending down to pick a couple of cornflowers, Will felt suddenly inadequate.

Allsopp the driver appeared on foot, near the church road, and waved once to signal 'time to go.' Will felt the hour had passed like a minute, and wanted to have said more. Clutching a large bunch of wild yellow Chrysanthemums and some striking blue Cornflowers, they headed back reluctantly towards the vicarage.

"You know in medieval lore, it was believed that a girl who placed a cornflower beneath her skirt could have any bachelor she desired." Alice remarked. "That's how the flower acquired its other name, *Bachelor's Button.*" Will glanced automatically at her skirt and blushed when she looked at him. She laughed and taking his arm one last time, put one of the darkest blues in his waistcoat button hole.

"There we go farm boy. More appropriate for a bachelor than my skirt."

"Will, *please,*" he managed to say defensively. She stopped and kissed him unexpectedly on the cheek. The lightest of touches like a snowflake caressing a leaf that completely dissolved his resistance; and yet at the same time left a very firm memory inside his soul.

"I'm just teasing silly," she whispered, and then pushing his blond hair away from his eyes added, "you know that flower deserves to be on a uniform with someone so handsome." She kissed him again on the cheek and her eyes bored into his for a moment and then she turned away, leaving him stunned.

As she walked off to join Allsopp he shook himself out of her spell and called out. "Will I see you again Alice?"

Half turning she replied, "I hope so *Will,*" emphasising his name. "I think we might come to watch the regiment march off from here on Monday week. Will you be there?"

The words coming back at him were a challenge as much as a simple question, and Will nodded and looked at the flower.

When he looked up to speak again, Alice and her driver were

already past the church and heading to the vicarage. She never looked back.

Chapter 6 – Sign him up

"How old are you Davison?" the Sergeant asked, staring at him. Will blinked momentarily as if coming out of a trance unaware exactly how he had come to be here. "Haven't got all day come on, come on."

"Eighteen," Will stuttered.

"Eighteen? And my old lady's the Queen of Sheba!" It was the fat corporal sitting near the fire in the Star Inn, that mocked him. The unpleasant looking soldier downed the remains of his third ale with a satisfied belch, and brushed a persistent crumb off his brown uniform jacket, straining to contain him. The Sergeant raised an eye at Will.

"Seventeen," he replied quietly, "but eighteen in January."

"And you're keen to join up you say?"

"Yes sir."

"Hmmm. Got any brothers already serving?"

"Yes my oldest brother James. He's a lieutenant in the Coldstream Guards."

The Corporal choked on the dregs of his ale with a loud guffaw. "This gets better and better. A farmer is an officer in the Guards? Pull the other one. You'll be telling me you're related to royalty next."

"What's his service number," the Sergeant asked, noticing the sincerity on Will's face.

"Yes we can check the records here for all the local men so you better not be lying sonny," the Corporal chipped in, still enjoying making Will uncomfortable in front of everyone. Will tried to clear his head and remember what James had told him in the barn when they were listening intently to his tales of training at the barracks...

His mind was a whirr of thoughts about the station and his time with Alice; his walk back towards the farm, with her words about him being in uniform still

45

smarting. The outbreak of laughter from the Star Inn that caught his attention. He recalled pausing in the porch listening to the creaking of the sign above in the strengthening wind, its repeated groans taunting him as he hesitated outside. His purposeful stride inside, undone in an instant when the pub went silent and all eyes turned to him.

Then he had spied the soldiers by the dusty unmade fire, their large recruitment books splayed out across the oaken table in front of them amongst a scattering of empty plates and glasses. His legs became stone until he felt a hand on his shoulder and turned to see Danny there, pint in hand, smiling and breathing beer fumes into his face. He was holding on, more to steady himself than to be friendly, though sober enough to sense why Will was there.

"Want a drink before you do it Will?" Danny had noticed the flower and touching it with his glass added, "She will love you more if you do I'm sure." They both smiled. The smile that old friends do when words are not required. "Does your Dad know?"

Will shook his head. Danny let out a low whistle of foreboding, knowing the scene that could play out soon in Mill farm; but as Will took a step back, his courage deserting him at the mere mention of his dad, Danny propelled him forward saying "Now or never mate!" And here he was.

"11150 sir," Will replied, the number suddenly coming into his brain.

"What's that lad, your position in the school exams," the corporal stated reaching for the jug to refill his ale glass with a grunt.

Will stood awkwardly in front of the soldiers, trying not to look at them directly but his eyes took in every detail. He saw the tall recruiting sergeant had a scar on the back of his neck that had not healed cleanly. As he thumbed the pages in the evening light, his right hand also had a tremor when not in use.

At forty five, Sergeant Langley had served in the Boer wars, and was a veteran of two campaigns and several battles. Now enjoying a far less arduous posting in England, he was none-the-less a stickler for orders and detail, and methodically cross referenced the files in front of him. It was probably why he was chosen to lead the recruitment process, unlike his corporal companion, who was there to enjoy as much beer and trappings as he could.

Langley was however a family man, with five children at the barracks in Roussillon in Chichester, and was already yearning to return there in a couple of weeks when this particular task was completed. In that regard, as in his attention to detail, he decided to take this young blond lad seriously who wavered in front of him. He glanced at Will again in his Sunday best with the ridiculous over-sized flower head drooping out of his button hole, and sighed. Then a particular line in the service book made him stop short and his look turned to surprise. He cross referenced it with a London edition. Nodding, he read the entry to his colleague.

"11150. Davison. J.G. 2nd Lieutenant, Coldstream Guards. 4th Reserve battalion, 2nd Division, 4th Guards Brigade. Place of birth – Steyning, West Sussex." Langley put the book down. "Well it seems like the lad was telling the truth after all. We've got a family of fighters here not farmers Corporal."

The Corporal took a swig of his newly filled glass, and eyed Will up and down once more. "Sign him up," he shrugged.

*

It was exactly seven in the morning. The old grandfather clock, that had been a wedding present for the Davisons, still chimed faithfully away in the hall. It was something constant at least.

David leaned against the door of his bedroom and listened to the animated voices in the kitchen below. His mum and dad had been up all night it seemed to him, since Will had come home with his news.

"Do you think it's safe to go down yet, I'm starving!" Fred announced behind him. David turned round and shrugged, his own thoughts a turmoil of emotions.

Fred was lying on David's bed, still not dressed, and with his beloved box of toy soldiers spread out in front of him. Though most carried drums and bugles and were supposed to be in a parade probably, it didn't matter to Fred and his imagination carried them across the battlefield sheets towards the pillow fort with roars and clashes.

His brother Will had hardly slept that night and gone downstairs very early. As the noises from the kitchen had filtered up, Fred had sought reassurance in his older brother's room. David would normally have refused - his one sanctuary being precious to him - but today was different, and everything seemed to be changing in the Davison household piece by piece.

The remaining soldiers not killed by the imaginary foe, stormed up the side of the pillow, as their mum shouted up for them to come and have breakfast. This was also different, as normally they had to work for a couple of hours before being fed. David was well aware how time had slipped by, while Fred loved the extra play time as if it was a special occasion.

The side door slammed and David crossed to the window, pulling the curtain back and opening the shutter ajar. He watched his dad walk off towards the barn, the absence of hums and whistles quite apparent. He knew he should go down and help but sensed that his dad also wanted to be alone, the usual shout for milking time not forthcoming. "Better get dressed Freddie," he murmured as he pushed his wavy black hair from his eyes, blown there by the breeze.

He was unsettled and sort solace at the breakfast table, and without another word to Fred walked out and down the stairs. As he entered the kitchen David saw his mum washing up some plates and was relieved by this regular sight. Will sat at the breakfast table and was picking at some eggs and bacon that looked very sorry for themselves.

"Hello Mum."

Agnes turned as if startled and smiled. She looked tired and her smile didn't hide the stress. Brushing her hands on her 'pinny' she said, "There's plenty of eggs warming on the oven plate. Help yourself love, just mind the hot stove."

"Where's Dad gone?" David replied, trying to bring some normality into his thoughts.

"He's away milking. Late today, and the cows are letting him know about it."

"Does he need my help?"

"No, he said you boys can eat first and then just find him when you're ready."

Now David knew all was not right with the world. They were only excused morning chores on their birthday, and Christmas day; and even then they would often still help, as their dad would usually be in a really daft mood and up for play fights and fun about the farm. He watched his mum pick a plate up she had already washed and begin to wash it again. He turned away frowning and took some bacon and an egg from the top plate. It was very hot, and he scalded his finger slightly on the oven plate as he put the cover back on, careful not to curse. He sat at the table and tore a chunk of bread as his mum turned round.

"I'm going to go and check the chickens for eggs," Agnes announced. David saw how many eggs were already in and knew she had probably already done that once this morning but just smiled and nodded. "I'll be doing a load of washing too today so if you want anything cleaned up let me know. William is going to need his suit pressing. So much to do, I don't know where to start," she went on, as much to herself as her boys. "If I don't get cracking time will just run away I know it."

She paused half way across the floor and looked at Will sitting head bowed, his fork now motionless. "Try and eat Will," she whispered tenderly, "you need your strength now. David make sure Freddie gets some food down him too."

"Yes Mum." He watched her walk out of the kitchen and up the hall without another word. David wondered if she had forgotten the chickens but decided not to call after her and stay and chat to his brother instead.

"You okay Will?"

Will looked up, tired eyes staring through him. "Yes I think so."

"So you're going to do it then. Join up."

"I already have. No going back now."

"Mum and Dad very upset?"

"Yes. Seems like. Sorry."

"Yeh leave me to face the fire as usual," David chided, half teasing. He pushed some bacon between the bread and took a bite. Despite his internal upheaval he had to eat something to ease his nerves.

Will shrugged. "Don't you want to join up?"

"Of course I do. But we can't all go can we? Be no one left to run the country. Besides what about the farm…Mum…I promised." David faltered over the last part, regretting his words of the previous month.

"Well I didn't. James has already gone and I just have to do it."

"Is it because of that girl? That Alice?"

"No…perhaps…I don't know. It's just something I have to do. It feels right."

David softened looking at the torment in his younger brother's face. "Look Will, you have nothing to prove to anyone you know. Especially us. You're not even eighteen yet so they can't make you go, and besides it's only volunteers they want. No one is press ganging us. Dad could go there and see them. Get you out of it."

"Thought you'd be glad to see the back of me," Will muttered.

David walked round the table and sat on the edge near his brother. "Then you're daft as well as stupid if you think that. You may be a pain in the bum sometimes and rubbish at football, but as a brother, you're ok." They shared a smile and David gave him a pat on the shoulder.

Will looked up. "I have to go David."

David stared long and hard at him and then said, "I know."

Freddie burst into the kitchen and immediately grabbed a plate and started filling it with food. "Hey Will," he shouted, pushing some bacon in his mouth to eat while he filled his plate, "where's Mum and Dad?"

"Mum's on the chores, Dad's outside. We have to join him once you've finished stuffing your fat face!" David answered.

"Hey, that's not nice" Freddie replied, food nearly spilling out of his mouth as he protested.

"And keep your mouth closed while you eat, you pig."

David cuffed him playfully and then put his plate by the sink, his hunger gone, and grabbed his boots. He turned at the door and looked at Will who was staring at his plate once more. "Better go sort your clothes out with Mum, mate," he said. "At the end of the day someone's got to look after James I guess, he's too much of a romantic."

50

Will tried to smile but couldn't and David looked away, pulling his boots on. As he opened the door he shouted "Don't be long piggy," at Fred and then went outside, before he could reply.

Fred seemed to register that Will had not spoken to him since he came in for breakfast. He wiped some egg off his chin. "Alright Will?"

Will looked up from the other end of the table. "Yes I'm alright titch."

"You going to eat anymore brekkie?" Fred enquired hopefully.

"No I'm done, help yourself." Although in truth Will had eaten nothing at all since last night.

"Great. Dad says we have to go and help him once we finish breakfast. So I'm going to make it last as long as possible!" Fred grinned and then got up and scooped more food on his plate, making the same mistake David had and burning himself on the hot plate.

"Yow!" he yelled, and then shaking his hand as if that would ease the pain, sat down to eat once more. Will smiled at his little brother still immersed in the here and now. Fred smiled back though food encrusted teeth. That cheeky lopsided smile of his.

"So you really off then?"

"Yes next Monday."

"Shame you have to go," Fred said between mouthfuls, not understanding the enormity of the situation.

"I'll be back before you know it."

"That's a shame too," Fred teased, and Will laughed properly. Then after a pause added, "Look after Mum and Dad for me?"

"Of course," Fred spluttered and poured himself some water from the stone jug on the table and took some big gulps. Wiping his mouth again he added, "Everyone knows I'm in charge here anyway. You can count on me."

"I'm sure I can," Will replied, and pushed his plate away and got up to leave. "I won't miss you banging your head every day on my bed."

"I won't miss you parping off all night either," Fred countered. They both laughed, and Will ruffled his brother's wild hair, and went out to find his mum.

51

Fred found himself suddenly alone in the big kitchen. A rare occurrence. For a moment he continued to eat in silence. Then he paused and looked at Will's chair. He felt cold suddenly and shivered.

"Miss you Will," he said.

Chapter 7 – Sent Off

Will had not slept on his last night at home; tossing and turning until in the end he had risen before dawn to walk the farm once more. The summer frost crunched under his boots. The animals stared or chewed quietly away in that hour before dawn, eyes shining like sparks in the blue dark - their noises comforting to him as he walked. As the starlings and sparrows called out for breakfast, Will headed back to the house and found his dad dressed and waiting for him. Sally crouched by his legs, alert as ever. They milked the cows together with barely a word exchanged, and then joined the others for breakfast, although the nerves had killed his appetite.

Now standing at the bottom of Steyning high street, the atmosphere was even more unbearable. As he rightly guessed at dawn, it was turning into another hot day. He looked around and saw nothing but strangers in the large assembly of men. Most of his friends being too young currently to enlist. *Or too sensible,* he thought ruefully. Impatient soldiers moved through the group calling names, attempting to organise the new recruits ready to be marched off.

It had not been like this in church yesterday when St. Andrew's was full to bursting with young men from the town and their families. Will had known a lot of those men by sight at least, if not all by name, as most of them lived locally. Many had gone to other regiments though - old family ties pulling them back to enlist where they grew up or where family members were already serving. It had been a sombre occasion, and Will had seen plenty of tears amongst men and women.

As Will stood with the other men, some old locals staggered out from the Star Inn to shout words of encouragement and the odd drunken jibe. It unsettled him further and he looked for his mum and dad, standing a little way off in the crowd of families and onlookers. They were chatting to David. Fred was tugging at his mum to point out a cake stall set up nearby from the Model Bakery, his day like any other. Shading his eyes Will looked up. There was scarcely a cloud to be seen on this perfect blue morning, although the sharp wind reminded them all of winter's expected arrival.

Will felt suddenly very anxious and alone, trapped in the crowd of men around him. He wanted to run back to his parents and away from this place. He felt ready to throw up.

"I think the boys will struggle in the league this season."

The familiar voice made Will spin round and he found himself staring at the large frame of Archie. "Half the spine of the team is gone with us away," his friend continued, his face masked his emotions.

"Bunny," Will exclaimed with relief, as if seeing a long lost brother again. "I didn't know you had signed up too." They shook hands warmly.

"Couple of weeks back now. Been finishing up at the factory and then spent a few days up in Horsham with me mum's family."

Archie's dad had been an open cast miner over in Robertsbridge mining for Gypsum and other substances, but had been killed in a freak accident some four years back. Since then his mum had gone back to live with her parents in Horsham with his younger sisters. Archie couldn't settle though and soon after had taken lodgings and a job with the glass factory near Steyning even though only fifteen at the time. It made him very independent and head strong as many opposition football players and referees could testify to; and the occasional rowdy drinker in the Norfolk Arms!

Will was glad to have him here. A friendly face at last. He felt his nerves settle as they chatted about village news and Archie poked fun at some of the men gathered here who had come from all around the region to get the train down to Brighton. It had struck Will what a variety of ages there were too from young fresh faced farm hands to married factory workers and even some fathers and sons. He turned away from Archie scanning the crowd for one particular face.

A sergeant walked past, papers clutched tight to his chest and Archie tapped him on the shoulder.

"What's the camp like in Brighton then? Lots of beer and girls

I hope?"

"You're not going to Brighton Sonny Jim, we just change there and head up to Woking. And I'll thank you to call me Sergeant."

Archie was not used to someone speaking to him like a child and bristled at the man's tone, but the sergeant was equal in size to him and probably about ten years older and for once he backed down.

"Why Woking...sergeant?" Archie asked, trying to be more polite.

"Training camp for the 2nd Battalion is there. They marched to the sound of the guns in August and been fighting ever since. We need you lads as replacements. Now if you don't mind I've a schedule to keep."

Archie turned to Will, who had only been half listening, and raised his eyes. "Bit odd sending us north when the fighting's south. Perhaps we are just going to be in a holiday camp for the war. They said it will be over by Christmas!"

"He also said they needed replacements didn't he?" Will pointed out, trying to sound interested.

"Trust you to spot that. Anyway it will be what it will be. Old Jerry better look out when Bunny gets stuck in. Hey what do you say we challenge 'em to a match. Winner buggers off home?" They both laughed and Will relaxed more, and noticed his mum was smiling at him now and waved back.

Just then a number of soldiers started walking up and down the group arranging them into fours. As the men shuffled slowly into place, an officer appeared, splendid on a large white horse. Exchanging salutes with the sergeant, he gave the order to move off. Seconds later the local pipe band struck up a very lively tune which someone nearby said was called 'It's a long way to Tipperary.'

"It's a bloody long way if we are heading south to get there. It's in sodding Ireland," Archie quipped. All the men roundabout laughed and the sergeant shouted at them to settle down. Will knew that Archie would be very popular wherever they ended up, and was glad they were friends.

"Let the men be lively sergeant. We need good morale for France." It was the officer who called out. As they passed him Will chanced a longer look and noticed he had a scar across his face that went across his left eye.

"Sword cut from the Boer war they reckon. Won the Military Cross out there. That's Colonel Bradshaw. Good man."

Will looked round and saw a man he didn't recognise with barely any front teeth grinning at him and nodding at the colonel. His breath stank and he had clearly spent the night getting courage in one of the nearby pubs. Will decided not to engage him in conversation, and fortunately at that point their line moved forward and they headed off to the station, the band in full flow. Fred roared alongside them shouting with his friends, some of whom were marching too with sticks held proudly by their sides.

Walking along behind the band, with the large crowds of people cheering them on along the way, Will suddenly felt very excited. A surge of patriotic pride swelled within him, and he could swear he seemed taller as he marched along. He had hoped that Alice would come to see him as promised, but she was nowhere to be seen, and he pushed that disappointment aside, allowing himself to be lost in this joyous moment.

The daily life of Steyning came to a standstill to celebrate this moment. Shopkeepers paused to stand on well washed steps and watch the procession go by. As the men passed the church Will was amazed at the size of the crowd that had gathered on the green opposite to cheer them on, with various side shows and stall holders doing a brisk trade from the impromptu event. As the families that had walked with them merged with the townsfolk gathered here, it became an incredible mass of cheering shouting supporters that made Will's chest feel as if it was going to burst with pride. They reached the platform in no time, the men reveling in the pomp and circumstance of the moment, regardless of status.

The platform was a sea of colour and noise as if swarms of bees had descended on a beautiful walled garden of roses in one huge mass. Normal social order was lost as people from all manner of backgrounds came together to say farewell and jostled for position. The stirring tunes from the pipes and drums drew more curious bystanders in to the contagious air of patriotism. Even the footbridge that allowed passengers to traverse safely from one side of the station to the other above the tracks was crammed with people. Many local children gathered here, squashing their faces through the holes of the iron lattice work that crisscrossed across both sides of the bridge; their pink cheeks from the winter wind adding to the colourful spectacle.

The local cattle market was in full swing that day too, right beside the station. Men made the most of the large gathering to push through sales of beasts and fowl, the animals adding to the noise of the occasion. Will didn't think he'd ever seen so many people in one place and for a time had lost sight of his family all together. Then his dad appeared on the platform alongside David. Their experience of pushing farm beasts around made it easy to make a path through the crowd for Agnes and Fred. Their actions mirrored the men in the market next door as cattle and sheep were similarly pushed this way and that. Now at last the Davisons stood together once more, but already the train was loading.

"Fancy our boys being sent off." The high pitched voice made them all turn and Gladys Nightingale was there in her best Sunday bonnet, pinched nose and mouse like features twitching with pride. Her son Bertie stood with her, six foot tall and gangly, towering over her.

Archie leaned in and spoke to Will and David, "Well it's not new for me but it's a first for Will to be sent off!" They laughed, and then Archie murmured, "Young Nightingale doesn't look like he can fight his way out of the choir stalls never mind anything else. See you on the train Will." He smirked and nodded to Will's parents and leapt on the train without a second thought, pushing a couple of men aside to reserve seats for them by the window.

Will shook hands with David, and Fred gave him a hug. Agnes turned from her polite conversation with Gladys and now the tears came. She pulled Will in close and whispered some last minute advice lovingly in his ear before kissing him once more and stepping back. She knew she was embarrassing him in public but everywhere it was the same for once; mums hugging sons regardless of whether it was expected or not. Even Celia Goodman was risking her reputation at the choir to give her husband a furtive kiss. Without children Agnes knew it would be hard for her alone, and she expected the choir would bear the brunt of that!

Archie, sitting by the train window, was pretending not to notice any of this; although inside he wished his dad was there to see him off. Tony Bassett had at least been there though with some of the football team; Danny Boyd and Tommy of course had cycled up from their farms. Owen Entwhistle stood awkwardly in his butcher's apron. He had just walked off with the crowd and expected to face the consequences when he got back, though there would hardly be any customers at the moment. Archie had crushed each of their hands in turn with his ferocious handshake to make sure they remembered him.

Will turned to his dad and as they shook hands Harold handed his son a present for the train. Will already had some food for the journey, (which had been well received by Archie who was always 'starving'), but this was a treat apparently.

"Be more for you when you come back lad."

He placed it in his bag with the other food with a smile. He made to go and then on impulse turned back and hugged his dad. David exchanged a glance with his mum who was smiling tears of pride. Harold stepped back, nodded a couple of times and then said, "Mind how you go now. Look out for James and make sure you both come home safe and sound."

"Of course Dad."

"And write to your Mum."

As Will went to reassure his dad his words were cut off by the train whistle. It blew long and loud, and a guard shouted "All aboard." Walter Miller waved his green flag to signal time to go.

The whistle prompted a fresh roar of noise and as Will settled in his seat the crowd pushed forward on a wave of emotion. Mums touched their sons' hands; sweethearts hugged and kissed through half shut windows, and friends and family up and down the platform waved and shouted goodbyes. The band struck up with renewed enthusiasm, and Colonel Bradshaw saluted the men on the train from the raised platform where he had said some words of encouragement just a short time ago.

Agnes hovered and then Fred ran and jumped on the train door ledge and shouted "Bye Will" through the open window, and she reached in to pull him back from the train as it started to move. It allowed her to see her son once more and she took his hand walking a few paces with the slowly moving train. She didn't want to let go, the pain of separation growing inside her as the train pulled him away. She felt like the seventeen years had suddenly rushed past like the London trains did here, without stopping, and she wanted so much to have her baby boy back again. Harold stepped forward and embraced her, gently breaking the hold she had on Will with a smile and cradling her in his arms. She sobbed uncontrollably as they watched their son depart.

People were waving handkerchiefs now, and the train was a sea of arms waving back. It reminded Will of a slowly moving centipede the legs all going in different directions. The driver, sensitive to the situation and with safety in mind on this unusually packed platform, eased the train forward gently; though it strained against his touch with every creak and clatter, like a racehorse in the stalls, eager to be off.

Will couldn't stop the tears coming and he dabbed them with his sleeve, focusing on the crowd to distract himself. As he glanced over the sea of faces he suddenly saw Allsopp resting against the Pevensey's car beyond the station fence. He was furtively smoking a cigarette aware that all eyes were on the train. As Will watched his arm was grabbed again and he looked down to tell his mum to go and stared straight into the eyes of Alice.

"I couldn't go without saying goodbye," she said having to raise her voice uncharacteristically to be heard above the noise. "Mother had one of her headaches and declined to attend, that's why I was delayed. I had to bribe Allsopp to drive me."

That explained the cigarettes Will thought, transfixed by her smile once more. She looked beautiful in a yellow summer dress that matched the sun, and wore a straw hat with a yellow ribbon tied about it to match; the ends floating like kite strings behind her in the breeze.

"I really hoped to see you in the parade. I'm thrilled you joined

Will. So handsome…"

The train whistle sounded again, pulling at Will's heart. Though her words were lost it made him feel prouder than ever seeing Alice and he just beamed at her. She laughed then staring intently as before.

"Oh Gawd. Hurry up and kiss her for god's sake or she'll be dragged to France with the rest of us!"

Archie's jibe made him snap into action and he reached out and kissed her hard on the lips. She responded passionately, holding him with one hand and the train door with the other and they rode like that for a few seconds before she pulled away and stepped off. She seemed to do everything with grace, even now. The train was starting to pick up speed as the platform end neared, and she would have had to run to stay alongside, so she paused and simply smiled once more.

"Good luck Will, write to me won't you?"

He shouted that he would and then she was lost in the smoke and noise as the train pulled out of Steyning. He remained transfixed for a few moments and then collapsed into the seat next to Archie. He realised that she had pressed a note into his hand, and he sat staring at it while Archie grinned at him.

"Who was that vision of beauty then?"

"Her name's Alice. Alice Pevensey. Lord Pevensey's daughter."

Someone in the carriage said "Alright for some," and another said "Has she got a sister mate?"

"Well that's a turn up. Here we are shouting to milk maids and serving girls and you get Alice bloody Pevensey seeing you off Davison, you dark horse."

Will self-consciously turned the note over in his hands.

"Look Romeo, not wanting to spoil this tender moment but I always find love letters are much better enjoyed on a full stomach, so what do you say we tuck into your Mum's sarnies?" Archie grinned and Will laughed and reached into his bag for the food. As he did so he remembered the present from his dad and pulled it out first. He unwrapped it and found a bar of his favourite chocolate inside, with a short note from Harold that simply said, *There will be more waiting for you when you come home lad. Stay safe. Dad.'*

He held it for a moment and then Archie looked over and slapped him on the shoulder, and said "Wow, pudding too! I'm starting to like this war more and more."

"You won't say that when you get to the training camp. Once the sergeants get hold of you it won't be no laughing matter. And trust me war ain't fun." They looked and saw an older man sitting smoking a pipe, perhaps a veteran of some previous campaign, with a rugged face that made it hard to age him.

Archie took a huge bite out of one of Will's sandwiches and winked at him. "Don't pay any attention to that old timer," he said quietly between mouthfuls. "This war's different Will, mark my words. And those sergeants better look out when Archie Bunden turns up!"

Chapter 8 – Training

"You and your big mouth Archie!"

"Well not my fault they don't have a sense of humour," Archie replied between labored breaths. The platoon was on their third lap together of the parade ground, rifles held above their heads, as punishment for Archie's latest misdemeanor. The rain was coming down hard and in the wide open space the wind seemed to blow it straight in their faces without let up. It had rained almost from the time they had come into the barracks in Woking, a fact not lost on the men already missing the comforts of home.

They spent the first two weeks in endless drill, marching up and down; alongside mundane lectures on how to cook, make their beds, clean and press their kit, and other tasks that some found easier than others. The last two days however had seen them move onto the live firing ranges. One of the sergeants was advising them on how to shoot at distance and take into account moving targets and the effect of wind and other elements. Archie had taken this moment to 'break wind' very loudly.

"I see what you mean Sergeant. Something like that could put the whole platoon off, especially after last night's corned beef hash."

The whole platoon had laughed out loud...and now they were running.

As Will predicted, Archie was a popular figure in the camp. One or two of the veteran sergeants however, felt him too cocky and arrogant for his own good, as if their sense of humour was somehow shot away. In reality they just wanted to get the men ready for the harsh realities of what lay ahead, knowing full well it could make or break a man.

Indeed despite being here for less than three weeks, several of the men who joined up with them had left, either due to poor health or just being incapable of soldiering. One of the men sent away was Bertie Nightingale who had proved incapable of doing anything from basic drill to exercise, and the instructors were certainly not going to give him a rifle. Some men were moved onto reserve lists ready to be called upon if necessary, and it was mooted Bertie might get a desk job in a territorial base. Archie of course had been the one to say that "as he was as thick as wood, he might as well sit at a desk where he would feel right at home with his fellow trees."

He had been on 'fatigues' for most of the second week for that, which meant cleaning the toilets every day and other unpleasant tasks. But despite regular punishments from the sergeants, Archie maintained a cheery disposition and was always helping some of the other recruits to try and settle in. If he felt they were worth helping, and not "walking planks" like Nightingale! Will saw a different side to him in those times, although he also wished his friend would keep his mouth shut more often. Like now, as they ran around the parade ground for a fourth time in the rain…

*

That evening Will lay on his top bunk reading the crumpled note from Alice once more, though he virtually knew every line. Despite clearly being written in a hurry it was still very neat and far easier to read than his own basic scrawl. He closed his eyes and tested himself on the contents.

> *Will.*
>
> *I hope this little note finds you well. I was really thrilled to see you marching today. How handsome you looked setting off on this grand adventure! Please keep safe won't you? I'm sure you will. I really did enjoy our time together the other day. I will write to you often I promise. Please write to me won't you? Mother won't mind.*
>
> *I will miss you farm boy. I can't wait to see you again soon.*
>
> *A. xx*

There had been no new letter yet, although his mum had

somehow managed three. He was sure she was just really busy on her father's estate but resolved to write back that weekend in case she was testing him. His mind was on what to write when the Sergeant Major came into their particular barrack block without warning and marched over to Archie. Will fell out of the bunk and the whole block stood to attention.

"Stand easy men, Relax."

Company Sergeant Major Russell was one of those men who had been in the army since fourteen, and served overseas for a number of those years. He had hardly engaged with the recruits since arriving but was always on the periphery overseeing things. He was probably now around forty and they knew little about him to be fair. There were rumours of a wife and kids, who the men said had left him some time ago. He was not tall but stocky and with a handlebar moustache that was currently very fashionable. What struck Will was the speed he had crossed the floor and with barely a sound like a ballerina spinning across a stage.

As the platoon relaxed slightly the CSM sat on the lower bunk much to their surprise, and beckoned Archie to sit next to him as Will moved away.

"Every platoon has a joker Bunden. I've seen lots of 'em come and go. You may not believe it but I was a bit of a lad myself when a private like you, many moons ago."

Archie and Will laughed politely but now listened intently to this sudden outpouring of conversation. Indeed the barracks had fallen into a respectful hush that made Will think of walking into St. Andrews back home.

"The thing is to learn when to joke and when to concentrate. There are times to speak up and times to shut up and listen. Soldiering is not farming lad, although I daresay there are risks on a farm too. But when we get over there, and that time is coming soon enough, there will be precious time for jokes. Jokes can get men killed. Not paying attention here can cost lives over there. Probably yours and more likely than not, your friends too. I'm not saying you won't have time to relax, and God knows soldiers do that better than anyone. Fight hard, play hard, I always say. But mark my words when I say there's no place for fooling about in war. The sergeants have a job to do. To get you men ready to fight and in a lot shorter time than they would normally have. So work with them not against them, and save your fighting for the Hun. Is that clear son?"

Archie had been as quiet as Will had ever known him and nodded silently.

"I said is that clear private?"

"Yes Sergeant Major!"

"They tell me your farts are legendary Bunden. Is that so?"

There was an audible breathing out around the block as the mood lightened, and Archie said "Yes Sergeant Major," and managed a weak smile.

"Good. Then we will use you as our secret weapon before an attack. Just make sure the breeze is going the right way first." The men broke out in laughter at that point and Russell slapped Archie on the back before standing up. "Oh one last thing. The corporals tell me you have been helping the lads a lot when not playing the clown. I think a bit more of that might be just the ticket. So I'm making you a Lance Corporal and putting you in charge of this block. See to it that you don't let me down. Anything wrong in here and I will hold you responsible. Congratulations!"

With that he marched out of the block and all eyes turned to Archie. He sat dumb struck on the bed and Will sat next to him and said "Blimey, well done Bunny."

"It's Lance Corporal Bunny to you! And I can't believe he thought I was a farmer. What an insult! Anyway this calls for a celebration. And that's my first order."

They laughed then and rose together, and all the men headed off in a group to the mess hall for a drink. Sergeant Major Russell watched them go from the shadows behind their barrack block. He nodded in approval and then headed back to the Battalion HQ building, another problem solved.

*

The joking had continued of course after that. It was impossible for

Archie not to rise to the occasion from time to time, but something certainly changed that night. Will noticed a quiet determination grow in his giant of a friend. In truth the whole platoon seemed to be galvanised from that moment, and while other platoons of recruits worked hard too, the men of 'C' Platoon, No. 1 Company, stood out in all areas of their training. Indeed when their all too brief stint in Woking neared its end, they were awarded the best platoon in pass out. Despite a man from No. 3 Company winning the best recruit award from the officers, ("bloody teacher's pet" Archie had grumbled); individually several of the men in 'C' Platoon topped the scores, and their platoon won best barracks.

Will turned out to be a crack shot and took to the rifle ranges like a duck to water. He was proficient with the Lee Enfield .303 rifle but also equally adept with the Maxim machine gun they were training on; although the British were already using an improved version called the Vickers from the same designers in France. The Lee Enfield bolt action rifle was accurate to fourteen hundred yards it was said, and in the final shoot offs in training, Will hit a target at thirteen hundred yards, dead centre; more than two hundred yards further and far more accurate than anyone else managed.

One of the officers said he should be transferred to the machine gun corps in France, but the CSM said he would make a very good sniper with the Regiment and other officers agreed. Will himself was keen to stay with his own company and was happy to be offered this chance, especially when it came with a stripe on his arm and additional pay. When he walked back to the barracks as a Lance Corporal too, Archie's face was a picture. But then he realised they had just won the marksmanship award as well and Archie proudly chalked another mark on their progress board on the wall.

Now as the men celebrated passing out together in their barracks, a real sense of togetherness had formed. Normally families would have been invited to this event, but this was war and everything was different, time being of the essence. Just then Ernie joined them with the mail and as the names were called out, 'Davison' was shouted not once but twice. With nervous anticipation he took his bundle over to his bunk.

There was a package from home containing more socks, and notes from mum and dad and some scribblings from Fred. This time there was also a pair of gloves from his grandma that didn't quite fit. He was smiling about it when one of the older men, Cedric, suggested cutting the ends off the fingers and using them to keep his hands warm and steady in winter so he could still shoot. He thanked Ced and turned his attentions to his parents' letter. It was much the same about things on the farm and what David and Fred had been up to, and the usual bits of gossip from the village, centred around the Church and the Star Inn of course. No doubt old Gettings was in his element now.

Then the final paragraph made him sit up and take notice. His mum informed him that a Lord Lowther had raised his own battalions to boost the numbers of men joining, and that volunteers had flocked from all over Sussex to sign up, and were continuing to do so. She said they were being known locally as 'Lowther's Lambs,' and that there would be at least three battalions based on her beloved South Downs.

Will called out to the men sitting around and read this out, and others confirmed they had been told the same from home so it must be true. It prompted a discussion whether they should transfer to a battalion that seemed to be based in their own backyards, but the general consensus was they were still in the Royal Sussex, and that was all that mattered. The conversation then turned to who they knew that had signed up, and Ernie said he would write home and ask for names from various places and a few towns and villages were shouted out as he made a list.

Ernie Isaacs as the eldest son of a tailor, was in his element here. As Will watched him take down details attentively he thought if the young lad had a tape measure and a pencil behind his ear, he could be back in the shop attending to gentlemen callers, working on suit designs, rather than sitting in his uniform in a barrack block in Woking. It was no surprise when Ernie won the smartest recruit award either.

Will's mind turned to his second piece of post and with shaking hands he picked up the envelope recognising at once the perfectly written address. It was from Alice. Archie stuck his head over the bunk, stole the socks and made a disappointed face when there was no chocolate this time. He saw Will mulling over the letter and recognised the writing too.

"Oh God, our sharpshooter's got a message from her majesty. We've lost him now for the rest of the day. Anyone fancy a kick around outside?" He dropped off as a number of the men shouted yes, mainly those without mail. A ball appeared from somewhere, and they tumbled out of the block, one of the men patting Ernie on the head as they did with a laugh.

Will should have been first out of the door but he hardly noticed as he read the letter and then read it again. It was full of news from Pevensey and mentioned the raising of the three battalions. Alice's father was a very good friend of Lord Lowther it seemed, and had been made a colonel in the new battalions. She enclosed a recruitment leaflet that was being sent out. It promised the men barrack blocks for training instead of tents, along with regular meals, recreation and good pay. It also said that friends would be kept together and promised 'return to work' schemes for all volunteers when they got home, in case they were worried about their jobs. Alice said that men had volunteered in hundreds apparently as a result. He could sense the excitement in her as she had written it.

The whole region seems swept up in this new initiative Will. More men sign up every day and I have agreed to help my father with organising it all. He's had to go to parliament with Lord Lowther more than once and someone needs to keep things running here when he's gone. Mother certainly isn't capable! I'm sorry that this work has kept me so busy I've neglected my promise to write.'

Finally she turned her attention to him, and thanked him for his lovely letter, and all the news within it. He read her words pouring over every mark and syllable.

'I am very proud of you Will. I loved hearing about your training and all the jolly fun that you have got up to. I am sure your parents must be terribly proud too. Have you been made an officer yet? You should consider transferring Will,

and then we could be close while you trained. I have spoken to Father about you joining the South Downs as an officer but he said they need men with experience to lead. Which is understandable I suppose, though quite rubbish. He did say if you joined Lowther promises fast promotion for all and I am sure I can influence that! Please consider it for me.

I do hope to see you again very soon. I miss my farm boy. It's not the same without you here. Please write again and forgive my tardiness.

Your Alice xx

Will was unsure why the tone of the letter bothered him. He couldn't put his finger on it and was cross at himself. He didn't like being called farm boy, but decided he was being over sensitive. He vowed to write straight back and tell her about his success and that of his platoon. Even so her letter pulled at him inside, and as he turned the question over about transferring, he absent mindedly looked out of the barrack window and saw Archie and a number of men roaring about with a football.

Could he leave them now? he pondered. *God he did miss her and longed to hold her again and kiss her, but he was here now and had new friends. It would be a wrench.* He started to write a reply, stopped and started again. He began with the news of his promotion first, as if stalling for time on the bigger question.

"Davison."

Will looked up and saw Sergeant Campbell from the HQ building in the doorway. He jumped down and said "Yes Sergeant?"

"Is that Bunden leading the riot on the playing field?"

"Er yes Sergeant. Well they are playing football that is."

"Well as that probably makes you the senior man here *Corporal* I'll tell you," the Sergeant replied, with some sarcasm in his voice. Will blushed as there were still half a dozen men in the barrack older than him, except for Ernie who had stopped scribbling and stood rigidly to attention.

"Company's been called up. In fact they all have. We leave tomorrow and sail for France at the weekend. Better get your kit all squared away and then I suggest you write home and tell your Mum not to wait up."

Will was stunned and the other men all stopped and stared at the Sergeant. They knew this was coming but the news still had an immediate impact.

"Yes Sergeant. I'll tell them all."

"Good. Oh and Davison. Better tell the men to get a few drinks in too. They are going to need it. I'll not expect to put my hand in my pocket in the canteen tonight." He raised his eyes and then turned and walked out.

That was that. There was no decision to be made now. Will abandoned his letter writing and went out to where Archie was arguing that tackling should include pulling people to the ground if he wanted to. He spoke to him on one side. Archie announced the news to the rest of the men with a shout and there was a great cheer. Will's first feelings of dread on hearing the news were blown away by Archie's infectious enthusiasm and he immediately joined in the game. The men roared up and down the pitch without a care in the world, and were soon joined by others as the word spread.

For once the rain had stopped and the sun shone down on this group of men, pulled together by circumstance. They were fit, and bronzed like Greek Gods, and eager to 'get stuck in' to the enemy. To a man they felt invincible.

From his window on the second floor of the HQ building, CSM Russell sipped tea and watched the men charge about. He smiled at the camaraderie, and yet a part of him felt sad as to what lay ahead for them. He knew the news from France, and it wasn't good. Nor were the casualty lists for the Royal Sussex, among the many other regiments, already mounting up from the first battles. *This was war and this was what they had signed up for*, he told himself; and despite inadequate training Russell felt sure they would do their duty when the time came. *King and Country*, that's what mattered. He took another swig of tea to swish away his moment of weakness, and then returned to the matter in hand of transporting these men to France as soon as possible.

Chapter 9 – Pre-Match Nerves

W hile the training camp in Woking had been a far cry from the comforts of home to the men, it was a palace compared to the transit camp they waited in now in Folkstone. Their barracks were no more than glorified large canvas scout tents with rows of mats for beds on the damp muddy floor. When being allotted their space, the Quartermaster had told them compared to a trench it was "heaven," and they would "learn that soon enough."

The rain had returned during the day. October always was a wet month, which only added to the gloom of the dull and lengthy journey by train and truck to their embarkation port. Their high spirits of the last forty eight hours were somewhat dampened by the new surroundings in Shorncliffe Camp, literally dampened it transpired, as the water was now dripping freely through holes in the canvas roof.

"Trenches?" Archie stated. "Nearest thing to a trench that QM has been in is a trough he sticks his fat snout in every day. It's a wonder there's any food here at all for the real fighting men." As ever he found a way to lighten the mood. "Look we've been told to rest this evening before anything happens tomorrow. I have it on good authority from one of the orderlies that there's a smashing little café down the road near the sea that stays open late. What do you say we go there and pass the time, rather than lie here like a bunch of sponges waiting for boiled beef and carrots in a tin?"

Will needed no second invitation, and before long a large group of them had assembled by the main gate, mostly from 'C' Platoon, though for Ernie and one or two others it was a risk not worth taking. Ced came into his own though, blagging a story to the camp guards on the gate to get them some time out, softened with a few cigarettes and a small bottle of rum his wife had sent him before they left Woking. By the time he'd finished they had a lift down to the front on one of the army trucks too; a medical wagon going to pick up more supplies from the dock.

As they rattled down the military road towards an area by the sea appropriately called Sandgate, Will looked around at the men sitting chatting who over the last few weeks he had come to know. Though most of them were not what he would consider friends, and to them he was probably still just a young lad, they shared a common bond now. The training and its purpose bringing them together in a way that just felt different to the friends he had back home. But there were one or two besides Archie that he had grown closer to, including the serious Ernie back in camp.

Cedric Longworthy, apart from being the hero of the hour, had taken a shine to him it seemed, and was a father figure to a few of the younger lads; always there with a friendly word of advice or helping hand, and never one to shirk a night out. His thick brown hair was betrayed by greying sideburns that showed the age, and of course the moustache was in full flow so only his bottom lip was ever visible. Ced had worked in a number of areas, including farms and mines over the years so was instantly a hit with many of the men of the regiment and without doubt Will saw the bond with Archie. They sat together now singing some well-known tune but concocting lyrics that would make a mermaid blush, each trying to outdo the other. Though Will didn't understand all the words yet, their meaning was obvious and he laughed with the rest, enjoying the moment. As the chorus reached a crescendo, the truck suddenly lurched to a halt, the medical orderly banging the side of the door and telling them to bail out.

They leapt and stumbled out of the back in a relaxed happy group, some arms around each other continuing their conversations, others striking up cigarettes. In front of them was a blue and white café, seemingly freshly painted, with signs outside advertising the tantalizing array of delights to be had if you cared to come in and linger a while. It had a number of large wide windows looking out towards the sea on one side that offered uninterrupted views of the Channel. Despite being after five in the evening, there were still a number of customers inside, and lamps had been lit to keep the creeping gloom at bay. Outside the late October sun still kept a final vigil over the beaches, as reluctant to leave as the couples walking along its golden promenade.

The men went in, Archie at the front as ever with a shout of "Aye Aye" in that familiar Sussex twang of his. Will stared at the sunset which exploded into the sea like a firework finale he had watched with his family once at a show in Horsham. Smiling at the memory he paused to look up at the sign hanging over the door. *'Maggie's'* it said simply in large white letters on a blue board. He pushed the door and went in.

The café was very nicely laid out with a selection of square tables each with four chairs set at intervals across the wide wooden floor. The tables all had blue and white checked table cloths on them matching the façade of the front outside, which added to the seaside feel. At one side of the café by the large windows Will had seen from the outside there were a couple of longer tables with benches which the men had poured onto and were now jostling and shouting without a thought for the other customers round about.

"Hello, can I help?"

Will turned to look at a pleasant dark haired lady probably in her late twenties who stood by the counter, notepad in hand. He was temporarily thrown by her appearance. Soft warm eyes and a welcoming smile, were framed by wild black hair that despite being tied back for work in a ponytail, still fell rebelliously around her ears.

"I'm Maggie. Maggie McRae. Are you here alone or with the school party by the windows?"

Her humour made him laugh spontaneously and he pointed to the group and raised his eyes as if in apology.

"Aye well take a seat and try not to break anything. I'll be over in a minute." Her Scottish accent now shone through and Will wondered why she was all the way in Kent as he made his way between the chequered maze to his friends.

"Here he is," shouted Archie as if on a football field, and Will winced as he looked at the poor families sat nearby. "Just in time to pay!" The others all laughed and Will sighed and climbed onto the end of one of the benches just about managing to squeeze his legs in. Maggie came over hands on hips and said, "Right gentlemen what would you like?"

"Aye Aye" said Archie again and the men sniggered.

"There's an offer we can't refuse love" said Ced.

"Oh I do apologise boys," said Maggie, "I mistook you for gentlemen. You soldiers are all the same." Some of the men laughed again at this, and Will smiled at the fact she could clearly hold her own. "Perhaps you'd rather my brother served you?" She nodded to the counter where a large brute of a man was hacking at a joint of meat with a carving knife to make some sandwiches up. He was about six foot six and twice as wide and cast a warning glance in their direction, knife poised in the air. Other than the dark hair there was little to suggest they were siblings but it put the men in their places and they calmed down a little.

Cedric was undeterred however. "No offence Miss. Maybe you can sit on my knee and we can start again?"

"That's very kind of you but you're old enough to be my father, and my husband wouldn't approve, even though he likes me to help the elderly." The men roared at this and Archie gave Ced a slap on the back.

"Let's not keep Maggie waiting lads," said Will, "and besides I'm bloody starving."

"Maggie? How do you know her name Davison?" one of the men from 'A' platoon called out, a small skinny man called Luke, who had tagged along with them.

"She told me when I came in. I assume this is your café miss?"

"Yes it is," and she smiled warmly at Will once more.

"Hasn't been here five minutes and already he's on first name terms. We have to watch this one Ced," Archie shouted.

"Always the quiet ones," one of the other men agreed.

Will blushed, and seeing his predicament Maggie told them to "leave the wee lad alone," and started to demand orders, until the men fell into line one by one, ordering drinks and food. Most went for the special of the day which was a beef salad with some new potatoes, although there was a spattering of requests for sandwiches and a couple went for fish and chips. All accompanied by beer. Will

74

was last and she came down to the table end rather than shout across the group.

"What about you?"

"Will. My name's Will Davison miss. And I'd like the fish and chips please."

"Of course, and you can call me Maggie. I'm not a teacher. Or Mrs McRae if you prefer." She smiled again and her face transformed once more. She was not a classical beauty like Alice, Will thought, whose face was fragile like an English rose but could transform a room with a simple flicker. Maggie was pretty in a different way entirely. He imagined the fields of heather on the Downs that you could wander through often, and not appreciate what you were seeing, and then suddenly something would happen to make you aware of it, like a rainbow after a storm, and you would be transfixed and never look at the place the same again. It made him feel warm inside and then he realised she was speaking.

"Shall I come back?" she laughed.

"What?"

"I was waiting for you to order your drink?"

"Oh sorry, beer too."

"Are you old enough Will?" she winked and as he started to mumble a reply she walked off to the kitchen.

Will saw Ced smiling at him and he smiled back embarrassed. Then the men descended into talk of the war and life back home. Some of the men from the other platoons were being teased about how it felt to be with the top soldiers but generally the spirits were high, and as one of the waitresses served the beers the noise levels increased. At one point Will caught Maggie as she was clearing a table nearby and asked where she was from.

"I'm from Inverness," she replied perching on the edge of a table. "My husband, Stewart, is serving in France with the Cameron Highlanders. When he went over the water last year I came down to Dover with him. My wee brother was already living here so I decided to stay on and help Angus with the café." Will raised his eyes at the description of Angus as 'wee,' and as he looked at him he spotted a blonde girl of no more than four or five run out from the back kitchen into the bar area.

"Do you have children then?" he asked pointing to the girl.

"Och no," she said with a slight blush. "That's Angus' wee bairn. There's enough here to do without fussing about my own little ones, though I daresay that might change when my man returns." It was Will's turn to blush now, and she changed the subject quickly noticing his discomfort.

"When do you go?"

"Tomorrow or the next day they told us."

She nodded and patted his knee. "That accounts for the high spirits then."

"More like pre-match nerves I think," said Will.

"Aye something like that. You like football then I take it, or is it rugby?"

"Football," he said beaming.

A couple of families left while they were chatting, smiling and shaking Angus' hand and Will was surprised they had lasted as long as they did.

Maggie stood up and called out, "Au revoir."

"Excuse me Miss but were those people Frenchies?"

"Sorry?" She was clearly still thinking of her conversation with Will.

It was Luke who had asked, and he continued, "They weren't speaking English, sounded more French to me."

"Oh those people were Belgium refugees. They have been coming into Dover and Folkstone since the war started in large groups, and being housed hereabouts."

"Refugees," said Archie. "I thought we were winning this war?"

"Perhaps," said Maggie. But their homes are being destroyed in the fighting and they have had to flee for their own safety and leave everything behind. We are trying to help where we can with many other families, but it's not easy."

The comment was a simple one but somehow seemed to remind the men of what they were about to do, and the enormity of it, and the mood became somber all of a sudden.

Ced broke the awkward silence. "We should be getting back, the guard on the gate said it was a good thirty minute walk."

"There is a bus goes from the corner of the road on the hour," Maggie offered helpfully, aware she had caused this downturn in events.

"Thanks Miss but the walk will do them good. Help sober them up before we get back just in case the CO is waiting."

"CO?"

"Oh, that's short for commanding officer. Sorry. How much do we owe you?"

"I'm sorry I don't know all these terms despite my husband being in the army. I'll get the bill for you."

They pooled their money and paid Maggie, with a number thanking her and apologising for the noise. There was a hushed discussion amongst the group and some grumblings. Archie leant in close to one of the other platoon members with a growl, and then Ced turned and handed Maggie another collection of coins.

"For the refugees Miss."

They left much quieter than they came, as if mirroring the way the troops came and went from the front. Maggie smiled the tears away as a mixture of emotions and thoughts flooded her mind. She hated this perpetual cycle of men already, and hoped the war would be over soon, and her dear Stewart would return safe and well.

Will was the last to leave, shaking her hand politely and saying thank you to Angus, who paused and smiled at this young blond lad who had taken time to chat to his sister.

"Stay safe laddie," he said, then ducked under the door into the kitchen and was gone.

"Goodbye Will Davison," Maggie whispered as he put on his regimental cap and walked out. He wondered if he had upset her with the question about children and was going to turn and say something, but then the door slammed in the wind and it made him jump inside. Without looking back he set off after the others, head bowed against the freshening gale.

*

On Mill Farm at that precise time the Davisons were all asleep, late nights being a rarity even when the Star seduced Harold to stay sometimes. But the storm had come in as predicted and the barn door threw off its temporary latch aided by the mischievous wind, and proceeded to bang against the wall.

Harold woke with a start and pulled his weary bones out of bed, and stumbled down the stairs and outside. It was a starless sky full of anger and foreboding and he knew the cattle would be scared enough without the door going. He paused to try and light a cigarette but the wind denied his lungs the pleasure. He cursed still trying to stay half asleep after only being in bed a couple of hours. His eyes adjusted to the gloom and stumbling forward he traced the well-worn path to the barn and then lighting a lamp that hung on the wall, he set about fixing the latch once more.

*

As Harold was struggling with the latch, James hurled himself into his French dugout as a third bomb landed nearby in quick succession with a loud bang. The roof of the timber structure shook with the blast, and soil and debris came down on the officers' heads sheltering inside, emphasising the fragility.

"Bombardment's started again Sir. Using whizzbangs too this time. No casualties yet."

"Thank you Davison," the colonel seated at the map table replied, "get yourself some tea and then listen in."

"Thank you Sir."

James went over to the stove and took the simmering pot off with a nearby rag and poured some black tea into his mess tin. He was joined at the nearby brazier by Harry Johnson, and allowed the fire to warm through his soaking jacket.

"Still alive James old boy?"

"Still alive Jonners," David replied with a grin. It was a ritual exchange they said every day when one or the other returned from a wire party or a reconnaissance patrol. As lieutenants they were regularly given difficult assignments such as taking men out at night to repair their wire lines, or to stop the Germans repairing theirs and listening for signs of enemy movement. All of which carried high risk and regular casualties, not just from snipers and fighting with raiding parties which they had done on more than one occasion, and with great credit; but from being caught in the open when the Germans launched another bombardment as they had now. James' section had literally just dropped back into the trench after two hours in No Man's Land when the shells began to fall.

"If you two love birds have finished, I'd like to start the briefing." James and Harry exchanged smiles and turned from the fire's warmth to face the colonel who was standing by the map table, pointer at the ready, with a captain of artillery, and their own Major Grenville-Peters, or 'the old GP' as the men called him affectionately. Old being a trench joke as he was only twenty eight last week, and yet everyone knew what the war did to them. He did however speak quietly and intelligently that reminded James of their family doctor, George Corbett, back home.

"It's quite obvious with this nightly shelling that Jerry is going to try another counter-attack any day soon so I want the men ready and alert at all times, and double sentries in post. If Jerry's not out tonight foraging about, he could be getting ready to try a push tomorrow, but if the wires are intact who knows. We have two more days then we are being pulled back and relieved by the Irish Rangers on the 18th I am told. Spot of rest and chance for the men to get a bath and some warm clothes. God knows the beggars need it. I know I do. But only forty eight hours if that, then we are moving north. What's that place again Major? Wipers?"

"Ypres sir. It's pronounced Eepers or Eeps I think they said."

"Stupid names. What's up with Oxford and Cambridge? We're descended from Normans and yet our names are far more sensible what? Anyway there's a big show on and we're being pulled in to show the lesser regiments what to do."

The officers nodded and smiled politely, and as the colonel went on about the big push further north in this ridiculously named location, the bombs continued to thump down, sometimes close, sometimes further away. No matter how many times the men went through this it was impossible not to flinch when one landed nearby as they all did now, with the roof shuddering again. James had seen more than one dug-out take a direct hit and knew that if that happened your number was pretty much up. More often than not having clawed wounded men out himself with his bare hands from their muddy tombs, he had decided early on it was better to die than survive in that state.

He allowed his mind to wander back home, as he often did to blank the deadly knocking. He imagined it was just his dad banging another fence post in. His thoughts turned to Will having had the letter from mum some time back, telling him that he'd joined up too. He gazed at the colonel's map and wondered where his young brother would be sent in this hellish landscape. *Please Lord somewhere other than here.*

James knew he should write home too and acknowledge his mum's updates. Since their first action he had struggled to know what to write other than he was well and missed home. There was nothing of his daily routine he wanted to share with his parents. So he tried hard not to think of home and the letter always remained unfinished.

*

At that moment Will was thinking of France as he climbed onto his makeshift bed in Shorncliffe camp. He listened to the rumble of thunder off the coast that Ernie had been told were the big guns at the front, though no one believed him. For once Will didn't go to sleep thinking of Alice, but of James. He hoped his brother was safe, and that he might see him soon. And then an image of Maggie with her shining eyes standing next to her man mountain of a brother, appeared surprisingly in his thoughts for a moment, until very quickly exhaustion brought sleep.

Chapter 10 - Playing for your country

The bugle sounding 'reveille' interrupted him as he was about to score for England and Will rolled angrily off his bed. He bumped into Archie who was still sound asleep on the floor between their mats. Archie awoke with a burst of swearing and grunts and then everyone was up and awake. One of the camp sergeants appeared almost simultaneously.

"You men have an hour to get some breakfast and get your things together. Your colonel came in last night while half of you were at the beach and wants to brief the regiment at 0700. You're sailing today."

"Excuse me my good man. I wondered if I could extend my check out time for another day or so. It's so very nice here and I haven't really had time to see the sights." Archie had spoken in a very posh accent and the Sergeant made to roar into him, and then checked himself looking round the group of men in various stages of undress, who were now all smirking.

"Unfortunately we're fully booked sir," he replied walking up to Archie, "but don't worry as I've organised you a nice cruise, followed by a foreign holiday where you will get plenty of chance to sight see."

"That's jolly decent of you."

"Isn't it." The sergeant leaned in. "Now shift your arse."

With that he walked out and the men set about sorting their kit, talking in hushed tones as they did.

"You're a one Archie," Will said, seeing his friend pause, and noticed just for a moment a look that was almost fear on his friend's face.

But in a flash it was gone and Archie bellowed out, "All right who's nicked me bleedin' socks!" and all was ok with the world again.

*

81

They gathered at 0700 hours in the main parade square in camp. Over two hundred men in six platoons, Will's platoon with A and B making Number One Company, and D to F forming Number Two Company, with a further platoon of support troops from various regiments including medics, orderlies and so on. The camp Chaplain spoke first leading the men in prayer and offering blessings for their safe return and assured success, as the soldiers knelt awkwardly on the hard ground.

"God fights on the side of the righteous and knows our cause is just. His angels will lead you into battle."

"I'll believe that when I see it," somebody muttered under their breath amongst the kneeling men, and there were murmurs of agreement.

Archie whispered to Will, "Germans are Christian as well aren't they? Let's just hope God doesn't like them more than us or those angels might come in the other direction!" They raised their eyes to one another.

"Silence for the colonel."

The men now all stood again. A dog barked in the distance, and the wind carried the sound across the uniformed statues waiting for the colonel to speak. Once more the colonel was on his immaculately groomed white horse, and it was rumoured the horse would be going with them to France, leading to yet more jokes. Harry Enright who'd been working over at the stables in Lewes was delegated to befriend the horse and find out any rumours from it.

"Get it straight from the horse's mouth Harry," Archie had said. Harry was not the brightest spark despite being a good stable hand, and had said "yes," before he realised he was being set up. Ced offered to go to the 'Nag's head' instead as he reckoned he could find out far more news there. And so it went on.

Colonel Bradshaw cleared his throat and spoke up.

"Men. You are going today to take part in a great adventure for which the Royal Sussex Regiment is already fully engaged. They have carried the Regimental name with honour into yet another field of battle and no less I expect from you. I do not ask my men to do anything I would not do myself, and so I will be going with you to the front."

Despite the previous jokes, the men were impressed by this. The colonel spoke with a clear strong voice, his upper class background clearly evident in his perfect pronunciation and polished accent. Yet he had also served with distinction and that endeared him to the men now arranged before him, despite the gulf in class.

"I have no doubt you will serve your country well and uphold the great traditions of this regiment when called upon to do so in France. We have halted the German charge at the gates of Paris and pushed them back already. Victory is only a matter of time. If needs be we will chase the Hun back to the very heart of Germany itself." The men cheered as the colonel continued.

"I know many of you like sport. Some of you have even represented your country. Well very soon you will all be playing for your country in a manner of speaking. It is a competition we must win and will win. If they take a set we will win the match. If they score a goal, we score two more. And while they may take the odd wicket, eventually we will bowl them out. Am I right?"

The men roared their approval now, and the colonel continued without waiting for it to die down.

"The try line is in sight men. But it will not be gained easily I'm sure. We know the enemy presents tough opposition, and without doubt some of you will be injured in the struggles ahead. Some of you will not return. But I expect you all to face the enemy regardless without fear and without thoughts of anything but success. If you fall, know that other men will rise to take your places, as you do now for those gallant men of the regiment who have already paid the ultimate sacrifice. We cannot fail men. Or we risk losing everything we hold dear."

The colonel delivered his speech with stirring passion and the men felt eager to get over to France and into the enemy. But Will was probably not alone in being at the same time unnerved by the matter of fact way Colonel Bradshaw told them that without doubt many of them could be wounded or killed.

"Good luck to you. For King and Country!" The soldiers cheered and echoed the cry, to boost their own courage as much as sounding patriotic.

The chaplain blessed the men and then they were dismissed to board the trucks down to the docks. There was excitement and nervous tension in equal measure and it was tangible in the air.

*

"I know what I hold dear," Archie said, as he joined the platoon assembling near the main camp road, "and I'm not getting it shot off for the politicians sat in London." Some men laughed but Will frowned at his friend.

"Shush Archie, don't let the officers hear you say that. You mean you won't fight?"

"Didn't say that did I, William old boy? I just said I'm not fighting for those fat lumps sat at home playing war over a sherry, while we are sent off to fight it for real."

"So why are you here then, *old boy*?" Ced asked sarcastically. "You one of these new communist types?"

"God no. More bloody foreigners. I'm here for me mates like the rest of us yes? I'm here for the boys from Sussex, and Steyning in particular. And I hate Germans of course."

A number of men said "Here, here."

"Ever seen a Jerry Archie?" Ernie asked.

"In pictures yes. They look right miserable sods." His booming laugh rubbed off on the men around who laughed too, eager to lighten the mood. Will was relieved that his friend was just joking, having been afraid Archie didn't want to go.

"Besides," Archie said, slinging his kit bag over his shoulder as the order came for their platoon to mount up, "I hear French wine is delicious and far too good for Jerry to drink. So that's got to be worth fighting for right? I'm off to save the bleedin' vineyards." With big smiles the men marched off to the waiting trucks singing as they did so.

*

The dock was a press of men and vehicles, voices everywhere shouting commands and requests for help. Mixed with the volume of noise from the men waiting to board the boat, it was absolute uproar. Tempers were frayed as things were lost or broken and schedules were missed. The men from Sussex weren't the only soldiers at the dock that day. There were groups of men from a number of other regiments too including the East Kents and the Hampshires, as well as several London Battalion detachments, some of whom had been diverted once already from other embarkation points.

Friendly rivalries boiled over, and here and there officers or comrades had to step in to break up fights and maintain order. Eventually the command came for the Royal Sussex to board the boat, and they did so painfully slowly up two single gangplanks which just exasperated the situation for those on board and those trying to clear the dock.

As they filed up slowly onto a rapidly filling boat, Will thought of the animals going to market back home and wondered if they suffered the same emotions of fear, confusion and indeed claustrophobia as the men squashed into every available space. He suddenly remembered the train load of sheep that had passed them when he was in his grandad's yard on their last visit, their black faces pressed out through narrow gaps. Were they now simply 'lambs to the slaughter' as well?

He recalled Alice's last letter, squashed in his top pocket, and the news of her father joining the new Southdown battalions known locally as 'Lowther's Lambs.' Seeing the men crowded here, and thinking of those sheep, he wondered if the name was a blessing or a curse.

Eventually having missed one tide already, the boat was loaded up, and the gangplanks removed. With a loud blast on her whistle, the ropes were released and the Steamship Victoria set off with her precious cargo. Will was amazed how the thing stayed afloat with so many men and so much equipment stowed on board, most of which seemed to be on the main deck. They were able to find themselves some space near the front however, Archie and a couple of the bigger lads ensuring there was no discussion; and were grateful they

85

weren't shut away downstairs with a lot of the others.

Will's thoughts of 'Lowther's Lambs' reminded him of home and he decided to pass the journey writing back to Alice, and to his mum and dad. He sat down against the side of the boat and rested the paper on his knee and settled into his task. The sea calm and still after last night's storms, was a deep inviting blue, and as the ship pitched gently up and down many of the men drifted off to sleep.

A noise from the sky made him look up and he saw lines of Canada geese flying in formation overhead, their incessant chatter breaking the tranquility of the moment. He smiled at the similarity between the geese and the men down below. Their incessant squawks reminded him of the noise on the dock. The birds were all blindly following their leader in lines, as the men did as they boarded their ship, trusting the person in charge that they knew what they were doing. As he watched, with some unspoken signal, the geese all changed direction away from France.

"Think they know something we don't," Ced remarked, who had noticed the birds from his own perch on a supply crate. Then he too dropped his head to search for sleep.

Will turned his gaze away from the sky and watched the English shore line shrink behind them. The white chalk cliffs sinking into the horizon like a trap door closing on an intrepid adventurer. Now the only way was forward, and he wondered when he would ever see home again.

Chapter 11 – Digging in

The Sussex men had gone by train to St. Omer from Calais when they had first arrived. Will spent much of the journey lost in thought looking at the landscape flashing past with the myriad of sights and smells. However were it not for the occasional foreign sounding names on signposts as they went in and out of towns, he thought they could just as well be in the English countryside; and somehow the sight of men toiling in the fields calmed the nerves he had felt on board the cramped ship. The leaves on the trees were well established in their autumn coats. Oranges and reds blurred together as the train roared towards the distant sunset, whose bloodshot crown now mirrored the landscape they passed through, seducing the unsuspecting men towards the darkness that followed after.

They had completed the last leg of their journey by truck, and were now based at a large camp in Neuve-Chappelle. Despite the obvious signs of war preparations, the base had seemed okay at first, with the men being used for a multitude of work tasks. There was hot food, dry tents and even allocated times for baths. Will didn't mind the conditions any more than the other men and he was used to manual labour, so just settled into a routine that seemed not dissimilar to a day on the farm. Digging certainly came naturally to Will and he set about it without complaint and was soon marked out by the officers as a good example.

For the first few days they were either humping supplies back and forth from the trucks that came up daily from the supply depot at the rail head, or repairing parts of the main camp that had been shelled. They were over half a mile away from the front line trenches in this main supply base, but every now and then the German's long range guns fired into these rear areas. The men were also sent forward to repair the communications trenches that ran back and forth to the front line. These were prone to more damage the closer they got to the front but more often than not just collapsed in places from the perpetual rain. Here Will began to see the men who had been at the front since August moving back and forth between the rest camps and the front line. He heard the camaraderie between them, but every now and then one would catch his eye as he worked, and something in their stare made him feel that their singing masked the reality of what was actually going on somewhere up ahead.

At the end of their first week the men were briefed about the current situation by a Major from the Second Battalion of the Royal Sussex who had come over to France in August. He had advised them that following the defeat and retreat from Mons, the British Expeditionary Force, or 'BEF' as they were commonly known, had halted the German advance near the Aisne river and then both sides had suddenly ground to a halt. What they had expected to be a fast mobile war became a stand-off suddenly with trench systems springing up almost overnight as both sides dug in. The Germans had adapted to this much quicker than the British inflicting large numbers of casualties, and had then tried to outflank the army to the north. The British and French armies countered this move, playing 'catch-up' to this new form of warfare, and both sides pushed their lines further and further north in what the Major described as the 'Race for the Sea.'

Will watched Major Brown's haggard face as he carried out this briefing. He seemed worn out already with the situation and not overly optimistic despite some rhetoric to the contrary. He was very tall, well over six feet and while his uniform seemed relatively clean Will noticed he had thick dried mud on his legs from the knees down, and if rumours of the conditions at the front were to be believed he must have come from there only recently. The Major didn't ask the assembled troops if they had any questions when he finished, he just turned to the waiting officers who had come over with them and said, "Well, you have your orders. Carry on and I will be back by the weekend."

They continued their manual laboring tasks for the next few days. The monotonous work gave Will time to think about home, and especially Alice. He wondered what she was doing right now, and as he reflected on their moments together he felt suddenly anxious. He had not heard from her since they were in the training camp but that was not unusual as they had moved so quickly from place to place. He managed to dash off a note before they left England to tell her of their departure and that he would write soon; which he vowed to do now as he took a break from the digging.

*

During this time they were also trained on trench warfare, and how to listen at night for enemy movement. Experienced men showed them how to set deadly traps on the wire and in shell holes to catch out enemy patrols, as if they were simply baiting traps for the vermin on the farm. They learnt how to distinguish shapes and sounds at night, and friend from foe potentially; and to know the different types of shells as they came in and where they might land. Some of the men didn't pay much attention as it seemed like any other training; the reality not having sunk in yet despite the constant sound of firing no more than a mile away.

Will sensed the change. With every day that passed now, he began to feel the sounds and smells of the farm back home were moving further and further away. So he listened to everything attentively, as did the street-wise men amongst the platoons like Archie and Ced. They saw the regular stream of casualties coming back down the line from the front, and befriended the thick moustached regulars with jokes and cigarettes to glean all the extra knowledge they could.

Two things then happened in twenty four hours that brought the reality crashing home to all of them, whether they had been paying attention or not. First they were ordered to take their place in the front trench, and then the platoon suffered its first casualty.

*

Rising from his tent as the bugle signalled the start of another day, Will spotted Major Brown striding purposefully through the depot in the first light. He noticed he walked with a slight stoop that belied his actual height. No more than a few minutes later the Company Sergeant Major and his staff were calling the men to fall into the mess hall once more at the double. The 'mess hall' being the local town hall that had been 'commandeered' by the British army when they arrived, along with several other buildings of note. Not least the Mayor's house which was now the headquarters for the British senior officers, much to the French Mayor's disgust; probably owing to his well-stocked wine cellar there, that affected his decision making on many an afternoon before the war.

This time it was their own colonel who addressed them, the Major standing respectfully to one side. Will realised the major was clearly the more informed of the two men, as the colonel frequently turned to him to confirm points as he relayed them.

"So in short gentlemen, we are to provide fresh troops to the Second Battalion who have been hard at it since August," the colonel continued, "and in this particular section for nearly three weeks on the front line. Casualties have been high and the Battalion is depleted and sorely in need of new men. We will relieve them by company so they can rest and recuperate by rotation without too much disruption, so you will have experienced men with you while you get up to speed. The Cameron Highlanders have been to our left for the last month and had a hell of a pounding I can assure you and they are soon to be replaced by new men from the London Rifles."

He stopped again to make sure the men were following him and to listen as the Major leaned forward and whispered something else in his ear. The colonel nodded almost imperceptibly and continued, his voice echoing off the walls of the tightly packed meeting room; its walls resplendent in fake renaissance floral wallpaper that clashed garishly with the brown uniforms of the men.

"Several of the other regiments that were here are also reducing their numbers or have moved on altogether so we want this change round to be as smooth as possible so Jerry doesn't spot any changes. The main fight may be going on further north but don't think for a moment the Hun won't try and pour through here if they get wind of the fact we are weakening our defences. Is that clear men?"

As the men nodded and said "Yes sir," Ced leaned in from where he was sitting behind Archie and Will.

"Aren't the Camerons the mob that sweet jock lass from the café said her husband had gone off with? What was his name?"

"Stewart," Will answered without hesitation.

"That's the one. Maybe we will bump into him and can tell him we saw his missus."

"Aye Aye" said Archie with a wink, "but I'd leave out the bit where you asked her to sit on your knee Ced."

They laughed together.

"Something you'd like to share gentlemen?"

The voice of the CSM brought them sharply to attention. They hadn't noticed Russell walking quietly up to them as they chatted during the colonel's briefing.

"I suggest you focus on what the colonel has to say, and you may learn something that will save your life. More importantly I don't want to have to write to your mummies and tell them you died because you didn't bloody listen. Clear?"

"Yes Sergeant Major," they echoed as one.

"Good. Now shut up."

*

A few minutes later as the men were dismissed and told to prepare to move to the front by company, one of the new Lieutenants called out for Harry Enright.

"Private Enright"

"Sir?"

"Fall out and report to the colonel. Special duties"

"Yes sir."

Archie's veins nearly popped out of his neck as he caught up with Harry in the melee of men pushing out of the hall, and pulled him to one side. Will thought he was actually going to explode and got Ced to pull him back.

"Oi Enright. What does he mean special duties? Are you in trouble?"

"No nothing like that Archie," Harry stammered, cowering more than a foot in height below him. "I took your advice that's all."

"What?"

"This should be good," Ced whispered.

"Keep moving there, hurry up you men." The officer that had called out Harry's name was now pushing the men towards the exit and out, and so the group had to walk together as Archie waited for his answer.

"You said I should get close to the horse," Harry continued, regaining some of his composure, "so I spoke to the CSM who approached the captain."

"To do what? Talk to the colonel's horse?" Archie continued, one eye raised sarcastically.

"No. To be his groom."

Archie stopped dead in shock and Will and Ced bounced off the back of him like two flies hitting a window.

"You have got to be kidding me?"

"No Archie."

"Get going you men, I won't tell you again. It's not like you need some big goodbye scene, you'll see him when you're next back here whenever that may be. Enright report to the colonel at HQ now."

The lieutenant smiled at his own poor attempt at humour. He was probably no older than any of them but had been through the right schools and gone to officer training and now was clearly enjoying being in charge. He was carrying a monocle favoured by the older officers, to try and make him look more senior Will guessed, but he thought it looked daft on this young man. He had very short blond hair as well, plastered to his head in a manner that seemed to accentuate his rather large thin nose.

"It makes him look German," Ernie had said dismissively as they had queued for breakfast a few days before. Will disliked him instantly. The lieutenant reminded him of a particularly unpleasant teacher he had had back home called Mr Bickerstaff, who had taken delight in humiliating any boy that got a question wrong on a daily basis, and Will had been no exception. The officer was called Dunn, and as other ranks are prone to do, he was quickly nicknamed Lieutenant 'Hun' after Ernie's remark about his appearance.

As the men formed up to march to the trench lines, having rapidly pulled all their kit together, it began to rain solidly again. Heavy continuous lines of rain like steel rods coming down to soak everything in seconds. 'C' platoon was in the middle of the line of men, and they watched Harry walk off with a couple of officers towards their horses, laughing and chatting as he did so. They thought they saw him glance at them guiltily for a moment but the scene was blurred through the curtain of rain.

"Un-bloody-believable," Archie said through clenched teeth. "Special sodding duties."

"Always the quiets ones 'eh Archie," Will said echoing what the men had said to him in Maggie's café a couple of weeks past, when he had been the brunt of the teasing.

"That's right lad," Ced agreed laughing as they marched off.

"Sod off the lot of you," Archie said and they all laughed then, though inside they were envious of Harry's luck.

Chapter 12 - Changing Round

In the half light of dusk, Will walked up the communications trench to the front line with the other new recruits. Half a dozen of the original BEF troops accompanied them. Having reached the second line of trenches they halted for a brief rest break and some rations, and a further briefing by company from the Sergeant Major; before playing the usual waiting game while orders were sent back and forth about where they were to be used. Then the new men were split up and posted all along the Sussex sector, and for the first time in ages Will was parted from Archie and Ced. Ernie was with him at least but they walked with barely a word exchanged as this close to the front sound carried, and they had been warned more than once not to attract the attention of the German observers.

As they approached the main trench the floor dipped down sharply and suddenly the boardwalk was gone under a foot of water, and they had to slow down so as not to lose their footing. They turned right and made for some 'dugouts' that were to be 'home' for the next two weeks or so. The trenches were crowded with men everywhere moving back and forth or gathered around their positions. Ernie slipped and stumbled trying to get out of the way of some men moving purposely forward. Will caught him but as he pushed himself up off the side, a rat disturbed by his actions jumped into the water near his legs and swam off. He shivered and pushed the horrified Ernie forward behind the others.

Will was well used to rats from the farm back home, but for Ernie this was clearly a huge wake-up call to their new surroundings. The smell was also quite overpowering here, the attack on their nostrils adding to the farming memories for Will as he instantly thought of his dad muck-spreading across the fields on a hot day. Ernie wrinkled his nose and tried to move forward faster, though the smells of waste and decay in these cramped trenches were inescapable.

Their 'dugouts' were cut into the side of the trench walls with wooden supports to stop them collapsing. Planks and sandbags made up the roofs for protection against the shells. Will was grateful his was dry at least and they were sectioned off in twos or threes and told to stow their kit. Which was a joke as there was nowhere to stow it, so they learnt quickly from the other men to dig holes into the dugouts and make temporary shelves. They noticed some men had acquired rope and other bits of wood to make things to hang kit on, to keep it dry. Others simply stuck their bayonets in the mud banks and hung uniform on them. Above all else they were told to keep their rifles clean and dry. The words of the Quartermaster in Shorncliffe echoed in Will's mind...

"It's heaven here compared to the trenches..."

Will missed his bed and Freddie banging his head every morning. Not for the first time he regretted his rash actions in joining up. He had just closed his eyes to think of home when a sergeant stuck his head in the dugout.

"Listen up you two. Make the most of the lull in shelling and get some rest. You'll be taking your turn on sentry duty soon enough. We make no exceptions for newcomers here. Oh and don't forget we are less than 'alf a mile from the German front line. Jerry don't need much excuse to lob a few shells over. So no unnecessary noise or you'll have me to deal with. Even if I'm dead. Understand?"

They nodded wide eyed and he went to leave, then paused and looked back. His face softened slightly. "And keep yer bleedin' 'eads down newbies."

Will didn't feel he could sleep. He was fighting a feeling of claustrophobia after a lifetime in the open air. Ernie didn't even want to sit down, and the sergeant's words had just added to his rising terror. So Will dragged him out and they went up the trench to try and locate their friends. More than once they were told to "keep their heads down" as they passed up the line by the soldiers on watch, and they noticed that the height of the trench varied in places so they had to keep stooping from time to time for fear of presenting a target.

As they passed a number of dugouts the scene was the same. The new men trying to sort out their kit fumbling about in a state of shock and the 'old hands' sitting about smoking, playing cards, talking in hushed tones or cleaning their weapons. Even had it not been raining the gloom in the trench was tangible.

About a hundred yards along the trench they found Ced, and just opposite in another hole Archie, and the mood lifted immediately.

"Davison! Pull up a chair, we've just ordered lunch," Archie shouted jovially from where he was sitting on the mud floor with one of the regulars smoking. Ced, smiling under that wild moustache came over to join them, and they exchanged handshakes all round. The dugouts here were raised to keep the water at bay, and Will instantly climbed in and sat on the floor, the mud no bother to him. Ernie remained standing, however, the water lapping round his shins in the trench.

"These are better than where we are," Will noticed, "me and Ernie have some work to do to convert our hovel into this grand mansion." The man sitting next to Archie smiled approvingly.

"This is Albert lads," Archie said, "he's from Yeovil originally. Moved to Littlehampton after a girl but it didn't work out." The men said hello and Albert offered Will a cigarette.

"Not for me."

"You'll smoke 'em soon enough in this hell hole lad," Albert replied, although his cough suggested they weren't benefiting him too much either.

"Albert's been here since the start. Happy to show us the ropes."

"Do you hate it?" Ernie asked directly.

"Not as much as you'd think," Albert said squinting as the smoke from the cigarette stung his eyes. "Lost too many good men already and it makes a change to be stationary. Spent the first few weeks getting our arses kicked by Jerry and running away, always retreating when we wanted to stand and fight properly. Least here at last we have a chance to do that. Chance to gather our thoughts and regroup. Makes sense to me, though the chow could be better."

"Chow?" said Will.

"Food lad. No hot food here. Tins and powder mostly. That's why we can't wait to get back to camp. Hot food, hot baths, hot nurses." He laughed and the men smiled. Albert's lilting West Country accent and easy manner endeared him to the new men instantly.

"Why can't we just get a stove going. Boil some food, make tea like they taught us in training?" Ernie asked innocently.

Albert looked at him with pale blue eyes, clearly deciding how to react to the newcomer. He sighed and said, "It's the smoke lad. Some men try and do it deep in their holes. Easier further back in the support lines. Officers have better dug-outs than us, and rumour has it some of them have fires going in braziers. But we tried it too when we first dug in. Jerry zeroed in on a wisp of smoke and their howitzers dropped us some sugar for our tea. Blew twenty men to bits. I've been a bit more cagey since then."

Ernie was stung by Albert's words and his mood worsened. He just looked at the place where his feet would be, the dank foul water slopping round his ankles.

"It's not as bad as that," said Ced sensing Ernie's depression, "my room mate says they send hot food up from the back when they can, sometimes every day. So get your order in early." He slapped Ernie on the back and told him to come and sit with them out of the water.

As they walked off, Albert said "That's true enough but they don't always come regular anymore, and sometimes don't have enough for everyone and we draw lots, or it's cold when it gets here. Just didn't want to raise the lads hopes is all. Better to be pleasantly surprised."

"Well I don't think you raised his hopes Albert, you cheerful sod," said Archie teasing him, and they laughed again.

Just then the CSM appeared with Lieutenant Dunn. They were speaking with the platoon Sergeant, who had told them to rest earlier. There was a brief exchange during which the Sergeant appeared to express surprise and shake his head, and then Russell and Dunn moved on down the line. Will kept out of sight, not wanting to be seen by the Lieutenant, and he noticed a number of the regulars duck down into dug-outs to avoid being seen also. *Or avoid being picked for something,* he thought.

Sergeant Albright was a pleasant enough sort who had also come to France with the Regiment in August. He had apparently won the Distinguished Conduct Medal near Mons, holding a position against the advancing Germans to allow the majority of the battalion to retreat. He was not a shouter like most Sergeants but spoke quietly and firmly to his men, and unlike some, took time to ensure the new men were sorted out. He had a friendly face and was similar to Ced in his features and mannerisms Will thought, but above all he instilled confidence and the men hung on his every word.

"Ok listen up men, pop your heads out. No use hiding. Come on you lucky lads I know you can hear me, out you come."

Men's heads appeared reluctantly all along the line. It reminded Will of seeing the rabbits popping up all over the field back home in the first light of day. "X and Y sectors have sentry and patrol duties tonight. Exact orders will come through directly, but we'll have several parties out checking the wire and listening for Jerry from the forward posts. The rest stationed here through the night for any signs of enemy movement and to provide cover."

The Sergeant looked at the mix of old and new faces for a moment. "You old timers can show the new ones what to do in the days ahead. As we are changing round, we need the newbies up to speed as fast as possible but tonight it's experienced men only. Give 'em chance to learn something. All section leaders report to me in thirty minutes. I want the machine guns cleaned and loaded too. Rest of you check your kit in the meantime, and get some food while you can."

There was a rumbling of moans and groans but the trench became alive with activity. He climbed out and the Sergeant saw him.

"Davison isn't it?"

"Yes Sergeant."

"Well visiting times are over son. Get back to your own billet and sort your kit. You're going to be in one of the forward posts tonight on sniper duty. Need your eyes on the far trench. From what I've heard you're a crack shot."

"Thank you Sergeant."

"Don't thank me son. It's not a prize. And you lot better not be bad luck. Just heard your colonel hasn't had the best of starts so let's hope that doesn't transfer up here."

"What do you mean Sarge," said Ced, already busy checking the working parts on his rifle were still clean just in case.

"Your CO. Colonel Bradshaw isn't it? Lost his horse today. Jerry lobbed some shells into our rear camp to keep us on our toes. Does it from time to time. Almost hit the hospital to, the bastards. But apart from a couple of store huts didn't do any real damage luckily except the one direct hit on our stables. Killed a couple of the horses including his. He's on foot like the rest of us now I suppose." He went to carry on down the line.

"Any men hurt?" said Will suddenly feeling a knot of anxiety well up in him.

The Sergeant paused and said, "Just one. Very lucky considering all the men moving through there currently heading up North. Colonel's groom if you can believe that. Private Enright I think his name was. Killed with the horse. Now carry on all of you, clock's ticking."

As the Sergeant moved off Albert took another long drag on his cigarette and turned to the men there. "Just goes to show, no point worrying about it boys," he remarked. "If you're number's up, it's up, no matter where you are," and he took a stone to his bayonet and began to sharpen the edge.

The four men looked at each other - Will, Ernie, Ced and Archie - absorbing the news. While they had not been anywhere near the incident when it happened the loss of one of their own platoon triggered something inside each of them. If the reality hadn't sunk in already it did now, crashing in as devastatingly as the stable shell.

"We better get on," said Will, breaking the sad silence and they shook hands once more.

"Take care up there Will," Ced called, as the group moved to their own dug-outs. Will looked back and nodded, a tear dropping imperceptibly to merge with the murky water around his boots, as he trudged away.

Archie watched them walk off, still deep in thought. "So much for special duties," he muttered.

Chapter 13 – Patient approach

Ernie was not coping well. He was fit enough and had managed basic training, albeit hardly the top of the class, but this was very different. They had not been in the front line more than a few days and he was already struggling. In the training camp he had excelled in appearance and drill. His attention to detail and presentation immaculate at all times, if not obsessive. In training when not on exercise it was drummed into you that cleanliness was next to godliness; and most of the time they had worn old uniform or PT kit when outside anyway, keeping their issued uniforms for drill and camp wear.

Ernie was slim and unremarkable in appearance, except for his mop of red hair perhaps, and needed glasses to read and see anything clearly. He was not strong like Archie, or a great shot like Will, but what he lacked in physical prowess he made up for in appearance and brains.

But here in the trenches the priority was survival. Staying clean was almost impossible and yet every man tried to do what he could to avoid infection and sickness. Regular baths were in short supply and hot water often non-existent when at the front. The winter weather was well set already and the rain was constant. Mud was everywhere. In their clothes, their kit, and sometimes in their skin. Then there were the rats and lice that carried disease with them and thrived in these conditions.

At first the men were appalled by the conditions, doing everything they could to stay clean and free from lice, and keep the rats at bay. They tried every trick the older soldiers knew, but still they failed. In time it became part of the normal routine, itching and scratching and occasionally delousing themselves only to find they were back within hours. They could never get rid of all the lice eggs, and their body warmth was perfect to hatch them out again. 'Shrugging' became a normal feature of parade or where any men were gathered, as their bodies responded almost mechanically to the lice crawling about them. Their feet were constantly wet, their clothes caked with mud, and their appearance far from the parade ground of only a month ago.

The men hated it, and deep down inside they didn't accept it, but they put up with it as it all paled into insignificance against the one common aim...staying alive.

For men like Ernie though, this was a double whammy. Being in the trenches was hell enough. Being unable to get clean was a nightmare he couldn't wake up from.

Ernie had a younger sister, Amelia, who was almost sixteen, but their father pinned his hopes on Ernie from a young age growing the Isaac dynasty with him. Trained in Saville Row in London, Jeremiah Isaacs opened a shop in Shoreham which was soon successful enough to move the family to a large house in Steyning, where their son, Ernie, attended school briefly before going on to Christ's Hospital. At eighteen however, he rejected university in favour of joining his father in the shop, to Jeremiah's absolute delight.

It was with no small concern therefore when Ernie, like Will in his own way, announced less than a year later that he wanted to join the army. Despite being anything but a sportsman, Will still took a liking to the immaculate Ernie. Indeed he owed him indirectly for unwittingly establishing his place in the platoon. As Will passed sandbags forward to Archie to repair a dugout that had recently been shelled, he cast his mind back to the incident from the day before...

They had gone to a holding camp to draw stores for the front. Following a roll call, as the soldiers started to head off to work, one of the men from another platoon made an aside about Ernie.

"Christ will you look at little Lord Toff over there. Don't know what he's doing here slumming it with the likes of us commoners. Am sure his daddy has more than enough stashed away to buy him a commission. That's if they take his sort in officer's school I suppose." His friends laughed.

Will knew that Ernie's grandparents were Jewish but paid it no attention, and went over to confront the man.

"Is there a problem private?"

"No problem Corp."

"I hope not. There's enough going on as it is without us sniping amongst ourselves."

"Just me and some of the lads were wondering if young Isaacs was Jewish is all." His friends sitting around started to snigger.

"Does it matter?"

"No. Always good to have a money lender in the battalion if we're short of a few bob." The men laughed openly now, and the man's pockmarked face grinned widely buoyed by his friend's support. He sat jacket open, thumbs tucked in his braces, challenging Will.

Will was aware Archie had stood up, and gave him an indiscernible shake of his head not to interfere.

"Stand up private."

"Bit young to be giving orders…owww!" Before he could finish his sentence Will hauled him to his feet by his braces, and leaned in close so his friends couldn't hear exactly what was said next.

"I said stand up private. Not too young to know a troublemaker when I see one and deal with him. Last time I checked, the enemy were on the other side of the trenches. I look around here and all I see are Sussex men. Regardless of social or religious backgrounds. All fighting for the same cause. We need everyone pulling together here or else. Do I make myself clear?"

He had gripped the man's skin through his jacket now and he winced with pain, and said "Yes corporal," through clenched teeth.

"Good. Now sort out your uniform and carry on."

Will turned away his heart pounding in his chest, and his hands sweating, but as he looked at his own platoon and the smiling faces of approval he knew he was one of them now for sure. Ced made a show of saluting him and they walked off together to carry on their work.

Archie wandered over to the soldier Will had spoken to, and gripped his arm to his side so the officers couldn't notice.

"A word in your shell like sonny. That there corporal you spoke to is my friend. Anything you say to him or the platoon you say to me.

Even if I'm not there. Understand? And trust me, mate, you don't want me as your enemy. You'd be better off with Jerry. I'm not saying this to you as a corporal. I'm saying this to you as someone who will smash your bleedin' face in the next time you so much as look at us the wrong way."

He twisted his arm for good measure and without waiting for an answer went off whistling. The man was white with shock now so that his face looked like a series of small red craters on an ashen moon. His friends picked up their kit and went back to work silently, the bravado of a few minutes ago blown away. Lance Corporal Will Davison however, was seen as a recruit no more following this incident. Now he just had to prove himself in battle.

*

Cleaning his rifle for a third time, Will looked over at Ernie. The rifle was spotless but it passed the time and took his mind off the night's work ahead. Ernie was trembling and Will was unsure if this was due to the damp or fear. The company were going out into No Man's Land again on 'mischief patrols' and Will was detailed once more into a forward post as a sniper. So far his first few evenings had passed with hardly any incident and the last patrols had come back intact. But enemy activity had been seen to be increasing opposite them in the last twenty four hours and this was confirmed by a report from one of their planes that had swooped about over the German lines, until the fire from the ground had proved too risky to continue.

Needless to say both things together led to the top brass in headquarters requesting a closer look, and maybe grab a prisoner or two, as if it was just some simple task. Archie had commented they should just walk up to the Jerry trench and knock politely and ask a couple of them over for tea, which as ever had gone down well with the men roundabout. The CSM had then informed them that a number of the new lads would also be going out tonight, including Archie, and he could put his theory to the test!

Ernie however was no longer laughing at anything. He had been assigned to one of the sections on guard in the main trench to offer fire support in the event of counter attack or a quick retreat. Will could tell that he was not ready to go out on patrol yet and might put the operation at risk, and this seemed to be noted by the officers, so several of the more nervous newcomers like Ernie were kept amongst the main force in this sector. But sooner or later he would have to be risked, especially with the regular battalion troops being taken off the line for a rest. Moreover Will was concerned whether he could actually fight at all, especially if they were attacked themselves. But then again deep down they were probably all wondering that.

*

The storm clouds that had hated them by day now wooed the men as darkness fell, blotting out all semblance of light from the moon and stars, and improving their chances of success in the task ahead.

"It's a perfect evening for a walk," Sergeant Albright said to the assembled men, trying to inject some humour. The men muddied their faces and took off any kit that wasn't needed, or more importantly might get caught out in No Man's Land. The 'old timers' - most of whom were under thirty themselves - checked the new men to ensure their necessary items were secure and wouldn't make any noise. Some wrapped cloth round the ends of their rifles to prevent mud getting in and others loaded up with extra ammunition and bombs. Just in case.

Will watched all this from his forward observation post where he stood with Lieutenant Dunn, and two other sharp shooters, next to a machine gun team that had been alert and ready for the past thirty minutes. *Just my luck to get stuck with Lieutenant Hun,* he thought to himself. *Doesn't bode well.*

Four teams of six were going out and Ced and Archie were in one of them, along with Albert and it was soon clear that two regular men would go out with four of the new ones to show them the ropes. They were to check the wire in different sections, listen for Jerry patrols and if possible any movement from their trench, and lay traps and warning 'bells' in some of the shell holes. These in essence consisted of crude devices of cans and broken bottles in the water, and anything that might jangle on the wire if someone pushed through. Here and there string wire would be attached to grenade pins and then tied to small posts until the tension was taut so that anyone tripping on it would dislodge the pin from the grenade and set off an explosion.

"The trick," Albert said with a number of the new men gathered round him, "is to remember where you left the sodding traps and mark them, so you don't set them off yourself when going the other way!"

As the men had blinked in silence absorbing this cheery news he continued. "Which is never easy when you're being shot at, nor to remember which shell hole might be filled with broken glass as you dive head first into it! Especially the way the landscape is changing every day with the shelling."

He gestured over his shoulder to No Man's Land with his thumb, and with a raise of his eyes he walked off to the parapet to slap more mud on his face, leaving them to dwell on the night's work ahead.

*

Archie stood next to Will as they waited to go. Will could hear his breathing and knew that Archie was anxious.

"Are you scared Will?" he whispered.

"Of course," said Will, "aren't you?"

"Me? Nah," said Archie pulling a mock offended stance. Then after a short pause he said, "I'm bloody terrified."

Will looked at the dark shape of his friend and even here in the blackness he seemed large. But he knew he was also just as scared as anyone else, and reached out and patted his arm.

"Just do what the others do and don't take any risks Bunny."

He saw Archie turn to face him but couldn't make out his expression.

Lieutenant Dunn leaned in. "Silence. Zero hour. Time to get cracking. Sergeant lead your team out, the rest follow. Get on your sights Davison." Will brought his rifle up and looked through the enhanced scope at the darkness ahead.

Sergeant Albright nodded and turned to his group and tapped the first one on the head who did likewise to the one behind and so on. Then ever so slowly he eased himself over the top and the rest followed one by one, spreading out slightly as they slid forward into the black mouth of no-man's land.

Archie's group went next, Albert leading off, as one after the other they slipped over the edge like foraging snakes. Ced went last and as he passed him he nudged Will and gave him his watch.

"Time us," he whispered right next to his ear. "Then I will try and beat my personal best next time." There was a flash of white teeth and he was gone too. As he quickly put it on his wrist, Will wondered if he had passed on the watch to time them, or in case he didn't come back.

Will could make out Archie's shape crawling forward like a large lumbering tortoise and then within moments they were swallowed up and gone. Each time a group passed him the noise seemed to amplify ten times and he was trembling with tension that they would be discovered, but in a minute all the men were out and the silence returned. Will didn't know if hearing nothing at all was worse or better and he constantly checked Ced's watch which seemed to move painfully slowly like the men it timed.

Will thought he heard a sound ahead in the void, but there were always noises at night, and it could be any number of things. The silence returned, and he relaxed his grip on the rifle assuming his anxious mind was playing tricks on him. Then Lieutenant Dunn appeared by him. He had obviously heard it too.

"That might not be us, stay sharp." The machine gunner pulled the firing parts back into position slowly and the click sounded like a door slamming.

"It's cat and mouse out there. A patient approach is the key," the Lieutenant whispered. "You have to fight the desire to move quickly or you're going to wind up dead, and never move again."

The officer spoke as if in a lecture hall back in camp to no one in particular but Will wasn't really listening anyway. He scanned the blackness ahead as his eyes adjusted more and he found ghostly shapes appearing slowly. The more he focused the more they seemed to move and change. There was a ruined building off to the left not more than fifty yards away he thought, though it was hard to tell distance, and some shattered tree stumps of varying heights further in front. But mostly it was just a dark curtain waiting to rise on the next deadly act.

Will's heart was thumping against his chest and he was sure it could be heard. He scanned the blackness again through his sights, and something made him pause. He went back to the line of tree stumps.

Was he mad?

He felt sure last time there were four stumps close together and now he could see five. Perhaps his eyes were adjusting more. It clearly wasn't becoming light but the shapes were there.

He watched.

And waited…

The 'stump' moved. Just for a moment, ever so slowly, it leaned to the left and back again. *The wind?* he thought. The storm was still in the air. Then as he watched again, there was a discernible second movement and the 'stump' waved something forward. Now he knew for sure.

"Lieutenant," he hissed without turning round. "Movement ahead. Just to the right of the clump of tree stumps." He felt Lieutenant Dunn move in close to him and slowly raise his binoculars. The first man slipped down and vanished but as they watched a second took his place and it was clear they were moving towards them.

"Ours sir?" Will asked.

"What time do you have Johnson," the lieutenant asked the second gunner holding the machine gun's belt of bullets.

"0225," the man replied barely audible to anyone but himself.

"Too soon. Unless something's wrong. But if they are not one of our groups then they will crawl right amongst them."

"Should we send up a flare sir," Johnson asked.

"Wait."

The lieutenant thought for a moment and then tapped one of the other sharpshooters on the shoulder and told him to go back to the main trench and tell the captain they may have company and to be ready. As the lanky figure of Jenkins slipped away quietly, taking time to watch where he stepped, Will saw the lieutenant take out the flare gun from the box next to him.

"What if they are ours sir?" Johnson whispered. "We will light 'em up for the Jerries."

"I'm perfectly aware of that Johnson you buffoon. Now silence. Davison keep watching and see if you can make anything out. Anything at all."

Will nodded and he noted with some admiration that throughout the tense actions of the last couple of minutes the man on the machine gun hadn't moved. He hadn't spoken or joined in the debate. He had just sat tense and ready, waiting for orders. Will thought his name was Philips, but he wasn't sure.

"They must be ours," the lieutenant muttered almost to himself "or they'd have bumped into our lot already."

Will looked again at the trees. He saw a spike on one of the branches.

Odd.

It moved, and the spike was on top of a helmet. Will felt giddy and his head span, and his heart began beating so fast he thought it was about to explode. He'd never fainted in his life but felt he might, so held the side of the trench for a moment to steady himself.

"Jerries sir. They're German."

"What? Are you sure man?"

"I can see a spiked helmet on one of them now."

"Christ. Are you sure Davison?"

"Yes."

Though wracked with fear Will's voice was now calm and assured and it was the trigger to set the lieutenant into action.

"Flare out," he said, and fired it into the air. To give his own troops a few seconds warning, he cried "Alarm," all sense of quiet now irrelevant as the flare roared up.

After that the world went mad in a flash of brilliant bright burning light. The whole of the ground in front of them was lit up and over a dozen Germans were illuminated no more than twenty yards ahead strung out between their position and the tree stumps. They started to dive for cover instantly.

Before the lieutenant had even shouted "Open fire," the machine gun to Will's right burst into life with the most horrendous chatter right next to his ear, that made him duck down. There were screams and shouts and bullets now started fizzing back at them from positions out on the field ahead.

Will recovered his position and saw shots coming in from both sides of the Germans as the British patrols opened up after probably recovering from the same shock as the Germans. Despite being on high alert, discovering the enemy right amongst them must have temporarily thrown their patrols for sure, and he heard someone shout out to watch where they were shooting as there was a danger of shooting across the Germans heads at each other.

The machine gun stopped to reload and Will saw several men break cover and run away. They were clearly fleeing for their lives now finding themselves trapped and hopelessly outnumbered. It was no good, the machine gun opened up again and Will saw three Germans shout out and fall down. Then the air became alive with buzzing like swarming bees and suddenly there were a great number of flashes from further out.

"Jerry trench is awake. Sergeant get your men back here on the double." Dunn wasn't worried anymore about noise and had to almost scream to be heard.

Will suddenly realised his friends were out there and the fear returned. It occurred to him then that he hadn't fired a single shot yet and he checked his safety was off and took aim. There was nothing to see close up and so he fired indiscriminately towards the far trench. Someone in No Man's Land threw a grenade and there was more screaming and further shots. As the main British trench returned fire *en masse*, it became clear to Will that there was a battle within a battle, with the important one for him out there in the dark middle ground.

A man came running towards them screaming. There was a shout to get down, and Dunn said "Hold fire he's one of ours."

Will realised it was Luke from 'A' platoon and he had clearly panicked and just run for it. He got within ten yards of the trench and then leapt the last few strides like a salmon. Will was amazed that anyone could do that, even when scared, and started to speak. "Christ Luke…"

"He's dead son." Philips said.

Will stared at him not comprehending at first. Then he realised the force of being shot had hurled him forward. He looked at the lifeless figure of their colleague lying sprawled in the trench and the shock came rushing in.

"Face forward Davison. Keep looking for targets."

Will wiped sweat from his eyes and looked again. His night vision had been affected by the flare, and as its glow faded, he struggled once more to make things out in the darkness ahead. He saw a shadow kneeling by the tree stumps taking aim. Despite the darkness the shape was still clear but he couldn't determine which side the man was on. He hesitated, saw the gun flash and heard a grunt next to him. He turned and saw Philips fall back from the machine gun, hit through the shoulder.

Despite the added sandbag protection round the guns as they were so vital, a bullet had found its way through. Will didn't know if it was the man he'd seen or any number of bullets flying about from the opposite trench. It could have been a lucky shot or something more specific. The machine gunners were always targeted for obvious reasons. Johnson stopped feeding the belt and dropped down to try and help Philips.

Will scoped his sight again and saw the 'shape' reloading. His finger trembled on the trigger. So different from training. Sweat running down his head. His finger wouldn't move.

A voice came to him then. Danny's voice. "It's now or never Will." He held his breath as they were taught and squeezed the trigger. When the smoke cleared the shape was gone. He didn't have time to ponder the moment as Lieutenant Dunn grabbed him and said, "Davison can you use that thing?" nodding at the Vickers gun standing idle.

"Yes Sir."

"Then bloody well get on it and let those bastards have it."

Will propped his gun on the trench wall and took the gunners seat as the lieutenant started feeding the gun. He was amazed the officer was supporting him and not the other way round, but took confidence from that. Will's tremor was gone and he aimed towards the flashes from the far trench and opened up, feeling the power of the gun in his hands.

As he did so their men started to slide and throw themselves into the forward post taking advantage of the dark once more to head to safety. Will tried to look more than once for his friends but saw only strangers covered in mud, their shouts and curses making the post a chaotic mass in moments.

"You men sort yourselves out. Any wounded get to the first aid post, the rest of you get to the main trench and report to the captain."

Will continued to fire but everywhere the guns were falling silent as the skirmish came to a close.

"Hold your fire Davison."

Just then Sergeant Albright fell into the trench with another soldier, dragging someone with them. Will thought at first it was a casualty and then realised it was a German prisoner. He looked terrified.

"Managed to nick one of the buggers sir. Where do you want him?" A third solider slid in and landed on the German who was cowering on the floor. The man shouted out.

"Well done Sergeant. Send him back down the line for questioning."

The Sergeant nodded and said "Longworthy, you and Baker get this man back to HQ. They'll know what to do with him. Then back here and no skiving off."

Will spun round at the name and saw Ced. They smiled at each other and Will slipped the watch off his wrist and tossed it to him with a huge sense of relief, before they dragged the prisoner off down the line. It was only after they had gone that Will registered Ced was bleeding down one side of his face.

"Casualties sergeant?"

"Could have been worse Sir. Two dead out there. Two of the newbies got too far ahead in No 3 party. Couldn't get to them. I think one of the other groups have some wounded. I'll need to check on their status. I'm missing one man from number four party too I think."

"I need a proper count as soon as you can Sergeant."

"Yes sir. Number one party also had one killed I saw."

Dunn nodded at Luke's body.

"Ah right, there he is. I'll get him moved sir."

The silence was eerie once again now but there was the unmistakable sound of men groaning out in the dark and it made Will shiver. Then closer to home came a louder groan and they all remembered Philips.

"Johnson help the sergeant get this man to the dressing station. Get back to the line sergeant and send some fresh men up to take over the watch here and move this body away."

"Sir."

Sergeant Albright looked exhausted as if he just wanted to lie down with Luke and sleep forever, but he shouldered his rifle and bent down to help lift up Philips who let out a fresh groan. As they shuffled slowly off the lieutenant turned to Will.

"You're handy on that thing. But you'll have to improve your shooting to impress me boy. You were far too slow to shoot, that's if you hit anything at all. All very well being a sharpshooter in training but out here's where it counts."

Despite his dislike of the lieutenant the words stung, and his overwhelming guilt at perhaps shooting a man was compounded by his failure to fire initially that may have led to Philips being shot. Even now he struggled with his conscience as to whether he could even shoot someone again if asked to. He knew the lieutenant was right and it made him feel even worse. If he had been given five hundred lines by the officer he wouldn't have been surprised. *Thou shalt not freeze in a fire fight Davison.*

He remembered once being made to write out hundreds of lines because his chair had squeaked as he sat on it during a talk by Mr Bickerstaff. Though it wasn't deliberate, other boys had laughed and the teacher had exploded with rage and kept him behind after school. *I must remain silent at all times unless told to speak.* The sound of the chalk scraping on the board writing that line brought back painful memories, from the task as well as the cane. He smiled at the irony of the importance of silence here now, but his dislike for either man wasn't diminished.

Then, like now however, he kept quiet and suddenly it dawned on him what the Sergeant had said… *"I'm missing one man."* Archie!

Right on cue there was a sudden explosion of movement and a large shape loomed over the trench side and fell in followed by a fresh round of shots. The lieutenant was startled and grabbed up Will's rifle.

"Wait sir he's one of ours. It's Archie."

"Bunden. Nearly mistook you for a Hun. What happened to you?"

Archie sat on the trench floor for a moment and Will wondered if he was going to speak. He was clearly thrown by the whole incident. Then he seemed to snap out of his trance and looked up.

"Sorry I'm late sir. I was over on the right with another man when it all kicked off. He panicked and ran before I could stop him."

"Yes you're sitting on him." Archie lurched forward cursing.

"It's Luke from 'A' platoon," Will said.

"That makes three dead then," Dunn continued, "and no count on the wounded yet. Costly night's work. But at least we stopped their endeavors and I'm sure the top brass will appreciate the prisoner." He seemed to mull that over for a moment and then said, "Right you can stay here with Davison and keep watch until the relief team comes up. I'm off to make my report and check on the rest."

"Yes sir," Archie replied standing up.

"And keep your head down or you'll end up like him, pointing at Luke's lifeless body. Carry on and keep your eyes peeled." He stepped over the corpse and stalked off.

"Hello Bunny. Welcome back," Will said once Dunn left, trying to sound casual as if he didn't care as much as he did.

"Hello Will, fancy seeing you here." They shook hands briefly then Will climbed down and took up his more familiar rifle, taking comfort in its cold embrace.

"Thought we'd lost you there for a minute. Though I guess you were too heavy for them to capture and carry off anyway."

Archie laughed then, and the relief was evident in his voice.

"Don't mind admitting I was worried for a moment myself. Not very friendly these Jerries. Apparently you can't just wander up without an invitation after all."

They both smiled and continued to look ahead.

After a minute's silence Archie said "I still think we should just challenge them to a kick about."

Will started to laugh and then a voice behind them said, "And I'm telling you if you make any more noise up here I'll be the one doing the kicking!"

It was Sergeant Albright and he'd returned with half a dozen men to take over the watch.

"Right two of you on the MG, the rest take up station here. Corporal Barnes sing out if you see anything. I'm off to check the other posts."

"Yes Sarge."

"And you two jokers can have the pleasure of taking your fellow recruit here back to the rear dressing station. There's a temporary mortuary there where they will record his death and sort out his personals, and then he'll be buried at some point. Take a good look gentlemen. Lose your head out here and that's what you will become. Food for worms."

They dropped their heads but as the Sergeant walked past them he turned for a moment and looked at them.

"You survived your first night patrol. That's something. There will be many more like this in the days ahead. Without doubt if the Hun are out foraging about like that there's an attack coming and it could be tomorrow. Take advantage and grab yourself a hot meal while you're back in camp lads. Then straight back here for first light. You earned it."

With a brief nod Sergeant Albright disappeared into the maze of trench lines, the darkness swallowing up his footsteps. Will grabbed Luke's legs and Archie picked him up under his arms, the jacket sodden with a mixture of water and blood, and they set off back to the main line, glad to be out of the forward post for now.

"He's not that bad, the sergeant," Will said.

114

"No, true, and I did learn something."

"What's that Bunny?"

Archie nodded at the man slumped between them, who just a short while ago was eating fish and chips in a Folkestone café.

"You have to be alive to laugh."

Chapter 14 – The Muddy Field

The wind shouted in his face repeatedly. Hard gusts that distorted sounds and forced him to brace himself against the sheer power of each blast. He stood squinting into the morning fog that stubbornly refused to budge in this natural onslaught, despite being chased around the fields by the mischievous wind. He was desperate to prevent more dust and debris from getting into his eyes as it swirled about, and then thankfully, just for a moment, the wind dropped.

Will paused, allowing himself to open his eyes fully and risk a look. Straining he thought he could hear the shouts from across the field as the attack went forward. He glanced up as a moment's brightness in the clouds winked at him like a torch.

Oddly a thought came to him. "The calm before the storm they call it William." He heard his grandma's voice in his head warning him of impending doom, and for a moment he was transported back to that tiny railway cottage, nestled on the end of a row of dark stone houses.

The rain came suddenly. Splashing the memory away with real venom, lashing down on the fields and soaking them all to the skin in seconds. With this new ally, the wind returned with renewed vigour, and Will set his teeth and raised his eyes, as if to acknowledge his grandma was right again. The rain did little to dissolve the mist either, which still skulked across the ground like a large grey sheet hijacked from a washing line.

He wanted to run. Find shelter. Get away from all of this. But he knew he couldn't, and wouldn't. He was the last line of defence. Behind him only Ernie was visible, shivering with head bowed, as he too struggled in this natural bombardment. Ernie may have been better off than him back home, but with his wild red hair now plastered to his face and his clothes drenched against his skinny frame, he looked forlorn. Will wondered if he too wished in that moment they could be transported back home.

A shout made his senses snap into life. It was a warning from somewhere ahead. Their attack had clearly broken down and now they were falling back this way. More shouts, the sound of clashing and cries becoming urgent. With sight and sound impeded it magnified the danger and he could feel his fear rising.

Blast my luck he thought, and then to encourage himself as much as anyone else in earshot shouted, "Come on boys fight!"

He saw them before he heard them, three ghostly forms emerging from the murk and mud, advancing on him, their shouts whipped away in the maelstrom of cries – wind and man merged together. *They had broken through!* He looked about but no-one was near. Not near enough to intervene that he could tell. His back felt cold as the icy realisation that it was down to him alone to do something crept up his spine. If they got past him, Ernie was finished. He was barely coping with anything these days and for certain he wouldn't be able to stop all of them.

As if to answer him more shapes appeared from the mist coming on fast across the field. Not that you could call it a field. The grass had long since been lost when the first winter storms and the constant tramping of boots had pressed the greenery out of the earth as if through a sieve. Now it was just a churned series of mud framed holes that even farmers would hesitate to plant; which could break a man's ankles in seconds with a wayward step. But it didn't stop these men charging across it once again. Whether the others were friend or foe Will didn't have time to find out, as he had to act. He looked at the leader of the ones out in front, clearly in control and shouting to the other two in support.

He had to stop him, he told himself despite his fear. *If nothing else it might hold up the attack. He couldn't deal with all of them but if he got to the leader, then there was a chance his side might rally. They couldn't all be lost ahead; some of them must be near surely?*

"Don't let them shoot Will!" The panicked voice of Ernie shouted somewhere behind him, and then more words followed but they were gone, torn apart in the wind before they reached him.

It mattered little as Will's brain had already triggered his body into action and he was off across the ground like a leopard. He had always been fast, the quickest at school, but now that was being put to the test in the harshest of circumstances.

The mud clung to his boots slowing him down and he cursed the wind that slowed his pace still further, jostling him so hard he felt like he was pushing through a crowd of angry protestors. He was close but not close enough, and he saw with despair that the leader had seen Ernie and was indeed getting ready to shoot. *God no come on!* he urged himself, pushing his freezing aching limbs forward.

Suddenly he realised that they hadn't seen him yet. *Incredible,* his brain flashed, and with a surge of excitement Will understood that the wind gusting in his direction was masking his movement - muffling the muddy strides and lung searing breaths as he pressed on - taking the sound of his charge away from his target.

Ten yards now…five…

Come on, come on, his mind urged. He saw the leader was taking careful aim, factoring in the distortion of the wind. *No!* his senses screamed. Will launched himself the last few paces in a desperate slide, and just as he heard the familiar thud of the shot he reached the startled assailant.

He had timed it to perfection. He saw the shock on the man's pockmarked face as he appeared suddenly from the mist; his greying beard parting to cry out in alarm through yellowing teeth, as his confident smile died in an instant. Will heard the double crack as he connected with his attacker just as he shot; and saw the football deflect wildly off target and away into the mist.

"Brilliant Will," Ernie shouted, and suddenly people were running in all directions around him, friend and foe.

A hand pulled him up and he felt a thump on the back. "Awesome mate," said Archie, pushing his hair away from his eyes, which was stuck to him in a patchwork of rain and sweat. "You saved a certain goal for sure." He flashed that cheeky smile of his he threw out so easily in any situation, and ran off.

Smiling to himself now Will looked up to see the attack had swung back their way again and the lads were moving forward. He glanced down to where the captain of the 'opposition' still lay in the mud confused and dazed.

"Merry Christmas Fritz!" he laughed, and pulled him to his feet. He shook the rain and mud from his hair and wiped his face. He no longer felt the cold, and inspired once more, he slapped the young German on the shoulder and with a wink set off running again to catch up with play.

It was Christmas day 1914, and at the exact time his grandma was saying grace over lunch where they were all gathered at Mill Farm, praying for a speedy and safe return of the boys to the village, Will charged into the grey curtain's embrace, lost in the wind and rain in moments.

*

In Steyning, the Davisons had tried hard to have a relatively normal start to Christmas day. Although the absence of the two boys had dampened the usual excited flurry of present opening, Harold and Agnes were determined that the war was not going to stop them celebrating Christmas.

Harold had just done the basic chores required knowing everything else could wait on this day, and ensured the cows and sheep were sorted early so the family could enjoy presents over breakfast, before going to church as ever. Despite having a stocking nagging him to be opened, David still went out to help his dad with the animals before succumbing to the magic of the day. By which point Freddie had already roared through the gifts left on his bed in minutes.

*

Later that morning Steyning church was full to bursting and Harold noted that there were even more occasional visitors than usual. Special services like this always drew in even the most hardened farmers, and of course there were visitors to the town in the congregation, like at Easter. But this morning there seemed to be more people than usual and it was not lost on Harold as he chatted to his dad on the way back to the farm that the war had led to a significant rise in religious fervour, if only to pray for safe returns. Harold was not a deeply religious man, but he was a man of principles and he attended church because it was the right thing to do, and because his Aggie insisted. However recently even he felt some comfort in the weekly attendances.

Without doubt the appearance of casualty notices in the newspapers, and the wounded soldiers returning to the region, brought the harsh reality knocking on every hearth. It was only to be expected that in times like this people would turn to God. If anything though, the early German successes had increased the patriotic fervour in the nation and the recruitment numbers were surging, which was mirrored in Sussex with Lowther's Battalions.

"People seem to have forgotten this was all supposed to be over by Christmas," Harold remarked to his dad, as he carved the meat for lunch once their duty in church was done.

Harold's parents had come down to stay as ever on Christmas Eve and Joan had seemed particularly determined to ensure Christmas went ahead as if nothing was different to previous years. She had been overly enthusiastic in her singing of carols in church, drawing a frown from Celia Goodman in her reserved pew at the front, and Joan continued the refrains unabashed as lunch was prepared. She insisted on reading to Fred from her childhood copy of Charles Dickens' 'A Christmas Carol,' even though he was much more fidgety than he used to be when listening. After she had said her own personal grace over lunch, she repeated the famous phrase from the book, "God Bless us, everyone."

For once it had seemed more poignant than usual, and David noticed it had set his mum to tears and she had taken to busying herself at the sink moving pots about. Despite the attempts at normality none of them could hide from the fact that two of the boys were not only absent, but in danger, and it remained an ever present feeling throughout the day; like a shadow in the corner of your eye that you could never quite see. There had been letters of course, not always reciprocated, and several parcels had been sent to France, so they remained confident the boys were okay. But despite their best efforts the house was not the same this Christmas day, nor was it in thousands of homes across Britain, and indeed Europe.

*

Lieutenant James Davison of the Coldstream Guards played another defensive stroke out to 'mid-wicket' which just happened to be near the ruined chapel wall, and ran instinctively when his partner at the crease shouted "Yes!"

He gauged correctly that despite only being ten yards from the ball, the additional helping of plum pudding the regimental quartermaster had eaten an hour earlier during the officers' Christmas lunch, would indeed impede his attempts to reach it and throw it back. As they came back comfortably for a second run, with RQM Bedlow struggling to pick the ball up, James smiled at his friend.

Harry 'Jonners' Johnson stood pipe in mouth at the other end, as if on the lush playing fields of Eton, and not this mud baked yard behind the lines at Ypres. As Jonners stamped down a broken muddy divot with the end of his bat, James paused, stepping back from the crease, and reflected on the bizarre nature of this Christmas day far from home...

For the Guards' regiments in the trenches at Ypres, the early morning had not brought the usual harsh 'wake-up call' from the enemy guns but instead the sound of Christmas carols floating to them gently across No Man's Land. Their men had responded in similar fashion, words replacing bullets, the rough voices bombarding the enemy's ears with peaceful intent. The world had held its breath in those first hours of Christmas dawn and white flags had appeared on both sides to reinforce the desire for a halt to the fighting.

An unofficial truce was hastily convened, although everywhere officers and men alike remained sceptical and nervous. But James and Harry had been two of the first to step into the eerie silence and approach their German counterparts. The exchanges had been brief. Hardly any of them spoke German and the officer they shook hands with, after some hesitation, spoke little English either. He was a Captain of the East Prussian Grenadiers from Bavaria they established called Heinrich, but little else could be fathomed, despite some scurrilous attempts by Jonners to find out unit strengths and plans much to James' amusement. Heinrich either didn't understand or else was wise to their line of questioning.

"Oh well best be getting along. Pleasure meeting you old boy," Harry said, and tipped his helmet politely which he felt preferable to actually saluting.

"Ja. Auf Wiedersehn. Good bye English," Heinrich replied and then added, "Passen sie auf ihren kopf."

"I beg your pardon?" Harry said.

Heinrich motioned to his head and then ducked down.

"Oh he's telling us to watch our heads I think," said James.

"Ha! Is he by Jove? Not if the Guards have anything to do with it," Harry boasted. "You watch you don't get your 'kopf' shot off first, Fritz old chum." He made a gun action with his hand.

Heinrich feigned a mock surrender, though the antagonism was quick to flash up in his eyes, the previous polite exchange fading in a moment. As the two friends moved towards the English trenches, James on an instinct turned back.

"Hauptmann," he called, remembering his lectures on opposing ranks' names.

Heinrich looked back and James standing tall gave a smart salute.

"I'm Lieutenant James Davison," he said.

Heinrich paused, and then straightened his helmet and brought his heels together with a sharp click.

"Heinrich Meyer." He returned the salute, smiled for a moment, and then walked off.

Others in their sector had exchanged some food and cigarettes here and there, but the main purpose had been to organise time to search for missing men, and just regroup. In all twelve bodies had been recovered but many more still remained posted as missing, either captured or lost to the earth for good. The fighting here had been particularly intense and bloody up to November, and even with the onset of winter the clashes continued through December. The traditional expectation of 'goodwill to all men' was not so easy to instil in so sombre a setting, despite the Chaplain's best efforts. The truce however was still as welcome as the Red Cross parcels and packages from home, and men took time to escape their reality in a variety of ways on this sunny Christmas day.

"Spotted my googly the cad, wasn't giving much away," Harry had said to James on their way back to the trenches. They picked their way carefully for fear of treading on traps or a lurking unexploded bomb in the mud; of which plenty littered the area ready to share their 'presents' on this particular day.

"And what may I ask is a googly?" James asked with a raise of his eyes climbing back into their trench.

"Well in laymen's terms it's when you pretend to bowl one way and disguise it so you bowl another. You know like a trick shot," he continued noticing James' blank look.

"Ah right, of course" James replied helpfully, still not entirely sure what his friend meant.

"Impressed you speak the lingo though, James old bean."

"Oh, Steyning Grammar. Had a kind language tutor. Just seemed to have a knack for it."

"Jolly good show. Might come in handy when we push on through to Berlin in a few weeks. We'll need it for ordering at the restaurants when we get there!"

James snapped out of his early morning memories with a warm smile, and focussed once more on their impromptu cricket match. Harry still puffed away chirpily on his pipe. He had found the tobacco from Heinrich to be much to his liking and complimented the Bavarian adversary on his choice of pipe filler, as he hit the latest delivery for four. The ball bounced out across the 'Devil's Highway,' as the road to the front had been named hereabouts, and the Chaplain of all people strolling by, picked it up and threw it back.

"Good arm Reverend! Fancy a hit?" Harry shouted out.

"No thanks Jonners. I'm batting for the Lord today. Perhaps another time."

Harry waved with an impressed smile at the Chaplain's retort, and moving the pipe to the side of his mouth, shouted "Play" and resumed his stance.

Captain Ernest Wyman, MM, was Chaplain to the 1st Battalion the Coldstream Guards, and had won his military medal at Ypres, going out under fire to give the 'last rights' to badly wounded and dying men. Despite being hit in the leg at this point himself, he still helped to carry back a wounded man. The act had endeared him to the soldiers, and silenced the quizzical tongues about the role of a pacifist priest in war.

The 'Reverend' Wyman however was made of strong stock, as his parish in Enfield would attest to. He came from a family of bishops and vicars who could trace their lineage back to the time of Henry VIII, and support for the birth of the Church of England. A struggle against worldly powers was in their blood, and Ernest was no exception preaching with a strong voice that God was on their side. His rhetoric both inspired and reassured the men in equal measure. He was a great character to have in the Battalion and as the realisation began to dawn amongst the men that this war would not be over anytime soon, he would become a beacon of hope for their salvation and sanity.

As the reverend walked off towards the mess tent anticipating the taste of leaf tea with milk for once, following the arrival of fresh supplies, his attention was drawn to the sound of an engine grinding away overhead. He looked up to see a German plane circling them. It was not the first plane he had seen, as his Uncle owned one up on his estates near St Albans and they had visited once to have a look; though he had not trusted his faith to go up in it. But he still marvelled at man's latest invention and watched it circle once more, its triple wings eclipsing the sun on each pass. The fact it was an enemy plane unimportant to him in that moment of wonder. *No doubt taking reconnaissance photos for the artillery,* he mused momentarily, but there was nothing much he could do about it, and so continued his stride forward to the tent.

"Tea waits for no man," he said out loud as he approached the tent smiling.

A loud whistle made him stop and instinctively crouch down and he saw the men near the tent dive for cover. The observer in the plane had in fact dropped a single bomb aiming for the supply dump they could see in the hope of hitting shells and setting off a chain reaction. They had missed by some distance with the wind taking the bomb away and the tea tent was blown to smithereens in moments. Though caught in the open, the reverend was still some two hundred yards from the tent and was unharmed physically by the sudden disruption to his Christmas thoughts. Mentally though he was more than a little put out by the loss of his fresh cup of tea. He stood up to his full height of six foot two and, taking out his glasses from an inside pocket, surveyed the damage.

"Bother," he stated out loud with a shake of his head, and noting that there appeared to have been no other casualties except for his choice blend of Indian tea, he said a small prayer of thanks and returned in the direction from which he had come.

Harry got up off the ground where he had flattened himself at the non-striker's end, and looked around.

"Any casualties private?" he shouted to the stunned kitchen hand surveying the tattered tent contents scattered about the outfield of their pitch.

"No sir," the man shouted back.

"Jolly good." He picked up his pipe from the ground and examined it and then looked over to James.

"Still alive old boy?"

James was dusting himself down from the rutted trench he had dived into a few moments before.

"Still alive Jonners," he retorted, marvelling at the resolve of his friend who had already picked up his bat and was tapping away at a clump of earth near his wicket to flatten it out.

"Fancy blowing up the mess tent on Christmas day! Just not cricket what?" Harry smiled at his own joke and then realised James was shaken by this event, and thought for a moment. "How about a tot of rum Davison? We'll call it a draw."

Chapter 15 – Rusty cups

For the Sussex regiment at Neuve-Chappelle however, their festive experience had been far more vociferous. Many of the men now occupying these trenches had been spared the earlier battles of the war, and were only a few weeks in position, and were yet to experience the full horror of the 'front'. The mood was certainly enhanced by the arrival of parcels and letters from home right on Christmas Eve, together with a significant number of charitable donations from church groups and other organisations. In X and Y sectors it was no different and Will was delighted like many of them to get a package from home.

Will's now famous *parcel from home* was even more exuberant than usual and he was impressed how much his mum could fit into one box as well as the fact it had arrived intact. Men started to gather whenever a Davison parcel arrived. There were socks and gloves from his Gran of course, and two bars of chocolate from his dad. Three types of homemade jam and some honey which he might exchange later, were carefully wrapped within, and as he opened them he could smell the scents from their fruit garden and pictured the bushes they came from clearly in his mind. Blackberry, Strawberry and Gooseberry aromas were released into the dugout as each lid was opened in turn. The addition of fresh tea with sugar and biscuits, was welcomed in several of the dugouts roundabout where Will's home parcels were now eagerly anticipated. Of course it was a race to share any before Archie came bowling down the trench to claim his share!

Fred had included a drawing of Will singlehandedly chasing the German army away, which looked a similar landscape to their bedroom back home but made him smile anyway and he managed to prop it up on the 'shelf' in his dugout. Men had taken to Will's easy manner, and the old hands were soon helping him with planks and bits and pieces to put things on and shore up the hole properly. He also managed to swap a beer crate for some gloves only a day ago, and sat on it now. The men were less sure about Ernie, being sickly and clearly so out of place here that he presented a risk. But being with Will earned him a reprieve.

Under the jams there was a long letter from his mum with lots of village news, not least of which involved Celia Goodman putting on a performance of Gilbert and Sullivan's 'Pirates of Penzance' in the church, to raise funds for the war effort.

'Though of course she's cast herself as the young leading lady at forty four,' Agnes wrote, *'so I think the play is more for her than the war effort! But it keeps me busy with the rehearsals and costume making and what not.'*

Will smiled. He found comfort in the fact his mum was enjoying herself and the apparent normality of life back home. He read on with real interest at the fact most of his old football mates had signed up to the Southdown Battalions, as Lord Lowther's initiative was formally called. They were going to merge with a battalion from Hampshire apparently, coming together under the title of the 116th Brigade.

Danny Boyd had joined up, *God help them,* and Tommy and Owen too. Their manager Tony had also volunteered but was told he was too old, and he had protested for the rest of the day in the Star Inn! Will laughed out loud now as he read through the list of names his mum rolled out.

The factories and farms are feeling the pinch now, and some of the younger lads and retired men are stepping in to try and keep them working normally. Both the Miller boys have gone, much to Walter's disappointment, but he's decorated the whole station in bunting and flags and proudly displays recruitment posters in every window, God bless him. Our David and Freddie are of course very busy about the farm, although you know the winter months are always less demanding in terms of crop rotations but harsher for the animal welfare. Freddie is doing his bit too of course, but we miss your help as ever Will, though I would rather you were just home safe and sound. Please take good care of yourself my lovely boy.'

Will turned the page where his dad had penned a few words. While he wrote sparingly as ever, the words were always carefully chosen and full of pride. Will was surprised his dad mentioned they couldn't hold David back from the war for much longer. He was putting plans in place to share a couple of the labourers part time from the large Eastwood Farm across the way in Findon. They had known the family for many years. The Eastwoods had three girls who did more than their fair share around the farm, and could also afford to employ several farmhands; which meant even when a couple had gone off to join the Southdown Battalions they had been largely unaffected.

Will popped some chocolate in his mouth and pondered about David and where he would go. As he put the box to one side he noticed that stuck underneath it was a separate letter from Alice, and his heart instantly started to beat quickly. He settled down on his 'bunk' in the deepening dark of Christmas Eve and found just the sight of the envelope brought the magical mood of his early years on this special night flooding back. The letter started to her *'Lovely Farm Boy'* which he no longer took issue with, and savoured the familiarity of the words. It was more loving it seemed to him than usual and amongst the bits and pieces of home news, she expressed more than once her desire for him to look after himself and keep well.

'...We have received news recently that two of the 'beaters' who work the grouse for the shoots on our estate were killed in November, and one of the local policeman has lost a brother, poor man. I do feel for the local families affected by this. We simply have to win Will, so that these men don't die for nothing. You must win Will! Above all else, you must stay safe too. Please promise me you will take care. I simply couldn't bear it if I heard anything happened to you. I really hope this whole ghastly event will be over soon...'

Judging by the continued rounds of hunts, tea parties and shooting on the estate Alice went on to tell him about, Will did not think the Pevenseys were suffering unduly so far in this 'event,' but he could tell she was affected by it none the less. He wondered how her brother was and vowed to ask about him when he wrote back.

'...I am getting very excited about Christmas, and I hope wherever you are that you still get some lovely presents sent to you. I would send something Will, but I'm not sure exactly where you are, and worried it might not find you. You will let me know this letter has made it safely to you won't you?

I'm hoping for a new horse to race at the steeplechase next year. Father has promised that I can go eventing with him and we might go to the Isle of Wight 'Grand National' next March if it isn't postponed. Father is a friend of Baron Seeley on the Mottistone estate there. (Did I tell you that before? I can't remember what we did and didn't chat about half the time, silly me.)

Anyway they are both as competitive as each other - in riding and in politics — you know how men can be, especially after Baron Seeley deserted the Conservatives for those awful Liberals! I think I definitely take after Father for my competitive nature. And my stubbornness from Mother! Don't answer that William. Father thinks Seeley may have already gone to war himself, so I might not get to ride there after all, but he is going to check. He's not getting away without my present. I really need a new horse. It's so exciting isn't it?'

Will knew very little about horse racing, and less so about politics, but the content didn't really matter as much as the fact she was thinking of him. Alice then wrote about her father's work with the battalions in Sussex, and how splendid they were, and that over a thousand men had volunteered. She teased him as ever about the fact he should become an officer or at least transfer across. Will began to wonder if that was a hint that if he did transfer she might like him all the more.

'Did I mention we are to host a grand ball at the Hall on Christmas Eve for all the new battalion officers and other distinguished guests that Father knows? Mother is fretting terribly about it all, so much to do, but I think it will be simply wonderful don't you Will?' All those men in uniform — how exciting! Are you jealous you are not here now? I bet you are. How frightful of me to tease so. Sorry. I know you are being very brave and doing your bit Will. I do think about you often.'

Will saw the letter was two weeks old and realised the ball would be happening right now and could not help but feel a pang of jealousy. Then as he turned the final page he found a cutting from some form of magazine stuck to it. There was a picture of a gorgeous blue ball gown on it, and she had written on the side that she was going to purchase this for the ball and hoped he approved.

He did approve very much and wished all the more to be back in Sussex, and more directly in Pevensey Hall. She ended it then with another note for his welfare and safe return and was sending him her love. She signed it *'Your Alice'* with three kisses. In that moment Will forgot all the difficulties of his situation, and fell contentedly asleep clutching her letter to his chest. He dreamed of swirling round a large ornate ball room lit with sparkling chandeliers, with a beautiful girl in a blue dress staring into his eyes, and that smile that could melt the hardest heart.

*

The Sussex men had also started Christmas Day with carols thrown back and forth between the two armies from the early hours, and then a white flag had appeared from the German trenches. Colonel Bradshaw had nodded to their Battalion Major, Percival D'Arcy, and boldly he had climbed out while all guns trained on the far trench for any sign of trickery.

There was none, and in moments the Major was shaking hands with the Hun and the men from both sides poured forward with faltering steps. Will and his platoon were soon in the thick of it, and it transpired that among Ernie's sartorial talents he could also speak some German.

"See I knew we brought you along for a reason Ernie," Archie said with a slap on the back that sent him stumbling forward. "Never mind the fighting, get chatting and see what you can scrounge!"

Men then went back and forth between the lines getting rations to swap and sharing photos and mementoes from home. Will saw Ced resting against one of the broken barbed wire posts with a couple of German soldiers exchanging and trying various cigarettes.

He smiled and waved at Will. It felt very surreal but wonderful, and as if to highlight this moment the sun had broken through the early morning mist and bathed the whole scene in brilliant joy.

Will spotted a German standing off to one side and went over to him. As he approached he saw he was not much older than himself and also had a mop of blond hair under his helmet.

"Hi. I...am...Will," he said, offering his hand and speaking deliberately slowly.

"Hello Will. I am Erik. Erik Bauer. How are you?" the German replied fluently while shaking Will's hand.

"Blimey you speak English!"

"Yes my father was a ship's architect in England for some years and I was born there, and went to an English school until they moved back to Munich in 1910."

"So you're English then. What are you doing in that trench," Will said without thinking.

"English by birth yes, but my parents are German and my homeland is Germany. I am in the right trench, as you put it."

"If you say so Erik."

"I do Will, the trench of the winning side."

At any other moment Will might have risen to this, but Erik smiled and they both laughed. Erik pulled out a picture of his parents from his top pocket, and talked about them and Will found himself transported from that place as he too told him about Steyning and the farm and his family. They could have been sitting by the river that rushed impatiently through the Mill's canals, like two school friends, were it not for the mud that sucked about their knees keeping them in the here and now.

"Do you like Chocolate?" Erik asked, pulling out an unwrapped bar that looked as if it had been bashed on the way to its recipient.

"Do I ever!" Will replied not able to hide his delight.

"We both do as a matter of fact," came the booming voice of Archie who had noticed the prolonged exchange and wandered over to see what his friend was up to.

"This is Archie. Archie meet Erik."

"Hello Fritz," said Archie with a cheeky grin.

"Hello Tommy," Erik replied not in the least bit put off, "I am a Gefreitner, a private like you?" he added, looking at the two men, and giving them both some chocolate.

"Name's Archie, not Tommy, and you don't ge-frighten us mate," Archie added cheekily. "And this man is a corporal I'll have you know Fritzy."

"Erik was just saying he's in the winning trench," Will mumbled through a mouthful of half chewed and very rich chocolate, trying not to laugh.

"Oh is that right!" Archie replied, raising up to his full height. Then swallowing the chocolate he paused, just as Will was concerned things might get tense. "Bloody good this Will, you need to write your folks and tell them you want this brand."

Archie turned back to Erik and helped himself to another piece without asking, his mind now a whirr of thoughts. In a much more jovial tone he said, "Winners is it? We'll see about that." He spun round and shouted across the field as if in the park back home with no thought for the situation. "Hey Albert did you find it?"

"Yes we're on," his dug-out companion called back with a *'thumbs up,'* and with that he kicked a football in the air and all hell broke loose.

The match that followed, if you could call it that, mirrored the very essence of the struggles in the trenches. The match swung this way and that in a series of mad charges, individual tussles, and mass brawls, with both sides claiming victory. Will was particularly focused on the last point having played in defence for most of the game and was adamant that they won convincingly eight goals to five. In truth once the early kickabout, or scrap, (in which no one had counted the goals) had become a more organised game, everyone seemed to take it more seriously.

Erik turned out to be an outstanding keeper, saving a penalty and several very hard shots from Archie and Albert, who were prowling around up front and not afraid to throw their weight after the ball frequently. In conversations as the game had gone on, it transpired that in Erik's Royal Bavarian Infantry Corps there were a number of national footballers, three of which were opposite them in the trenches. This was obvious as despite the encumberments of the mud and their heavy boots, several of the Germans could clearly play very well. Will loved every second of the game, and when he managed to get a boot to a mad scramble after a corner kick, and saw it fly past Erik between the makeshift posts, he jumped for joy. In that moment he was just a young lad enjoying a game in the park with a group of mates. They all were.

The game fizzled out as the opposing officers called time on the exchanges, worried that a General from HQ might appear at any moment once word filtered back, and take a dim view on events. Reluctantly men from both sides drifted back to their own trenches. Here and there quite a few were in opposing trenches enjoying a hospitality and welcome that no amount of force seemed to have achieved so far. The irony was not lost on Ced as they traipsed back to their dugouts laden with German gifts.

"Typical isn't it. Spend hour after hour day after day sat on our arses in the mud, trying to dodge bullets and bombs, while the top brass decide where the next great plan to end the war will be unleashed. And here we are left to our own devices for a few hours, without any shooting, and we gain more ground and more chance of peace than they ever will. And without any casualties!"

Will nodded clutching a second bar of German chocolate and looked back at Erik as his new 'friend' made his way back to the far side of the field carrying some of Will's rations and a pair of his grandma's gloves with the fingers cut off. They waved one last time, Will smiling as the red fingerless gloves were still visible long after Erik's features had become indistinguishable.

"Aye maybe you're onto something there," Archie continued, "though I'm not sure that big lump in defence would agree there were no casualties. I left my mark on him alright." They laughed together and jumped down into the forward trench. Archie threw an arm round Will, noticing how he was still glancing back to where Erik had been moments before. "She's not one for camouflage your nan is she mate. I'd call that a good trade getting rid of those target markers for some choc."

"Think we can risk a brew up," Albert said more relaxed for once given the occasion, "who fancies some tea, fresh from home in a Christmas parcel?"

There was a chorus of excited voices and the men in this section grabbed what cans and cups they could and gathered round. Will grabbed Ernie and pulled him in amongst them, hoping that the day's events had helped to settle his mind a little and make him feel included. Without doubt as the weeks leading up to Christmas had gone past he had become more and more withdrawn, and with each fresh artillery barrage on their sector, his trembling had increased.

A hush descended on the group for a moment as they were lost in the smoke of the make shift stove with dreams of home. As the milkless tea was handed round, the men shared some of their delicacies from home, and some of their newly acquired German gifts. It was Will who spoke up amongst the group.

"My Grandma always used to say, *'God Bless us, everyone'* on Christmas Day," and a number of men smiled and nodded.

"It's a shame Harry's not here," said Ernie, the occasion not lifting his gloom seemingly. Though in truth he was also still harbouring the resentment of only having received a card from back home with a few terse sentiments, and no gifts like many of the men. His parents still expecting him to give up this foolish venture and come home.

"Yes, and Luke," another voice echoed from the group of men, clearly a platoon mate of his from training.

"Ah well, I say Merry Christmas everyone today, friend and foe, alive or dead," Ced announced cheerfully to stop them getting too morbid, and they all clinked rusty cups.

Archie looked out over No Man's Land to where only a short while ago, men from both sides had been engaged in friendly banter and games without a thought for uniforms and countries. He smiled as if pleased with himself, and jerked a thumb over his shoulder as he got a refill on the tea, adding a tot of Bavarian rum from an earlier exchange.

"I always said we could settle this with a footy match."

Chapter 16 – The Post

A week had passed and 1915 had arrived for Will not with laughter and music as in years gone by, but with an uneasy silence as the Christmas truce had ebbed away like rainwater in the dank earth, and the war had continued once more. Shells and bullets became the only things exchanged as the days passed, and the mood became all the more sullen after the euphoria of a week ago. In Will's trench Albert remarked that the words from *'Silent Night'* that they had sung so emotionally, were particularly ironic given the latest bombardment.

Sergeant Albright appeared and was carrying an unusual amount of kit on his back.

"Listen up my sections I have good news. We are out of the line for a fortnight. No home leave I'm afraid but time for some relaxing down time and a hot bath. God knows you lot need it. Not you farmers though of course. You're happy as pigs in the proverbial no doubt."

"Yeh I had my bath in June Sarge," Ced shouted down the line, and the men all laughed.

"Exactly. Now keep the noise down and get your kit together. And keep your heads down too. Snipers are busy today looking for targets to say *Happy New Year* to!"

"Who's replacing us Sarge?" Will asked as he started to get his things together.

"Indian Regiment coming in for the duration so that should challenge those of you staying here."

"Indian Regiment? Are they lost?" Ced called back.

"Or desperate," Archie added, wandering forwards as the news filtered down the line about the break.

"Neither. They are tough as old boots. Been fighting up in Ypres before Christmas and just coming back into the line after a well-earned break. Saved the situation up there more than once I hear and at great cost. One of their number got the VC. So suggest you mind your manners with this lot."

The men paused at this, suitably chastised, and set about packing up ready to be relieved.

"Well if they cook as well as they can fight I guess they can borrow our holiday cottages for a while!"

"Always the last word 'eh Bunden," the Sergeant said. "In that case you can help Perkins with the Officer's cases. Jump to it."

"Thanks a bloody lot Bunny you idiot," Albert muttered and they doubled past Will's dugout crouched low, Archie raising his eyes to him as they passed.

*

Two hours later they were walking single file down the communications trench to the rear camp as the last of the Indian soldiers from the Meerhut Division passed them heading to the front. There were brief nods and exchanges along the way but the usual banter and insults the differing regiments would normally swap on meeting never came forth.

Will simply looked in wonder at these men from the other side of the world who were here in France. They marched with turbans instead of helmets, dark eyes staring determinedly forwards from brown skinned faces. As the Sussex men passed them, covered in the grime and mud of France, Will mused how they must all look the same regardless of race or culture, and how the war broke down all barriers eventually despite men's efforts to the contrary. Many of these Indian soldiers wore medals as testament to their previous courage, and still more showed signs of battle on their faces and hands, scars still healing…on the outside at least.

As they reached base camp the men were told to stand down, and dispersed into various locations like lightning, not wanting to wait around to be collared for any 'special duties.' They had all learned that lesson the hard way through poor Harry's example. Archie went to check on the food situation, and Ced suggested a hot bath before they did anything else which was the first time they had seen Ernie's face light up in weeks.

"Need to delouse and get some fresh clothes. Apparently they are gonna burn this lot! I can't imagine how good that's going to feel."

Will was tempted to join them, his back itching immediately as if to highlight their ever present passengers, but he was prepared to bear it for a little while longer for a few moments of solitude.

"You go ahead Ced and I will catch up with Bunny when he's back. I want to find somewhere quiet out in the open, not in some dank hole and look at Alice's letter again. Maybe get off a few lines before we all get too drunk."

Ced smiled at his young friend, noticing how much he had grown up already in the few months they had been together. He said simply, "Okay my friend, enjoy."

Will watched Ced grab Ernie by the collar and drag him off saying something to him that he couldn't hear from where he stood. He knew the rest break couldn't have come at a better time for Ernie, and relieved of the burden of looking after him for once he wandered over to a small grassy mound away from the main camp area and sat down.

He took out the letter and slowly read it once more, savoring every sentence and looking at the fading photo of the dress in detail. Will wondered how the ball had gone and once more felt the pang of jealousy that she would be there with lots of young officers no doubt. He chose not to dwell on that thought and lay back in the afternoon sun, which defied the winter month. He let its warm rays caress his face, while a gentle breeze lulled his senses. His thoughts drifted away from Alice to home and family and bowls of steaming homemade soup by the log fire in the kitchen; Sally stretched out around his feet, her work done.

An unexpected shadow loomed over him darkening his delicious memories and he stirred uneasily.

"Here he is lads. Our own Sir Lancelot off with thoughts of rescuing his damsel in distress no doubt."

"Oh it's you Bunny," said Will, as the grinning face of his giant friend loomed into view. "I was just dozing off nicely thanks very much. Did you fetch any grub?"

"As a matter of fact I fetched beer instead courtesy of some new friends and thought we could go and get the food together. Where's Ced and the tailor?" Archie said looking round, using the nickname the whole company had adopted for Ernie, though they were all a world away from London's Saville Row.

"Oh they went to have a hot bath first. You know what Ernie's been like about the lice. He may be in there scrubbing for hours." They laughed as relaxed as ever and Archie beckoned some men forward.

"You'll never guess who I bumped into in the cookhouse." Will blinked into the sun as the group approached but didn't recognise any of them. He then noticed one was wearing Sergeant's stripes and went to get up.

"Och, dinnae fret yerself laddie. We're off duty like you are here. All pals together like."

Will looked at Archie as he explained. "These lads are Cameron Highlanders from the Highland Division. Passing through on the way to new winter quarters. And that fine looking Sergeant is Stewart Macrae. This is me mate Will I was telling you about."

Slowly the jigsaw came together in Will's brain and he blurted out, "Maggie's husband."

"Ha Ha. That's right laddie the very same. And I hear she's been looking after you all in her café."

"Yes she was very kind. As was her brother."

They shook hands and Stewart introduced a couple of his fellow Sergeants. Then the five of them sat down on the grass bank, beer bottles in hand, and spoke about home and their experiences to date.

"Her brother was a scary sod that's for sure," said Archie.

"What Angus? Och just a wee gentle giant. More scared of our Meg than anything else. She's a feisty lass though that's for certain when provoked, if you get ma meaning?"

Stewart waved his beer bottle in their direction as his spoke as if to emphasise the last point. Archie raised his eyes at his friend.

"She was very kind to us" said Will, polite as ever, not sure if that was the right answer.

"Aye she is that laddie," Stewart said with a smile. "Huge heart and a smile to match."

"She's got a few huge assets your Maggie," said one of his companions with a cheeky wink, his wide grin revealing a mouthful of ragged teeth.

"Aye maybe. But I'll thank you to keep your mind off them," Stewart retorted with another wave of his bottle.

Will found himself blushing and to change the subject said "It's very good of her to help your brother. Does she miss home?"

Stewart took a long swig of his beer and said quietly "It's not as simple as that laddie. My brother-in-law lost his wife eighteen months ago and she's stayed to help with the wee bairns until he's back on his feet."

"Oh I didn't know."

"No bother."

"Then a toast to your good lady," said Archie raising the volume once more. "May you be reunited soon."

They clinked bottles and sat in silence for a moment, and then the voice of an orderly carried to them shouting "Mail call."

"The post! Not that there'll be anything for me but you never know. Where's bloody Ernie when you need him. It's the only sodding job he can do well."

"He's in the baths Bunny," Will said reminding him.

"Typical. If you want something doing, do it yourself I guess. Oh well I'll go, and grab some more beer on the way back," Archie said heaving himself up reluctantly. "Then am going to grab a bath myself. Put you lads to shame once I get my kit off."

Will rolled his eyes.

"Charlie go and see if there's anything for us too," Stewart said to his cheeky companion, the man's curly black hair shaking like a mop as he nodded in reply.

"Aye alright Stewy."

Archie lumbered off chatting to his new companion to catch up with the orderly and Will and the other two sat in silence for a while just enjoying the down time. At length Stewart asked Will when they had come to France and where they had been, and Will told him of their brief experiences to date. He mentioned the football match on

Christmas Day and they found they shared a common love.

"Alec here and me are Caley lads through and through. Though Charlie there's an Inverness Thistle nut," he said nodding after his companion they could see talking a couple of hundred yards away with the mail orderly.

"Aye the traitor," Alec chipped in, who up until now hadn't spoken at all.

"Caley?" said Will. "Are they in Inverness too?"

"Och aye laddie. Caledonian F.C. Proud Scottish football since 1885. Founder members of the Highland football league. Have you no heard of 'em?"

"What Caley? Why would he?" said Alec with another aside. "Useless bunch of bastards."

"Aye but our team none the less," said Stewart. "And better than those thistle Jacobites. Should never have let 'em join the league."

"Aye right you are there Stewy."

Will confused with the men's banter, just smiled an apology for not having heard of their illustrious team.

"Who do you support then Will?"

"Oh I don't really have a favourite club. I play for Steyning in Sussex, so I just follow our teams in their different age groups."

"We could adopt you then as a Caley fan," said Stewart. "But you're English so you might bring us bad luck!" The two highlanders laughed and as Will smiled awkwardly he was relieved to hear the booming voice of Archie returning with Charlie. He was shouting before he got to them, lugging a bag containing what looked like half the post for the company over his shoulder. No doubt he'd just grabbed everything, too impatient to wait for it to be sorted out. Charlie was also carrying a crate of beers.

"Well just as I thought! Sod all for Archie Bunden again but good news Davison, your Mum's sent a new year parcel! Might be too soon for her to get your letter asking for a different brand of chocolate, but we can always trade your socks in for some ciggies."

Will stood up as his friend approached, his booming laugh and running commentary making more than one head nearby turn round.

"Jesus. Is he always this loud laddie?" Stewart asked alarmed, as

Will set off to meet him. "I'm not surprised your sector has been quiet. Probably scared Jerry off."

"Oh he can be louder trust me," said Will smiling over his shoulder as he walked forward.

"I heard that," Archie replied with an even broader grin.

But no one heard the first shell land.

*

Much of what happened after was a blur to Will. He remembered a sensation of falling as in a dream, with no sound at all and just fragments of memory all thrown together and jumbled up like his dad's sailing boat jigsaw in the box back home. When the noise returned he was sitting propped against a stack of food crates with two or three of the company around him, and a pretty dark haired nurse attending to a cut on his arm.

"He's coming round miss," someone behind him said. He went to look round but it hurt to turn his head and he winced with the pain.

"Easy now. Stay still," the pretty nurse remarked with a smile.

"Where am I? What happened?" Will mumbled.

"The camp was shelled. But you're going to be okay. I think your arm may be broken but otherwise just some cuts and bruises, and maybe a sore head for a while. You were thrown back a way and knocked out, but you're a lucky boy. You landed on foraging hay for the horses." The reassuring smile came again. "I'm just fixing your arm in place for now."

She finished a makeshift sling round his neck, firmly but gently working with expert hands. Will was convinced he was dreaming, only half taking in what she was saying, and he tried to wake himself up.

"There, all done. I'm going to get you moved to the hospital tent. Won't be a jiffy."

"What's your name," Will asked, trying to get a hold on what was going on.

"Teresa."

With that she stood up and he watched her legs disappear out of view. Slender pretty legs he thought, with a strange feeling of guilt for Alice, and then they were blocked from view as a couple of pairs of soldiers legs came running towards him and dropped down by his side. Ced's face appeared, a concerned smile under the wild moustache. Albert was with him, his hair wet and his moustache trimmed. They didn't have a spot of mud on them, and they both looked as if they were in their Sunday best.

"It's definitely a dream," Will muttered, his head beginning to throb more. He tried to get up but felt suddenly faint.

"Easy Will. Lay still," Ced ordered, gently easing him back against the crates. "We were in the bath house. Just got out when the shells hit. You were knocked out sparko apparently. Nurse says you're ok though."

But Will could see he was frowning as he looked at the blood on his arm and forehead.

"Came straight over," Albert added. "Thought you'd all copped it."

Something white and soft landed on Will's face and he went to brush it off but his arm was too painful. Another one landed on his left hand and he looked at it. His head began to pound now and he tried to distract himself looking at the white falling petals.

"It's snowing," Will said dreamily. "Fancy that. A white Christmas after all, just a bit late."

"It's not snow Will. It's paper." Ced stated, exchanging an anxious glance with Albert. They paused as they saw their friend trying to process what had happened. Ced struggled to know what to say next.

"It's bits of the mail," Albert said looking down at the ground.

Will's mind suddenly spun as his memory came rushing back with a bang and he tried to get up again.

"Archie!" he shouted out loud, and caring hands went to hold him once more, to stop him moving.

"Where's Archie?" Will shouted again, the panic rising in him. He looked imploringly at Ced. Two soldiers arrived with a stretcher and went to pick him up. He pushed the first one away, and grabbed Ced with his unbandaged arm. "Tell me where he is. He's alright yes?"

"Will," Ced paused, searching for the words. "The shell landed right next to him. Some poor bugger from the Camerons was killed instantly, and Archie took a hell of a knock. He's not dead but it's not good Will. He's in the hospital tent now and they are getting ready to ship him off to the port if they think he will make it."

Will's head spun wildly. The mixture of panic and concussion rolling over him like a storm cloud crashing in across the Downs. He lurched forward and threw up. The regurgitated beer violently splashed the boots of the men around. Ced held his shoulders and then helped the stretcher bearers lift him carefully onto the canvas sheet stretched between the two poles. He patted his head.

"Did you see him?" Will said fighting a rising sensation to be sick again.

"They wouldn't let us in the tents Will," Albert was saying, "then we heard you were involved too and came running over. We feared the worst when we heard someone had been killed, until we saw you sitting up."

"I need to see him," Will said through spasms of pain, as he was hoisted into the air and taken off.

"Soon," Ced replied patting his hand and then he spotted Will's helmet lying off to one side and went over to get it, grateful of the moment alone to compose himself.

As Will was jerked across the muddy camp floor towards the hospital tent he looked back and recognised Stewart kneeling on the ground twenty paces away. He recalled speaking to him and felt some relief that he was alright. The Scottish Sergeant looked forlorn, oblivious to his surroundings, or the fact he was squatting in the mud which clung around his legs. He knelt with his bonnet gripped between his hands, head bowed, staring at something crumpled on the ground.

Will saw a body lying under one of the harsh wool blankets they had draped over his legs. Though he knew Charlie wouldn't care anymore about the way it made the men itch.

Chapter 17 - The Dressing room

Despite Will being classed as 'walking wounded', the doctor that saw him remained concerned about concussion, and so kept him in the hospital tent for forty eight hours for observation. It turned out his arm wasn't broken, but the doctor had quickly established he had in fact dislocated his shoulder. While telling Will this and distracting him with news from the front, he expertly reset it. Will felt a giddy sensation of sharp pain followed by relief, and didn't know whether to be angry or grateful for that.

His first night in the hospital tent passed in fitful sleep; the groans of the men a constant reminder of his current predicament and the bigger picture. He noticed Ced had left his watch with him again, clearly stopping by at some point when he had succumbed to sleep. While meant as a kindness it only served to heighten the depressing boredom of his enforced rest, watching the hands chase each other round the clock face in endless monotony.

Though the tents were crowded, and men were constantly being brought in, Teresa did her best to look after Will when she could. The nurses and doctors were clearly overworked and Will was shocked at the amount of men in here and the number of casualties, which was not something they had been aware of up to now. Especially having not been involved in a full scale battle. More harrowing was the number of men being moved out, and not always alive. It made Will fearful for his friend.

Teresa told him that the hospital was a centre for a number of sections, and men were being brought here daily from up to twenty miles around. Primarily because they were close to the main road that ran direct to the rail head from where they could be transported quickly to the coast and a boat home. But some had to endure miles of uncomfortable transportation just to get here from the front, and Will felt a fraud for taking up space and time.

"You have just as much right to be here as anyone else Will," Teresa reassured him, but he was keen to be up and about as soon as he was allowed, and she could see it in his eyes.

"You're here until you're told otherwise soldier," she advised him more firmly.

It was the first time someone other than a Sergeant or officer had called him soldier, despite the fact she knew his name, and it made him feel different inside somehow. The doctor came past and spoke briefly to Teresa about Will. They looked at his notes together and he felt like a small child once more, being spoken about but not involved.

"Seen but not heard, that's what children should be!" The voice of the schoolteacher came into his head once more, and he shook it away angrily.

As soon as the doctor moved away Will asked about Archie.

"Private Archibald Bunden. Do you know what happened to him? Is he alive?" Will's pleading face now cleaned of mud betrayed the youth inside the uniform.

"He's alive Will." Teresa paused while folding some starched bed sheets on a trolley nearby. "But he's very badly wounded. Multiple shrapnel wounds to his arms and legs, and he can't walk. They are not sure if they can save his legs. I'm sorry." She softened as she spoke, but the manner of her words pointed to someone who had passed on news like this many times before.

"Where is he now? Can I see him?" Will had asked quietly, tears swarming in his eyes. Teresa came and sat on the end of his bed.

"He's away to England on a hospital ship Will. We shipped him off as soon as we got the bleeding under control and got him stable. We gave him what we could for the pain to try and ease the journey. He had one lucky break. The large piece of shrapnel that probably killed the man next to him lodged in his mail bag and that took the full force of the blow. Without that he'd be dead for sure."

"Oh God."

"Is he a good friend of yours?"

"Yes. Very."

"I'm sorry Will. If it's any consolation he wasn't conscious. With luck he may stay asleep for some time. He can't have felt anything at the time, it was very sudden I'm told. We were all caught out by the blasts. We lost a nurse like that last week."

Will looked up at her. "Was she a friend of yours too?"

"No just someone I worked with here in France. It doesn't make it any easier though. You expect it on the front line, but back here the sporadic shelling still has the ability to shock. Just some bored German officer lobbing shells to pass the time and look what happens. The world's gone mad."

Will watched her screwing up a towel in frustration. He guessed she had probably worked through the whole night without a break and was clearly struggling.

"Are you with the Red Cross?" he asked, trying to change the subject.

Teresa dropped the towel into a basket. "I am attached to them here yes. But I was a nurse back home too. A staff nurse in a military hospital in Aldershot. We came out here after a couple of months of the war breaking out. Seemed the right thing to do."

Teresa turned back to the trolley of bed linen. Will realised the conversation was over.

Will felt lost, as if part of him had been blown away in that stupid moment out there in the camp, just when they were supposed to be relaxing. Sporadic shelling was rare behind the lines, designed to cause disruption and irritation but nothing more. His anger built up. *The shellings usually followed a set pattern of early morning and night time bombardments. It was an unspoken war time courtesy, everyone knew that. There were rules. This was wrong. Stupid.*

Teresa must have seen Will looking distraught and turned back once more. "If he survives the journey he might be alright you know. He looks strong and they can do wonders in these hospitals back home. I worked in one and the medical staff were marvelous. Don't blame yourself. It was just one of those stupid things. Wrong place wrong time. The longer you are here the more you will accept it. It's the nature of war Will. It doesn't pay to dwell on it too much."

She placed the last sheet on a trolley and walked off with a quick smile. A shout of "Nurse" from a far bed taking her away from him.

In another time and place he knew she would be quite a catch. The uniform only seemed to accentuate her full figure rather than detract from it. She had stunning brown eyes and wore a red lipstick that contrasted starkly with her surroundings but accentuated her lips as she spoke. Will thought it quirky how people held onto certain things to remind them of normal life. A pipe, a cricket ball, lipstick! He'd seen it all. For Will it was chocolate of course. Teresa's 'look' was further framed by waves of brown hair that would no doubt fall to her shoulders, were they not scraped back in a bun for work... but none of that mattered now. Archie was gone and maybe even dying as he sat there and he could do nothing about it.

"Bloody war," he mumbled as he shifted uncomfortably on the bed trying to sit up more, his mind churning over what Teresa had said. *He wouldn't just accept it. Not where his friends were concerned. Wrong place wrong time. What did that mean anyway? The whole bloody war felt like that at the moment.*

Will looked at a man in the bed opposite. He was asleep and had a frame under his bed sheet to keep it off his legs but it wasn't pulled over all the way. Will realised he had no legs below the knees. There was a tag on his arm Will had learnt meant that the solider was a priority to be shipped out. He stared at the stumps under the sheet and shivered, appalled at the sight, and thought of Archie again. That could be him soon. *Bloody Jerries*, he thought and at some point drifted off to sleep.

*

He was woken sometime later by a soldier moving past on crutches supported by two colleagues, who stumbled and fell onto his bed momentarily. As Will came to with the man's friends apologising to him he was greeted by the sight of blood oozing from bandages on the soldier's lower leg. A nurse ran over to help, calling for the doctor as she did so. They moved on down to the far end of the tent, the man groaning in agony with each step, having to be almost dragged by his friends.

"Bastards," Will muttered, looking at the wounded man, the

anger rising in him once more. It was becoming light outside. He must have slept through the night again but it had done nothing to brighten his mood.

"That's no way to greet your mates," a voice said, and Will spun round and saw Ced and Albert moving in to the bed.

"How you doing lad?" Albert asked, looking around the tent and wincing at the sight.

"No breakfast in bed then?" Ced added, trying to be cheerful. "Better not tell you what me and the lads have just stuffed away then."

"The nurses say they will try and get us some food soon. Been mainly water and biscuits so far. Not that I'm hungry."

"Am sure we can sneak you in something stronger than that lad," Albert said. "Sure you're not ready for that cigarette now?"

"No thanks. Not for me. Not now."

"Suit yourself."

Will noticed the bed opposite was empty once more and wondered if the man had been moved away in the night, or was buried in the rapidly expanding cemetery outside. That reminded him of the Camerons and he asked about Stewart and Alec.

"They moved on last night," Ced told him. "We don't know where they were going, and they didn't either I think. Great shame about their mate. They said they'd known him since kids. Grew up together. Now he's just out back with a temporary cross. Must have been hard to leave him here."

"Yes awful," Will reflected.

"The Sergeant, Stewart, told us he'd write home to his sister and let her know he's okay and tell her about Charlie. He said he'd mention Archie in case he passes through Folkestone on the way home, but the medics think more than likely he will go to Blighty instead. Big hospital there for the wounded."

"That's decent of him," Will said, looking at the pair of them. "Blighty is Brighton right?" They nodded and he made himself ask about Archie not wanting to hear the news.

"All we know lad is he was alive when he left here and he went off by train to a port," Albert answered. "Still trying to find out where as I said, but it's chaos here as you know and finding any news is nigh on impossible with all the censorship. They'll as likely know in England before we bloody do!"

"That's something I guess. I've been fretting all night he might be lying outside with Charlie."

"Not Archie. He wouldn't give those Hun the satisfaction you know that! Anyway you shouldn't be fretting with these pretty nurses to look after you," Ced retorted with a wink.

"As if. Hey where's Ernie by the way? I've been meaning to ask."

"Good question Will," Ced replied, raising his eyes. "Last time I saw him was when we came out of the bath house and the shells landed. He's not dead we know that much! Some of the lads said he was in the nosh house later on in the day. Bit of a mystery currently but he can't have gone far"

"Damned if we know," said Albert, "Needs a nanny that one. Bloody kid shouldn't be here, more trouble than he's worth."

"He's a good lad Albert, just scared."

"Ain't we all? Got trouble enough without looking after the Tailor. He'll probably turn up down the road in some Frenchie village shop sewing uniforms for the frogs."

"Good luck to him if he does I say," Ced replied. "Speaking of trouble, look out the Hun's inbound!"

The three of them looked up as Lieutenant Dunn and Sergeant Albright appeared in the tent chatting to the doctor and looking over the men. Ced and Albert gave Will a last pat on the arm for good luck and said they'd be back later and shot off in the opposite direction. Men pleaded for help as they passed through the tent. As they reached the end Will saw Albert turn back and throw a packet of cigarettes to the nearest soldier and told him to pass them round.

"Gawd bless ya mate," the wounded man shouted, his accent and badges marking him out as a London Rifles Brigade man. It reminded Will of the dodgy fairground man at Steyning fete last summer. That seemed like a world away now.

"Well well, Davison. Got yourself into a spot of bother what?" The voice of Lieutenant Dunn made Will look round sharply.

"Er, yes sir."

"Caused me no end of paperwork I can tell you. How's the arm?"

"It's sore sir, but not too bad."

"Good, good. Well the doctors say you should be out tomorrow so come and report to me at the Mess and I will find you some things to do."

"He's on leave at the moment sir," Sergeant Albright chipped in, "and the doctor said he suffered concussion and needs to rest."

"Stuff and nonsense. Needs to work to keep his mind active more like. Rather than malingering here."

"He's not in any shape for manual labour lieutenant. He's had quite a blow, not to mention shock." The voice of Teresa made them all turn round.

"I see miss. Well that's as maybe but.."

"It's Staff Sergeant Halliday sir, or staff nurse when I'm working. I gave up being a miss when I joined the army as a nurse."

Dunn was clearly flustered by this but recovered his poise and continued regardless.

"I see...nurse. Anyway the concussion hasn't affected his legs and arms that much. So I'm sure he can do some fetching and carrying and what not. Light duties. Nothing too taxing and if he's around camp he can always come back here if needed."

Will knew he wouldn't be given an easy ride by the Lieutenant but didn't want people arguing on his account.

"It's fine Sir. I'd get bored sitting around camp day after day so I'd rather be busy. I'll come and report to you as soon as I'm out of here."

"Good-o. That's the spirit. Get some rest Davison. Right sergeant let's continue. I've got a report to do on our lot before lunch, and don't want to be late for that. Sausage and mash today I'm told."

Dunn moved on without a backward glance, and the sergeant raised his eyes to Will and dutifully followed.

"I'd like to get him under my care for a few hours," Teresa said, clearly still angry. "He's no right to do that, you need rest."

"I'll be alright. But thank you anyway. And for all you've done."

"That's okay Will. Now rest up and I'll see about getting you some tea." She flashed a red lipped smile and went off. Will watched her go before lying back once more on his bed to let the time tick by. He tried to think about home and what would be happening now, to try and drown out the constant moans from the men around him.

*

On Mill Farm David was also surrounded by noise. He had just finished getting the cows out into the lower meadow after breakfast. He lit a cigarette and watched the herd meander off grazing. They were lowing constantly as they did and no doubt it sounded like they were distressed to anyone passing by, but he knew the cows were content. He still didn't smoke when his mum was around. His dad knew he did and whether his mum did or not, he knew she wouldn't like it, so always tried to light up out of sight. He inhaled the fumes deep into his lungs and felt its calming effect. It was a cold crisp start to the day and as he exhaled, the smoke mingled with his frost kissed breath and floated away.

He had told them finally over breakfast that he was going to sign up with the Southdowns and the reaction had been better than expected. They knew he wanted to. It had been there in the background since the summer. His dad had asked him to wait until the end of the month and help with some urgent repairs and he had been happy to do this. The relief at finally telling them felt like a real load off his back.

The letter from Will which had arrived yesterday, written just after Christmas, had certainly helped smooth the way. The stories about the Christmas truce in many a similar letter delivered that day had given families in the town fresh hope that the boys would be home soon and it would all be over. Old Gettings had stated with conviction to a bar full of regulars last night that an armistice had already been signed. It might all be over before he got there but he still wanted to go. The fact Lord Lowther was promising 'hot food and real beds for all recruits' until they went, and also local training, had certainly softened the blow with his mum. Besides, many of his friends had signed up so he couldn't stand by and watch them go, even though he knew there was more than enough work for him here.

David closed the meadow gate and looked up to the top fields where he could see his dad working on the crumbling stone wall, clouds of smoke ebbing forth from the kneeling figure, mirroring his own breath. Glancing at the house he wondered about going to check on his mum but saw Fred in the kitchen chatting away to her, and so set off up the track instead. He wasn't sure what to talk to his dad about or what he would be thinking but he knew they could work together in silence. Though it was only mid-morning, the relief at finally telling his parents washed all the tension out of his body and he resolved to have an early night.

Unlike Will struggling to find peace in the hospital tent, David would sleep as solidly that night as the granite rock his dad was hefting up ahead. It was a time of true contentment that he would always struggle to recapture.

Chapter 18 - The right frame of mind

Ernie was missing.

A week had passed since the dreadful day when Will had been injured but he was healing quickly. The cuts and bruises he had suffered were already disappearing and there had been no worrying side effects to the concussion thankfully. The main issue had been with his shoulder, especially being right handed, and though he had tried to use his left to write, it had been hopeless. However he was conscious he must send something home. Will was worried that with other people writing home too, news might reach his family that he had been hurt before he had a chance to explain he was alright. As his recent letter had been so upbeat just after Christmas he knew this would cause even more concern to his parents, so he was determined to send a note himself.

This proved to be a challenge not least because of the discomfort in his arm, but also because Lieutenant Dunn had been working him round the clock like his personal slave since his release from the hospital, and he found it hard to get any time to himself. He had hardly seen or heard from his friends since working in the officer's mess, and was therefore oblivious to the drama unfolding within the camp.

Salvation from his enslavement came in the form of Teresa once more, who required extra help with fetching and carrying supplies from the railhead and got one of the army doctors, Major Philips, to request Will to join the working party. Dunn had objected of course as it impacted on his daily routine, but the Major had outranked him and it had been a short conversation. Will didn't wait for a second invitation and went off with the other men to get the fresh batch of medicines and equipment. He knew some other poor soul would be dragged in soon enough to wait on the lieutenant.

Now away from the main camp and with the trucks all loaded,

he sat down and finally managed to slowly pen a few lines home to let them know he was alright. He hoped to find out some news about Archie too. He had asked Teresa to help when they last spoke but she agreed with his friends that getting news from back home was painfully slow. All she knew was he had probably gone back to Brighton on a boat from Boulogne, but of course she would try to find out where he had been shipped to.

Will paused to let the cramp in his hand subside, still struggling to form proper words with his right hand. He shook his head looking at the messy scribble on the paper in front of him, having always prided himself on his neat writing. As he folded the note and finished the envelope he looked up to see who he could pass it to, and saw a familiar figure walking up the lane towards him.

"Hello Will."

Ced greeted him smiling, as much as was possible to tell under the ever blossoming moustache. "I heard you had escaped your jailor and been sent to the depot so I thought I would wander down and catch up. I brought lunch!" He produced two large pieces of sausage and some crusty bread in brown paper and proceeded to make a couple of rough sandwiches with them, handing one to Will. "Courtesy of our finest chefs!"

Will patted him on the shoulder and they sat down relaxed as ever in each other's company. He took one of the rough sandwiches from Ced and leaned back looking up at the sky. The winter sun was very bright and he put an arm across his face to shield his eyes as he looked about. A robin settled on a fence post nearby, unperturbed by the presence of the two men, a doomed worm wriggling uselessly in its beak.

"I know how the worm feels," said Will ruefully.

Ced glanced to where his friend was looking and wasn't sure if he meant being stuck with Dunn or the whole war in general, but laughed regardless. He looked at Will.

"Ernie is missing."

Will sat up immediately. "What proper missing you mean?"

"Yes been gone for three days now. We are on leave yes, but it's not like Bournemouth beach is it where we can just wander about at leisure with an ice cream. They took a roll call yesterday as you know and realised after going through the people working duties like yourself, that he wasn't assigned anywhere. We did a scour round the camp with Sergeant Albright first trying to keep it under wraps but he was nowhere to be seen.

Will shook his head. "Oh no."

"So the sarge had to tell the captain and he called in the coppers. The Military Police were sent to go and search the local establishments."

Will raised an eye quizzically so Ced continued. "You know bars, brothels that kind of thing. Most of the men are allowed out for relaxation and what not in the day, but they all have to be back for last post. There's a few spots in Béthune that are popular if you know what I mean. And sometimes the lads get *carried away* as it were, or too drunk and have to be fetched!"

Will had not been interested at all in going to the bars, and even less in the brothels some men were drawn to any chance they got. He felt guilty enough just looking at other women like Teresa, regardless of whether Alice would ever know, and frankly wasn't fussed about any of the common vices the men used to ease the days; smoking, drinking and the like. He would sooner be kicking a ball about any day of the week. He couldn't believe for a moment Ernie would do that either and Ced seemed to read his thoughts.

"Of course the Tailor never turned up anywhere. We never expected him to, unless he'd had a complete change of personality so he's been posted missing officially. There's even a rumour he's taken himself back to the front so someone's been dispatched back up there to talk to the Indian Brigade and our relief companies just in case."

"Poor Ernie."

"Albert is chuffed to bits as he had a wager running on it with a few lads that Ernie would be the next to go. Such a git."

"What now then?" Will asked despondently.

"Well the MPs will keep looking but frankly the captain said this morning he has too much on to worry about one man, and he'll deal with it when and if he turns up. Meanwhile I think we are all for the heave ho shortly."

"Heave ho?"

"Moving on. New posting. They want us up at Ypres."

"Oh joy," Will said sarcastically, then added, "Won't be the same without Archie. And as much as he's a pain I will miss Ernie."

"Nothing's the same without Archie lad. Camp's like a graveyard without him. Hit the company hard I think. More than anyone cares to admit. As for Ernie. He's better off out of it I say. But God help him when they find him."

"Do you think he will be in trouble?"

"Not half. They take desertion seriously you know."

"Ernie isn't a deserter he's just lost."

"You know that and I know that, but try telling those bleedin' officers that!"

They sat in silence for a while, watching the clouds chase each other across the sky. There was a mixture of bird songs here when they took time to stop and listen, and somewhere someone was hammering a post into the ground. Whether it was for the war or a farmer refusing to acknowledge what was going on around him, they couldn't tell, but for all intents and purposes they could have been in the fields in Steyning. The robin returned looking for dessert to follow up his worm lunch. He eyed the crumbs from the sausage sandwiches eagerly, and hopped a few paces further forward. Ced stood up brushing himself down and the bird flew the few yards back to its watching post.

"Well if you're done here we best be getting back. Camps a hive of activity after the order arrived to pack up and if you haven't been summoned back yet you will be soon, so best show willing."

Will picked up his rifle slinging it painfully on his left shoulder as the right was too sore. Ced reached down and grabbed his pack and the two men set off back up the lane towards the chaos of the front, Will still clutching his letter to his mum.

Behind them the Robin chirped triumphantly as it flew to the flattened grass where the bread feast awaited. It sang in the sun and its mate answered it from the nest in the hedgerow nearby, the eggs safe and warm under their mother's embrace. They were used to the noise and activity here and carried on their lives happy in the moment, without a thought for the future. Before eating the Robin glanced cautiously around once more, instinct always ensuring it stayed alert, and watched the two strange creatures moving away. Content all was safe and they wouldn't return, the bird pecked at the ground several times before grabbing a large crumb and flying off.

As Will and Ced approached the camp both men had their minds very much fixed on future events. Albert saw them coming back into the camp and hurried over to meet them. It was rare to see the veteran hurry anywhere.

"They've found Ernie."

"What? Where?"

"Is he alive?" Ced asked, voicing a fear that several of the men had held unspoken.

"Very much so," Albert replied. "Believe it or not he was fishing apparently when they caught up with him just a couple of miles away. Reading a book by the river with a makeshift rod."

"Good grief."

"Where is he now?" Will asked, instantly concerned.

"They've got him locked up in a shed over near the mess hall. Dunn is going to haul him in front of the Major tomorrow. Wants a full court martial as an example."

"Oh for God's sake, what a joke. He can't be serious. Clearly he's no deserter, he's just sick." Will looked at his colleagues for support but they looked at the ground unable to share his optimism. "He's just not in the right frame of mind that's all. You know this lads don't you?" Will was almost pleading as the other two men struggled to find the right words to give him the reassurance he sought.

"I'm sure it will all be fine Will," Ced responded, meeting his friend's eyes and trying to look calm.

"I'm going to speak to Teresa and see if she can help," Will continued. "Maybe some medical report or something. Will you see if you can speak to him Ced? Reassure him. See if we can get him anything?"

"Of course lad, leave it with me."

They watched Will hurry off towards the hospital tent.

"Between you and me Ced, I'm not sure it will do much good. His best hope is they have too much on to bother with a trial, but that might go against him."

"What do you mean?"

"I mean old Hun wants his pound of flesh and they may just shoot him as a deserter and be done with it. Bigger fish to fry and all that, and the Major won't want to have this stigma on the regiment."

"Bugger." Ced shook his head. "Well let's see if we can go and see him like the boy asked. Cheer him up at least?"

"Ok but I'm not getting put against the wall if push comes to shove. Not for the Tailor. Not for anyone who hasn't the stomach for it."

"I know Albert, and when the time comes you better help me make sure Will doesn't get dragged in either."

*

That evening Will paced relentlessly about in the camp. He had been unable to find Teresa when he went to the hospital tents as she had been on a rest break and had gone to Béthune with a couple of other nurses. His friends had likewise failed in their mission, being prevented from seeing Ernie by the MP on guard, and it had left Will feeling helpless.

He leant against a crate of newly delivered vegetables that smelt past their best to someone with a sense of smell honed on the farm, despite the contents being labelled 'fresh'. He remembered his letter home and had just emerged from the operations dug-out where he had passed it to a mail orderly, if nothing else than to pass some more time until morning. Will knew sleep would not come easily to him tonight. The dug-out being one of the key hubs of the base was set below ground, despite being some way behind the front, and Will knew all too well why now, given the events of the last week.

It was home to three rooms below ground and a mass of orderlies were working on communications and supply tasks. There were also a number of officers here too engaged in various tasks, who had moved from the Mayor's house as the shellings continued. It was chaotic and noisy and he wondered if this was what it would be like in an ants nest when the Queen decided it was time to move on.

The noise intensified the oppressive atmosphere, and Will had felt suddenly claustrophobic and giddy and pushed his way back up the steep ramp to the sandbagged entrance and now leant back gasping in the cool night air. He was about to head off when he spotted a female nurse with a mass of untied black hair approach the entrance. An orderly emerged insect-like from underground and bumped into her, before dashing off with a shout of "'Scuse me miss!"

Teresa half spun, half turned with the impact and was about to shout after the man when she saw Will by the crates.

"Fancy meeting you here," she said regaining her composure with a broad smile. "How are you Will?" He stood up immediately and came forward.

"Ernie's been found. They've arrested him. Albert reckons he might get court martialled," he blurted out in reply.

"Calm down soldier. I heard about your friend. I did try and look for you before I went off shift but you must have still been at the depot. I was going to have a look for you again once I was done here but looks like you found me first." Will smiled, but it was a weak smile.

"Ced told me. I came to find you but they said you had gone to Béthune. I didn't get chance to thank you for getting me away from Dunn."

She made a motion for him to be quiet and nodded to an officer sitting nearby smoking a pipe who Will hadn't noticed before. "That's alright," she said lowering her voice, "Any update on your friend?"

"No none. They won't let us speak to him. I am really worried about him Teresa. But he's no deserter he's..." Teresa put her finger to his lips and shushed him again, as his emotional outburst began to draw quizzical looks from men hurrying past. "Let's chat over here."

As they walked away from the dug-out he noticed angrily more than one of the soldiers nearby prod their mate and nod at her. Someone in the shadows muttered, "lucky blighter," and another let out a low whistle. She stopped him out of sight by a set of supply tents.

"Sorry about that," he mumbled.

"Why? It's not your fault. Just ignore it, I do. Besides they are just little boys away from their Mums," she added with a cheeky smile, "I can handle myself don't worry." Will felt embarrassed again and assumed he must just be a little boy too, to her.

Teresa sensed his unease. "Look I will speak to the medical officer and see if we can get something written down to hand in at the hearing tomorrow. You know like a report or something to say he's been affected by the injury to his friend and such like. Bound to be in shock. It might help."

Will felt buoyed by this. "Would you? That would be terrific."

"I can't promise but I'm sure we can do something to try and get him some support. From what I hear the Major is a decent sort. He was a lawyer or something before the war but he's not an ogre, and he might let us hospitalise your friend with a bit of persuasion."

"I owe you again."

"Oh shush. Now go and get some sleep or you will be no use to yourself let alone anyone else. The regiment is moving north tomorrow isn't it? You won't want them to catch you falling asleep en route!" She squeezed his shoulder for reassurance and he winced with the pain.

"Oh God sorry Will. I forgot which one you had hurt. Some nurse I am," she said laughing.

"It doesn't matter," he replied lying, as the constant dull ache reacted instantly with a more sharp pain.

She leant in unexpectedly and stroked his shoulder. "There, that better?" she asked with a disarming smile, the teeth flashing white in the gloom.

"Much" he responded, going as red a beetroot and grateful for the darkening sky that hid his embarrassment.

They stood there silently for a few moments as another orderly rushed past into the evening sky carrying several dispatches.

"I must be off back to work," Teresa said to break the silence, having waited for the other soldier to disappear out of earshot. "I'm on the night shift tonight. I swapped with one of the girls who needed the break more than me. That's why I didn't go into town."

"Oh I see," he nodded. "Will you, I mean the hospital, be heading north with us tomorrow too?"

"No I don't think so. Too many men to look after here and there is talk of moving us into a more permanent structure as we are too crowded. Don't worry though, I am sure there will be other nurses wherever you end up corporal."

"Not like you," he said inadvertently.

"Of course not Will. No one's like me. Now get off back to your mates and good luck tomorrow at the hearing."

He was about to say something else when the pipe smoking officer appeared and walked past them. They saluted him together and he responded curtly and looked as if he was about to stop and question them, but then hurried on. As Will looked round Teresa was already walking away towards the dug-out. He wanted to call after her or follow her as her company soothed him greatly, but he thought better of it and turned towards their billets.

Teresa paused at the tunnel entrance. She looked back in the direction of where the young corporal had disappeared. "Remember your training Teresa dear," she said to herself, "don't get attached to the men."

Chapter 19 – Up against it

The hearing was not going well. Apart from the fact the Major was under pressure from Headquarters to get little short of a thousand men from companies of the Sussex and Hampshire battalions resupplied and organised, and moved up to Ypres, he now had to deal with a personnel issue.

Major Marshall Bluffington-Sykes, or the Right Honorable Bluffington-Sykes, as he was known before the war, was originally a Justice of the Peace for his local council in Windsor and Eton, before also training formally in the law. His work in Windsor, and his former attendance at Eton school in the 1880s, had brought him to the attention of several peers of note, of whom he could now count Lords and Generals and even His Royal Highness the Aga Khan amongst them. He had attended more than one Royal function in Windsor castle, and despite not ever feeling totally at ease in those circles he was able to converse genially and in an informed manner.

At forty four, had he joined the military from university he could have expected to be a colonel or higher by now, but having only joined the army in 1914 and with no formal military training behind him he held the honorary rank of Major; and that only after some words were said on his behalf 'behind closed doors.'

Marshall was however as affable in the army as he had been in school, and brought a level headed sense of fair play to his legal and military duties that was born on the playing fields of Eton, where he had starred at both Cricket and Rugby. This all served to strengthen his position within the Army Service Corps, or ASC as it was known, to which he had been assigned upon receiving his commission. There had been a number of regiments willing to take him but as a nine year old boy he had been stirred by the tales of the heroic defence of Rourke's Drift in the Zulu war, and of the actions of Acting Assistant Commissary General James Langley Dalton in particular who was awarded the Victoria Cross. Although not a line officer Dalton had fought bravely and assisted in the defence of the small hospital post against overwhelming odds even when severely wounded, and this had drawn Marshall to the ASC as it had shown him that all manner of men could serve in the armed forces.

His attention to detail, coupled with the fact the role was critical to the movement of men, animals and supplies made him a notable figure in the Division. Not least because he was responsible for the movement of the officers' personal items, including their horses and the mess silver! Here at Neuve-Chappelle he had become somewhat overworked as his reliability and ability meant officers naturally gravitated to him to get their work done.

However there had been a number of incidents during his time in the region caused by the recent random shelling that had made his life very difficult, not least the destruction of one of the stable blocks. More recently bombing of some storage areas and mail tents lead to several key functions being rehoused underground, and an already chaotic administration function, had threatened to descend into total anarchy. Having just got that all squared away and working once more, they now had to up root everything and move it north!

In truth though Marshall was looking forward to a change of scenery, as he had started to feel this area was a curse to his logistics operation, and if he managed all this without too many mishaps he was told he could be moved into HQ to work from there. Today however there were a million and one things to do and he was feeling overwhelmed enough as it was without Colonel Bradshaw, knowing of his legal background, dropping a desertion case on his desk...

"Man of your renown, should only take you a few minutes major," the colonel had stated over a sherry the previous morning. "Some young lieutenant from the Sussexers says it's an open and shut case of desertion. In which case just find a wall out the back, throw him up against it and be done with it, and let's get back to winning the war what?"

Marshall had sipped his sherry and not said anything in the moment, reflecting on the way life was suddenly so cheap when it came to ensuring the mess silver and sherry arrived ahead of the army.

"It might not be as straight forward as it seems sir," was all he had offered during the brief exchange.

"Possibly Major, but don't make it any more complicated than it is. These trifling matters can't detract from the issues at hand, and we don't want a whiff of any dissention in the ranks getting back to HQ, let alone the newspapers. I'm sure you understand the position. More sherry?"

Marshall had simply nodded, as he did now, quietly reflecting on the situation and the poor wretch standing in front of him in the Quartermaster's 'office' which was in the cellar of a farm house, and the only place currently that wasn't overrun with soldiers and workers. He knew these young lads were under tremendous strain, being a long way from home and the life they knew, but it was no different for him. He also knew there had been plenty of cases of men going 'walkabout' already and the army was full of shirkers. He studied Private Isaacs again and wondered if this was another test by his colonel, and whether his transfer might rest on it.

Ernie looked a long way from the smart tailor's son who had enlisted some months before. Unshaven and in a uniform he had been in for some days he looked more like a man returning from the front than one who had supposedly been on leave for over a week. But for someone who took such pride in his appearance and was normally so clever, the soldier standing before the major was a pale imitation of that man, which did his cause no good whatsoever.

Lieutenant Dunn had presented the facts of Ernie's disappearance with some embellishment, and when the major had tried to ascertain why Ernie had gone absent, he could barely muster a sentence in his defence. If it wasn't for the fact that Will knew he had never taken a drink in his life he would swear he was drunk. He seemed completely out of it and mumbled incoherently, which Dunn pointed out was due to guilt.

Will had initially felt a ray of hope when he had gone into the hearing as Lieutenant Goodman was acting as the major's aide.

He had not seen Theodore Goodman since they had set off for the training camp last year and he had spotted him kissing his wife goodbye on the platform despite the public setting. In training the officers and men had been kept apart and he had been far too busy to worry about anything except getting through each day successfully. If Goodman was at Folkestone or on the ship over with them he never saw him. After that he must have been detailed to another sector or company, or even the ASC. Will had smiled at him to try and establish a rapport but the man had looked straight through him and just stuck to his task of minuting the meeting.

Will suddenly recalled that once when he was a small choirboy with his brothers they had heard Celia call her husband 'Teddy' outside the vestry, and he had chased them off angrily when they all laughed. But he pushed it aside as he was sure Goodman didn't even recall who he was. He certainly wasn't giving any indication that he was going to speak up for or against a Sussex lad.

Will was called upon to speak briefly on Ernie's behalf as a character witness, which helped Marshall to feel that he had at least given the boy some sort of a fair hearing. But as Will began to speak for his friend and tried to read from a hastily scribbled statement signed by several of his colleagues, he was interrupted not only by Dunn but by two messengers from Colonel Bradshaw asking for updates on the Division's progress. He wanted to protest but as a low ranking soldier he had no ability to do so and he felt inadequate once more.

Marshall looked at the young corporal reading falteringly from a scrap of paper in front of him and sighed. *This is a long way from the courtroom in Windsor,* he thought depressingly. He stared at Will, nodding absent mindedly but without hearing what he was saying as his thoughts were now elsewhere. It was clear to Marshall that the colonel had completely forgotten what he was doing this morning, or more probably didn't care. His mind began to wander to the many tasks requiring his attention. *He was wasting time here,* he thought to himself.

The emphasis of the character statement was lost and Will had a horrible sinking feeling that he was fighting a losing battle on his friend's behalf. He looked round hoping that Teresa or someone would appear with a medical report but no one came. Ced leaned forward from where he stood just behind his friend.

"It's no good Will. Evidence is all against the lad and he can't even explain himself why he ran off. He's not a great soldier either which doesn't help. He's a risk and officers don't like that."

"He's our friend Ced and we have to help him."

Ced gave him a resigned look. "Let's just hope he's lenient eh?"

As if to undermine that point Lieutenant Dunn spoke up. "Sir. If the Corporal is finished may I sum up?"

Dunn continued without waiting for an answer to press home his advantage, and tapped into the Major's concerns about the day ahead. "I am concerned that this matter takes up any more of your precious time than is necessary sir. The man was absent without leave and has no excuse. I accept he wasn't in a front line post but the fact remains he disobeyed orders at the first sign of trouble, and if he can run away here from just a few shells what might he do when faced with a full scale attack? If he leaves his post when we are under attack he could put lots of lives at risk."

It was a strong point and Will's heart sank. He tried desperately for something to say but his mind was blank.

"Alright, alright," the Major said with a world weary tone to his voice. He shuffled some papers as if looking for an answer on his desk, and then clearly came to his decision. He looked directly at Ernie, his face expressionless.

"Private Isaacs I find you guilty of desertion. While the repercussions were not serious, your actions are not those becoming a soldier in the Royal Sussex regiment, despite the loyalty of your comrades here in this room. You have been unable to explain your actions and I share the lieutenant's concerns that were I to allow you to return to your unit you might do the same thing again."

Dunn looked delighted at this and could barely contain a smile spreading on his lips. Will felt sick to his stomach and Ced put a hand on his friend's shoulder to steady him, knowing how the young lad might react.

"I am also aware," the Major continued "that if your actions are to go unpunished, this kind of careless disregard for authority and order could spread to other troops. I therefore have no alternative but to sentence you to…"

"Bluffers!"

The Major was stopped abruptly by the shout from the back of the room, and was about to respond with an outburst of his own at this unauthorized intrusion when he recognised the man who had entered unseen. "Good God," was all he could say and all eyes turned round to see who the new voice belonged to.

Standing resplendent in full dress uniform was a captain of the Coldstream Guards, his 'Sam Brown' officers' belt gleaming across his chest in the gloom of the cellar as he followed protocol and smartly saluted the Major. He then tucked his hat neatly under his arm and removed his gloves and held them in his other hand along with his baton, and smiling broadly stepped forward. Will and Ced looked at each other in complete astonishment neither knowing who this officer was or why he was here. The soldiers in the room, including the lieutenant all snapped to attention as he came forward.

"Sorry to burst in unannounced old boy," the Captain continued offering his hand, "but I came over here forthwith as I have something relevant to this case, but I had no idea you were here. Small world Bluffers what?"

"It's major in here, *captain.*"

"Oh quite, sorry sir. Just delighted to see you again. Unexpected and all that."

"Well indeed. That's as may be," Marshall said giving the captain's outstretched hand a brief shake. "Anyway what the devil are you doing here Harry, I mean captain, and how are you remotely involved in this private's case. The Guards are not in this sector?"

"No that's right. I came down on a spot of leave with a friend this morning early as the lark, looking for his brother, and we heard what was going on. Spoke to some delightful nurse who press ganged me into service on her behalf. Not that it would have taken much pressing!"

Harry Johnson gave a broad smile that would have disarmed most ladies and endeared him to the Surrey Cricket board in equal measure. A board that had given him his first county cap when they had played against Middlesex some five years ago, who just happened to be captained by the Right Honorable Bluffington-Sykes. They discovered over a delightful tea in the pavilion between innings that they were both *Old Etonians* and the friendship had been formed. Not least because Harry had been the first person since Eton to call him 'Bluffers' without even thinking twice about it when introduced.

Marshall had a flashback to the precocious young talent who had followed up a quick fire fifty not out with an even faster wit. He had gone to congratulate him over tea on a maiden half century as the opposition captain to which Harry had replied, "Bluffington what? Bit of a mouthful. I'm Harry Johnson but everyone calls me Jonners. Appreciate the words Bluffers old man. Shall we take tea together? Splendid spread."

The memory caused Marshall's impassive face to break into a spontaneous grin and he was genuinely pleased to see him and clearly doing so well. He cleared his throat trying to restore some vestige of formality in the room.

"Well Captain, you come in the nick of time. I was just about to pass sentence. If you feel you have some bearing on this poor boy's future speak up."

"Sir, no disrespect to the captain, but is this appropriate given the circumstances and the fact the captain has said he doesn't know Isaacs?" Dunn questioned frustratingly.

"No offence taken lieutenant," Harry said stepping in front of him and stopping him speaking any further. "I have here a medical report from the hospital about Private Isaacs that Staff Nurse Halliday was due to present this morning but owing to the requirements to get the walking wounded up and out following the order to move the Division onwards, she has been delayed. It's produced by the leading medical officer I'm led to believe. May I submit it major."

"Hamilton's signed it?" Marshall commented, sensing a way out of this ridiculous situation and referring to Colonel Hamilton, the senior Royal Army Medical Corps man in the sector.

"Yes sir, so I believe."

"So that's your nurse's name eh? Halliday," Ced whispered with a nudge. "Seems like you have a way with the ladies everywhere we go lad. I need to keep close to you. Some of that charm might rub off." Will blushed slightly but still kept anxiously watching the major for what he would do next. He couldn't relax yet.

Marshall scanned the document in front of him. "It appears Private Isaacs is suffering from a debilitating nervous condition caused by severe shock and requires urgent medical attention not a firing squad. Indeed it is recommended that he is sent home for a period of time for treatment, whereupon he can potentially be rehabilitated back into the frontline in due course. Saved rather than lost it would seem." He paused reflecting on the fact that he had almost condemned the boy to death with a stroke of his pen, and how another signature had saved him. Such were the margins of a man's life in war time. "Perhaps this should have been looked into more thoroughly first lieutenant rather than waste everyone's precious time with a hearing as you put it?" He peered round the captain looking disparagingly at Dunn.

"But sir," the lieutenant began to protest.

"Unless you feel qualified to challenge the opinion of the senior medical officer for the Battalion, and are content to waste more of HQ time on the matter?"

Dunn fell silent, the mixture of shame and anger clear to see.

"I thought not. Captain, thank you for bringing this matter to our attention. Davison get Isaacs over to the medical tent right away and get him assessed. Lieutenant you may go. I am sure you have many more pressing and arduous tasks to be getting on with."

As Dunn saluted and slunk away, still seething about the outcome, Will stepped forward with Ced to take Isaacs gently by the arm.

"Ah yes Davison. I almost forgot," Harry said turning to him.

"Sir?"

"Perhaps Major another soldier can deal with Private Isaacs here as the Corporal has a visitor I brought with me?"

"Of course Captain. Longworthy help Isaacs over to the hospital tent and then report to the RSM for orders on the move."

Will felt elated at the outcome of the hearing and grateful to the unknown captain who had intervened, but at the same time he couldn't help but feel a pang of jealousy that he wasn't going to be able to see Teresa again. If only to thank her for her help.

"Are you sure I shouldn't go too major? I am probably closest to him."

"No Longworthy can manage. You have business elsewhere it seems. Now dismissed all of you. Let me get on."

The soldiers in the room started to file out and Ced followed leading the bewildered Ernie, totally clueless as to how close he had come to a firing squad. As Will made to follow, Harry touched his arm. "You'll find your visitor having a quiet smoke outside. Make sure you mind your manners now." He smiled and turned back to speak to Marshall, and Will walked out even more mystified than he had been during the last few minutes.

Marshall was already in conversation with Goodman about what to prioritise next when Harry strolled up and sat on the corner of the desk.

"Good to see you Bluffers. Keeping well I trust? Family all good?"

"Very well Jonners thank you. I'm pleased you joined up. The Guards are perfect for you."

"But am I perfect for them?" Harry said with a laugh. "Anyway couldn't miss the big show. Just not on. Not being an Old Etonian and what not."

"Quite," Marshall replied smiling again and feeling more relaxed than he had done in the last month.

"Fancy a late breakfast Bluffers?"

Marshall looked at his pocket watch weighing up the options and work ahead of him. It was inscribed on the back by the Middlesex team of 1900, after another solid year under his Captaincy. It had been with him ever since and had kept time in many different circumstances. A half hour break wouldn't hurt, especially after the stress of the morning and he had been working since reveille sounded at half past five.

"Why not," he smiled. Then he became aware of Lieutenant Goodman still scribbling away discreetly behind him.

"Lieutenant, why don't you see about getting those stables finalised and on the move. I'll catch up with you shortly."

"Sir." The Lieutenant saluted and walked out as well.

*

Theodore Goodman was not an Eton, Marlborough or Harrow scholar and as such wasn't deemed to be in the same 'club' as other officers. Although he had excelled at Christ's Hospital school he knew his apparent local education would hold him back when promotions came. His older brother was the Squire of the estate back home, and at fifteen years younger Theodore always considered himself to be an afterthought. He never wanted to ask if he was a mistake or a guarantee in case something should happen to Ernest. Everyone knew his father didn't want his two daughters inheriting the title and lands.

Theodore wasn't close to his brother and on everything except special occasions fell in line with the community and simply called him Squire. Certainly Ernest had inherited the full force of their father's chauvinistic traits. But ironically his love of whiskey and parties, and disregard for women had left him without a wife or heir, whereas their two sisters were married with children aplenty between them. His own beloved Celia had never been able to have children and so it would probably fall that the estate would pass to one of his sisters or their children anyway. He didn't care. Oh Celia loved the idea of being the lady of the manor of course, but they were wealthy enough without the responsibility and after everything he had seen here in France, he didn't care about land or status.

But he was happy to do his bit and frankly even happier not to be in the front line currently. So he played the game and went about his work with a quiet efficiency content not to raise his profile too much. His sole purpose was to survive this whole crazy misadventure and go home to his Celia in one piece. Often at night he would think about just taking off when he got back. The two of them. Starting again somewhere and just living life to the full. He had written home more than once about it since arriving. Maybe they could travel and see some of the world. Maybe. He had to survive first.

Goodman passed the young corporal in the doorway of the

171

farmhouse, pausing before going out into the rain in the hope it might stop.

"Davison. Your Dad has the big farm in Steyning on Mill Road doesn't he?"

"That's right sir," Will replied straightening up in the officer's presence.

"He's a good man your father. Your mother's in the church with my Cel… I mean my wife."

"Yes I believe so Sir."

"Any more of your brothers joined up or just you?"

"Just my oldest brother and me so far sir."

"Two's more than enough for any family to worry about. Is he in the Sussex?"

"No sir, a Guard's officer like the captain inside."

"Commendable. Well let's hope we can all meet back in Steyning church again soon." Theodore paused with a wistful smile and then exchanging a short salute strode off into the rain.

Chapter 20 - Holding on

"Corporal Davison."

Will saw the officer move out from the shadows of a small hut off to the right of the farmhouse where he had been sheltering from the rain. The officer wore a dark greatcoat that almost covered the length of him, swirling about his legs as he walked forward, the collar pulled up against the elements. It was raining so hard his shadowy form was almost indistinguishable as he moved forward, but the bright brass Lieutenant pips were still visible on his shoulder glinting in the gloom, and instinctively Will saluted. The officer returned the salute, the same brown leather gloves snapping up to his forehead, that the captain had worn inside.

"At ease little brother," James said as his handsome face appeared into focus and moved under the cover of the porch.

"James!" Will exclaimed and hugged his brother instantly without a thought for protocol. James ruffled his younger brother's hair affectionately and returned the hug, his time in France rekindling the bond between them that age demanded should be more reserved. He had already seen so many young men wounded or killed that he felt an overwhelming relief to see his younger brother fit and well.

"Ahem." Harry coughed politely as he came out with Marshall to head over to the mess for a late breakfast, hoping that everything wasn't being packed away just yet. Will and James sprang apart. But if the Major had seen them he didn't mention it, and just said "Davison you can take an hour off from duties while you speak to the officer there. Report to the RSM when you are done and catch up with your section. I'll cover for you in the meantime."

"Yes sir. Thank you sir," Will replied clearly delighted.

"I'll see you after tiffin old chap," Harry said with a warm smile to James. "If I'm not here I'll be skulking about the hospital tent getting my fillings checked by the nurses." He hurried to catch Marshall, laughing as he went.

"He won't get any joy from Teresa," Will said moodily. "More than likely knock his teeth out."

"Teresa?"

"The staff nurse in charge at the hospital tent. The one who got the report for Ernie today."

"Ah right. I see. Is that a spattering of jealousy I detect in my kid brother?"

"Don't know what you mean," Will replied blushing, "Oh shut up anyway."

"Fine way to talk to an officer I must say. I'm only teasing Will. Shall we sit inside out of the rain and catch up? I haven't got long."

"Yes please."

They moved inside the farmhouse and found that the sitting room contained a single broken sofa, one of its cushions rotted completely with just the springs sticking out. There were a couple of wine crates upside down nearby that had clearly been used before. James found a rag and dusted one off and then put his coat across the half of the sofa that still functioned for Will to sit on. They sat down smiling at each other not knowing where to begin.

"You talk funny now," Will began, "all posh like."

"And you sound just the same as ever. It's only my officer training I guess," James explained, suddenly feeling self-conscious. "I have to speak a certain way in front of the men. They expect it."

Will raised his eyes at this.

"I'm still James underneath. Don't you worry."

"I think men would follow you regardless of how you speak James, for what you do. You've always been a natural leader." His older brother smiled at the compliment. It was genuine and from the heart. Unlike the shallow words of praise from some of his senior officers passed to men they barely knew to supposedly make them fight harder, he knew that Will only ever said what he meant.

Will did indeed look up to his oldest brother and he admired so much in him that had they not even been related, he would have still followed him as an officer without question. There was no jealousy for the differences in rank, only a brotherly pride and an

174

unspoken love. He looked at him now. James was resplendent in his Guards' uniform, with the long greatcoat removed, and sat with a confident air despite being perched on an old crate. He had a pencil thin moustache that accentuated his extremely handsome face, the short brown hair and hazel eyes shining out above a frame that had filled out even more since he left home. He definitely had the broad shoulders of his father and Will knew that were he to walk into St. Andrew's church back home looking like this, all eyes would be on him. His brass buttons shone out as the rain suddenly paused its onslaught and the sun raised a sleepy eye over its dark clouded bed.

'Honi Soit Qui Mal Y Pense' was around the Guards' regimental crest which framed the badge imprinted on every glittering button. Will thought it fitting that they should have the same words as the Royal Sussex did around their own crest. He remembered these words from their Latin classes in school. It was one of those phrases that stuck in his head though at the time he hadn't fully understood it. He recalled that the translation was something like 'Shame on him who thinks evil of it,' and suddenly it occurred to him that it was rather appropriate for anyone who disapproved of a farmer's son being made an officer.

"Anyway I couldn't miss today now could I?" James continued.

"What do you mean?"

"Don't tell me you've forgotten?"

Will looked blank. The events of the last few hours had crowded any other thoughts out of his exhausted mind. James produced a bottle of brandy as if to prompt his younger brother's memory.

"Happy Birthday Will," he said with a big grin. "I do believe you have come of age to take a touch with your brother."

In all the emotion of events post-Christmas, Will had completely forgotten about his birthday. Back home he would have been woken by his parents coming in singing 'Happy Birthday' with a gift or two, and some homemade biscuits and a glass of milk. His mum singing in her beautiful soprano voice, his dad grumbling enthusiastically propped by the door, and Freddie changing the words as ever; as much as he could get away with. It never changed even as he grew up and he loved it just as much, so never asked for anything different. There would have been chocolate too, and a cake. A wonderful chocolate cake and white icing. He sighed and then took the bottle from James and had a big swig to fortify himself against the memories.

The brandy burned the back of his throat and he coughed with the sensation, but it still felt good inside, and his brother smiled that devilish smile of his. Content in the moment they talked on about their parents, and David and Freddie, and what they missed about home. They laughed about memories of working on the farm and some of the scrapes they got up to in the town, like long lost friends suddenly reunited once more. For though it was only a few months since they had last seen each other, the nature of the war made every day feel like a month, and every month a year. And looking at the physical changes in a lot of the men after they had been in France a while, this did not seem so fanciful a notion.

James told him how Harry had commandeered a car to come over having just recently been promoted and insisted on driving, giving the driver the day off. Whether he actually had any real experience himself appeared dubious once they began, James recounted.

"I felt more scared sitting next to Jonners as he flew about the roads on the way here than I have since I came to France," he remarked laughing. "I may walk back! Honestly I wouldn't have been surprised if we had ended up on the German side."

He asked Will then about the men he had joined up with and his friends from Steyning. Will talked about the Southdown battalions and how a lot of his friends he had heard were now with them but that they were still in England. So he spoke about his time in France and about the great football match at Christmas, and James said that some of their sectors had had a truce too. But they had played cricket not football at Harry's insistence and not with the Hun.

"Can't trust the buggers not to bowl round the wicket with a grenade," Harry had purportedly said, and that was that.

Talking about Christmas Will's thoughts naturally then turned to Archie and he updated James briefly on events since they had come out of the front line. Will talked a little about Ernie's case though he knew his brother was only showing a polite interest and was probably full of worries of his own, and it became clear that the more he talked about things in the present the gloomier the conversation became. So he switched track and moved the conversation onto Alice and her letters, and it seemed to snap James out of his melancholic trance.

"So are you telling me that you might be Lord Pevensey one day if you marry into the title?"

"Ha ha perhaps, so you better start being nice to me or else."

"Or else? Or else what little brother," and James jumped up suddenly and grabbed his brother and started play fighting with him. They could have been in the attic room at home.

"Ahem. Excuse me but isn't striking an enlisted man a court martial offence?" The brothers sprung apart once more at the sound of a voice in the room, and were relieved to see Harry standing there, water dripping off the bottom of a very expensive non-army issue coat. They all smiled.

"We have to go *lieutenant*," he said emphasising the fact that he was now a higher rank.

"Yes *sir*," James replied sarcastically and then hit him across the stomach with one of his crisp leather gloves.

"Oof! Pleasure to meet you young Davison," Harry said, and shook Will's hand warmly. "James talks about you often. I hope we can all meet again soon what? In Berlin perhaps." He smiled and walked out whistling to where he had parked the car.

James turned to Will. "Look after yourself won't you? Keep writing home and I will do the same and then Mum can tell us what each of us is doing! Because I doubt very much if the top brass know where we are supposed to be." He smiled and squeezed Will on the shoulder once more, and then put his coat around his shoulders.

"David told me I have to look after you," Will said looking sad now.

"Well then, make sure you do! And the best way to do that is to stay alive yourself. So no silly heroics because I'll be damned if I'm going back to milk those bloody cows every morning just because you're shot." It was a veiled attempt to make light of the situation but Will appreciated his big brother's attitude as always and wished he was going with him.

"Goodbye Will."

"Goodbye James…Sir."

"That's right, and don't you forget it Lance Corporal."

He strode off to where Harry was waiting in the car with the engine running. As he got in Harry went to roar the car forward but the back wheels were stuck in the mud and began to spin. He called out to two soldiers sitting under a tent nearby working on some machinery part and ordered them over to give them a push. The men reluctantly obliged, and this time with their help the car rocked free and set off across the farm yard to the road beyond, showering the two soldiers with clods of muddy earth.

"Thanks awfully," Harry shouted above the noise of the car, without a backward glance at their mud spattered rescuers. As they roared out onto the road Will saw James look back briefly and thought he caught a glimpse of a smile. He started to wave but they were gone too quickly. A last cry of "Tally Ho" from Harry carried to him on the wind before the engine noises faded away.

The rain returned and Will sighed deeply. It had been fabulous to see James but his departure had only heightened the growing homesickness he felt following the events of the last two weeks. Without Archie to cheer him up he missed home more than ever now. He spotted the major returning from his break with Harry and tried to smarten up and pull himself together.

"Everything in order corporal?"

"Yes sir."

"Good show. Then off to the RSM at the double and get yourself ready to move out."

"Sir."

Will jogged off across the yard towards the main camp area where he could make out the shapes of dozens of men moving back and forth in the rain. He could hear the RSM's voice breaking through the weather's relentless drone with his own thunderous commands, and he felt a sense of impending doom drawing him back into the war once more. At the last moment something made him stop, and without a second thought he changed direction and jogged down the slope towards the hospital tent.

He found Teresa sitting in the small rest area behind a makeshift screen to one side of the main hospital tents. She looked tired and her uniform was covered in dirt and blood and she was attempting to wash her arms in a small bowl of water set on a table with a rough bar of soap. Despite this she smiled broadly when she saw Will, drying her arms with a worn towel hanging on the back of a chair.

"Hello Will, you boys seem to have a nose for timing." He looked at her quizzically and she pointed to a stove he hadn't seen before. "The kettle's on. I hear on the grapevine that felicitations are in order?"

"What?"

"Many happy returns of the day?"

"Oh yes. Some birthday!"

"Well fancy a cuppa anyway birthday boy?"

Will felt himself unwinding in her presence. Teresa's ability to live in the moment, which probably served her well out here, worked its charm on him once more.

"Well I haven't got long but okay. I have to report back and get ready to move shortly. I just wanted to see you."

She smiled.

"Ah yes you're off today aren't you. Well we have fresh milk courtesy of one of our nurses Alice who has struck up a friendship with a local farmer. He leaves milk for her every morning in exchange for a smile and a wave and some broken words of French!" She laughed but saw Will seemed distracted.

"Have I said something wrong?"

"What? Oh no. Just the name Alice. Reminded me of someone back home."

"Oh I see, a sweetheart?"

"Not exactly. Well...maybe."

Teresa took off her bloodied apron and dusted down her blouse. She poured two teas and added some of the precious fresh milk.

"Sugar?"

"No thanks."

She handed him a warm cup and perched on the table, holding her own with both hands and blowing on it gently so her red lips pursed. He wondered if she did it on purpose but she continued to chat casually.

"Well you don't sound sure?"

He pondered this himself for a moment, taking a couple of gulps of tea that was still quite hot. Teresa waited politely for him to answer, pretending to look at some notes on the table.

"That's because I'm not really," he said eventually. "I know she likes me but she's very rich. Not sure what she sees in me."

"Oh I think you underestimate yourself. I've seen the way you care about people and girls like that in a man. A sensitive side. You seem quite popular here and are making friends in high places."

"How do you mean?"

"Well you had a Guards officer asking after you earlier and he was only too happy to help with your predicament with Ernie. Ced brought him down to us by the way. I'm delighted it worked out well."

"Thank you yes. It was a huge relief and that's why I'm here. To say thanks again. Really. You saved his life with your note."

"Oh don't mention it." She poured a little more tea for them both and he could see she was pleased with the compliment.

"And I think the Guards officer was more interested in you than me miss."

She blushed a little and said, "He wouldn't be the first!"

Will wanted to ask more but a doctor appeared at that moment.

"Sorry to spoil your break Staff, but I need help with one of the new patients."

Teresa smiled apologetically at Will, setting her cup down. "I have to go Will. Ernie is over in one of the far beds but we gave him something to calm him down. He's sleeping now. They say he will be shipped out tomorrow back home."

"Thank you." He put the tea down and followed her into the main tent and the mass of men and beds. The smell of the cramped area hit him instantly. He had not noticed it when he had rushed in from the rain, distracted by his purpose, but pausing here now he was shocked once again at how poor the conditions were for these soldiers. He thought how frustrating it must be for Teresa and the other medical staff to try and attend to them like this. He moved through the rows trying not to make eye contact until he came to Ernie who was indeed asleep in one of the cleaner beds near the entrance.

Will thought he looked peaceful at last and was glad his friend would soon be away from all this. He patted the sleeping form of the young tailor affectionately on his shoulder and pulled the blanket up round him to try and do something for him in that moment. He became aware then that he needed to be elsewhere and went to walk out.

He hesitated at the tent entrance the rain continuing to come down hard, and now there was an icy edge to it that made it even less appealing. Teresa came over.

"I nearly forgot to tell you in all the excitement."

"What Teresa?"

"We had a dispatch from England, a report on the latest casualty clearing lists we sent back. Your friend Archie made it back to Brighton okay and he's now in the main hospital there. They said he's serious but stable. Which I think means he has a good chance of pulling through. No amputations reported so fingers crossed eh?" She smiled and touched his arm briefly then said, "I have to go."

"Me too. And thank you again."

"You're welcome and I hope it works out for you with that girl. You sound quite smitten."

One of the doctors moved close to them speaking to a soldier in a bed nearby, his face completely wrapped in bandages except for his eyes and mouth. Teresa changed her informal tone just in case.

"Oh and corporal…"

"Yes staff?"

"Happy Birthday."

Will pulled on his hat, and smiling walked out into the rain heading over to the barrack area where he could see a number of his company moving about. Despite the icy drops stinging his face he felt better now and ready to face the world again. As he approached the barracks he could see some trucks had been brought in and the men were loading all the kit and equipment onto them. The familiar figure of Ced came up to him with two large sacks over each shoulder

"Here grab this, the RSM's on the warpath and you don't want to be caught being idle." He threw him one of the sacks and they fell into a line of men loading up the trucks.

"Once these are done we grab our kit and start walking."

"Aren't we going in the trucks?" Will asked hopefully.

"Don't be daft lad. They are for the officers and the kit. Equipment has to be kept clean and dry. More important than us." He gave a wry laugh and heaved his sack into the back of the nearest truck. "It's just a short forty mile hike for us lot."

"Oh great," said Will as he threw his sack in.

"I saw Ernie. He's asleep now. Looks better already."

"Lucky sod. Wish I was. Still good luck to the kid I say."

"I thanked Teresa for her help," Will added.

"Ohhhh, I wondered where you had vanished to!" He laughed and winked as they picked up a large crate and manhandled it towards the trucks between them, slipping on the muddy floor that was fast becoming waterlogged.

Will ignored the jibe. "My brother was here with the Guards captain. It was great to see him again."

"That's good to hear lad. Is he an officer too did I hear right?"

"Yes he is."

"I really am going to stick close to you then. I'm glad we know each other young Davison. I might get a ride in that truck after all." They laughed together handing the crate up with some difficulty to the soldiers waiting up inside the truck.

"Teresa told me she'd heard about Archie."

"Oh?" Ced stopped, and looked at his young friend.

"Yes he made it back okay. In a main hospital now she says. They think he will pull through."

"That's great news." He looked visibly relieved and stood for a moment shaking the rain off his coat in a futile gesture, as it would be soaked again in seconds. But it allowed him time to gather his thoughts. He clasped Will on the shoulder with a smile. "Come on let's get going. And God help those poor nurses when he wakes up."

Chapter 21 – Dropped.

Harold climbed the last few steps and leant back against the rock. Beyond the top wall of the farm the land climbed away onto the open moor of the South Downs. He liked to come up here when time allowed to a small standing stone that stood against a rocky outcrop like an immortal sentry, from which you had a clear view right across Steyning and on towards the sea. When the boys were younger he would often bring them all up here for a break from work and rest on the rocks while they charged around in the bracken.

He smiled at the memory. Hearing their voices echo off the rocks as they ran about. His little lads. Not little anymore! The thought pulled at him despite the pride he felt in their achievements. He looked round suddenly as if anyone nearby would be able to read his thoughts. There was no one of course, and he took a long hard pull on the cigarette.

Although now in his mid-forties Harold usually found the climb effortless. Sometimes he would continue on across the top to Chanctonbury Ring from which you could see for miles in any direction. Old Gettings was convinced he'd seen all the way to France up there once on a fine summer's day. You could certainly see the sea, as he could now from here, but he'd never seen France. However since his boys had gone over there, he had looked for it on more than one clear day without success. He used to look north towards London when James had gone up there, now he always found himself gazing south.

He felt the climb more than usual today. He had not been sleeping well of late since David's departure, and his back troubled him daily. He didn't like to feel hampered in anyway, especially with his health, the responsibility of the farm always weighing down on his shoulders. So he pushed himself harder to work through the discomfort.

It was Easter Day, 1915, and the church bells of St. Andrew's had been ringing joyously since early morning, shaking off the sadness of Good Friday with peal after peal of celebration. They called the town to join them in rejoicing in the risen Christ, although Harold wondered up here alone with his thoughts if the more sombre tone of Good Friday was more reflective of the people's mood than today. He would head down in a moment. He lit a fresh cigarette and looked at his farmhouse, where the thin wisps of smoke rising from the kitchen chimney highlighted the fact the mornings were still cold despite the welcome return of spring on this early April day.

It had been a successful start to the year for the Davisons and Harold smiled proudly at the number of sheep supporting one or two lambs each. The old ram from Tulip farm was still clearly up to the task he thought to himself with a smile, as indeed was Joe Eastwood's bull. It had cost him a small fortune as ever for its 'services' but with half the herd already pregnant it was money well spent and he was more than happy with that. It wasn't the same without the boys though, and the farm felt quiet despite the constant noises from the livestock. He looked once more out towards the sea.

"Oh well Harold better get a shift on," he said out loud.

With a sigh he pushed off the rock and stubbed out his cigarette on the ground, careful to ensure it was out even though the bracken here in the shadow of the stones remained damp with dew. Aggie would be fretting about them being late for church he thought to himself, and no doubt Freddie would be doing everything in his power to avoid going. As if on cue he saw his wife appear briefly in the doorway, a sign it was time to make a move. Even way up here he could feel the irritation in her stance that he was a good few minutes up the hillside. He gave a wave so she knew he had seen her and set off.

It looked like she had her blue summer dress on, though it was hard to tell exactly. He hoped so. He loved that dress or to be exact he loved her in it, and the memories it brought back to him of romantic times together. The warm glow it fostered within dispelled his aches and pains in a pleasant analgesic, and Harold sang as he strode home.

*

An hour later the three Davisons walked up the daffodil lined path towards the church, a stream of local people mingling with them from various directions. They smiled and chatted to a number of friends and made small talk about the weather and the flowers in the churchyard, and even the latest amateur dramatic revue in the town hall. Anything to avoid the main subject on everyone's minds.

Walter Miller stood near the entrance and Harold noted as he walked up the path from the road, that people had started to avoid him which he felt was unfair. In his dual role as station master and telegram officer he had inherited the unenviable task of having to deliver telegrams to families whose sons, and sometimes daughters too, had been wounded or killed in the war. Often before any other official notification was sent to them by the War Department. This made it worse as he was unable to give them any more information than was in the telegram at a time when anguished parents searched for answers. Harold stubbed out his cigarette discreetly and walked up to shake his hand in a show of support.

Walter had just finished posting new names with the Vicar on the noticeboard near the dark oak door, prior to the service starting. The real blessing so far was that, after the first couple of months of the war, it had remained a reasonably short list.

"Are you not coming into the service Walter?"

"No Harold, I've a train due at lunchtime and some things to sort before then."

"Service will be over by midday and you've got a young lad helping you anyway who can do the crossing gates."

"I know but I think people will enjoy themselves more if I'm not lurking at the back like some harbinger of doom."

"Oh nonsense man. You can sit with us. Can't he Aggie?"

Agnes had been holding Fred's reluctant hand while she scanned the noticeboard for the fourth time that week. He was pulling at her like a dog on a leash keen to get to a fresh scent, and at her husband's call she let him go. Freddie ran into the church to catch up with a couple of his friends. She shook her head and turned back.

"What was that love I didn't hear?"

"I was saying Walter could sit with us now that his sons are away to training couldn't he?"

She guessed her husband's purpose knowing him so well, and aware of the stigma that was attaching itself to this poor man.

"Of course he can, and you should come back for lunch afterwards too. I've made a special Simnel cake which I know you like."

"That's very kind of you Mrs Davison but I really must be off. I don't trust young Dempsey to mind the place for too long! I trust your boys are all well?"

"Yes very well thank you. And yours?"

"Enjoying training so I hear. Along with your David too yes?"

"That's right," Harold answered, "though we don't know yet when they will go overseas. He wrote to us and said there was no news yet but they are all keen to go."

"Impetuousness of youth. Maybe it will all be over soon anyway."

"Let's hope so," Agnes said.

"Well good day to you."

"And you Walter. Take care."

They watched him walk off head bowed, and then joined the stragglers walking into the church as the single bell now tolled to tell everyone the service was about to start. Inside they managed to catch Freddie on his third circle of the font chasing young Charlie Abbott from the tobacconists, whose oldest brother Bill had gone over in August '14.

Harold reluctantly dragged Fred into one of the rear pews, while his wife dashed forward into the vestry to join the other choir members. He caught a glimpse of Celia Goodman scowling as she went in, but saw his wife smile sweetly and guessed she was apologising and probably blaming him. *It was always a guarantee to get sympathy if you blamed your husband,* he mused. He looked down at Fred now, and pondered on the fact that a year ago he would have had at least three sons there even if James had not come home for Easter.

As the vicar welcomed everyone from the front of the church, the choir began to process round the aisles following the cross, and the service started. As the first hymn began Harold suddenly had a terrible thought that he might never have anyone other than Fred with him here again. He dismissed it instantly shivering as he did so and tried to throw himself into the first hymn with as much gusto as he could manage. The hymn that had been chosen was 'How Great Thou Art,' and as the congregation sang the words "I see the stars, I hear the rolling thunder," the emotion of the war came over him at last and he hugged Freddie for all his sons.

*

After several weeks of constant movement up and down the lines, the post finally caught up with the men of the Royal Sussex Regiment on this bright Easter day. The post drop was always a moment of mixed emotions now for Will, the joy of receiving news from home tempered by the constant reminder that it was the mail that caused Archie to be so badly injured in the freak shell burst.

They had been cheered recently by an exchange of correspondence Will had received with Teresa back at the hospital camp, through an army courier. She told them that Archie was going to be okay, despite his injuries requiring numerous operations, although his rehabilitation might be a long process. His right side was particularly bad with multiple breaks to his arm and leg, and some internal damage where pieces of the shrapnel had gone into him. However the mail sack had indeed saved his life and miraculously no major organs had been hit.

Teresa advised them however that despite the surgeons skill it was still unclear if he would walk properly again, and certainly not without sticks. The friends had rejoiced in the news he was alive, and only Will understood the mental impact this might have on someone like Archie who loved his football so much. He remembered now the scared man all those months ago going out on his first night patrol, and knew that underneath the brash exterior the self-doubt lurked just out of sight. As it probably did in all of them.

Now the mail finally arrived, there was a glut of letters and packages. Will was delighted to see several pieces land on his lap while they were on a rest break in a local farmer's barn. He picked his post up and his rifle and moved out into the early morning air, keen to look at it before the scheduled communion service in the old church of Saint Michel later that morning. They were a couple of miles from the front line here and the landscape seemed quite untouched and beautiful. The early morning mist still caressed the grass and a buzzard rose lazily from a tree top as he approached and swooped low over the ground. It did not care too much about being seen, as if it too was keeping the peace intact.

Will watched it fly serenely away and then perched himself on the side of a low water trough and sifted through the mail. He saw to his delight there was one from Alice dated over a month ago, and though he was angry it had taken so long to find him, he couldn't stop his heart beating faster and it was all he could do to stop himself ripping it open immediately. He placed it carefully on the floor and reached for his mum's letters. There were three of them all told and he worked out the dates in order and began. The first carried birthday messages from the family and a number of friends. Agnes had got the church ladies to craft a very pretty card with some long faded flowers pressed to the front. He smiled despite the fact the belated gesture was long past its prime and made a mental note to tell his mum it had arrived intact. Fred had enclosed a handmade drawing with another picture of Will winning the war single handed. *If only it was that easy,* he smiled to himself.

Finding a familiar bar of chocolate he popped a piece in his mouth and lost himself in the tales of life back home, much of which was dominated by David's decision to sign up with 'Lowther's Lambs' and his first letter back to them about the training. Will smiled at the irony of him joining a battalion Alice was involved with through her father, and wondered if David had even met Lord Pevensey. Then he reflected on his own training and felt for David going through all that. While the conditions here were much harsher, they had settled into a steady routine now, with very little action to speak of, and he was not envious of his brother going through basic training. He wanted to tell him it could never prepare you for what went on here, but he knew the censors would never allow such talk.

"We were all very sorry to hear the news about Archie," his mum wrote, "but glad to hear that he is on the mend. How is your shoulder now? We have been very worried about you and hope you are well and keeping safe."

Will rubbed the shoulder automatically that still twinged occasionally, but didn't affect his aim anymore. His dad had written "Be careful son," on the side of the page. There was some old news about Christmas and more gossip from the village. The show had apparently been a roaring success even if Celia had written the press article herself!

The second letter contained a longer note from his dad as well as a very rushed scribble from Freddie with some more pictures he had done at some point. Will looked at them all warmly. There was news about the livestock and the hope of new lambs and calves on the way. His mum's letter was shorter but he noticed the difference in their handwriting was quite marked, and had visions of his dad writing his note on one of the walls while walking about, such was the irregularity of lines and letters. She thanked him yet again for his previous letter, which he noted was probably a gentle nudge to write more often! He was looking again at one of Freddie's attempts at a biplane dropping exploding sheep onto the Jerries, when Ced walked up.

"Hello Ced, news from home?"

"Oh aye. Our lass is busy with the kids as ever and her work in the school. She's doing more time there now half the teachers are off to war."

"How old are your kids now?"

"The twins are twelve and my young girl is nearly nine."

"Growing up fast."

"Indeed. I have something here that may be of interest."

He passed over a grimy note that was simply addressed to Ced Longworth, 1st Battalion, RSR, France.

"God knows how it got here."

"Who's it from?"

"Have a guess. Only one idiot would spell my surname wrong and address a letter to France!" He laughed then and as Will pulled the note out he saw instantly that the signature was Archie.

"Oh wow," Will shouted and stood up. He flipped the note over and said "Is this it? A page and a half? There's barely four words to a line!"

"Well when you look at the picture I think he's done well to get that much down, although in truth I think he was probably bored after the first ten words. Not much for writing our Bunny."

Will scanned the brief tatty note that had probably been half way across France unintentionally. He read it aloud:

'Aye aye! How are you lot doing? All good here and making slow progress. Can't sleep much but glad to be up and about once more. Food good. Sun shining. There are some good perks. (See photo). I have everyone organised as you would expect. If you get shot try not to get killed and ask to come here. Ha ha. Don't miss any of you at all. Much. Bet you all miss me. Archie.'

"Like a hole in the head," Albert said, who had wandered over for a chat and caught the gist of the words. "I've slept great since I stopped sharing with him. He snored louder than the shelling."

Although like the others it was obvious he was pleased to hear he was ok. A few other men had wandered over with Albert, the post having shaken them from their fitful slumbers, and they were also keen to look at the note.

As Will passed it round smiling, he asked to see the photo. It was taken outside one of the wings of Brighton Hospital clearly. Archie still looked in a right state. He was in a wheel chair with one leg in plaster sticking out in front of him and his right arm likewise plastered to the shoulder and pinned out similarly in front at a right angle. He looked gaunt and had clearly lost a lot of weight. But the smile was unmistakable.

"No wonder he didn't write much," Will said, "he's not left handed."

"Never mind that," said Ced, "look at the cheeky bugger."

They all peered at the photo and there ranged about him were no less than eight smiling pretty nurses, with a sister holding the wheelchair and grinning.

"He's bloody set that up," someone said behind Ced.

"Too right he has. Trust Bunden to fall on his feet."

"Well he was blown off them technically," Albert said wistfully.

"Nine lives though. Landed alright. Just like a cat!"

They laughed and some of the men sat around the water trough now and began smoking. The sun was starting to break out and teased them with the promise of warmth to come through the mist's seductive veils. They immersed themselves in the morning glow having learnt some time ago to grab these moments of luxury whenever they could.

Will noticed that the last item was also bulky with the promise of more treats from home. Ced and Albert saw that too, and told him to hurry up and open it. But there was no food this time or indeed more chocolate, although the note did promise some *"next time for Easter."* No gloves or socks either but there was a woollen hat. He tried it on. It was lovely and warm but too big.

"Won't stop anything in that if you go over the top. You need to ask your nan to use steel not wool," one of the older men called Rawlins commented.

"Doesn't fit anyway," Will replied, "still it's the thought that counts eh?"

"I got some biscuits from home, another man said. "I'll swap them for the hat. They are a bit crushed mind."

"Happy with that Franko," said Will, "crushed or not," and threw the hat over to the tall lanky corporal at the back. *Franko's* real name was actually Barry Jones, but at six foot six, and with an enormous forehead he had been rather unfortunately dubbed 'Frankenstein' in training by one of the instructors some years back and it had stuck. Now here in the mud of France it had been shortened as these names always are to something more manageable and affable. Franko tried on the hat and it looked as if it had been made for him. He beamed joyously and snuggled down against the barn wall with a brew.

"Another happy customer," Will muttered, and then as much to himself as the men nearby added, "Oh I almost forgot. My Mum's sent a newspaper cutting through too."

He unwrapped the inside pages of the local Sussex Herald, scanning various notices and a butcher's ad and then saw his mum had scribbled something across one page – *'Some sad news from home. I think you knew him? xx '*

He scanned the pages and then said "Oh God." The men

roundabout looked up and Ced asked him what was the matter. He looked at them and started to read:

It is with great sadness that Jeremiah and Cecilia Isaacs announce the death of their beloved son, Ernest, who tragically took his own life on March 16th, having recently returned wounded from France. A service of remembrance will be held at the Synagogue in Hove, followed by a dedication at the Memorial gardens in Shoreham where a tree will be planted by his sister Amelia and her class mates from school. Afterwards all are welcome back to Ham Lane to our shop for a light supper. 'Yea, though I walk through the valley of the shadow of death, I will fear no evil, for Thou art with me; Thy rod and Thy staff, they comfort me.'

Will passed the paper to Ced and looked around at the men, tears in his eyes, some of whom couldn't meet his gaze.

"Oh Christ Will, poor kid," was all Ced could say, as he took the paper and looked at it.

"I didn't know he was Jewish," Rawlins muttered.

"What with a name like Isaacs you daft sod?" Albert retorted.

Rawlins looked sheepish and raised his eyes and turned away.

"I thought he would be safe when he went home," Will remarked, struggling to control his emotions.

"Will. We all knew Ernie wasn't right to be out here but credit where credit's due, he joined up and gave it a bash and he didn't deserve this. I'm sorry. We all are."

Will nodded and a number of the men got up now and started to shuffle away, one or two tapping him on the shoulder as they did.

"I'm sorry Will," Rawlins said. "Speak first engage brain after, that's me all over," he continued. "Perhaps we can have a collection or something and get something sent?"

"Yes perhaps. And don't worry, it's the damned war that's done him in, not us." He tried to smile to reassure Rawlins who hung about not sure where to put himself.

Soon only Albert, Ced and Rawlins and a couple of men remained with Will. The mist had all but burned off now and the birds were in full song and many swooped around them to catch the waking bugs on this golden spring morning. Will felt in that moment that they were like Ernie's soul, flying this way and that without seemingly a care in the world, free from all the pain and suffering below. He hoped that was true of everyone when they died here.

Ced folded the paper up and was about to hand it back when something caught his eye. He looked at it again.

"Oh shit," he said suddenly. He looked even worse than he had a moment ago and glanced at the others who were all staring at him, before passing it back to Will.

"On the other side," he said tapping the page. He was almost stuttering as he spoke which unsettled the men who knew him to be so steadfast.

"What is it Ced?" Will asked, that sense of doom knotting his stomach again suddenly.

"On the top of the announcements page...it's just not your day lad."

Will stared at the paper.

His mind folded in on itself. He opened it out fully and couldn't believe he hadn't seen it before. If his mum had seen it, she certainly hadn't mentioned it or made any attempt to hide it. But there it was in bold letters at the top of the page that carried news of Ernie's death in the Obituaries.

*'**Engagement**: Lord and Lady Pevensey are delighted to announce the engagement of their daughter Alice Isabelle Maud, to Lieutenant George Archibald Grenville Wilson of the Sussex Yeomanry...'*

He didn't read the rest. He felt sick and stood up. Rawlins leaned in over his shoulder gawping at the paper Will held limply in front of him.

"Oh stone the crows. She's only gone and dropped him. And publicly too."

Albert saw the headline and grabbed Rawlins by the scruff of the neck and pushed him away. "So help me Rawlins but sometimes I wonder whose side you're on."

Suddenly the birds swooping around Will's head were a great annoyance to him, and he futilely swatted at them with the paper as he strode away. They heard him shout "Shut up damn you," scrunching the paper into a ball and throwing it away, and a number of the other men looked up at this sudden outburst on such a peaceful morning. Ced went to follow him but Albert caught his arm.

"Give him some time alone to vent."

"What if he does something daft?"

Albert considered this and then said, "Nah, he's got common sense at his core that one. It's gonna hurt like hell but he probably knew like we all did that it was just a lovely pipe dream. All the same…" He motioned to one of the fellow snipers in the platoon. "Harris you've got sharp eyes. Go keep a watch on young Davison for me but stay out of sight if you know what I mean."

"Yes Corp."

"I'm not so sure he did think that way. He's only young, and dreams can come true you know," Ced muttered as they watched their friend stomp off across the field, his shadow Harris trailing him at a safe distance. Albert turned to walk away and then saw the unopened letter from Alice start to blow across the yard from the trough and stopped it with his foot. He passed it to Ced who shook his head when he saw it.

"Yes Ced, they can sometimes, but not out here."

Chapter 22 – The Gloves

The Royal Sussex had moved back down towards their old lines near Neuve Chappelle shortly after Easter. In their absence there had been a major spring offensive in the region carried out primarily by the Indian Army Corps who had taken over their sector shortly after Christmas.

The initial attacks had seen significant successes. The British army had taken time to plan the attack in detail and in some sections several key objectives were taken. It had been even more revolutionary by planning combined attacks with the Royal Flying Corps who cleared the area of German aircraft and then set about bombing reserve troops and artillery behind the German lines to aid the advance. Even in a section where the attack had gone in the wrong direction, the bravery of the Indian troops, and the fact the supporting companies followed them in error anyway, meant here too parts of the German front lines were overrun.

However as had often been the case with the war to date, the initial successes had not been exploited and the Germans had recovered to recapture a lot of the ground taken. The French attack that had been due to go in to the south was cancelled and supporting British brigades could not spare troops as first planned. Even so it was seen as a tactical success and the Garhwal Brigade of the Indian Meerhut Division once again distinguished itself.

The Sussex rested now in an old trench in woods not far north from where Will had first been posted, outside a little hamlet called Estaires. They joined two companies of the Hampshires who were holding this position while the Sussex moved in and the Indian Corps moved out. Will and Albert were stuck in a forward lookout position, while the main body of troops were briefed and set about making camp. A small party of men had gone off to investigate a large copse of trees ahead of them.

Between the two groups of trees there was a wide overgrown field which had presumably been cleared for arable work in the past, with some sort of abandoned farm machinery off to the right. The wild grass here grew as high as a man's shoulder in swathes and it reminded Will of a regiment on parade lined up ready for inspection. As he surveyed the open space ahead he noticed wild cabbages and purple headed broccoli growing amongst the grass and realised that at some point this had clearly been someone's dream, now gone to seed.

Behind them Colonel Bradshaw had called his officers together and had met with counterparts from the Indian Division who had been involved in actions in this area. There was a brigadier with them and he looked magnificent in his uniform complete with the traditional turban, and the most marvelous moustache that circled several times at the side.

This section was unusually quiet being some distance away from the scenes of the previous intense fighting. Consequently the trenches were not as intricate here, relying more on barricades in the woods and shallow dug outs behind, so the men were set to deepening the trenches. A field telephone was set up and run out to where Will and Albert were stationed in their forward look out post. The two friends were currently digging into this further as well, and building some sandbags in front that had been hauled out for them by Ced and Franko with no end of banter.

"Now we've got you tucked in for the night, I'm off for a nice shave in that cold shallow stream back there, and a lukewarm mug of coffee. All the comforts of home eh?" Ced quipped, as he dumped the last bag and headed back to the woods behind.

Albert stuck two fingers up at the retreating men, grumbling that they had got stuck with sentry duty once more, and then settled the last sandbag in place. He looked at his young comrade, staring into the grass, and couldn't help but worry. He had been very withdrawn since the news he received at Easter; the double whammy of Ernie's death and Alice's engagement had clearly had a profound effect on him. He tried to distract him once more.

"Any idea what's going on Will?"

Will shrugged but said nothing.

"Well they are clearly planning something judging by the big pow-wow going on over there." Will glanced back but still didn't speak.

"As long as it doesn't involve any more walking eh? Be nice to sit tight for a while."

"Don't care either way."

"Look lad sooner or later you have to move on. Life always does. Being like this isn't doing you any good. We all liked Ernie but he wasn't cut out for this soldiering lark and no one could have predicted he'd go and top himself."

"I should have taken better care of him. I thought he'd be safe…" Will said suddenly. His voice trailed off and Albert looked about and saw no one was watching so he put his rifle down and gave Will an affectionate grasp on the shoulder. He took out a cigarette and lit up.

"Sure you don't want one? Might help?"

Will looked and then shook his head.

"I did love her you know."

"I know kid. Haven't wanted to pry but did you ever read her note?"

Will shook his head and then paused before pulling it out of an inside pocket. "Ced gave it to me. I keep looking at it, thinking if I read it the facts might change, that the article might be a dream. But I know it isn't, and whatever she says in here won't change what's happened and what she's going to do."

Albert took the letter glancing at it as his young companion talked.

"Want me to read it for you?"

Will shook his head and looked away again. As Albert took another drag on his cigarette he noticed one of the Indian officers had broken away from the group and was studying the far wood line through his binoculars. He had his arm in a sling, presumably from the fighting, and was struggling to set them up to use. Albert thought about going to help him but decided not to interfere. *Never wise to volunteer for anything,* he mused, and the Captain sorted himself out eventually. He saw the officer wore a slouch hat favoured by some of the Indian divisions who didn't wear the turban. The officer wasn't looking in their direction but Albert stubbed out his cigarette just in case, nipping the end off to kill the light to save the rest for later. He picked up his rifle as Will continued.

"No doubt she met him at that bloody officers' ball at Christmas. I had a bad feeling about it, despite her letters to me calling me her *farm boy*. I hate officers!"

"Amen to that lad. Though they're not all a bad lot. Not his fault I guess. Just the right man in the right place to take advantage. But it still sucks."

"Yes."

"You know my ex, Beatrice, told me we'd always be friends too, and that was four years ago and haven't heard from her since!" He laughed mockingly and for once Will smiled.

"No bad thing at the end of the day. Didn't make it any less rubbish at the time mind."

"You said you'd followed her to Sussex from Dorset?"

"Yes, that's right. She was a teacher and got offered a decent job in Littlehampton through her uncle at a girls' school. I was teaching too at the time, doing well, and was Head of the English department." He nodded at Will proudly, and puffed his chest out theatrically, aware he was distracting him from his own misery.

"I helped her find some lodgings and we agreed once she was settled I would hand my notice in and go and join her. We corresponded by letter and everything seemed to be going well. So after a couple of months I discussed the situation with my Headmaster who was a lovely man. He said he had a friend in Chichester who was governor of a grammar school locally, and could get me a job there teaching English probably. I was so excited I took some leave to surprise her and went over for a couple of days."

"So what happened Bert?"

"When I turned up at the house she wasn't in and a man answered the door with his pipe and slippers on basically. She came to my lodgings that night and tried to fob me off on the door step with some stupid excuse about him being her mentor, but I could see he was used to being there and knew what was going on."

It took a moment for the penny to drop and then Will said, "Oh no. Well at least I was spared that."

"Yes, I heard later he was the landlord of a number of the houses in that area and had been involved more than once before with his new 'lodgers.' Maybe I should have knocked him out but I just walked away. I guess I was in shock trying to take it in."

"You should have."

"Nah he wasn't worth it. Besides it was better in the long run. Like I said not his fault for chancing his arm. Just the right man in the right place at the right time. She wrote me a note as I say about always being friends and being sorry. I think she meant it. Said they did love each other. But like you, it didn't help at the time. I'd already dropped off the edge by then. It was all a right mess, so I fell into a bottle and sobered up in the army." He raised his eyes with a sardonic smile and looked out towards the far trees.

"Actually tell a lie, I did hear from her a couple of years later out of the blue. Got a letter at the barracks. Said she was on her own now with a baby and asking after my health. He'd done a runner obviously when the baby was due. She wanted to meet up but I wrote to her and said no. I wished her well. I did miss her but couldn't put myself through it again. I don't blame her for it now. Not healthy to harbor these things trust me Will. Besides I had a mate in Littlehampton reckons she got back with the bloke sometime after that, and might even have got married. Good luck to them I say in this bleedin' mess. If you can find happiness grab it. I'm not a pipe and slippers man anyway so it was probably for the best."

Will wasn't so convinced about the last part and thought Albert would make a great dad, and was just saying that to convince himself as much as anything, but he let it pass with a nod and a smile. It was unusual for Albert to speak so much in one go, and they both seemed relieved when the patrol appeared out of the woods over on the left and headed back across the field to where the battalion was brewing up. It allowed them to focus on something more practical once more. As Will watched them trail in, the Sergeant at the front broke off and headed over to see the colonel. They disappeared and Will envied them the opportunity to rest and eat. It would be another couple of hours before they were relieved but clearly the patrol had found nothing as their return was so casual. He noticed the Indian officer had also watched their progress but still stayed where he was arcing slowing back and forth with his binoculars.

He was aware Albert had fallen silent, and Will looked at him now peering forward under his steel helmet and realized that everyone had their stories to tell. You never knew what people had gone through unless you had known them for a long time and even then, they didn't always tell you everything. He realised how easy it was to judge someone's personality without taking time to understand what made them like they were. He had always seen Albert as a grumpy old sod. Helpful yes but not lively or fun, and here he was talking about romance and how he had had such plans for the future. Will felt guilt in that moment.

"Why didn't you go back to Dorset then? You hadn't left the school. I'm sure the Headmaster would have understood."

Albert had clearly been reflecting on it too. "I should have. He was a lovely man. We had known his family for years and he had always been good to me. Stupid pride I guess. Didn't want to go back and face my colleagues having had a woman do that to me. With the benefit of hindsight I should have. I still might after the war."

"Yes you should. I can't believe you taught English."

"Lived and breathed it. But this isn't the place for Shakespeare or Tennyson now is it? So I keep that to myself. And don't be all morose like me Will. Make the most of the here and now. This war's not going to last forever and you'll be back home on that farm before you know it chasing sheep!"

Will laughed now and felt the tension that had lived in his chest for the last fortnight starting to ease. "I'm sorry I've been miserable lately Bert."

"Don't worry about it lad. Just don't make a habit of it. Not like you're short of female admirers now is it. You seem to attract them like flies with your baby looks. All wanting to mother you." They laughed together now and as they did a group of pheasants broke cover from the 'regimental' grass a couple of hundred yards in front of them.

The birds flew towards them quickly in a low arc, their mocking repetitive calls crying out to each other as they did so.

"Think they know something we don't," Albert said with a grin. The two men followed the flight of the game birds and noticed the Indian officer nearby watching them too. He leaned back as they flew over him seemingly mesmerized by their flight, as the men often were by the seemingly trivial everyday things. Anything that held some link with normality took on greater importance out here.

"Probably wishing he had his gun to pop a brace for the officers' table tonight," Albert muttered and Will laughed out loud now, the relief in his previous tension palpable to him. As they continued to watch grinning together the officer seemed to over extend and stumbled backwards and they both laughed spontaneously even louder at this.

Then they heard the delayed crack.

They spun back to face the woods instantly ducking down, the familiar sound snapping them into heightened alert, scanning the field ahead.

"Someone is shooting but not at the birds," Albert said, stuffing Will's note into his pocket.

"Sniper," Will agreed nodding.

The officer cried out now, he had been shot but not killed and as the shock wore off the pain came in. There were more shouts now from behind them; commands, urgent orders being given and one more plaintive cry from a fellow Indian officer who charged forward with another man towards their stricken comrade.

The voice of Sergeant Albright broke through the confusion, "Get your heads down. Stay low and watch your sights. Check those weapons."

Another cry rang out, followed more quickly this time by the crack and Will and Albert looked round to see the second Indian officer fall lifeless to the ground. The soldier that had been with him stopped dead in his tracks and threw himself flat and started crawling back towards the woods. A number of their men started firing blindly at the far trees, some of the rounds even hitting the ground not far in front of where Will and Albert were sheltering.

"Shoot straight you bastards," Albert said as one hit the edge of their sandbags and then they heard the familiar tones of Company Sergeant Major Russell calling them to order and to hold fire.

"Bugger," Albert said.

"He's just leaving them," Will cried, watching the Indian soldier slither back to safety.

"He's smart lad. He'll only end up dead too. It's what they want. Lure us out into the open. Can you see them?"

Will scanned the woods through his sights but could see nothing but shadows. The Germans had the sun behind them too which gave them an added edge.

"No nothing."

The pitiful cries for help of the wounded officer came out once more. He had been shot through the side, but was clearly still very much alive.

"Clever lad this one. Wounded the officer to get us out where he can pop us off one by one. And he's got the sun behind him. Nice little ambush and we've walked into it."

They heard the colonel's voice now ordering the men to get the Indian brigadier away to safety and to try and get some artillery on the area.

"Oh great, now they are going to start shelling us too."

"They know we are here Bert yes?" Will asked anxiously.

"I hope so lad!"

Although only a hundred yards forward of their lines, they felt terribly exposed now, but knew that were they to try to run back, it was more than likely one or both of them might be shot. Then again if the shells started falling down short they would have to make a dash for it regardless!

"We might have to see that famous speed of yours soon Will," Albert said, glancing back nervously to the tree line behind them and then back again out in front.

The field phone buzzed and Sergeant Albright's voice crackled on the other end. "Can you see where the shooter is men?"

"Not yet Sarge."

"We are going to try and draw his fire. Stay low."

"Okay."

"Not like we are going to get up and have a stretch now is it the daft sod," Albert said, as he replaced the phone. At that a number of men behind them fired controlled bursts over their heads into the woods beyond. And some raked the grass fields too. But there was no reply. There was a call for cease fire and the eerie silence remained. Except for the groaning of the officer to their left.

The two men knew not to make any gestures that would pinpoint them anymore than was needed, and that sound was more easily distorted. They had seen a lad put his thumb up once before and it had been shot off by a sniper, so they kept low by design.

The phone buzzed again.

"Anything."

"No nothing at all yet."

"Keep looking. We may call in some artillery and if we do you'll have to keep your heads down lads unless you fancy dashing back."

"Understood Sarge."

Albert hung up once more. "So damned if we do and damned if we don't eh? He's a clever lad this one."

"Might be more than one Bert," Will said without breaking his gaze from the space out in front; remembering the machine gunner all those months ago on the night patrol who never lost focus, even when speaking.

"A team you mean?"

"Yes, or even more than one team."

"Trust you to always look on the bright side. Perhaps they scared him off anyway. Might have been a scout."

"No. Too accurate for that," Will said.

"I know," Albert replied," but we live in hope."

As if to answer there was another crack and the officer screamed again. This time he was shot in the leg. Another wound not meant to kill.

"Bastard," Albert said.

There was a pause and then Will said, "I've got him."

He had now developed the calmness that came over him only when he was in moments of extreme concentration, when all other external factors were put aside. It was something he had taught himself to do when taking penalties in matches, and since then it just seemed to kick in instinctively. Right now he didn't care about Ernie or Alice or Archie. If anything those events spurred him on. There were no nerves here. No internal debates about whether he could shoot or not. He was in the zone.

Albert looked at the young lad with admiration for he knew he was a crack shot, despite his youth. He focused in himself.

"Where?" he whispered.

"The scattered machinery two hundred and fifty yards to the east of us. Just for a moment a glint. Spotter's sight."

"So it is a team. We can call it in, lob some shells on and Bob's your uncle."

"No too risky. They are close to the woods there and could scarper before we know it and just come back after. Or they might be sat in a dug-out for all we know. More importantly we could get blown up too!"

"That's a compelling argument you make there young William, so what do you propose. I'm all ears."

"We need to draw him out, make him show himself so I can get a shot away."

"Agreed."

Will looked at Albert.

"Oh…you're joking right?"

*

Back in the woods the colonel was pacing up and down, his officers aware of his frustrations and equally concerned to get things moving.

"RSM any news on the blasted artillery."

"Nothing further sir. HQ said they can't get any guns into our sector currently. Needed elsewhere," CSM Russell replied. "We could try and work round them with small parties and flush them out sir?"

"Blast. HQ orders are to push forward and through those woods ahead before nightfall. Apparently we're now behind schedule as it is and every hour we delay Jerry could gain ground. Marvellous!" Bradshaw exclaimed sarcastically. "Dig in, push on. Does anyone have a clue what's actually happening back there I wonder?" It was a rhetorical outburst and there was a polite silence from the colonel's assembled subordinates. He regained his composure thinking hard.

"Scouting parties will take too long CSM. That Indian captain will be dead in a couple of hours. Besides those woods behind could be full of traps."

"Begging your pardon sir."

"What is it Sergeant?"

Sergeant Albright had approached the group and the CSM now beckoned him forwards.

"One of my company, Longworthy, who is working the field comms believes that the lads stuck in the forward post might have a plan," Albright said to the colonel. "One of them is a sniper and has asked him for a diversion."

"Who's up there CSM?"

Russell raised an eye to Sergeant Albright.

"Lance Corporals Davison and Higgins Sir."

"They are lance corporals Sir, and one of them has yet to prove himself."

The new voice was Lieutenant Dunn who had suddenly spoken up from the back of the group, seizing his moment to undermine Will and not wanting him to get any glory.

"What do you mean by that lieutenant?"

"I'm just concerned that Lance Corporal Davison is up to the job sir. I've been with him before on night operations and…he struggled shall we say."

"That was a long time ago sir, with respect," Albright replied clearly angry, "and from what I recall he did sterling work with the Vickers after the gunner had been shot."

"Well that's as may be but we are not using machine guns today."

"Look can the boy shoot or not," the CSM interrupted without any protocol, looking at the Sergeant.

"Yes Sir."

Lieutenant Dunn went to speak again but the colonel put his hand up.

"Enough of this. I'm not running a debating society in Hyde

Park. Men are dying and I don't want to lose anymore. Whatever he proposes get on with it."

*

A few minutes later it was all set and Will looked at Albert.

"When they open up you can take two steps no more. No heroics Bert. He's very good remember. He will see you and fire but if the diversion works he won't be looking at us and will rush his shot. That's all I need. But flatten out yes or you'll be too big to miss even with a hasty shot."

"It's not as easy for us old timers to dive about like you, you know. Just don't miss lad."

They shook hands and nodded at each other with a steely determination. Albert flashed the tin lid back to the woods again, its glint from the noon sun indicating they were good to go to save time using the phone, and Ced nodded to the Sergeant. "He's ready."

Sergeant Albright nodded too and waved a hand to the CSM.

Company Sergeant Russell blew his whistle, several machine guns opened up, and the men all let out a loud roar and from the two ends of the line they hurled a number of grenades forward as far as they could.

The grenades exploded either side of Will and Albert and for just a moment it looked like the battalion was going to charge forward.

"Go," Will shouted and Albert dashed out the back of their small dugout and took two steps towards the officer as if going to his aid and then hurled himself forward. There was a whizz past his right ear as he fell, and the ground kicked up in front of him followed by a distant crack of the rifle's retort.

Will played the scene out in his mind. The German sniper hearing the shouts and the guns opening up, his mind assessing the situation; and then the explosions either side causing him to swing his rifle back and forth. The momentary pause while he decided whether to run if it was a full attack, or perhaps try and shoot a couple of officers first and then go. Then he would notice Albert break cover trying to rescue the wounded officer, and his decision would be made to shoot that

206

A doubt entered Will's mind that if there were several Germans one might not be distracted and just fire as soon as Albert appeared, but he went with his hunch there was only one sniper here, perhaps two men at most. He aimed at the machinery. He saw the flash from between two old rusty farm rollers and fired. In that moment he had no doubts about what he was doing. There were no nerves. He was just focused in the zone. Practicing his skill like he did back home in football training, taking free kick after free kick long into the evening shadows, after the rest of the team had gone off to change. He had trained for this moment too. Until he was perfect.

Will was using the standard issue Lee–Enfield rifle; a bolt-action, magazine-fed, repeating rifle that was the main firearm used by the military forces of the British Empire and Commonwealth during the first half of the 20th century. It had been the British Army's standard rifle from its official adoption in 1895. It was often referred to as the 'SMLE,' which was short for the common 'Short Magazine Lee-Enfield' variant. The Lee–Enfield took its name from the designer of the rifle's bolt system, James Paris Lee; and the factory in which it was designed, the Royal Small Arms Factory in Enfield. This particular rifle had been refined several times since 1897 and Will had the latest Mark III version complete with extensive sniper scope. It was a very powerful weapon capable of firing a round at two and a half thousand feet or eight hundred yards approximately a second. It could hit targets easily up to three thousand yards away, and had been known to fire much further, but was deadly accurate at anything less than half of that distance.

Will estimated the German sniper was no more than eight hundred yards to his right, or less than a second to a speeding bullet. The rifle had a ten-round magazine capacity using .303 rounds which enabled a well-trained rifleman to perform the *'mad minute;'* firing twenty to thirty aimed rounds in sixty seconds, making the Lee–Enfield the fastest military bolt-action rifle of the day. In training however the men were expected to be able to shoot between twelve and fifteen well aimed shots in a minute. Will could shoot twenty rounds a minute or one every three seconds. The combination of outstanding characteristics of man and weapon meant only one outcome.

Albert turned to look from where he lay prone in the field upon hearing Will's gun. He opened his mouth to ask if he got him, and then saw Will fire again and looked over to where he was shooting. As soon as Will had fired the first bullet he had reloaded instantly just like training, and as he did so a German soldier broke cover and ran for the woods. Will fired again within a few seconds, almost a luxury for him to steady himself and aim, and this time they all heard the shout as the German fell forward dead.

"Outstanding shooting," the colonel said, looking at the scene through his binoculars. "Sergeant Major I want both those men promoted to full corporal. Battle field promotions on the spot. Send a patrol out to check the bodies and get the medics to Captain Amdullah poor fellow."

"Are we sure he got them, sir?" Lieutenant Dunn enquired.

"Oh I think so lieutenant, considering both our corporals are standing up!"

Dunn blushed as he saw Albert was running over to the wounded captain while Will moved slowly towards the German position.

"I think we can safely say he's up to the job sir," Russell said quietly to Lieutenant Dunn, moving off to sort out the Battalion now this hold up had been resolved. He had watched this young lad since he came into his training camp in Woking, and continued to be impressed with his progress.

Will and Albert gave each other the thumbs up and Will moved cautiously forward, the sweat running down his back from the tension of the moment. He came upon the soldier who had tried to run away and saw that he had hit him clean through the back, the bullet immerging through his chest in a large hole killing him instantly. A noise made him spin round, the adrenaline still pumping through his veins but it was Ced who had come forward with a small scouting party to check the bodies and move forward.

"Well done lad," he said admiringly.

"Thanks Ced," Will replied, "though it was Bert who took the risks."

"So he should, he's expendable" he grinned.

"Sniper's here sergeant. Shot through the head." Franko shouted, who had reached the second body by the farm machinery ahead of the rest. Sergeant Albright was following on and looked over to where Will and Ced were walking across to them.

"Well done Davison. Impressed the colonel. You've got some formal news coming."

Will smiled, and as he approached Franko called out to him.

"Hey Will."

"What is it Franko?"

"You're never going to believe this but this sniper you shot was wearing red fingerless gloves, just like your Grandma sends you sometimes."

Chapter 23 – Caught Cold.

It was undeniable. Will's bullet had been unerring in its accuracy and had hit the German sniper just under the left eye. The force had blown the back of his head clean off and sent the helmet spinning some ten feet away. No doubt the sight had made the second German flee from shock. But despite the gaping wound from the bullet there was no mistaking the man lying dead at their feet. It was Erik.

His blond hair now lay matted by blood around his face and Will rolled him onto his back so that he was more recognisable. He crouched down by him and placed a hand on his chest. He unbuttoned his top pocket and sure enough there was the faded photo of his parents standing proudly with Erik and another boy with some mountains in the back ground. He noticed now there were skis on the floor behind them and realised it must have been a holiday in happier times. Such was war, and it could so easily have been Erik looking down at Will and photos of his family, or indeed that dress he thought to himself, which would have caused some eyebrows to raise. He replaced the picture and stood up.

Ced, understanding the connection, came over to him. "You okay Will?"

Will looked at him and frowned, as if pondering the question. He didn't answer straight away choosing instead to shoulder his rifle and take out the notes from Alice, and the photo of the dress she had sent, which he had kept in his jacket pocket all this time. He looked at them briefly before ripping them all up and throwing them away, watching them scatter in the light breeze and fall among the untendered crops. He sighed a deep sigh and looked back at his friend.

"Yes Ced I'm fine. But Archie was right you know. We should have settled this whole bloody business with a kickabout."

Ced watched the pieces of paper disperse amongst the tall grass and untendered crops and nodded, agreeing it was the right thing to do with silent assent. He patted Will on the back as their sergeant barked some new orders.

"Right you lot. Fall in and back to the woods. We have orders to get set to march on before nightfall."

Sergeant Albright brought the reality of the moment in once more, and the men moved away. Will lingered and stared at Erik one last time, before echoing Archie's cheeky retort. "So long Fritz."

As they walked off Rawlins bent down and pulled the gloves off Erik's lifeless hands. "Too good for you Jerry me old mucker," he muttered. "I'll be having those back where they belong." He stood up trying to squeeze his large hands into one and as he pulled his arm out in front of him his eye line caught movement ahead of him on the far side of the field. At first he thought it was just the grass swaying back and forth and then he realised it was men, dozens of men emerging from the woods opposite.

"Jesus bloody Christ," he said out loud and the words made the small group of men with Will turn and look back.

Will saw Rawlins scrunch up the gloves and thought he was frustrated at first that they did not fit; but then he noticed he was transfixed by something away to the left and was beginning to point. Even more surprisingly he broke into a run and Will looked to where he had pointed. He caught his breath. Emerging from the woods were literally hundreds of German troops, many with rifles slung on their shoulders in relaxed order, clearly believing like they had done that the area was unoccupied; and with the same intention of pushing forward to take up positions in the woods where the Sussex now rested. They had not spotted the small detachment of men at first because they were off to the edge of the clearing and partly obscured by the machinery. But when Rawlins began running it caught the attention of those on the far left and there were shouts along the line. Someone behind him said "Bollocks," and the whole group instinctively broke into a run, even before the Sergeant began telling them to shift themselves.

There was an immediate outburst of firing from the Germans, ragged at first as they began to cotton on that the fields were occupied by more than rotting vegetables. Will paused and looked back.

"Rawlins come on," he cried. But it was already too late. He was some fifty yards behind the others and was hit multiple times before he had gone ten paces. As his body hit the ground the red gloves flew out of his dying grasp mimicking the life-giving blood being driven out of him. He never moved again and with a wrench Will turned on his heels and ran for his life.

As they reached the woods the situation was chaos with men 'standing to' along a wide front. No sooner had they entered these woods that morning and begun to dig in, than the Sussex had been ordered to take a line further forward across the fields in the second copse some half mile hence. Consequently, they had barely begun to improve on the shallow defences that were in place here, which the Hampshire Company had been holding for them temporarily. They were caught totally unprepared as most of the men were now packing up kit to move while some had been detailed to make a reserve line here and were still digging and chopping timber for barricades.

The Germans having recovered from their initial shock were now advancing in good order, firing controlled volleys as they came, and the deadly 'rat a tat tat' of machine guns was starting to add their weight to the hail of bullets. The only saving grace currently was that the machine guns were restricted to firing on the flanks for fear of hitting their own troops, and clearly like the British, their heavy guns were not yet making an appearance in this sector.

Several men were already dead or wounded and the colonel standing in the signal tent that had been erected in the middle of the woods knew they were caught cold. He turned to his adjutant then.

"Captain Archibald, get Brigade HQ on the line, signal urgent. Tell them Jerry's counterattacking north of NC near Estaires. And send a runner back to the holding area in Estaires. There's a company HQ set up in one of the houses and some of the Indian troops may still be there. Major D'Arcy is in the village sorting out our replacements so find him if nothing else. Make sure the man you send has the exact location for a bombardment and stress upon him to tell them Jerry is attacking in strength and we may not be able to hold."

The captain looked startled for a moment at these last words. Coming from the colonel who was always so bullish and resolute, to hear him talk of failure was unheard of; but he also knew he was a very good judge of a situation and that made the words even more of a shock. He hesitated not knowing what to reply.

"Today captain, if you please."

As the captain scampered off to find a runner, the colonel checked his Webley six shot revolver. He saw Lieutenant Dunn crouched down behind a large Cedar tree and strode over to him.

"Dunn get yourself over to our right flank and organise the men to fire controlled bursts back. There's a company of Hampshires there so liaise with their officer and get those machine guns working. Then try and get some men to work round their left side and get some flanking fire in. If nothing else stop Jerry moving up on our flank. Use half the company if necessary, five sections should do it, but make sure you only send half the men so they are not too exposed."

Bullets struck the trees nearby and Dunn hesitated.

"And stand up man. You're an officer in the Sussex not some Johnny private. Set an example."

Dunn set off towards the right side, but the colonel saw him crouching low again as more bullets smashed into the bushes round about and another two men cried out and fell dead nearby.

Angrily he shouted "Company Sergeant Major." He only used the CSM's full name when on parade or when something serious was occurring and the CSM broke off organising the men and ran over at the double. By now the first lines of Germans were coming to the end of the grass fields, and the British troops were returning fire but not in any controlled fashion and many were having to take cover behind trees and in ditches as the trenches were proving ineffective.

"Sir," Russell said, knowing even here in the woods not to salute now for fear of drawing attention to the officer as an obvious primary target.

"Sergeant Major we need to hold here for as long as we can until we can get some artillery support. I've sent a runner in case the signals are delayed and hopefully he may rustle up some reserves too.

The Indian Brigades are still no more than a mile behind us all being well. Work with Captain Wittering and get the men firing in volleys. And get those blasted machine guns talking."

Russell nodded and immediately ran off again.

*

At that moment Sergeant Albright and his party came scampering in from the right and ducked down behind some broken fence line, trying to regain their breath.

"Rawlins didn't make it," Will said.

"Poor lad," said Albert.

The Sergeant looked round for where they should report, and a number of bullets started to hit the fence.

"Christ they are right on us. Flatten out and fight here while I try to find an officer."

Before he had gone five yards Captain Archibald appeared.

"Sergeant, give me one of your men, I need a runner to get back to Estaires and tell them what's happening here. We are trying to get though on the phone but the lines are down I think."

"Franko you've got long legs, let's put them to the test. Shift yourself."

As Franko went off with the captain, the pair of them crouching low, the Sergeant moved off again.

"Stay here, keep low and shoot as many of those pointy hat bastards as you can."

The fire from the woods slowed the advance of the Germans now as their own casualties began to mount and they started to crouch in the long grass or lie down for extra protection but they were exposed here and it looked like the Sussex could hold. Russell, noticing the change in momentum, began walking up and down the line, encouraging the men and organising the fire.

"You're the best bloody shots in the whole British army. You let those heathens know it. Pour it into them men and get those bloody machine guns chattering."

The CSM inspired the men to relax and their training kicked in trading rapid volleys with the Germans and killing dozens of them in the front waves. He noticed one of the younger officers, a Lieutenant Harris, picking up on his words doing likewise over to the left and grunted with satisfaction as the machine guns started their deadly harvest of the enemy.

Lieutenant Dunn came across Will and Ced and the rest of the group firing from behind the fence. He crouched behind a tree and shouted at them.

"No use cowering there men you need to get forward and join the fight properly. The colonel wants those machine guns from the Hampshires aimed at the Jerry right side and then some men to move up and flank them. You can do that while I go to the guns."

"But sir there's only eight of us," Ced called back, "chances are the woods are crawling with Jerry too now. Do we take some of the Hampshires with us?"

"Can't you see the situation is desperate soldier? If we had hundreds of men you wouldn't be cowering back here and we'd be attacking, so get forward. You're supposed to be crack shots so you can do the work of fifty men."

Will and the others set off back to the right from where they had come.

"Cowering? Bloody bastard was hiding behind a tree himself, and those guns are already firing so what's he going to do?" Ced grumbled as they ran forward.

"Lieutenant 'Hun' would direct fire from the channel if he could," another man said and they laughed as they slithered down a bank and ran up to the thin line of Hampshire soldiers firing from a natural stream bed that ran through the south of the woods here. Their lieutenant stopped them and asked what was going on and they explained their orders.

"Flanking fire? Just the eight of you? That's ridiculous. You can take one of my sections but I'm down to sixty men here."

"Sixty sir? But you had two companies we were told."

"There were, but one of them was sent back to rest when your battalion showed up and they were both under strength to start with. Our captain went with them to report and get new orders and sort out supplies for us. He sent one of our lads to advise your colonel but he was in a briefing with the Indian fellers, so reported to one of your lieutenants."

"I don't think the colonel has any idea how thinly stretched we are here," Albert commented. "We need to tell him personally or we could be in trouble if Jerry spots it sir."

"I agree, better from one of his own though. One of you men go back and see him."

Will and the others looked at each other and it was Ced who volunteered.

"I'll go. Senior head needed and I'll try and find the CSM first. He will listen."

"Good idea. Better carry on," The young lieutenant said. "Corporal Attwell. Take half a dozen men and go with the Sussex chaps here into the woods. Colonel wants some flanking fire. But if you meet any heavy resistance fall back here and tell me, and we will regroup. Hopefully by then we will be reinforced."

The men shook hands and the joint party set off moving further right first so as to avoid being seen by the main German force. As Albert took off he called to Ced, "And make sure you skirt round Dunn on your way, he's more trouble than the real Hun out in front!"

"Dunn?" The Hampshire officer said. "That's the feller my man reported to."

Albert and Will exchanged looks as they ran off.

"You know what, Ernie had him pegged right all along!"

*

He was breathing harder now. The woods rose steeply away from the clearing towards Estaires and Franko was struggling with the exertion. They had been so relaxed on the march into the sector that he hadn't realised they had dropped down so much in the woods. His legs began to ache painfully as he pushed them on and his throat burned with the sudden increased demands on his lungs. He paused momentarily near the summit, sweating profusely and wishing he had left his pack behind for the sake of more speed but knew the sergeants would never forgive him if he had. Hands on his knees he gulped in air and then behind him the sound of shooting rushed into his senses despite the blood pounding in his ears.

He looked up. The trees soon thinned out down the slope and he could see the rooves of Estaires no more than half a mile hence. Even nearer he could see the main trench lines that ran in front of it with obvious sentries moving about. With a final gulp of air he hurled himself forward down the track, the lives of his friends adding to the pressure his body felt once more.

*

Private Guptha of the 39th Garhwal rifles, 7th Meerut Division, looked out over the ramparts of the forward trench lines at the lush green fields in front of him. Behind him the village was a hive of activity as the Division got ready to move, but he was unperturbed by it as much as some of the officers seemed to be, as it was nothing compared to the crowded streets of Delhi back home. In fact he often smiled when some of the Englishmen complained about the crowded conditions as despite the obvious squalor he found it quite bearable.

At home he had four generations of his family living with him in little more than a handful of rooms, and since being married two years ago he had not been alone with his wife except on their wedding night as they shared a room with her two younger sisters. He smiled to himself now reflecting on the fact that there were times here he had more privacy than back home, and slept better!

But recently his mother had written saying the work started in New Delhi in 1911 was coming along tremendously well and his father had them in line for two of the new homes there as a respected foreman on the works. He was excited at the prospect of having a room just for him and his beautiful Kaila when this crazy war was over. He missed the heat though. Despite the extremes of temperature back home the winter here had been long and very, very cold. And the rain lasted for weeks, not just the occasional hard downpours during the Indian season but weeks and weeks without

217

end. Now as May approached it was still cold; he could not believe it and shook his head. *Where was spring, where was summer?*

Behind him one of their working parties was knocking down some fencing to enable the artillery to move forward that was due later that day. He glanced back casually and wondered if anyone knew what was going on. The infantry were being moved away while their artillery was coming here. *Ridiculous!* He frowned as the echoes from the banging continued after the men had stopped and he looked round again. Several of his comrades peered over the rampart up the hill towards the woods. A captain, mid shave, appeared and wiped the remaining lather off his face with an old towel. Frowning he reached for his binoculars and scanned the top of the ridge. At that exact moment Franko burst out of the last line of trees heading down the hill, and following him like a rolling thunder of death, the sound of firing came clearly to the ears of the men in the trench.

"Bugler, stand to," the captain called without hesitation, and the bugler blew the call to arms. The trench filled with men in moments and behind them there was a momentary pause in the hectic activity in the villages as the notes bounced off the buildings, and then the whole place sprang into action. Private Guptha thought it looked as if a fox had burst into a chicken coup with the men scattering in all directions.

"Eyes front, and hold your fire," the Captain shouted, "He's a British soldier."

*

Moments later Franko was marching up the street with the captain and they found Major D'Arcy hurrying forward with Brigadier Mathur of the Indian Corps. The captain saluted.

"This soldier is a runner from the Sussex regiment up ahead sir. He reports they have encountered a large number of the enemy advancing towards them through the Aubair woods, and need support immediately. They have called for artillery without success."

"Damn those guns," the Major said.

"Yes Major, and ours are still in a queue waiting to move

forward," the Brigadier added. "We are being beaten by paperwork." The Brigadier then regarded the sweating man in front of him, but appreciating the need for calm in this sea of chaos, waited for him to catch his breath and then addressed him.

"What is the enemy strength soldier?"

Franko had never been spoken to by a Brigadier before and paused struggling to know what to say.

The Major assumed he didn't understand the question, and prompted him. "The Brigadier wants to know how many Germans there were private."

"Oh, right…thousands of 'em sir."

*

Will's group made their way round a large sunken pond which the slow moving stream fed into, and pushed on towards the woods opposite trying to go in as wide an arc as possible. Despite the large area that had been cleared in front of their positions, the far woods extended like a crescent moon shape on each side of the clearing so that they almost encircled the crops, but there was still a wide gap on the right side where presumably the farmer had come and gone to tend the crops. They dashed across it now hoping they were far enough not to be spotted by the Germans and came to a halt in the trees on the other side, trying to control their breath to listen for signs of movement. All appeared quiet, although the sounds and shouts of fighting just across the way made it difficult to know for sure. The lurking shadows of the wooded interior was unnerving after the bright sunshine in the field, and with so much vegetation, the men were clearly on edge.

They had not fought in woods before which required a very different approach, as it was easy for anyone inside the woods to look out but far harder for the troops entering the dark interior to know who or what awaited them, and indeed to see in. They paused for a moment as their eyes tried to adjust to the gloom, their ears sensitive to every falling leaf and twig that might signal danger.

"Slowly does it men, move forward in twos," Corporal Attwell said. They moved through the tangled forest floor almost from tree to tree stopping to listen as they did so, their senses on high alert. Their fears battled against the pressures of time to try and get round the right side of the German force and relieve some pressure on the comrades fighting behind them. Will hoped that Ced had managed to get to the colonel by now and advise him of the weakness on the flank.

About a hundred yards in with the advantage of looking out into the field from the sheltered wood, they could see wave after wave of German troops moving forward.

"This is far enough," Attwell whispered. "Let's spread out here along this line and hit them with grenades and rifle fire." He motioned to the men to fan out either side of him, and indicated with actions to throw grenades and then fire five rapid volleys into the Germans before retreating. Will and Albert moved towards the end of the line of men and got into position where they could see through gaps in the trees in front of them to fire. Will took out two grenades and placed them on a tree stump in front of him, and then checked his rifle as a matter of routine and rested it against the tree next to him.

As he went to pick up his first grenade there was a sound of a twig snapping distinctly to his right and he froze. He moved his head ever so slowly and looked ahead, but there was nothing. He looked back at Albert and he was looking too but the rest of the party were focused on their grenades and what was happening in front of them. Will knew there were plenty of animals and birds in the woods despite the fighting and it could have been anything but he felt a chill in his neck and risked leaning further to his right for a better look. But he could still hear nothing and it was so dark it was almost like fighting at night in here.

Corporal Attwell saw that the two men were not ready and signaled down the line to find out what was amiss. As each man beckoned to the next one the man next to Albert hissed to get his attention. He turned to see all the men looking at him and the corporal raise his eyes as if to say "What's up?" As Albert raised his arm to point behind them, Will heard another twig break and went for his rifle.

The first shot passed through Albert's outstretched arm and

continued into the chest of the man facing him with a dull thud. He looked at Albert, eyes wide with shock, and collapsed forward into the undergrowth, the men watching him stunned by the unexpected turn of events. Moments later the darkness erupted and dozens of German rifles opened up on them.

"Christ they are in the woods," the corporal shouted, and then cried out as a number of rounds slammed into his body and the man next to him.

"Throw your grenades...and get...out of here," the dying corporal shouted with rasping breaths, the pain wracking through his body.

The men didn't need telling twice and some threw their grenades wildly at the advancing Germans and others just ran. Albert was on the floor swearing and holding his arm but still had the foresight to grab a grenade and throw it over Will's head. Will had been lucky. In reaching for his rifle a number of bullets had slammed into the tree it was resting on and he fired rapidly now, hitting one of the leading Germans and causing the others to pause as fire came from a new angle and the confusion grew.

But now the Germans in the fields were alerted to the firing on their flank and a number of them started advancing on the woods firing as they did so, and another of Will's group was hit in the back and fell forward dead. It was every man for himself now and he shouted "Go, go." He took advantage of the exploding grenades to reach down and grab Albert. He was bleeding freely now down his left arm.

"Can you walk Bert?" he asked anxiously.

"If you get me on my feet lad I can bloody run."

Will smiled grimly and hauled him up, pulling his bad arm over his shoulder and they took off as fast as they could zig zagging through the trees, like some bizarre three legged race at the fete. Albert was grimacing with almost every step but Will knew he had to get them out of the woods before he could think about checking his friend's wound or they would both wind up dead.

He had an idea and paused briefly resting Albert against a broken tree lying at right angles to the ground, its rotten trunk long since cracked under the weight of time. He took aim through his sights and fired at where he had left his two grenades unused on that flat stump some distance behind them. He didn't miss and the explosion was sudden and dramatic causing a large piece of tree to uproot and killing or wounding several of the Germans passing nearby. The unexpected explosion in the middle of the Germans caused them to halt instantly. At that very moment some of the Germans, alerted by the shooting burst into the woods from the fields and in the chaos started shooting at their own troops, and this bought Will a few more priceless seconds before they chased after them once more.

Battles can often depend on timing as much as luck and both elements were to work against the Sussex men now. As Ced ran up to the colonel, the machine guns on the left were stormed by the Germans with grenades and both fell in quick succession. The CSM saw Lieutenant Harris draw his sword from his pack and fall hacking and slashing as the enemy poured over them. The colonel alerted to the explosions realised the situation was now becoming desperate.

"Sergeant Major take two sections and send them to prop up the left side and then have the men withdraw by sections. Firing lines if you please."

"Right you lot, every other man from 'C' company get over to the left and reinforce the north end of the line and listen to the orders. Be prepared to fall back on command. Shift yourselves. Rest of you prepare to fall back by sections."

CSM Russell continued to prowl up and down the line, occasionally stopping to shoot himself, knowing full well that this was no time to show fear or weakness. He had been here before, and thoughts of home and hearth were pushed aside as the need to lead by example came to the fore. Once more his organisation held the German tide at bay, and the Sussex began to pull back in an organised fashion. The Germans were reluctant to follow them uphill in the trees, against concentrated fire, but were driven on by their own officers.

Ced ran up gasping for breath and Captain Wittering stopped him.

"Where do you think you're going at a time like this?"

"I must speak to the colonel urgently."

"He's a little busy right now soldier, what's so damned important."

"Right flank won't hold unless reinforced and the Ger…"

"Nonsense man," the Captain interrupted him irritated, "there's two companies of Hampshires there at least."

"That's just it sir, there isn't. They were sent back to rest and resupply. There's barely sixty men over there and less now probably. Their officer sent me for help."

The captain went pale. "Come with me."

They ran over to where the colonel was standing above the line, bullets now starting to ricochet off the trees roundabout.

"Sir."

"What is it?"

"This man's from the southern end of the woods. Says the Hampshires pulled back earlier. Less than a company holding that side and they need help."

"What? Why wasn't I told?"

"Their officer said he sent a runner sir he…"

"Never mind that," the colonel said, cutting Ced off once more and turning red with rage, "there isn't anyone to send. We've lost out guns on the left and I've sent additional men there. Did you see Lieutenant Dunn?"

"Briefly sir."

"Well get back there and tell him he has to hold with what he has and keep those machine guns going at all costs. Do you hear? At all costs, or we will be surrounded. We will blow the whistle when we have made the top of the ridge and he…"

The bullet took the colonel on the left side entering his heart and killing him instantly. He collapsed holding his revolver which had never been fired.

"Oh my God," Captain Wittering said staring down. Ced checked him and said "He's dead sir."

"Well don't just stand there man. You have your orders. Get over to Dunn and tell him to hold."

"When do we pull back sir?"

But the captain was no longer listening. He strode off down the slope shouting "Sergeant Major!" and Ced was left alone with the dead body of his former commanding officer. He had a brief memory of the man sitting proudly on his horse on Steyning green; veteran of the Boer war, his life's experience wiped out in a single shot. He felt the weight of futility wash over him as bullets snapped about in the trees behind, and then he turned and ran back down the hill, thinking only of his friends now.

Chapter 24 – Counter attacking

Will and Albert stumbled on through the trees but the blood was flowing freely from Albert's arm now covering them both, and he began to struggle to stay conscious. Will paused behind a large Cedar tree, its branches outstretched as if asking *'Why? Why these foolish men were so intent on killing each other.'*

He propped Albert up and then bent down and rapidly undid one of the puttees wrapped round his lower leg, allowing the trouser leg to sag down unchecked. *Uniform be damned now,* he thought. He quickly took off his bayonet and cut the material in half, discarding one part and then tying the other around Albert's upper arm as a tourniquet to staunch the bleeding. His friend winced as he did so, unable to suppress a groan. A bullet smashed the branch above his head and more followed and they both saw another of their comrades cry out and fall as he attempted to flee.

"Can't be helped Bert sorry," Will said, "Have to stop the bleeding. Now we have to push on. Can you walk?"

Bert nodded but the confidence of a couple of minutes ago was clearly draining with the blood and Will realised he was weakening. One of the Germans charged past nearby ahead of his comrades, clearly excited by the chase, caution forgotten in the moment. Will picked up his rifle and calmly fired twice into his back and he fell dead without a sound. It made the others stop mid-flight and take cover not knowing where the shot had come from. Albert smiled admiringly at the young corporal.

"Only one thing for it," Will said slinging his rifle on his shoulder once more, "Hope you don't weigh more than a sack of spuds."

With that he reached down and lifted Albert onto his shoulders, one arm and leg either side of him, and grunting with the weight set off forward once more. Bullets whistled past but somehow from within Will found the energy to break into a run and began to zig zag through the trees, the shouts of the enemy hot on his heels.

As Will headed desperately back, Ced stumbled into the gulley where the Hampshires held on, waiting for support. He ran over to the young lieutenant who was now firing a rifle from one of his own dead soldiers.

"Is anyone with you?" the lieutenant asked.

"No and they won't be coming either, they can't spare anyone. And it gets worse."

"What do you mean Longworthy?" the voice of Dunn from behind him made him spin sharply and Ced saw the anxiety on his own lieutenant's face.

"The colonel's dead sir. "

"What? Utter tosh. He can't be. How do you know?"

"I was there, I saw it. The captain's organising a controlled retreat."

"A retreat? Then we need to pull back now."

"We were told to hold sir."

"Hold? The colonel is dead and the regiment is retreating, we have to go now." Dunn then looked at the young second lieutenant and said "Get your men together."

The closest soldiers had stopped firing and one of the machine gunners paused hearing the exchange and looked round waiting for orders.

"What about the guns," the Hampshire officer said, wavering between the situation and his senior lieutenant's command.

"With respect sir we can't," Ced countered, "The captain reiterated what the colonel had said, that the machine guns must cover the retreat."

"Don't argue with me soldier. This is no time for heroes."

"But sir, our lads and some Hampshires are in the woods still over there."

"He's right," the young lieutenant started to say, and then there was a huge blast as a grenade exploded nearby. The nearest machine gun team was wiped out and the Hampshire officer was blown backwards several yards into the bushes.

The Germans had seized the pause in fire to storm forward,

and at that unfortunate moment the three remaining men from the Hampshire section burst from the woods to their left. The Germans spotted them and turned their fire on them and the men were cut down yards from the trees. Ced looked on forlornly towards the far woods but no one else emerged.

"Well that solves the problem of your friends clearly," Dunn sneered in his face. "And that will be the rest of us if we don't move now, so any more objections and I'll have you on a charge. You're lucky I don't leave you here." He glowered at Ced then screamed above the chaos. "Pull back! Retreat. All of you."

Dunn was already running as he shouted the last commands, and seeing their own officer down and this one running back, the men broke and fled after him. The second machine gun was abandoned and without the withering cross fire from the flanks, the Germans in the centre surged forward with renewed vigour. Ced glanced once more towards the trees for any signs of his friends but the area was now swarming with German troops and he knew the situation was hopeless and turned and ran with the rest.

*

Russell heard the guns stop and assumed they were overrun, and then heard the roar from the emboldened Germans in the field only a hundred yards or so below them. He did a quick analysis of the situation and then turned to the colonel's adjutant, Captain Archibald.

"Can't hold them now without artillery or machine gun support sir. We'll just be sacrificing the men for nothing. Chances are they are over the flanks already and if we fall back at this pace we could be surrounded and wiped out. I'll keep two sections here as a rear guard, keep them thinking. You and Captain Wittering can pull back to the village with the bulk of the men and cover us when you get there. We need to let HQ know Jerry is counter attacking here in strength in case our runner didn't make it."

"You know what you're saying Sergeant Major?"

"Yes sir but better thirty men than the whole battalion. I'll detail two men to carry the CO's body out with you. Best get going now sir."

Captain Archibald looked grimly at his best soldier and then saluted and the orders were given. The majority of the men turned and moved quickly up the ridge as the bullets intensified. As Russell watched them go bullets ripped past them again and he saw Archibald cry out and fall. Men rushed to his aid but he never saw him rise and his face frowned with the concern it was already too late to pull back. He doubted if any of them would make it back and when he turned round there was a line of anxious faces looking at him from the score of men left behind, clearly all thinking the same thing. Russell forced his face into a smile, the large moustache flicking upwards.

"Right my lucky lads. Let's buy the battalion some time. Make 'em think the whole bleedin' 5th Army Corps is firing down on 'em." The men seemed uninspired and he tried another tack. "No heroics though mind. Not expecting us to fight to the last man. When the time comes if we can't get away I'll let you know when to surrender. Which will be shortly after we reach the pearly gates! Any questions?"

His men responded now with suitable grim smiles and the odd laugh and no questions came as they settled into their positons and set their sights once more. They could see the Germans congregating below them, firing steadily, ready for the final assault up the hill. Despite the situation Russell couldn't help admiring the courage of their enemies. He had assaulted more than one position himself uphill in the Boer war and knew it took real guts to do that. "That's proper soldiering," he murmured appreciatively.

He thought briefly then of Ginny back home and his lads running around the garden in their treasured married quarters. He smiled knowing a lot of the men thought his wife had left him years ago, unable to live with such a hard man; this being his reputation amongst the Battalion. In truth he did nothing to change that as his private life was just that - private. But when he was home he was anything but the gruff Sergeant Major and was putty in the hands of his family and very house proud.

Such a big house they had acquired with his promotion as well, he reflected smiling. How they had laughed in bed that first night after bathing the boys in their own full size bath with running water.

"No more tubs by the fire for us Genevieve old girl," he had shouted, beer bottle in hand in his long night shirt.

"Oh I don't know Geoffrey," she had said with seductive eyes, "that old tub had its moments." He felt her warm hands run across his stomach then…but somewhere below a bugle blew a menacing note, and he shook the scene away. He set his face and strode forward as the Germans troops charged.

"Ready…

Aim…

Fire!"

*

Will and Albert burst out of the woods to cross the gap back to their own lines, at the exact time the Hampshire troops were pulling back. As the German troops pushed forward they didn't realise at first that the man running bent double with another man on his back was actually a British soldier, not expecting to see any enemy troops behind them now. As they approached the tree line however Will's luck ran out as the Germans chasing behind them broke cover, and began firing and shouting alerting their comrades to their flight, who subsequently started firing too. The bullets whizzed past them like flies and Will felt a sharp burning sensation in his left arm as one found its target and he collapsed swearing into the brush on the far side, Bert crying out with the impact.

Will rolled over and mercifully found the ground sunk slightly here and dragged Bert down with him. As the Germans moved towards him an officer appeared and ordered the main group to continue up the hill after the fleeing Hampshires and told a section of the ones who had been in the woods to follow where Will disappeared.

He had dropped his rifle in the impact and reached out and dragged it to him now. He checked it and found he only had a few rounds left in his pouches. Not enough to make a difference but he wouldn't go down without a fight. He looked up the hill and saw Lieutenant Dunn running up it without pausing, and knew as soon as he tried to make a move they would be cut down. He looked at Albert who was breathing heavily now and patted him on the chest.

"Looks like the end of the line Teach," he said with a smile, unless you have a few dozen grenades in your knapsack."

"It's artillery you need lad," Albert said, understanding their doomed predicament, though his voice was quite hoarse now, and his breath very laboured. "Unless…you have a machine gun… hidden anywhere about your person."

Will shook his head and sighted on the German officer still giving orders in full view. At least he would make sure his last contribution was a significant one. As he looked along the sight his eye was drawn to a shallow dug-out no more than twenty yards to their left, and in it sat the abandoned Vickers machine gun.

"Bloody hell," he said, "there is a machine gun."

Albert half turned to look and saw the Germans racing forward.

"You'll never make it lad. Best leave me be and make a dash for it. I can distract them perhaps."

"No I have to try Bert. But just in case use this."

He laid his rifle by his friend and went to rise up, and Albert made a grab at him with his good arm. Will flinched as Albert grabbed him on the arm that had been hit and he looked down to see it was now bleeding steadily; though to his relief it looked like the bullet had only nicked the edge of it.

Albert let go seeing his friend's discomfort. "Don't be a fool Will."

But Will was determined and patting him on the shoulder sprang forward crouching low.

The Germans saw the movement instantly and began shooting. Will ducked down and rolled over behind a log as several bullets smacked into it, and then crawled forward trying desperately to reach the gun but they were right on top of him now. A German soldier appeared suddenly and raised his rifle to shoot and Will saw him smirk at him. "Auf Wierdersehn Engländer." There was a sound like a firework going off near them and the German fell backwards with a shocked cry. The Hampshire Lieutenant appeared by Will firing his revolver at the advancing Germans. He was bleeding heavily down the left side of his face and his clothes were torn and bloody from the explosion. He was clearly badly hurt but had somehow got himself up and come to Will's aid.

"Get that gun...working Corporal. I will...cover you." The words came through gritted teeth as if it required a tremendous amount of effort to speak, and Will realised that there was no time to lose, as the officer could collapse again at any moment. He ran forward the last few yards and jumped on the gun. There was a shout next to him and the young officer ran forward firing the last of his rounds at their attackers and was clearly shot again, but threw the pistol in a last act of defiance. A German clubbed him to the ground and then they were on him. Will tore his eyes away from the desperate scene and checked the gun, feeding the bullet belt in, and making sure the actions were clear.

Incredibly the officer rose once more now slashing with a knife he must have been carrying but he was knocked back again and stabbed and shot repeatedly and with a final cry disappeared from view surrounded by a dozen of the enemy. One of them picked up his revolver and started waving it above his head mocking the dead man. Then the Vickers gun clicked as Will cocked the weapon and they all turned to see the deadly barrel pointing right at them; a British soldier with blazing hate in his eyes hunched over it, his hand on the trigger.

Some moved to shoot, others went to run, and still more screamed in terror, but the result was the same for all of them. Will began firing and in seconds had torn into the group killing every one outright before they had moved one step. He swung the gun round now in a controlled arc no longer caring about his own safety, his hate for the enemy in that moment driving him on. The bullets cut the startled German officer in half causing his men nearby to break and run, and the corpse collapsed with its mouth still wide open, his voice cut off in its final order.

The German soldiers here were caught in the open and though some tried to fire, Will shot steadily away at each of them in turn. One man clearly older than the others and probably a veteran rushed forward bravely with a grenade to stop this new threat, but Will saw him and shot him as he threw it so the grenade dropped near his feet and simply blew him to bits.

For a moment the fact Will was having to adjust the belt every few seconds caused it to jam momentarily, and he cursed fiddling wildly with the actions to get it working again. Then a bloody hand appeared on the ammunition box next to it and said, "Easy lad... short controlled bursts like they trained you...yes? I'll feed."

Albert had crawled over to join his friend during the action and now propped himself up against one of the sandbags, and with a nod began working the rounds into the gun. Will cleared the stoppage and looked across the tree line where the main body of Germans were rushing forward and opened up.

Over on the left CSM Russell and his small group were braced for the German onslaught when out of nowhere a machine gun began firing from over on their flank and decimating the Germans in front of them. Russell couldn't see the British gun that was firing from where they were but smiled in admiration. "Well I'll be. You little beauty." He looked down the hill and shouted to his men. "Pour it into 'em lads. If you have grenades throw them now and show them what the Sussex are made of." The Germans caught in a cross fire and desperate to escape the dreaded machine gun that was tearing into them in droves, fell back in disarray.

"Right fall back to the top of the ridge, you might just live to fight another day after all, thanks to that gunner. Move."

Albert nudged Will and pointed to the ammunition boxes. "This is the last belt lad. When it runs out we better had too. Sharpish like. Once Jerry realises the gun's empty he will swarm after us like a horde of bees, and they won't be in any mood to take prisoners."

Will nodded and reloaded, looking up the hill to the ridgeline which now looked a long way away. Throughout the woods here there were the shouts and cries of men engaged in hand to hand fighting. Despite Will's actions a number of Germans had already gone past on this side chasing the fleeing Hampshires and by the sounds of it had clearly caught up with some of them. He hoped Dunn had got his just desserts finally. *A bullet in the back would be right for someone like him.* Then he admonished himself for thinking like that, and commenced firing again.

By now the main group of remaining German soldiers had taken cover and rifle fire was beginning to come back at them, increasing all the time. They could tell from the direction of the shots that some of them were clearly working round to the woods opposite too, and using the darkness to their advantage to aim at the British pair.

"Time to go soon," Albert said "or you'll...get one in the kisser."

Will looked at his friend who had lost much of the colour in his face, and lay slumped heavily in the dugout his one good arm still pushing the bullet belt out of the box towards the gun. He owed it to him to try and get him out of this.

"Not going anywhere without you Bert. Couple more bursts then we'll dash up the hill."

"I would not wish any companion in the world but you," Albert said suddenly with a flourish.

Will looked at him quizzically.

"It's Shakespeare lad, always good...in times of crisis." He smiled now and Will looked at him once more in amazement, and then the gun clicked empty.

"Bugger."

At that moment the tree line opposite parted as a German pulled a branch to one side and a machine gun appeared directly opposite them.

"You can say that again lad," Albert said with another grimace.

Will looked round for his rifle and saw Albert had left it where they had fallen some yards back. It wouldn't help them now. He ducked down behind the sand bagged ledge and grabbed Albert to him, waiting for the inevitable explosion of bullets into their shallow pit. He tensed with fear against the inevitable searing pain when the bullets ripped through the weak defences and into the pair of them.

The explosion when it came was even more dramatic than that, and with screams the German machine gunners were blown back into the gaping darkness of the trees and swallowed up. Will and Albert looked up stunned.

"Our guns?"

"Can't be Bert there was only one shell."

They looked round as several Germans now appeared on the tree line opposite and began shooting at them. They were answered by an unfamiliar sound of rapid firing that came from behind where Will and Albert lay, causing them to duck back out of sight once more.

With a rush of leaves and dirt Sergeant Albright slid into view above them.

"Thought you boys might need a hand. Time to go though I think."

"Am I glad to see you Sarge," Will said with a huge sense of relief, and then added, "Higgins is hurt."

"Thank me later. And looks like you both need a bit of attention. Can you move?" Will nodded. "Well get going, I'll cover you."

He raised the unfamiliar gun and started firing it again. It was a Mark 1 Lewis gun with its distinctive top-mounted 'pan shaped' cylindrical magazine mounted on top, capable of rapid fire. It had been used at the start of the war by Belgium troops and then adopted by the Royal Flying Corps as a weapon of choice. It was not standard issue in the British army yet but there were plenty around that the veterans had 'acquired,' especially being able to fire five hundred rounds or more a minute in the right hands. It was designed to be fired lying prone supported by a tripod stand at the front, but weighing half of what the standard Vickers gun did, it could be fired while being held too, if you were strong enough. Which Sergeant Albright clearly was, and hefted it about as easily as the men did their own Lee Enfield rifles.

He began firing once more and Will lifted Albert up onto his back and crossed the few yards to where his rifle lay and picked it up too.

"Keep moving left in a wide arc towards the ridge," Albright shouted. "There are still a number of Jerries combing through the woods above us and when their troops regroup and come up again we need to try and slip round them."

Will did as he was told and glanced back awkwardly to see the Sergeant was now running after them. It was hard going uphill carrying Albert and he slipped more than once, grazing his knee hard on one occasion, and soon he began to struggle. The muscles in his legs were now burning with the exertion as they instantly remembered the hard work needed to carry Albert the last time, and cried out to Will's brain in protest. His heavy feet caught a root and they both slid back once more on the wet bracken, Will cursing his luck. He struggled to move under Albert's weight, fear of being caught making him panic, but then a friendly arm grabbed him and the Sergeant was at his side.

"Let's get him up between us Davison. Use your rifle butt for support like a walking stick."

They each hooked one of Albert's arms around their necks and carried him between them, and working together made good progress. More than once they heard the shouts of German voices and the occasional shot, but they reached the ridge without further incident. They looked down from the trees and saw the allied trench full of British and Indian troops. *Safety at last*, Will thought through exhausted eyes.

As they paused for a moment, all three men gulping in air, the woods behind them became alive to German voices once more, and they knew they were not safe yet.

"Sounds like Jerry has regrouped and is on the move again. Best move round to the left a bit more, follow that hedge line over there," the Sergeant said. "If we burst out of here now, liable as not we'll be peppered full of holes by our colonial brothers!" Will smiled and nodded and they turned once more to work their way round the ridge. As they did so they came face to face with two startled Germans, heading back to their own troops from the skirmish in the woods earlier.

"Look out!" Albright shouted and pushed Albert onto Will making them both fall over in a heap. He raised his gun in one swift movement as he did so and fired a burst from the Lewis gun at the same time as the Germans did likewise.

The Sergeant and one of the Germans fell backwards without a sound and the other one was frantically reloading his gun, fumbling with a bullet clearly scared. Will reached for his own rifle but it was tangled up underneath them and so instinctively he just charged forward and grabbed the German about the legs knocking him over, as he had done many times with his brothers back home.

The German started hitting him on the back now and half freed himself reaching for his rifle nearby. Will saw a piece of branch and desperately grabbed it swinging wildly at the man. He hit him once in the chest and then the German blocked the second swing and hit out at Will striking him on the arm and causing a shooting pain to fly up into his neck. Will swung the branch again harder this time and it smashed into the side of the man's face knocking his helmet off with the impact. But it seemed to have no effect on his opponent and he hit Will full in the face, knocking him on his back dazed.

As he tried to recover his senses the man climbed over him pinning him to the ground with his knees. He saw a sadistic smile now on a pock marked face. Hot sweat ran down the shaven head, freed from its helmet, and dripped onto Will's face. The German breathing heavily, wrenched his bayonet from its scabbard and raised it aloft in triumph. Will frantically looked round on the floor for something else to use to block it but there was nothing. He tried to raise his good arm but it was held down. The man shook his head tutting sarcastically as he did so and brought the bayonet down.

A shot rang out and the German convulsed wildly and Will saw the grip on the bayonet slacken and fall mercifully hitting him side on and rolling off his chest. As he watched dark blood appeared at the corner of the man's mouth and he began to slump forward. With an effort Will heaved him off and pushed him to one side. He looked over to Albert and he was lying half propped up on one elbow with Will's rifle in his arms.

"Christ thanks Bert! That was a close one."

Bert nodded as Will checked the two Germans. The shaven headed one was dead alright and when he went to the second one, he could see quite clearly he was also dead without a need to check closely, his chest full of half a dozen holes from the Sergeant's gun. He ran over to where their own Sergeant lay amongst the undergrowth. Percy Albright had been hit in the chest and lay quite still with sightless eyes gazing up into the spring sunshine, which now broke through the tree's canopy.

Albert had collapsed again and spoke without looking over.

"How is he?"

"He's gone Bert."

"Christ."

They sat in silence for a moment, Will looking at the eyes that had shown kindness to him so many times since he came to France, and recalled how just a few minutes before the sergeant had saved their lives.

"That shot is going to alert the Jerries. We need to move," Albert said to break the moment.

"What about the Sarge?"

"We'll have to leave him and try to come back for him later."

Will nodded and moved over to Albert picking up his rifle, and then heaved his friend onto his back once more.

"Off we go then Bert."

"Once more…unto the breach…dear friend," Albert replied quietly, being bounced up and down on Will's back as he shuffled forward once more. The aching returned almost immediately in Will's legs but at least from here on in it would be downhill, though the risk of slipping and falling was just as great.

They skirted the hedge line as their sergeant had said and as Will approached the trench nervously from its far side through the thinning trees, a sentry emerged only a few feet away and called out a challenge.

"Lance Corporal Davison. Royal Sussex with a wounded man. We were attacked in the woods."

He was waved through and saw to his amazement a hidden machine gun bunker that had been skillfully built into the trees here just yards from where they had been stopped. Will was glad it was one of theirs or they would have been killed before even knowing where the shots came from. They followed the soldier to a ramp that led down into the main trench, and walked down to where a British sergeant was busy giving orders to some Indian troops.

"Thought all of you were back," the sergeant said, breaking off from his briefing. "Those that were going to make it back. Any more behind you?"

"I don't think so sergeant, but it's chaos back there" Will replied struggling under the weight of his friend.

"Right well get yourselves off to the sick bay. Follow the trench along for fifty yards and then left into the communication trench and that runs back to the village and out. Ask for the building there. And keep your heads down. "

"Yes sergeant." As they stumbled off without anyone offering to help Will heard him continue his chat as if they were just walking past on a parade ground.

"Right so you heard what that soldier said. So anyone who pops out of those woods now is likely to be a Hun so get to it and look lively and shoot anything that moves."

Will hoped he had been right and that no one else was behind him, or they might get shot and he felt anxious suddenly. And tired. Very, very tired. He stumbled on the boardwalk and his legs gave way sending them both sprawling.

"God sorry Bert."

As he struggled to get up on the mud slicked boards, an Indian soldier bent down immediately to help.

"Careful Sahib, the path is slippery here. You are hurt. I will get some help for you and your friend. I am Private Guptha of the 39th Rifles," he said proudly.

"Thank you. I am Will. Corporal Will Davison. Can you help my friend first he's worse than me."

Guptha nodded and passed Will his water, and then called out in a language Will didn't understand for another soldier to help him. Will sat against the back of the trench wall and drank the water gratefully. As the Indians lifted Albert up he leaned forward to give him a drink.

"Here mate have a sip before we get off and patch ourselves up. We made it."

Guptha and the other man looked at Will and sadness grew upon their faces.

"I am afraid he cannot hear you Corporal Sahib. Your friend is dead."

Chapter 25 – Promotions

Hauptmann Dietrich Steiger led his men up through the woods to the ridgeline with an air of controlled aggression surrounding him. The fight in the farm fields had been unexpected and frustrating, despite being ultimately successful once more. He was angry with the information given to his regiment that there were no enemy troops within half a mile of this point, and more so that his fellow officers had been so blasé about the situation that they had not even employed skirmishers. It was as if the British had appeared out of thin air, and not for the first time in this ridiculously organised war, Steiger bemoaned the unnecessary losses.

Several of his incompetent fellow officers had paid for such arrogance with their lives in the area below them. He would not make the same mistake, Steiger thought smiling to himself now as they crested the ridge. Despite the bravery of the British troops, not least with those cursed machine gunners, his men had overcome their stubborn resistance and pushed on. His regiment had first bloodied the British at Mons, and had not been involved in a defeat yet. *Now he had assumed full control, that was not going to change today!*

His father had been an Oberst in the Franco-Prussian war of 1870 that helped unify his beloved Germany, and he had followed in his father's footsteps as soon as he was able. He served with distinction as a young *Leutnant* in China when the German detachment combined with ten other nations to crush the Boxer rebellion in 1900, and the promotions followed. Both father and son had winning in their blood.

He ensured they moved through the woods carefully, but not too slowly so as to stay hot on the heels of the broken English and keep the pressure on them. Casualties had been unacceptable but they had inflicted a larger blow to the enemy including a number of prisoners taken which would enhance his reputation with High

239

Command. He paused to relight his pipe which had gone out, while their skirmishers now pushed forward. The first rank of his men paused alongside him, trusting in his experience.

Steiger examined the family crest on the side, a present on joining the army from his family, and smiled as he lit it once more. He was not tall like his father but well-built and with the natural grace of a cavalry man, having originally joined the 17th Brunswick Hussars in his native Hannover. Which was another thing that irked him as he found himself fighting on foot, and his blond eyebrows twitched in frustration. *Give me a regiment of lancers*, he thought preening his fine moustache, *and I would ride down these English stragglers in moments and chase them back to the Channel!*

The sound of fresh firing from his skirmishers made him focus once more, and taking the pipe from his mouth he urged his loyal men forward. As he came to the edge of the wood his attention was naturally drawn to where his skirmishers were firing. The sun was now shining brightly overhead and he raised his hand to cover his eyes to look in the direction of the shooting.

He observed a group of British stragglers running hell for leather towards an old bridge that forded a small dry stream bed skirting round the village in front. No doubt it might fill up in times of heavy rain but it wasn't anything his men need worry about, and they had already forded large rivers under fire so his tactical brain discarded it instantly. The bridge wasn't wide enough for trucks and was probably an old pack horse bridge which was no doubt a throwback to the village's medieval origins. Steiger knew he would need to construct something far more robust once they were established in the village to allow the guns to move up, unless there was anything better at the far end.

He checked his map quickly and saw it was indeed the village of Estaires and his regiment's intended target, and he waved the line of men forward with his pipe. Anticipating the opportunity to have a hot bath in one of the houses below, Steiger nodded with satisfaction as the last two British 'Tommies' were cut down short of the bridge by his men's accurate fire. He strode forward blinking against the sun, and scanned the front of the village. He saw one of the British stragglers wave to something on his left as he crossed the bridge and he naturally looked in that direction. It was at that moment he saw the man-made entrenchments running north to south in front of the village, the sandbags covered in shrub and brush. As someone in them waved an arm in reply, Steiger froze, as the enormity of the situation appeared out of the shimmering haze below. Those men closest to their officer heard him simply say "Mein Gott," his pipe falling unchecked to the ground in his trance-like state.

Then the machine guns opened fire.

*

CSM Russell lurched over the bridge with the bullets hitting the ancient stonework and ricocheting in many directions. His dwindling rearguard party was scattered in front and behind him and he heard the cries from behind as at least another of his men was hit. He looked back and saw Private Bateman stagger against the bridge wall and then fall over it. There was no time to lose and frankly were it not for the machine gunner back in the woods, many more of them would now be joining Bateman.

"Are you the last Sergeant Major?" an Indian officer called out to him in very clipped English. Panting with the exertion of the run, Russell simply gave the officer a thumbs up and nodded. He saw the officer raise his arm and bring it down, the shouted command lost as his troops opened fire with rifle and machine guns on the German troops emerging from the woods.

"Take that you bastards," Russell grumbled under his breath, then told his remaining men to follow him into the village while he located one of their officers.

Nearby Will sat unnoticed with Albert's head cradled in his lap. Tears caused white rivers of sadness down his battle blackened face. The emotion and exhaustion of the previous hours exploded from him in sobs as he sat in the muck of the trench, the occasional medic and orderly moving back and forth behind the soldiers, not knowing whether to approach him or not. Albert had been hit in the back at some point while he was being carried, but had made no mention of it, nor complained of the pain. *Perhaps he knew he was already done for,* Will thought. In front of him Private Guptha was now firing steadily at targets somewhere ahead of him, unseen by Will on the trench floor. In that moment he didn't care, and as Guptha knelt to reload he said, "You should probably move out of here, and take your friend to the mortuary at the far end of the village. I am sorry Corporal Sahib."

"It's Will. And thank you."

"Rajiv." They shook hands and as they did so the scream of artillery shells roared overhead and flew into the ridgeline beyond them. Clearly the guns had finally arrived in range to be able to support them.

"Well better late than never I guess 'eh Bert," Will said speaking to no one in particular and ruffling his friend's hair affectionately. "Let's go mate," he added as he hauled the dead man up once more out of the mud and grime.

There was a shout of "Fix Bayonets," from somewhere along the line and all the soldiers instantly obeyed the command. Another barrage of shells flew over in a synchronised arc of death, and then the machine guns halted. Guptha looked at Will briefly as the young soldier hefted his dead friend into his arms.

"Well here we bloody go again. Back to those woods," he said, his head shaking as he smiled. "Good luck to you Will."

"Take care Rajiv and thank you."

A whistle blew and Guptha let out a roar that didn't match his previously gentle nature and it made Will jump. He watched him climb out of the trench as the 39th Garhwal Rifles surged up the slope towards the smoke filled ridge, still shuddering under the impact of the shells. Then he carefully lifted Bert up onto his shoulders adjusting the weight, and set off down the trench with him towards the rear.

"You can rest easy now Teach, no more lessons today."

*

"They are holding an inquiry this morning," Ced commented, as he sat down with Will and other members of their platoon in the large central square in Estaires the following morning.

"An inquiry? What about?" Will said puzzled, watching Franko spoon luke warm porridge from a mess tin into his mouth.

"Yesterday's defeat. HQ not happy about it at all it seems."

"Not exactly our fault," Franko chipped in spitting porridge bits over everyone, "seeing as we stumbled on half the bleedin' German army."

"Besides the Indians retook the woods," Will continued brushing the porridge remnants off his kit indignantly; not that it made much difference as they had been unable to even change clothes for several days now. "And they are now well established beyond where we were I'm told."

"Plus they've got the 3rd Division of the City of London Brigade up in support. So hardly a defeat at the end of the day," Harris added, munching on an apple he had acquired from one of the trees roundabout.

"Maybe but I hear Jerry guns are now pasting them hourly so it could all change hands again today who knows! More importantly a colonel got chopped and that can't be swept under the carpet. Major D'Arcy is up against it and has to put on a show for the top brass."

Will looked at Ced as his friend spoke and shook his head.

"They do know there's a war on right? People do get killed, including the officers." The other men nearby chuckled at this black humour. "Anyway if we are done with breakfast, and most of us have had extra from Franko anyway, I want to go over to the temporary grave site and sort out something for Bert." Franko looked sheepish and stopped eating. Harris spat the apple out onto the ground.

"Ew! Bleedin' maggots. Everything's rotten in this stinking war."

A number of the men there had lost friends the day before and the sombre mood reflected the fact the Sussex had taken a hard knock. Their pride as much as their numbers was severely dented.

"I'll go with you," Ced answered and a few other men who had liked Albert nodded too. Harris, who was still spitting bits of apple out at the back of the group suddenly piped up.

"Hold your horses Will, trouble inbound."

"It's Corporal to you," Ced corrected him firmly.

But Will didn't care in the moment having also spotted the Sergeant Major marching purposefully over to them. The men sprang to their feet.

"At ease men. Davison, Holdworthy, with me."

"Sergeant Major?"

"You're called to the inquiry. Come along I'll explain on the way." Will glanced at the other men and noted the concerned faces but turned and followed the CSM with Ced.

*

They approached an old stone warehouse building, towards the rear of the village, with large wooden doors and a first floor open hatch for a grain store or something similar, although the winch looked as if it hadn't been used for some time. The sides were covered in shiny green ivy that had surrounded the main entrance and were gradually threatening to overwhelm the whole structure. Russell had given them a brief overview of the basis for the inquiry as they walked through the village in the early morning haze. As the two friends followed the Sergeant Major up some stone stairs at the side, the railings rusting through neglect, he stopped at the top.

"Just one last thing Davison. I am told on good authority that it was you who manned the machine gun and prevented the battalion being overrun. Is that correct?"

"Yes Sergeant Major, with Private Higgins. But he died sir." The vision of Bert lying in the trench was still vivid in his mind, as was the moment he'd had to leave him in the temporary mortuary with strangers, and the pain clearly showed on his face.

"I'm sorry lad. Sergeant Albright too I'm told."

"Yes Sir, he came back to help us when everyone else was gone. Without him we would have been killed for sure." Will's voice broke now with the emotion of remembering the events of the previous evening.

"That's sad Davison I know. He was a good man. If they ask for your version of events in there just stick to the facts and keep it simple."

As Will nodded, his friend spoke up.

"We were told to go sir. Ordered back. I would have stayed…I thought everyone else was dead."

Ced looked at the floor unable to meet his friend's eyes, feeling the guilt more than ever despite the fact he had been following orders. He had wanted to talk to Will about it before but hadn't been able to find the words, and felt awful that he had pulled back thinking he was dead only to see him walk up the street that evening carrying Albert's body. They had rushed to help the young inconsolable corporal carry the body of their friend to the mortuary tent. Later after 'evening call' the men had sat drinking in silence, and no one had really spoken about the day's events.

Will gave his shoulder a pat and nodded at him sympathetically, breaking his sad reflections.

"Following orders lad that's all you can do," Russell stated in his baritone voice. "Was it the Hampshire officer that ordered you to pull back?"

"No Sergeant Major, he was wounded by a bomb blast. I thought he was dead until Will here, I mean Corporal Davison, told me later he had fought on. Lieutenant Dunn ordered us to pull back."

"Dunn? Are you sure?"

"Yes Sir."

"I see. Well mind how you go in there lads. Stick to the facts as I said."

Will and Ced exchanged puzzled looks at this, but the Sergeant Major opened the door at the top of the stairs and went inside. They went into an ante room where an orderly sat writing out some reports. The soldier stood up instantly when Russell entered, one of the papers swirling to the floor in his hurry, and he blushed as he gathered the papers up. Russell ignored the man and swept past him knocking hard on the internal door, and after a short pause was instructed to enter by a firm voice within. As they walked in they saw several officers sitting behind two desks on the other side of the wide room, with a couple of soldiers behind a further desk presumably making notes. Lieutenant Dunn was at attention in front of them; hat pulled down firmly in place, and was deep in discussion with Major D'Arcy and Captain Wittering.

The room inside had clearly been used for crop storage of some kind, as part of the left hand wall still had a pile of hessian sacks along it. The room had clearly been swept quickly so that a mixture of grain and dust merged together in piles along that wall. On their right the light from the pale morning sun shone in through the open hatch where the winch machinery was standing idle. The noise flooding in from outside alongside the golden rays of the sun, reflected the sounds of several battalions of men preparing for another day on frontline duty. Irish and Scottish regiments were now belatedly moving into the area, to attempt once more to give the Indian Corps a break from the front line.

The tramp of boots and shouts of hundreds of men added to the poor acoustics in the room that made it hard to hear anything that was being said between the officers. Will noticed gaps in the rafters above them and light blinked here and there indicating that the roof too was starting to show signs of wear and tear. *One direct hit and the whole place will probably collapse,* he thought. *Just my luck if it's now with me standing in it.* He looked at Ced and raised his eyes.

"Atten...shun!"

The voice of the CSM snapped the pair into statues in front of the assembled group inside. Will fixed his eyes high above them at a point on the far wall, as they were taught in training, not daring to look anyone in the eye. Russell gave a sharp salute and announced their arrival. Wittering looked round the side of Dunn and said, "Have the men stand at ease Sergeant Major. But hats on for the hearing."

"Stand at...Ease. Hats on."

Will felt suddenly nervous and wondered if his friend felt the same. Just then Dunn saluted and turned and walked past them clearly quite shaken, his face markedly pale in the gloom of the interior; but still managed to look at the pair with barely disguised malice.

"Sergeant Major. We'll speak to the men now. One at a time. Have the other one sit with the Lieutenant until called." Captain Wittering continued with the formalities as if they were in a barrack block in England. Will was sure he would have carried on even if the

Germans were charging up the main street outside.

"Sir." Russell saluted again and then indicated to Will to go and sit at the back of the room.

"Private Longworthy. Four paces forward and salute. March on."

As Ced strode forward Will turned and saw three chairs placed at the back of the room to the right of the entrance as they came in, which he hadn't noticed before. Dunn sat on one end. He moved back and sat on the other end leaving the middle chair empty between them, as much to give himself space as to observe some formal etiquette with the officer.

Will looked straight ahead allowing the noises of the men outside to wash over him. It was impossible to hear what the officers were saying to Ced and so he just switched off until it was his turn to be called. He was tired and just wanted to go somewhere quiet and rest. Above all else he wanted to be back in his room, climbing into his bunk bed, and munching on some chocolate or homemade biscuits with a glass of warm milk. He must have been smiling inadvertently at the memory as he suddenly became aware that Lieutenant Dunn was speaking to him, albeit very quietly so as not to disrupt the inquiry.

"I don't know what you feel you have to smile about Davison," he hissed, "perhaps you are just feeling smug that once again you have come through unscathed 'eh?"

Will turned to look at him now. The warm milk and cookies dissipated in moments like the dust specks dancing through the room amongst the sun's glowing beams. "Sir?"

"Funny isn't it how you survive while everyone else is killed. Maybe you carried Higgins on your back to protect your own skin. I heard he took a bullet for you."

Will's anger rose as he looked into the officer's sneering face, and he gripped the sides of the chair hard to stop himself reacting.

"Doesn't make you a hero Davison in my eyes. I know what you are. And you better make sure you don't go boasting to the major about your contribution in all this. You were just very lucky that's all and don't you forget it."

Will took a deep breath and considered his reply carefully. As he opened his mouth to speak his attention was caught by seeing Ced salute and do an 'about turn' and start to walk towards him.

"Davison, front and centre," the sergeant major called, and Will stood up.

"Mind my words Davison."

"Yes sir. Thank you Sir," Will said quietly, then added "I'm no hero sir. I just did my duty. We should all be able to look at ourselves in the mirror and think that shouldn't we, as the colonel once said." He marched off smartly forward as his words smacked into Dunn as if he had been slapped in the face. The lieutenant's anger was replaced by nervousness now, knowing what he had done in the woods, and he began to sweat profusely.

Will talked through the events from the moment he was ordered forward into the woods to flank the German main group. He did not mention that Dunn had wanted them to go alone, but said instead that the officers sent a combined force that was subsequently ambushed itself. He spoke uninterrupted until he got to the part where he carried Albert down to the trench and then Major D'Arcy raised his hand and said, "Thank you corporal."

"So it was Private Higgins that assisted you with the machine gun is that correct?"

"Yes sir though we would both have been killed had it not been for the actions of the lieutenant from the Hampshires, and then of course Sergeant Albright's intervention sir."

"Indeed." The major lent over to Wittering and murmured a few words. Will heard him say something about letters to families and that they should be put forward for a posthumous award.

"Agreed," the captain replied and then louder addressing Will asked, "So the rest of our troops in that section had scattered, is that right Davison?"

"They had pulled back sir," Will replied sensing he was being led down a particular line of inquiry. Then quickly added, "When we got there everyone was killed or gone sir."

"Quite. They had scattered. In your opinion if the troops had stayed do you think they could have held the flank?" Captain Wittering continued.

"Sir?"

"Lieutenant Dunn said it was impossible to hold the positon as the numbers were far fewer than we realised and some of them broke and ran when the guns were stormed."

"I am sure the lieutenant did what he felt best in the situation sir."

The Captain nodded looking him dead in the eye. "Quite so. Not what I asked though."

Will was concerned now he was digging himself a hole, and worse making Dunn look bad. Despite the fact he didn't like the officer the last thing he wanted was to antagonize him even more given his warning earlier.

"The Hampshires were depleted sir and Private Holdworthy went back to advise the colonel. I can't comment on what happened after we went forward but there were a lot of Jerries, I mean Germans, pushing through there."

"But you managed to get to the machine gun."

"Er. Yes sir. With the Hampshire lieutenant's help as I said. I didn't think really. Just had to try it. He gave his life for it."

"Well you saved a lot of lives with your action too corporal," the major now added.

Will looked embarrassed and didn't know what to say.

"Captain, did you say the colonel had promoted Davison and Higgins after their exploits with the sniper."

"Yes Major. Full corporals. Battlefield promotion."

"Excellent, just reward. And you will be mentioned in dispatches for this lad, mark my words."

"Sir. Thank you sir. Higgins too?"

"Of course. We will write to his family. Can you make a note of that Goodman?"

Being so focused staring straight ahead, Will hadn't noticed that the third officer was Theodore Goodman who was taking notes in the corner. He glanced down at him now and saw the officer smiling at him which surprised him.

"You're dismissed corporal." The major's voice brought him back, and the CSM marched out Will and Ced.

Outside Russell nodded at the pair of them. "Away to your billets and sort yourselves out lads. Well done again." He went back inside without another word, and as they walked away Will glanced back and saw Dunn emerge too from the shadows of the warehouse. He looked as if he might follow them and Will shivered as if someone had walked over his grave, but then Dunn turned and headed off in the opposite direction.

*

Back inside the officers were chatting amongst themselves more relaxed now, and an orderly was handing out sherries that had magically appeared from somewhere. CSM Russell stood at ease but was noticeably not relaxed, as soldiers never are in the presence of officers. Given the subject that had just been discussed he also found it hard to stomach they were now drinking sherry as if back at home in the mess.

"So he's a good man you say Sergeant Major?"

"Yes sir. Very reliable. The men like him too."

"Aren't you a Steyning man Goodman?" the Major now asked, turning to his right.

"Yes sir, born and bred in Beeding Manor," Theo replied trying to sound as grandiose as possible.

"And do you know this family at all? What is it again, Denisons?"

"Davison Sir," Russell interjected, somewhat frustrated on behalf of his soldier.

"Ah yes. Davison."

"Yes I do sir," Goodman replied. "Good farming family with four boys. Oldest is a Guards' officer I hear."

"What?" Captain Wittering spilt some of his sherry on his tunic in his surprise. "Damn and blast."

Raising his eyes at his Captain, the Major turned to Goodman. "Is that true?"

"Yes sir. Commissioned in '14, and been over here pretty much since the off I'm informed."

"Goodness me. But farmers you say?" Theo nodded, noting the disapproval in the Major's tone, that he often felt in the Mess having not been an Eton or Marlborough man.

"Well they clearly breed good stock in your town lieutenant." He laughed at his own joke and the Captain joined in a little too enthusiastically. Goodman smiled politely and saw the CSM do likewise.

"Anyway that's as may be. I don't know why he hasn't followed his brother into the elite, perhaps not as clever 'eh? But good to have him here. After all we can't all be officers what? And we can't have all the men led by farmers either!"

Even Captain Wittering squirmed at this remark so changed tack quickly.

"Well let's see how he handles the situation tomorrow as Dunn has asked for him to be on his squad."

"Indeed. Won't do him any harm to earn that new stripe straight away."

"He won't let you down sir." Russell added.

Goodman nodded and the Major sensed the support for the lad and moved to change the subject too.

"Sergeant Major, you are dismissed. Assemble 'A' company at La Gere Farm tomorrow morning at 0600 and ensure the Hampshires are there too as we discussed."

They exchanged salutes and Russell marched out, his boots clicking sharply across the floor despite the mud encased about them. D'Arcy watched him go. His thick black eyebrows creased in thought so that they met in the middle forming a dense thicket across his balding forehead. His head wrinkled in support as the frown spread; the additional lines of concentration like trenches marked on a map. Despite their moment of conviviality D'Arcy felt tired with the normal pressures of command exaggerated so much by the constant demand for reports and pressure for success.

"What do we think of Dunn gentlemen," he asked without looking at them, his piercing blue eyes still fixed firmly ahead.

"He's of good stock," Wittering replied. "Had a great grandfather who was a colonel with Wellington at Waterloo in an infantry brigade. The 'Bluffs' I think."

"But what do we think of Dunn?"

"Not the first time his name has cropped up in my reports sir, nor the first time he's crossed my path in inquiries. It's not been a great campaign for him so far." Goodman decided to speak aloud his concerns in the hope of support as inside he felt Dunn was an accident waiting to happen.

"Yes that's what worries me. Doesn't strike me as a born leader. You're both Lieutenants, and while I appreciate you haven't seen much action yet Goodman, you strike me as a far more steadying influence on the men than Dunn. 'Bluffs' or not."

D'Arcy's sudden compliment took Theodore by surprise and he stuttered a "thank you." He realised that the major noticed a lot more than it seemed and perhaps his attendance at the wrong school wasn't such a draw back in this hell hole after all. At the end of the day shells and bullets didn't discriminate between public and local schools as they were all learning to their cost.

"Keep an eye on him Wittering. Especially when we next get into the thick of it with the Hun. We must do what we must do tomorrow. Have to maintain order but there's a whiff about this I don't like and Dunn's in the thick of it."

"Yes sir," Wittering replied and then stood up as the major had already moved to leave.

"Oh and Goodman," D'Arcy said, pulling on his hat and wiping out the trench lines on his head with a smile.

"Sir?"

"I've recommended you for captain too. With immediate effect. Need a bit more clout around here with these young subalterns. You can help me with that, alongside Wittering. Bluffington-Sykes might be cosied up in HQ now but we will show them we can still run a tight ship out here too 'eh?"

"Yes sir. Thank you sir." Goodman returned the Major's salute, his eyes and mouth still probably wide open with the surprise.

"Carry on."

Chapter 26 – The Wall

L ater that evening the 'last post' echoed through Estaires; the notes from the unseen bugler rebounding off every dark hollow and doorway and rising up in the clear night sky, where the moon chased away the last vestiges of the sun. High up in the trees behind the village an unseen bird cried out in reply, calling its flock home for the night, their daytime routine complete once more.

In the lengthening shadows, a large group of men were gathered in the temporary mortuary on the main road out of the village where over fifty hastily erected wooden crosses of various shapes and sizes were in place on newly dug graves. Mounds of soft earth covering the still faces of friends and comrades who had also been called home one last time. Some of the crosses had helmets or items of personal importance hung about them. Others like the grave of Lieutenant Harris, aged just nineteen, had words inscribed in ink on the wood prior to anything more permanent. Most just had their name, rank and serial number.

Will and Ced stood with Franko and Ollie Harris, not related to the deceased lieutenant, and several other men around Albert's grave. Lifton, a private from 'C' company who had befriended Albert in training, was reading a small passage from the bible. He was a sidesman at his church in Shoreham and carried it everywhere with him. The men nicknamed him 'Preacher Paul' and he was known to spout forth passages he had learnt by heart after a few drinks, which always amused Will, especially when he preached about abstinence. Lifton finished now and the friends fell silent once more.

Ced reached inside his jacket and said, "I got something from the Quarter Master, when I was drawing stores earlier and we got chatting about what had happened in the woods. Turns out he likes a novel or too himself. Reads Tennyson and other people I can't remember. You know 'Charge of the Light Brigade' and all that," he added, seeing several of the men look blank at the poet's name. He noticed some lights of recognition flick on in their eyes as they huddled round the grave in the fading evening glow.

"Anyway he has a copy of some Shakespeare plays in a big book he pulled out of a chest in his tent. It's amazing what you find out about people in times of stress isn't it?" No one replied and his comment was rhetorical anyway so he continued.

"He showed me a copy of Romeo and Juliet and wrote out a passage for me that was a personal favourite of his. I thought you might like to read it out for our teacher here," Ced added, handing over a piece of note paper with noticeably trembling hands.

Will read it and looked at Ced and the impact was instantaneous. His eyes watered and he glanced away to where the sun had finally surrendered in an explosion of red waves along the far dark horizon.

"It's very apt," he said quietly.

"Let's hear it Will," Franko said and a number of the men said "Aye."

Will looked at them, and at the paper, and then at the grave of his former friend who until recently had walked among them. He arched his back as if Albert still clung to it, as he had done to life, during their flight through the woods only a short while ago.

"Ok. Here goes:

When he shall die, take him and cut him out in little stars,
And he will make the face of heaven so fine
That all the world will be in love with night
And pay no worship to the garish sun."

There were murmurs of approval and men from other graves had stopped at the words and come over out of curiosity and camaraderie. The silence hung respectfully in the air and Ced placed a hand on Will's shoulder and squeezed it once. Will hung his head and tried to picture his friend's moustached face but frustratingly could not, and so he just looked at the words once more, the sadness draped about his shoulders like a heavy cloak.

"Ah there you are Davison. I wondered if you lot might be up here." Dunn smashed through the silence with his grating tone and the men caught out, threw up a smattering of salutes and acknowledgements. Will's distaste for the officer was never more acute than in the ruining of that solemn moment and he clenched his fists as the anger rose up within him once more. Sensing that his young friend might do something silly, Ced stepped out in front.

"Can we help sir?" he asked, "we were told we were off duty."

"Oh I won't keep you men long don't worry." He looked disdainfully around and then stared past Ced at Will. "I need a squad for special duties tomorrow and as you are highly thought of it would seem, I asked the major if I could pick you Davison. Good test of your new stripe 'eh? What do you say?"

"I'd be happy to help sir, what is it we have to do."

"Uphold the honour of the regiment. Set an example to the Hampshires. Can you do that? I need a team of four men with you leading. Who else would you choose?"

Will didn't need to think twice and immediately called out Ced, Franko and Ollie. Despite the lieutenant's presence he felt excited at the prospect of leading a team, and not least because the major clearly favoured him.

"Longworthy, Jones and Harris. Excellent. Do you know La Gere Farm on the outskirts of the town by the western approach?"

"The one with the small pond by it? Yes sir."

"Good. 0600 sharp then. Be there in the morning with your team corporal. Rifles cleaned and loaded ready, and report to me in the main yard. Is that clear?"

"Yes sir, any kit needed? Rations?"

"Kit? Good heavens no. You're not going anywhere Davison."

He smiled then and turned to go.

"Sorry sir, but I don't understand."

Will suddenly felt apprehensive not least because Dunn looked smug, and the switch between calling him corporal and Davison was odd; without the fact they never went anywhere, even for an hour without kit of some kind.

Dunn turned back on his heels and looked at them all with mildly disguised contempt. "Oh you will understand soon enough. Enjoy your evening gentlemen."

As he walked away, Harris murmured, "Pompous arse." Then looked at Lifton and said "Sorry preacher!"

"Don't worry lad," Lifton replied under his breath, "He's going straight to hell that one, mark my words."

Ced watched the dark form of the lieutenant merge into the skulking shadows of the night. "I don't like it. He's up to something."

"Think we should go and see the captain and ask?" Will said, clearly worried too.

"No. Can't go over the head of the lieutenant. Just have to do what he says and turn up at six. Let's finish up here and get some rest. Need to be up early and make sure the rifles are extra clean just in case."

The men came together then and saluted as one. In twos and threes they drifted back to their tents, some choosing to stay and smoke, and chat to men from other companies. As Will and Ced walked back along the road through the village, they didn't notice their CSM watching them from a small window in one of the houses. Russell puffed on his cigar once more and inhaled the rich oak sensation, before blowing a cloud of smoke out of the window in front. He shook his head, the politics of war angering his thoughts when all he wanted to do was proper soldiering.

He picked up the new-fangled gas mask they were being issued with and shook his head before tossing it away onto the bunk, that lay immaculately presented in the dust covered room despite the circumstances. *Gas bombs and aero planes,* he thought to himself, *and machine guns that take the place of a hundred men. Why can't we just stand up and fight with rifles and bayonets like the good old days?*

He despaired for the soldiers under his command in a war that was being progressively fought from a distance with weapons of mass destruction. *Where was the bravery in that?* As he saw Will disappear out of sight, he pulled on the sweet cigar for comfort, and hoped that the young lad he had watched since training could cope with tomorrow's task. He was sure he could. Despite his young looks he showed a maturity beyond his years. He liked the corporal, and would be pleased if one of his sons turned out like him frankly.

Besides which, he owed him his life.

*

Agnes Davison set off early to church. It was barely six am but she wanted to make sure the flowers were all in place and pruned before the first communion of the day. She carried a basket with her with various pruning tools in and her own personal bible she used for comfort. As she reached the gate she paused and waved at her husband who was ushering the last cows in for milking. It helped him to keep busy she knew. As he spotted her and waved back she glanced at the house. It seemed so dark and empty these days but at least Freddie was there. She didn't like leaving him like this but had left a note with some milk ready in the fridge if he woke, and Harold would look after him she was sure. They would come to church for the family service at ten, and then perhaps a walk afterwards she contemplated if the weather held.

She pushed the gate open and went through, but the sudden rumble from the coast made her pause and look up. She knew by now it was the guns from France. They had never heard the sea from here and she shivered at the fact that guns so far away reverberated here. *Just how big did they have to be to be heard in England?* she wondered, and felt anxious suddenly at the thought of her boys over there amongst them. The gate unchecked, slammed shut and she yelled involuntarily surprised by the loud crack. Harold ran out from the shed looking worried.

"You alright love?"

"Yes Hal. The gate slammed shut...made me jump...sorry. I'm fine."

He nodded and went back inside. She realised afterwards he had come out with the milking stool clutched in one hand, Sally appearing a second later, alerted by her master's unusual stance.

She wasn't fine but gathered herself once more and set off down Mill Road towards the High street. Davey Binstead came out of his end terrace house ahead of her and set off sack in hand towards the Mill. It was one of the few places that still had to be manned on a Sunday like their farm. As they passed, he tipped his cloth cap and smiled. He rarely spoke but she knew he was a good neighbour and his presence reassured her in the hushed dawn street, while the deadly thunder rumbled on in the distance. But the gate had spooked her and she couldn't quieten the voices in her head that warned her of trouble, the anxiety welling in her chest with every step.

Their Cockerel called out from somewhere on the still dark farm. Its dawn cries offering reassurance rather than irritation for once. Agnes paused and wondered about going back home and asking Harold to walk with her. At times like these she appreciated his strength and wanted those rugged arms about her. But then she remembered Freddie, and knew he couldn't be left alone, and told herself she was being silly. So she took out her bible and clutched it to her chest for comfort instead, and quickened her pace towards the sanctuary of the church.

*

Will, Ced, Franko and Ollie arrived ten minutes before the instructed time of 0600 at *La Gere* farm on the outskirts of Estaires. They had been up well before reveille at 0530, the mood and task ahead not lending to sleep anyway. They were dressed in their best uniform available and their rifles sparkled in the early glow of the day. Will looked at the pond where a number of different ducks swam quietly back and forth as if uncaring that a war raged all around them. He envied their simple daily existence in that moment, and his thoughts turned to home. One of the birds quacked an alarm and several small black ducklings emerged from the reeds and sped across the water to their anxious mother. As Will smiled, the sergeant major appeared and told them to follow him round to the back.

In the pale glow of morning the house loomed dark and foreboding as they circled it, but they went through a side arch into a walled rose garden, stocked with a variety of flowers some in the beds and others creeping freely across the walls. Will knew that in the glow of the sun the place would look completely different. *Were it not for the war…*

As they emerged through a crumbling brick arch on the other side the four men came up short and almost bumped into each other as they found themselves in a wide area around which a large number of men were assembling slowly to quiet calls from sergeants and corporals.

"Wait here," Russell said, and walked off to speak to his opposite number from the Hampshires who were there in strength. Will saw the men were now assembling into ranks forming three sides of a square around the outside wall of the rose garden. The four friends looked around bewildered and observed a number of the men formed up were looking at them despite now being at attention. Will noticed their sergeant major and another CSM from the Hampshires sharing a smoke together and they shook their heads as he watched.

Captain Wittering appeared, with the newly promoted Goodman, and the men were called up to attention, more show than anything as they were already standing still. Another officer had appeared from the Hampshires and they exchanged salutes and pointed at the four friends.

"Whatever they're selling I don't want it," Harris said in his strong local accent, and Ced nodded.

A cockerel cried out from a barn behind them.

"Bit bloody late rooster, we're all up mate," Franko muttered, and the friends laughed half heartedly.

Dunn appeared out of nowhere like a Pantomime villain from the wings of a theatre. "Have the men form up sergeant major. We haven't got all day. The captains are waiting."

"Sir."

Russell walked briefly over to the four men.

"Right lads. Well done for volunteering. Not an easy thing. Let's get set."

"No one's actually told us what's going on sergeant major," Ced replied looking genuinely concerned now.

CSM Russell stopped dead and spun round.

"You're kidding right?"

"No. Lieutenant Dunn just came over last night and told Will he needed him and he picked us to help." They both looked at Will, and

Will nodded. Russell surveyed the puzzled anxious faces of the four men and shook his head again.

"Unbelievable."

He looked over at Lieutenant Dunn with real anger and puffed out his cheeks.

"Ok. Gather round." The four men moved in.

"And it's Sir out here today Longworthy, not *Sergeant Major*. There are officers on parade."

Ced nodded.

"The findings of the inquiry yesterday have laid the blame on the Hampshires on the right breaking and running which caused the Germans to be able to get round us and pressure the whole line. Specifically the machine gun teams."

"But there was only about sixty of them and Lieutenant Dunn ordered them to pull back," Will said becoming agitated.

"Keep your voice down lad. I know what you said and what you thought you saw, but the fact of the matter is you manned the gun after they had gone which means they could have held the line. Or at least pulled back in a more disciplined way."

"We know what we saw sir," Ced added and Russell flashed him a look to watch his place.

"It was luck sir that I succeeded," Will continued, "and thanks to their own officer and Sergeant Albright."

"Maybe but we have to make an example here. HQ have put pressure on the major. We can't run in the face of the enemy. And you lad didn't run."

"We were all scared sir. Everybody ran in the end," Ced muttered.

"In the end. Sometimes you have to. But that as may be the findings of the inquiry are that the machine gunners ran away in the face of the enemy and are to be shot for cowardice."

"Shot?" Will said shocked by the comment.

"Yes by firing squad. You four to be precise."

"Jesus Christ," said Harris.

"Sergeant Major if you please. The sun will be above us before we get started and the first man is coming out now." Dunn's high pitched voice added to the tension and bewilderment of the men.

Will felt sick, and his head spun as the facts lodged themselves in his brain. He looked at his comrades standing staring about them.

"Don't worry Will, you weren't to know," said Franko who for once actually understood the seriousness of the moment.

"Line up boys, come on," Russell said in a calming tone. "Here." He held out four bullets. "Take these. Now listen to me. One of them is deliberately a blank. So one of you won't actually shoot the man. Understood? Believe that to be you and you will be fine."

He nodded to them and walked off now to meet the guard party as a Hampshire soldier was led out between two military policemen, blindfolded with his arms tied behind his back. He had clearly soiled himself and looked a pitiful sight.

"Dear God almighty," said Harris.

"Poor bastard," Ced added shaking his head and loading his gun.

"Ced this isn't right. You know this." Will pleaded.

"Load your gun lad. There's no getting out of this one. We can debate the moral overtures later but if we refuse, likes as not we will just end up joining him. You know Dunn would love to have us against that wall given half a chance."

The condemned man had collapsed to his knees now and was sobbing quietly. The MPs reluctant to lift him back up.

"Oh for heaven's sake sergeant major have a word. He's disgracing his regiment now as well as himself." Dunn's words rankled with many of the men standing in still lines about him and the captain noting the mood called out.

"Company Sergeant Major. Get a chair brought from the house at the double and let the man sit down. And untie his wrists. I don't think he poses a threat."

A solider was dispatched off and Dunn clearly looked irked at this show of mercy. He walked over to the four friends standing in a line and came up behind Davison.

"Have a good look what happens to cowards gentlemen. As you are supposedly the best shots in the battalion you better do your duty today. Make sure no one flinches corporal there's a good fellow, or I will hold you responsible."

He sneered and walked off to the side as a chair was brought hastily from the house. Either the ground was uneven or the legs of the chair were, for it lurched forward at a weird angle when placed down and the soldier sitting upon it nearly fell off. The captain nodded to Dunn and he spoke up loud enough for everyone to hear.

"Private Grenville Finch, D company 1st Battalion, Royal Hampshires. You are guilty of cowardice in the face of the enemy and are hereby sentenced to death. Carry on sergeant major."

"Firing party ready." The four men checked their guns and raised them.

"Any last words lad?" Russell said standing over the man.

He shook his head, the ragged blindfold flapping about adding to the tragedy of the scene, but as Russell stepped back Finch suddenly shouted out.

"I'm sorry lads. I'm sorry. God."

"Aim."

Will's hands were shaking and he was gripping the rifle tight to stop himself dropping it.

"Mum I'm sorry!"

"Fire!"

There was only one crack. The training and marksmanship of the men over and over making them fire as one and they instantly pulled down their rifles and stood ready. The sound seemed to echo into eternity and Will realised they were all panting. Clearly in the tension they had all been holding their breath just like him, and now their bodies tried to shake it out.

Dunn walked over to the slumped figure and took out his revolver, firing one shot directly into his head as per regulations, to ensure he was dead.

"Only shot that bastard's fired in anger," Harris said.

"How did we get into this?" Ced asked quietly. "It's enough we got our arses kicked in the woods, and now we are helping Jerry by shooting our own."

Will said nothing as they carried Finch away. He was staring at a single white rose that had made the long climb up the far wall to be rewarded with the first rays of sun every morning. As it stood proudly at the top he focused on the innocence and beauty of nature and not the scene in front of him. He didn't realise that Dunn had come up again.

"Pretty isn't it Davison." The voice made Will jump. "Perhaps you were looking at that and not at the man in front. One of you missed completely. There were only two shots in him, and as one bullet was blank that means one of you missed. No doubt on purpose. If there are not three holes in the next one you'll all answer for it."

"The next one sir?" Franko asked, confused by the whole series of events.

"Yes there were two gunners found guilty Private Idiot. Jobs only half done. Now reload." He looked at Will as he walked off and nodded at the rose swaying contently in the early morning breeze. "Perfect colour that. White for cowards."

The sergeant major came up and handed out four more bullets as the second man was brought out behind him. They noticed not only were his hands untied but he wasn't wearing a blindfold either.

"Ok lads. One each. Same as before. And don't miss. Any of you." He looked at them all in turn. "He's a dead man anyway, missing won't change that. Don't make it any harder than it needs to be."

"Captain Wittering sir." It was the military police sergeant that called out, standing to attention in front of the second man.

"Yes what is it sergeant?"

"Prisoner has asked for a last request sir."

"A last...extraordinary." Wittering was thrown by this temporarily and for a chance to compose himself looked over to the Hampshires where one of their captains stood behind his men. He was looking at the ground making circles in the dirt with his boot, trying very hard not to watch the scene in front. He clearly didn't agree with what was going on but was powerless to do anything about it up against HQ orders. Unable to catch his eye Wittering spoke up.

"What is the request sergeant?"

"Prisoner would like to be able to sing while he waits for the end sir. His words."

There was a stunned silence and then sporadic laughter broke out from the ranks of men behind Will and the others.

"Hope it's something bloody rude about officers," Franko whispered through gritted teeth and Harris also laughed.

"The prisoner? What a joke, he's one of ours isn't he," Ced commented.

"Silence." The voice of the sergeant major brought an instantaneous hush from the assembled men.

But the ducks, on edge from the previous rifle fire, broke at this parade ground blast and took to the air above the house from the pond, quacking loudly in protest as they did so. Some young soldier in the ranks laughed at this and Russell merely pointed to one of his sergeants to deal with it and Will heard the pacing stick hit home.

"Captain Jessop?" Wittering called out once more to his Hampshire counterpart, irritated by the delay.

Jessop looked up and simply nodded curtly and then went back to his fascination with the earth beneath his boot. Wittering raised his eyes at Goodman and looked back at the sergeant standing waiting for a reply.

George Grenville Wittering was born in a barrack block in India. He had soldiering in his blood and his father was a retired colonel of artillery, who disapproved of his son's decision to join a line regiment. But his father did at least understand it even if he was disappointed; telling George as he embarked for France that he himself had refused to join his own father's regiment of Hussars, declaring an undying mutual hatred of horses. George's mother had followed the drum from Catterick to Calcutta producing four boys and an ailing daughter along the way, the youngest son succumbing to dysentery in India.

But George was the opposite to his doomed sibling. Strong, tall and dashing, and to the elder family members a man who clearly inherited his grandfather's cavalry gene. He was brought up on tales of heroism, and despite a sharp mind at school, the thought of following his eldest brother into law was never an option. With his parent's links and a General's patronage, who held his mother in great affection, he had a commission at seventeen. He earned his second pip through hard work, and by the time war broke out he had earned a captaincy on merit, no longer needing to rely on anyone's support.

He was twenty four and did not tolerate fools gladly, and cowards even less. But while he was a career soldier and knew what to say and when to say it, he was not blind to the limitations of leadership amongst some of the upper classes, and promoted fair treatment of the men whenever he could. He could do without moments like this therefore and resolved to get it done as soon as possible. Aware all eyes were now on him, he rose to his full six foot four, and spoke in a clear voice.

"Very well sergeant. The prisoner may sing. Within reason. Does he want a blindfold?"

"No sir."

Will heard someone behind him say quietly "Go on Triffo, belt it out lad," but no rebuke came now from the officers or sergeants.

Dunn called out again now. "Lance Corporal Edmund Triffit. D company,1st Battalion, Royal Hampshires. You are guilty of cowardice in the face of the enemy and are hereby sentenced to death. Carry on sergeant major. Prisoner may now sing."

The last words were delivered sarcastically but as Triffit began to sing, Will spoke out loud.

"Oh Christ."

'Oh Mary this London's a wonderful sight
There's people here working by day and by night'

"What is it Will," Ced hissed, seeing his friend had lowered his rifle.

"I know him."

"What?"

'They don't sow potatoes nor barley nor wheat
There's gangs of them diggin' for gold in the street'

"He was our referee," Will stated, staring wildly at him.

"What? when?"

"At our cup final in June. Triffit was the ref and he whistled this song at the end. I remember it because it's my Dad's favourite."

Ced struggled to know what to say but was spared the task when the sergeant major strode over.

> 'At least when I asked them that's what I was told
> So I just took a hand at this digging for gold
> But for all that I found there I might as well be
> Where the Mountains of Mourne sweep down to the sea.'

Triffit's lilting baritone voice and perfect pitch had transfixed everyone in the scene initially and then Dunn realised nothing was happening.

"What's going on sergeant major? Get on with it."

Sensing something was wrong, Russell's years of thinking on his feet and army life kicked in.

"Weapon jam sir, won't be a moment."

> 'I believe that when writin' a wish you expressed
> As to how the fine ladies in London were dressed
> Well, if you believe me, when asked to a ball
> Faith, they don't wear no top to their dresses at all.'

"Right what the blazes is going on corporal. Make ready."

"I know him Sir. From back home. He's a referee."

Russell stared long and hard at the young boy. Perhaps this was a step too far too soon for him, but instinct told him shouting would do no good here.

> 'Oh, I've seen them myself and you could not in trath
> Say if they were bound for a ball or a bath!
> Don't be startin' them fashions now, Mary Macree,
> Where the mountains of Mourne sweep down to the sea.'

Russell looked now at the condemned man. The forty one year old former referee was in full voice. Although working in Sussex back home, Triffit had always been a Hampshire man born and bred, and answered the call with everyone else from his old town. It was evident the man was as popular a soldier as he was a referee. Russell knew inside this wasn't right but orders were orders and that was all there was to it.

"You know him lad?" he said almost tenderly to Will who nodded.

"Then the best thing you can do for him now is shoot straight and true."

Will looked at him and as Triffit continued a new verse, Russell nodded at him and made a show of cocking and uncocking his rifle a couple of times and then put the bullet back in. He shouted "Clear," so the officers could hear, and handed the rifle back.

There are beautiful girls here-Oh, never you mind
With beautiful shapes nature never designed
And lovely complexions all roses and cream
but O'Laughlin remarked with regard to the same'

Russell took a few steps back and Dunn gestured at him to get on with it, as Triffit in full flow spread his arms wide as if in a concert hall.

"Firing party ready."

That if at those roses you venture to sip
the colours might all come away on your lip'

"Aim."

'So I'll wait for the wild rose that's waiting for me
Where the...'

"Fire!"

The four men recovered their rifles as Dunn strode over to where Triffit had been flung back against the wall; a red stain splashing colour on its dust coated grey bricks, where he had slid down to the floor arms still spread wide. He had three bullet holes through his tunic, tight around his heart. As Dunn delivered the *coup de grâce* with a shot to the head, Will sang softly finishing his verse.

"Where the Mountains of Mourne sweep down to the sea..."

Chapter 27 - Déjà Vu

The soft early morning mist clung to the uneven ground in front of the main trench showing no sign of lifting despite the sun's presence. The ferocity of the latest dawn bombardment had done nothing to dispel it and it rested motionless now across No Man's Land. *Like a sheet over a corpse in a mortuary,* James thought. He moved along the trench, pausing every so often to check on the men. A shared joke here, a supportive word there. James Davison was a very popular officer with the men under his command, and they had all celebrated when he was recently promoted to First Lieutenant.

As he approached the next group of men they sprang to their feet, which despite him being the officer of the day was unusual. He normally told them to ignore such nonsense unless a more senior officer was with him. As his own reasoning became a conscious thought, it triggered a warning and he spun round to see another officer walking quickly to catch him up. He saluted and was pleased to see all his men do the same.

"At ease Gentlemen," Captain Johnson said, and then shook James' hand.

"Hard night last night," he continued more quietly, "Thought you'd appreciate the company lieutenant after all those shenanigans."

"Yes sir, thank you," James replied.

The 'shenanigans' that Harry referred to had been an unexpected night attack by the enemy after two days of hard shelling. Despite their well-entrenched positions it had been a close run thing for a time, and the battalion had suffered a large number of casualties. While many were only wounded and fatalities were mercifully few, it still led to a depletion of experienced men, who were moved away for treatment.

As they continued down the trench Harry noted the weary look on his friend's mud spattered face, and patted James on the back.

"Still alive old boy?"

James stopped and smiled at his dear friend and nodded as the emotion of the night's fighting caught up with him.

"Still alive Jonners."

They paused then by several men who had a casualty propped up against the trench wall. A coat had been laid over his head and James knelt down and gently pulled it back.

"Who is it?"

"Wadey sir. Company bugler. Died just a few minutes ago."

"Why wasn't he taken back with the rest?"

"Too bad to move the medics said. He knew he was done for. So stayed and had a smoke with us."

James glanced at his friend and then the men standing around. He recognised Wadey now. The green eyes, their cheeky sparkle gone, looked through him for answers.

"I'm sorry," he said replacing the coat, "he was a good man."

"Sir. Thank you sir."

James stood up. "Okay, you and you, move him down to the rear and then get yourselves back. There's a consignment of biscuits in from the boats. Chocolate covered I'm told, probably en route to the Mess. Grab a couple of crates on the way back, and share them out for the men. Mention my name."

"Yes sir." The men smiled, as did Harry seeing how easily his friend managed the troops.

"We'll need a new bugler too," Harry added as the two officers began to move on.

"Phipps has volunteered sir," one of the men replied.

"Phipps? Dear God. I'd rather have the shells wake me than his racket."

The men laughed at this and the trench returned to its daily routine.

"Stealing biscuits now James?" Harry asked as they walked on, stepping carefully round a break in the trench boards where the water lapped unabated.

"Resupplying the troops Jonners. Since I got promoted my admin tasks have gone through the roof and it seems I'm in charge of tea and biscuits now too! So I'm making quite sure our company gets first dibs."

"Quite right too."

Harry paused then and took him over to a quiet part of the trench. They both automatically checked the trench lip was above their heads, fearing the sniper's spectre that hung over them twenty four hours a day if they stood still for more than a few moments.

"Speaking of admin, did you see the latest batch of reports that came through yesterday?"

"No. I was going to read them last night Jonners and then Jerry turned up uninvited."

"Quite. Probably heard about your biscuits." As James smiled Harry took a breath and continued. "Anyway the latest reports included something from further down the line at Estaires. Says the Sussex got quite a pasting."

James' eyes searched his friend's now fearing the worst.

"It's okay," Harry continued quickly, understanding the instant anxiety of his friend. "I've seen the lists. He's not on them. Quite a to-do though and some poor buggers from the Hampshires were shot for cowardice apparently for legging it during the battle."

James raised his eyes at this but wasn't really focusing. He was simply thinking about Will and whether he was alright. Sometimes the lists were wrong and sometimes men went missing and weren't listed for days.

Harry read his mind. "Listen, we are out of here in a few days for a spot of downtime. Shall I get us a car?"

James smiled warmly. "That would be much appreciated Jonners."

*

Will and Ced were walking at the front of their company along a main road they were told was the *Rue du Grand Chemin*. It had rained hard once more through the night and though the air was clear now as they tramped uphill the water poured down the road unabated, having come down too hard and too fast to be absorbed by the fields round about. Despite being a main road, the surface was cracked and worn in many places and it made the going harder than normal. As they pushed on trying to keep to the middle to avoid the gushing currents at each side, a motorbike came into view and quickly bore down on them. Anything unexpected triggered a nervous reaction in the men and several cocked their rifles and took aim before a sergeant near the front shouted he was a British dispatch rider and to stand down.

Sergeant Davis was new to the battalion and had been drafted in as a replacement for the fallen Sergeant Albright but as yet no one knew a lot about him. His orders were added to almost immediately by Captain Wittering telling the men to make way and get off the road, and with slow begrudging steps the men parted into the fields on either side.

The bike sped past, spraying water and smoke equally at the men on both sides as it went through, the rider staring straight ahead through goggled eyes unrecognisable save for his cap badge marking him out as part of the Logistics Corp. He had a scarf wrapped round the lower part of his face and a long coat with the collar pulled up against the elements that obscured pretty much all the rest of him. Thick gloves struggled to maintain the bike's forward momentum as the wheels continually lost their grip on the flooded broken tarmac, and the knee high boots could be seen working furiously to balance and steer the bike as it swayed back and forth.

As the bike passed Franko the rear wheel slipped sideways once more and showered him with grit and dank cold water that made several of his comrades roar with laughing. The rider put his right leg down to correct the motion and pushed off again, revving the engine just in time to drown out the string of profanities that came forth from Franko to send him on his way. Will and Ced watched him go, the line of men jeering and waving two fingered salutes at him as he passed each section in turn; and then the sergeant called them all to form up again with a nod from the Captain, and the excitement passed.

They started to walk first up the field edge, reluctant to return to the broken streams of the main road, but here the clay earth saturated by the rain clung to their boots like beggars, tugging hard at the heels with every step. When Ced almost lost a boot after barely a dozen strides he muttered, "Bugger this for a lark," and strode back across to the road where the majority of the men were now ambling forward. At which point the voice of Sergeant Major Russell came forth from almost the rear of the column, but with such volume and force that the whole line of men jumped as one; and dozens of rabbits enjoying an early morning graze after the overnight storm, scattered back to the safety of their holes, many of the men wishing enviously they could join them.

"Where the bloody hell do you lot think you are? Hyde bleedin' Park? You look like a load of French gypsies you useless lumps of lard. Sort those lines out now and dress off by fours, or so help me you'll be running the rest of the way!"

Within moments and with some quiet moaning the men fell back into a marching pattern and continued on, splashing through the water, as the sun finally came out in full.

Eventually they came off the road near a small village called Richebourg, as the front lines were far from straight forward here. They skirted the village without entering it and headed back up familiar paths towards their old base camp behind Neuve-Chappelle once more. May was in full bloom here, the trees thick with their bright green foliage, mocking their neighbours that stood blackened and bare only a mile or so to the east. Here in parts the land still remained untouched by the devastation of the war which made the contrast more startling, the colours more vivid, and reminded the Sussex men of their fields back home. The sun bathed the marching men in its warm delights and they sang heartily as their boots stomped out the rhythm driving them on. To the occasional French passerby who paused to observe the lines of men moving through their countryside, these men appeared without a care in the world, their songs masking the memories of recent weeks.

As they entered the camp from the north road the men had mixed feelings however and the songs drifted away behind them. The comfort of being back somewhere that they knew was tempered by the memories of those first skirmishes with the enemy, and of the losses of friends and comrades. For Will and Ced at the front, they were particularly hesitant about approaching the base, and Will felt that had it not been for the lines of men behind them pushing him forward he may have stopped altogether. He still felt awful about leaving Albert in the makeshift graveyard and the friends had vowed to go back one day if they survived and ensure he had a proper gravestone. The events in the woods and the subsequent horror of the firing squad however, made them all glad to be away from that cursed place.

As the men marched silently into the camp they could not escape the ghosts that came back to haunt them now. Will thought of Ernie fastidiously sorting his kit out for inspection back in training camp and how smart he always looked. He then recalled the ragged filthy man that had been found fishing by a river near here some weeks later, and despaired at what the war did to men and boys alike. Worse were the memories of Archie that lingered everywhere. Will could hear the echoes of his voice booming off every building from the mess hall to the billets, that seemed to penetrate the rhythmic stamping of their boots. He missed him now more than ever and his mood worsened.

As they passed the hospital area, the smiling figure of Teresa came out of the tents talking to a doctor and saw the men marching past. Spotting the unmistakable figure of Will leading the Sussex companies marching in, she could not stop herself from waving. In that moment the dark spell was broken and Will gave a furtive nod in return and could not believe he had forgotten about Teresa. Several of the other men had seen the pretty nurse wave, and cat calls and comments rebounded through the forward lines until a Sergeant called for quiet.

As they approached their old billets Franko suddenly spoke out from a couple of rows back. "You know this is like that feeling you get. What do they call it?"

"Déjà Vu," Ced replied automatically.

"Huh. What?" Franko continued, not understanding the French phrase at all. "No really there's a name for something when it feels like you've been there before."

"Déjà vu!" Ced stated again, the frustration evident in his voice at his friend's ignorance.

"What does that mean?" Will asked him quietly at the front.

"I don't know the exact meaning but it's basically when you have a feeling that you have seen something or been to a place before even though you haven't. I know it's not quite the same in this case as this is our old base but we're all feeling it. People say if you experience it you can predict what's going to happen next, apparently."

"Oh right," Will replied, then thinking about what happened here before muttered, "God I hope not!"

"Days are blue...," Franko continued pondering the words from Ced, having heard him incorrectly as ever. "Well they might be, but there is definitely a phrase for what I am feeling and it definitely feels like we have been here before!"

"That's because we have been here before you clot," Harris said and all the men laughed at this, their spirits lifted once more.

Chapter 28 – Run like the wind

Two weeks had passed since the men of the Royal Sussex had returned to their old base near Neuve-Chappelle. It had been a good time for the men to catch up on news from home and refresh their uniforms and kit, while the regiment was resupplied. Each company had a couple of days at the front line by rotation but the time passed with very little incident, which came as a blessing to many of them.

For Will it had been an enjoyable break from the intense stress and pressures of the previous months. The almost boring monotony of army camp life was a soothing remedy to his troubled mind. He had received letters from home as they all had, and a food parcel from Agnes, which for once he enjoyed almost all to himself, bar the chocolate he shared with Ced. He had been delighted to get updates on a number of his friends from the football team as well via David, who had written to their mum from the training camp, and she had forwarded it on to him.

He smiled thinking about those days back in training despite it seeming a life time ago now. He was jealous in a way of how relaxed and safe that time now seemed, though in the moment it had felt so pressured. Hearing about his old friends made Will think about football once more. It had been ages since he had last kicked a ball... *Christmas day!* He resolved to find one soon and change that.

Above all else the time in camp had allowed him to see Teresa again and without his previous guilt about Alice they had grown closer. Will felt a lot more relaxed and comfortable in her presence now. He wasn't sure if it was because he no longer felt the pull to Alice, or just that he had changed since they last met. *Perhaps both,* he mused as he told her everything that had gone on since they left the base, and also on the news from home. She had been sympathetic and caring, knowing when to speak and when to listen, as befitted

276

her status as a senior nurse. But also because it was in her nature to care, and despite being older than Will she was clearly fond of him.

She was more forthright in her opinions about Alice, as only a woman can be, but was sensitive enough to realise that he was not over her entirely yet and did not go overboard in her comments, instead blaming the war for so many sad occurrences and untold pressures. Will often drifted in and out of the conversation, either lost in the daydream swirls of steam rising from his freshly poured tea, or just staring at her red lips as they formed soundless shapes as she spoke. Occasionally she realised this and stopped and he became aware he'd missed a question or had just let the delicious sounds of her voice wash over him and caress his ears. But she never got angry with him, and just smiled or pulled him back to the real world with a teasing rebuke to continue their chats.

Staff Sergeant Teresa Halliday had learnt to adapt in this very masculine world in which she worked. She was strong enough to stand the jibes from the men and the demeaning comments from many of the senior officers, and still perform her tasks to a high standard. Will wondered if the bright lipstick hid the pain that came from some of the things she had to put up with, but it never showed externally, and if anyone did go too far she dealt with it. A firm but polite rebuff to an over amorous patient when needed. A strong word to a junior rank who forgot their place and didn't believe female soldiers had any clout. And for the senior officers who dismissed her opinions, a respectful reminder of her training and that she had earned the right to be there. If all else failed she pointed out that one day they may find themselves needing her to save their lives, and they wouldn't want her holding a grudge. It was a sobering riposte and usually did the trick.

As the days passed Will grew bold enough to ask her if she had anyone waiting back home or indeed a boyfriend here. She had laughed at the suggestion, saying she barely even had time to chat to him over a cup of tea let alone have any meaningful relationship. Then after some reflection had added that there had been a man back home at one time, but that when her training had got intense the shift work had not suited them. She alluded to the fact he was a drinker and that eventually they had just drifted apart and the war had at least given her the opportunity for a fresh start.

The days had passed with snatched conversations like this, sometimes longer when their duties allowed and on one occasion they had even managed to have a short stroll away from the hustle and bustle of the camp and the hundreds of prying eyes, though none of Will's friends begrudged him his new acquaintance. Teresa was very tactile often touching his knee as they sat talking as she made a point, or taking his arm when they walked but it never went beyond that. Will thought that on more than one occasion she was willing to kiss him, perhaps expecting it; but he was unable to find the courage that had served him so well in the recent battle, or that walked in his shadow when he went out at night on patrol. With Alice it had been so instantaneous, swept up in the emotion of the moment at the station and driven by her, so that he had not had time to think. Now he had a lot of time to mull things over and the more he thought the less bold he felt.

So the moments passed and as each one did it became more awkward for him to ask her. If it bothered Teresa she didn't show it. They continued to laugh and chat about things at home and their likes and dislikes, amidst the continual dark backdrop of the war. Sometimes he felt a pang of jealousy when she chatted and flirted with the injured men in the tents, but he knew it was just her manner, and her attempts to distract them from their awful wounds.

During one visit towards the end of his second week at camp, Will shared some chocolate with her.

"Well here's an occasion and no mistake. I must be a good friend if you are sharing your chocolate with me!"

"Yes but don't expect me to make a habit of it," he teased in reply.

"Don't worry I won't. It's probably just a bribe to get you a clean bed when you are shot anyway," she replied and they laughed again.

Teresa kissed him on the top of the head suddenly. It was the one solitary occasion she broke through the barriers, but before he could react she pushed him out of the tent.

"Takes a lot more than a few bites of chocolate to get round me corporal," she called after him and vanished back inside.

The orange glow of twilight accentuated the dark outlines of trees and buildings on the horizon as Will walked back from the hospital area. The colours were so striking and the shapes so sharp against the skyline, that Will thought it would be an artist's dream to paint such a scene, were it indeed safe to sit there and do so. Regardless there was a warmth to the evening that reflected the glow in his heart. As he floated back across camp smiling as broadly as the Cheshire Cat from 'Alice in Wonderland', Ced walked up to his grinning friend and informed the smitten Corporal formally with a salute that they were moving up to the front once more in the morning, for their next rotation.

"Won't do you any harm to spend a bit of time with your mates either," he added informally ensuring no one was watching. "There is a war on after all Romeo!"

*

The damp clung to Will's back like a child refusing to be put down, and he struggled to remember any sustained period of warmth since they had come to France.

"The weather can be a fickle friend at the best of times lads," Harold would often tell his boys as they worked with him on the farm. "Ask any farmer, it's the one thing we can't control. In the gloom of winter a sudden glorious sunny day can seduce the mind into thinking that summer has returned, and swarms of flies will appear to torment man and beast alike long after they are thought gone."

His dad's words echoed off the dug outs as Will and his friends lamented the freezing start to this June day that forecast another period of gloom and murk; the early morning fog skulking around the derelict landscape in front of them unchallenged by sun or warmth.

Their old trenches had been significantly improved since they were last in them, with larger, deeper dugouts and more permanent boardwalks and emplacements. While they appreciated the improvement in their temporary living quarters, the reason was not lost on them that this war was not going to be over anytime soon. Defences were being prepared for the long haul, and not to be fluid lines of advancement as was initially envisaged last year.

Will oversaw a section of the trench now with a dozen men under his care across five dugouts so that a couple of them had three men in, and the rest with only two occupants got stacked up with spare ammunition and supplies. Will had Franko with him and Harris. He had wanted Ced but chose instead to use his calm head with the other three-man dugout where the least experienced men were stationed, one of whom – Private Castle – had only come out in the New Year with the replacements. Most corporals and sergeants would have picked a roomier dugout for themselves, but it was testament to Will's nature that he "didn't ask the lads to do anything he wouldn't do himself," and so squashed in with his two friends.

He didn't anticipate being in the dugout that much anyway and sure enough, once the sergeants had been round passing out duties, Lieutenant Dunn appeared to further increase his load.

"Ah Davison. Thought I would find you loitering along here somewhere."

"Good morning Sir," Will replied as cheerily as he could muster, used to the sarcastic tone now.

"You've had your orders from the captain I trust?"

"Yes sir, the sergeants have been round. The men are all briefed."

"Good-O," Dunn continued sniffing the air dismissively. "Well see that you keep this area clear and your men sharp Davison. I am sure I don't need to remind you what happens to shirkers anymore do I corporal?"

"No sir," Will answered, the memory of Edward Triffit singing as he was shot returning to his mind once more, as it did regularly when he slept now. Two nights ago he had dreamt he saw Triffit in his referee's kit ,and the boys lining up to take penalties suddenly turned and shot him. He had awoken with a shout apparently but none of his friends had mentioned it, and when Castle tried to say something Franko loomed over his bunk and advised him it would be in his best interests to go back to sleep.

"Right well I'm off to the officer's dugout. But don't think I won't be watching what's going on."

There were terse salutes and Ced came out to add his formal greeting, and the men watched Dunn slope off whistling down the line. Ced ambled over cigarette in hand.

"Did our illustrious leader Sir Dunn-g heap have any stirring words for us on this fine summer day?" he asked, his play on the officer's name bringing smiles from his comrades.

"Yes to mind how we go." The men round about laughed at this. "Oh, and that he will be watching us," Will added.

"Bloody good these officers. Able to watch us from the insides of a deep dugout," his friend replied.

"How do we mind how we go corporal?" Castle asked, coughing as the fog got into his lungs.

"Strewth. God help us lad," Ced continued. "Don't be thinking too much will you, you're liable to cut yourself with sharp observations like that."

"Speaking of sharp observations, the sergeant major is inbound, so we best look lively," Harris said suddenly, and the experienced men scattered to previously assigned tasks.

Ced grabbed Castle and dragged him back to their dugout. "Best get the duster out and get busy cleaning son, and if you ask me where the duster is so help me I'll save Jerry a job and shoot you myself."

Castle opened his mouth to speak and then thought better of it and sat down to check his rifle. As Russell moved up the trench he saw the familiar blond framed face of Will and smiled.

"All quiet corporal?"

"Yes sergeant major, though it would be easier if the fog lifted a bit."

"Yes indeed. Too quiet for me. Keep the lads alert won't you."

Will nodded as Russell looked around, his expert eyes checking all was in order.

"Have you seen the lieutenant this morning?"

"Yes sergeant major. He was here just a couple of minutes ago. He's gone on to the officer's dugout."

"Has he. Well I better go and find him. We've got some new orders through so we've got a busy night ahead."

Will went to question what they were when Russell suddenly stopped and put up his hand for quiet.

"Silence men."

He leant against the wall of the trench and listened, frowning. Russell's unquestioned experience and nose for trouble made all the men instantly alert, the anxiety in the newer members palpable. Will strained to hear, his body tensed in anticipation of action immediately. Ced came out and stood very still, head down and cocked to one side as if to improve his hearing. Then all at once through the fog the dreaded sound was apparent to most of them at once, and as the screaming nerve-wrecking whines grew louder, Russell shouted at the top of his voice.

"Incoming! Get to cover!"

The men scattered into their holes as the first shells landed. Some soldiers just dropped where they were, choosing to play the percentages of being flat and in the open but a smaller target, than running back to their dugouts where the dreaded shrapnel could catch them. After the first salvos landed however and nothing hit the trench, they all went to ground.

Will sat listening to the 'crump, crump, crump,' as the shells landed nearby, waiting for them to get closer, to land amongst them. He noticed that Franko was shaking despite his huge bulk and knew he should think of something calming to say.

"Look on the bright side lads. While they are shelling us their troops can't attack. Even Jerry's not that stupid." His friends nodded without looking too reassured. "Unless they have the equivalent of Castle in charge in which case they might rush us at any minute." This made them smile at least but then all they could do was sit it out. The bombardment was unusual though, both in the fact it was short lived and more so because none of the shells appeared to come anywhere near them. Within moments of the last explosion dying away, Russell was out of his temporary hole and up to the lip of the trench listening.

"That's it boys. Up and out. Infantry will be using the fog to get up close. Get on the trench guns and prepare." The well drilled men poured out of their holes knowing that seconds were vital now. The machine gunners took up their deadly posts and everywhere there was the sound of rifles being loaded and checked. Captain Wittering appeared further down the line and propelled Dunn forward towards them while he went the other way barking orders. Anticipating what was to come, Russell shouted out.

"Company will fix bayonets. Fix…Bayonets!"

The men responded as on the training ground and dozens of the sharpened knives clicked into place on their rifle hosts.

The thought of hand to hand fighting drew mixed emotions from the men awaiting the grim task ahead. Some men were muttering prayers and others stood silently chewing or with heads bowed waiting for the orders. The machine gunners swept their weapons back and forth looking for the first apparitions to appear from the morning shroud. Castle threw up violently just as Dunn ran up pistol in hand, bent double despite being under the lip of the trench. He was lucky he missed the lieutenant by inches as he continued to be sick, though Ced raised an eye at Will as if to say "Pity."

"Get ready sergeant major," Dunn said, trying to sound authoritive, which was a completely redundant order, as the men stood poised on the firing steps in the trench in both directions already. Russell went through the motions though and made a show of checking and encouraging the men once more.

"I don't like it Sir," he commented, "shells have all fallen short and there's no sound of any movement. No whistles, bugles or bells from the Jerry lines."

"Poor shooting is all I say, though the captain thought it might be a creeping barrage at first."

If that was the case they would still be firing as their troops came forward surely? Will thought to himself, and he could see the sergeant major didn't agree either.

"Something's not right sir," Russell said continuing to strain his senses out over No Man's Land.

"Nonsense. Either they have lost their nerve or it was just another nuisance shelling and in the fog they have lost their markers." He looked around and stood up properly now. "Good practice for the men though what?"

Russell wasn't listening now and had gone over to the nearest machine gun team, raised above them in a strong fortified emplacement.

"See anything at all?"

"No sir. Not a thing."

Russell began to think Dunn might be right for once but as he went to walk back one of the team said.

"That's odd."

"What is it private?"

"The fog sergeant major. It's changed colour."

"Changed colour? What the hell are you talking about? Move over." He climbed up next to the gun team and looked out. He was going to reach for his scope, but he didn't have to. The wind was blowing directly towards them now and had increased in its strength, and was shoving the fog along with it. *Odd,* he thought to himself, *fog would normally disperse this way and that in a strong wind. But this is concentrated.* His mind worked through the scenario in front of him. *Shell smoke. Yes, thick smoke that's it. But that would dissipate too surely? And the lad's right it is an unusual colour. Yellowy green…*

He froze, as the enormity of what he was seeing for the first time dawned on him with a sick realisation. Then struggling to control his own unexpected panic he cried out.

"Gas! It's gas. Masks on!"

The trench descended into chaos as men searched around frantically for their recently acquired gas masks. One of the machine gunners grabbed Russell by the arm causing him to spin round angrily.

"What do you think…"

"I haven't got a mask sergeant major!"

"What do you mean no mask, private?"

"I wasn't issued with one yet sir."

"Not issued…?"

Russell looked stunned. The main gunner turned round and looked at him.

"It's true sergeant major."

"I don't understand." Russell looked frantically up and down the trench, and could see from the reactions that this was widespread as men started to panic and shout, some fighting over masks. He looked back at Stevens on the gun.

"They said it was one between two for now sir," Stevens said reading the disbelief on Russell's face. "They said those on duty could use them, and then swap with the next lot when they changed over. Not enough to go round."

"Not enough to go round?" Russell's anger was matched only by his shock and the fact this was rapidly turning into a disaster. "Why wasn't I told?"

Stevens shook his head and then the trembling gunner with him piped up. "Lieutenant Dunn knew sir. He was there when the RQMS dished out the stores. I was on kit duty."

Russell had to compose himself. His years of solid soldiering had never been more tested than in this moment. He took a moment to take stock of the situation and then saw Dunn coming up the trench towards him shouting at the men.

"Here, take mine lad," and he pulled the mask from the pack on his back and gave it to him. "Machine guns have to keep firing."

"But what about you sergeant major?"

"I'll be all right sonny, you just watch your front."

"Sergeant Major Russell. What's going on? Did you shout gas?"

"Yes sir coming right for us about three hundred yards out, and with this wind it will be here shortly."

"Rubbish man, shell smoke is all. You've caused chaos in the trench and Jerry's likely to attack at any moment."

"That's right sir but I've seen a lot of smoke in my time but never thick green or yellow. That's exactly how the Frenchies described it when they were hit in April. Whole regiments of French and African troops overrun."

"Oh tosh and nonsense. All bloody cowards the colonials we know that. Let me look. Probably wasn't anything as bad as they made out…"

Dunn looked through his binoculars but didn't need to, as the wind was whipping the deadly smoke towards them rapidly. For all his bravado he could see this wasn't ordinary smoke and the colour drained from his face.

"Did you know we don't have enough masks for the men?"

"What? Yes of course. Not enough supplies. We can make do."

"Make do sir? That's gas out there not rain. We can't share masks."

"Well get half the men in masks to man the trench and the rest can shelter in the dugouts and switch over if the men wearing them get hit. Anyone gets shot they can just grab a mask and keep firing. In the meantime just cover their faces with cloths or something. Yes that's it. Give the order."

"The men can't hide from this sir, it will kill or maim. We could lose half the battalion. And what if the men are only wounded and not killed, we can't pull their masks off."

"Oh don't talk rubbish man. You're panicking unnecessarily." Dunn then suddenly realised his own mask was back in the officer's dugout. "My mask! Right take over sergeant major you have your orders. I need my mask if I am to lead the men."

Russell watched him run off and knew he had to do something. Fast. He was scared but aware that dozens of sets of fearful eyes were now looking to him for comfort.

"Right listen to me. Those with masks, get them on. Stand to and look to your fronts." He pulled his own scarf out from his backpack dropping the pack on the ground as he did so. It would be no good to him soon. "Those without masks help the others, and then tie anything round your mouths for now while I figure something out."

He tied his own scarf round his mouth to show them he also didn't have a mask, and then spotting Captain Wittering further up the line caught up in the chaos of the trench, he set off after the shrinking figure of Lieutenant Dunn.

*

"Captain Wittering. Captain Wittering sir."

"Sergeant Major. What the devil is going on? Men are shouting about gas but there's no sign of the enemy. Where's Lieutenant Dunn?"

"Gone for his mask sir. Jerry's launched a gas attack. We have to move."

"Move? Move where?"

"Back sir, to the reserve trench. We haven't enough masks for the men and they are going to be wiped out if we don't. I've passed word for all the machine gun teams to have masks to cover our retreat."

"But that will leave our front line undefended. They can just walk right in."

"We can worry about that later sir but if we don't pull the companies back, right now, we won't have anyone left to hold the sector let alone this trench. You know what happened to the French in April."

Wittering pondered the consequences of surrendering the trench potentially without firing a shot, but he could see the gas was less than fifty yards from them now; and as if to undermine their desperate situation, the sound of whistles being blown from the German trench carried to them on the same treacherous breeze.

"Jerry's on the move sir."

"Right. Orderly get on the phone to HQ. Tell them we are under gas attack and the battalion is pulling back to the second trench. Ask them for covering artillery fire as the Germans are advancing. Go! Sergeant Major, get the men without masks out of here now down the communication trenches. The remainder to hold the line and give cover until the shelling starts."

"Sir. Sergeants to me!" Russell immediately started the flow of information up and down the trench and the men, reassured by decisive commands, snapped into action.

The orderly reappeared from the dugout. "Can't get through sir. Line's dead."

"Blast! Sergeant Major!"

"Sir."

"Line's down. We'll need to send a runner back to the reserve trench and see if they can contact HQ and the artillery boys. Failing that he'll have to run all the way back to the guns himself and tell them. Chances are we may be pulling back further as it is. We need someone that can run that far and fast. "

"Understood sir. I have someone in mind."

As he turned to go Wittering took his arm.

"You don't have a mask sergeant major. Get yourself back with the first wave and organize things in the reserve trench. I want someone there I can rely on anyway." The captain pulled on his mask and, with a distorted voice, now continued. "I'll hold here and as soon as I think you have had enough time we will come back. Anyone back there without masks move them out too. Understood?"

"Yes sir."

Russell didn't like this form of warfare and the sight of the men in their head gear made the whole thing even more macabre like some hideous fancy dress ball. Except that Death was about to crash the party. He turned to Bateman, the orderly standing nearby looking grotesque in his own mask.

"Right private, shift yourself down the line and find a Corporal Davison. Fastest man in 'A' company if not the battalion. Tell him what the captain has said. Tell him that I said our lives depend on it."

"Yes Sir."

"Oh, and orderly."

"Sergeant Major?"

"Tell him to run like the wind."

Chapter 29 – Personal Best

Sergeant Campbell watched the recruits go over the assault course at Woking Camp for the second time during this training period. Although they were used to the obstacles now, the addition of the logs he had given them to carry in their teams of four had really slowed them down. Some of the groups were struggling to even get the logs over the obstacles and were spread out over the course, while the rest were arguing amongst themselves about how to tackle each one. He smiled how something so simple as a piece of wood could affect the ability of even the fittest men to carry out tasks. These Southdown Battalions may all be willing volunteers but he needed these men to be able to tackle anything thrown at them; to work together to achieve their objectives, and to be stronger and fitter than the enemy. He clearly had his work cut out ahead of him!

One team however was flying round. Led by a brown haired lad who was not only strong but clearly leading the group, they were working together like clockwork and were some three obstacles ahead of anyone else.

The leading group approached the final obstacle – two sets of triangular poles forty feet apart set in the ground like inverted 'Vs'. There were wooden steps at intervals between the sides of the poles going to the top where a small platform allowed the men to pause. Here two taut parallel ropes were stretched over a tank of freezing cold water to another platform on the other side. The water tank was the final little present from the training team, should anyone not have the strength to get across. If any one of them fell into the water the whole lot had to go back to the bottom of the steps and start again.

As Campbell watched, the lead team lifted the log up the wooden steps, working in pairs on each step; passing and lifting, passing and lifting. They worked mechanically up to the top, and then they adjusted the log onto the ropes.

One of the men looked back at the trailing pack and said, "Right lads it's now or never, let's finish this."

Their brown haired leader shouted in support: "Yes come on. One last push!"

Two of the men swung across the ropes to receive the log at the far end. The other two then simply rolled it across lengthways and swung behind it nudging the heavy log along. As they reached the end they hefted the large piece of wood down the steps to the ground where they lined it up, and then hauled it onto their shoulders in one swift movement. Campbell admired how easy they made the task seem as the group broke into a final run, breathing hard as they pushed on to the finish line and collapsed finally on the ground next to the sergeant.

Campbell looked at his watch. He raised his eyes. A new course record. Over a minute and a half off the previous best time. He looked again now at the brown haired lad who had led this team with such ease, clearly respected by his peers and trusted to get them round. The group smiled at each other with unmistaken pride looking at their comrades still struggling across the course behind them.

"Okay on your feet you four. Get some water down you. It's Davison isn't it?" Campbell said to the leader of the group.

"Yes sergeant," he replied straightening up, his breath still coming in gasps.

"Any relation to a Will Davison we had through here last year?"

David nodded. "I'm his older brother, sergeant."

"Is that right. Interesting family," he mused, and was about to say something else when a cry of "Look out!" followed by a loud splash and even louder curses, made them all turn round. One of the teams dropped the log into the final pool, taking three of their number with it. The last man hung helplessly upside down by his legs on the ropes, until the strength failed at last and he too fell headfirst onto the thrashing group below.

"God help me," Campbell mumbled then turned to face David. "Well Davison, I am sure you will be pleased to know you just shaved nearly two minutes off the previous course record." As the men

290

cheered and slapped each other on the back, he added "Which was held by none other than your illustrious brother."

David smiled with glee now and couldn't wait to write to him and tell him.

"Thank you sergeant," he said.

Danny Boyd grabbed him by the shoulders and said, "Bragging rights down the Star Inn for sure now! That was a great team effort boys."

"All right you four away to the barracks and get cleaned up. You have the honour of no duties tonight as you won, and bragging rights in the mess hall too no doubt never mind the pub back home. One of the other groups will take your log away. Now I better go before they all drown themselves."

As he watched the four men jog off Campbell couldn't help but smile at the lad. "Give me a regiment of Davisons," he said to himself, "and I could shorten this war for sure." Then he strode off towards the obstacle course once more.

Owen Entwhistle had just broken the surface of the water for a second time struggling to get a grip on the side to clamber out. His bright ginger hair floating on the surface in stark contrast to the dank dirty water round about it.

"Right you bloody useless bunch," Campbell roared, "Stop swinging about like a load of drunken orangutans and get those logs moving!"

*

Will was still trying to calm the new men down when the orderly arrived panting in his gas mask. The wheezing sounds reminded Will of the pigs back home on the nearby Tulip farm, rather than any human occupant. Thanks to Ced's new friendship with the quartermaster they had managed to acquire additional masks and all but two of their section had them on. Will insisted that Castle have his mask and Ced had then given his away too, and they were arguing about this when the orderly pitched up and conveyed the message from the sergeant major.

291

"That settles it then. Ced you go back with the men here that don't have masks. Get 'em organised. Get going."

"Sod that, if you're duty runner someone needs to stay and organise things."

"Longworthy. You heard the whistles. No time to debate. That's an order. You get going, right now! Franko?"

"Corp?"

"Get masks off the new boys and send 'em back. Hand them out to the experienced lads anywhere you can. And tell Sergeant Davis what's occurring and that I'm off back on the captain's orders, as the phones are down."

Will saw the orderly was still here.

"Ok you delivered your message. Hop off back to your own section Private."

As the soldier ran off Ced moved in close to Will to protest, so as not to be overheard.

"I can grab one of the masks off the new lads and stay Will."

Will paused in the midst of dropping off anything from his webbing he didn't need. "No," he said firmly. Then grabbing his friend by the shoulder added, "I want you back there Ced. Out of it."

With that he turned and pushed his way down the line to the first communication trench where men were already starting to file away. As he did so the shelling recommenced in support of the German advance and this time the shooting was spot on. Shells landed all around the British front line trench and began to pepper the area between that line and the reserve trench. They had learned no doubt from earlier gas attacks that the effects would force men back, force them to flee, and they were wasting no time in hampering their efforts.

As Will moved painfully slowly down the crowded trench that zig zagged away from the front, a shell exploded directly in front of him no more than twenty yards away. There were screams and one soldier was blown right out of the trench.

He stopped momentarily, crouched low, his hands on his helmet pulling it down on his head anticipating the shrapnel. But none came, and then he was up and moving again before the smoke had even cleared. The voice of his old training sergeant came to him then. "Safest place to be after a shell lands is right where it just landed. They hardly ever hit the same place twice so if you're caught in a barrage follow the bursts," Campbell had said. "Of course if you do get blown up in the same spot don't blame me," he had added with that cheeky lopsided smile of his.

Will used this information to drive him on. However a few yards ahead part of the trench had collapsed and he could see the burnt remains of an arm protruding from the earth. He stepped round it, blanking the image. Another soldier lay shaking on the ground and as one of his comrades ran to him, Will saw the man's left leg was missing. He shuddered and instinctively went to help. Then paused, remembering his instructions - the words from the sergeant major coming back to him as the smoke cleared from the blocked trench...

It was vital he got back. Their lives depended on him. Don't stop for anything. And run like the wind.

Will weighed up his options. He'd lost vital seconds already. It was chaos here and to go back to the front line and try a different communications trench would take too long with everyone coming this way. Not to mention the gas. He had no choice but to climb out and risk the open ground. As he scrambled up the collapsed earth, with the sounds of groaning men all around him, the shells came screaming in again swooping down like birds of prey to pick off the easy targets below.

Will could see the reserve trench some two hundred yards away and his mind was a myriad of thoughts. *A straight sprint. What would that take him? What was his personal best at school? Twenty five/twenty six seconds? But he was much younger then. He could go faster now. Yes, but not in boots and weighted down with kit. Oh to hell with it!*

He crouched down feeling for the spring in his legs as another shell landed nearby, earth spinning high into the ground. He ground his boots into the broken earth for grip surveying the scene in front. The shells were coming down unrelenting now without any pattern. It looked a suicidal run and he closed his eyes for courage. In that moment he was back on the grassy track in Steyning school. The children all shouting and waving flags lined either side of the track.

Mr Moore the PE teacher, in his old bulging football kit, pushed his wavy black hair away from his face and raised his arm.

"On your marks boys…"

The whistle raised to his lips.

"Get set…"

"Go!"

Will was off like lightning. Anticipating the whistle as he had always done. He didn't see the shell bursts. He didn't hear the shouts of men in the trench behind him to come back. He didn't feel the earth as it lashed down on him from explosions all around. He was looking at the tape in front of him as his dad had always told him.

"Don't look left or right son. Keep your eyes on that tape. Don't stop, no matter what."

His arms and legs pumped him forward. He didn't feel the squelching mud underneath, only the firm grass of the track as he surged over the ground like a cheetah. Now the crowd were urging him on in front.

"Come on, come on" he heard them cry.

"Run lad, run," his dad was shouting, fist clenched anxiously near the finish line.

Another explosion nearby, and another. Death breathing down his neck, straining to catch him up, adrenaline and fear driving him on. Until with a final effort he burst over the line…and dropped down into the trench, gasping for air.

*

"What the bloody hell do you think you're playing at corporal?"

A sergeant was standing over him in moments, and nearby he saw a captain come out of a dugout and come forward drawn by the sudden rise in noise. "How you weren't killed I'll never know. You better have a bloody good explanation."

"Yes sergeant I have," Will gasped, struggling to draw breath. Then he saluted as the captain came up. He began to blurt the message out still panting with the exertion of the run.

"Sir… compliments of Captain Wittering… Phones are down…

Jerry has fired gas and they are following up with a full attack."

"Take a breath corporal and relax. Now, carry on."

"Only half the men in the front line have masks so the rest are being sent here, while the others hold until signalled to retreat. Captain Wittering has asked for artillery fire and for you to organise the line of defence here, and if necessary evacuate any men from this trench without masks too sir."

"Are our phones down sir?" the sergeant asked, looking worried at this report.

"No thankfully they are not. And it's a good report corporal and timely. Gas 'eh? The bastards. As it happens we've just had some additional masks sent up with supplies this morning. Sergeant get the companies moving and be prepared to deal with the men coming back too."

"Yes sir."

"You better grab one yourself corporal. Why didn't you use the trench?"

"It was blocked sir."

"And if our phones were down too?"

"I was to run on to HQ sir."

"I see. Well that was some dash you made. Sprinter are you?"

"Yes sir and a footballer."

"More of a rugby winger for me. But good show. What's your name?"

"Davison sir."

"Right carry on. You can help Sergeant Morris with your own lot when they get here. I dare say you beat them even with a head start." Will saluted again. "Oh and corporal?"

"Sir?"

"Did I see you dip as you got to the trench?"

Will smiled, realising what he must have done. "Shame it wasn't timed sir."

"Quite."

By now the British machine guns in the first trench were chattering away non-stop, and they were soon joined by rifle fire from the troops left behind. Will felt anxious for the friends he had left there and was thinking about heading back, when he heard the familiar voice of their sergeant major moving through the reserve trench immediately organising the men. He made his way to Will just as the first British artillery shells flew overhead and started pounding the German attackers struggling through the wire and mud in No Man's Land. Russell looked up and nodded approvingly and then patted Will on the arm.

"Well done lad. Saw your run. Took guts. Knew I'd picked the right man. Should give us half a chance now."

He was called away then to the Captain of 'D' company and as Will felt a sense of relief inside he saw the smiling moustache of Ced appear amongst the sea of men jostling back and forth in the crowded trench. As they embraced, a flare went up overhead. A command boomed out - "Prepare for covering fire" - and as it passed up and down the line, the men moved as one to the front of their trench. They could see the remaining soldiers left behind in their weird masks moving towards the communications trenches but they were bunching up and panic started to set in. The machine gunners waited until the last minute but then they too pulled back and as the guns fell silent the roar from the advancing Germans was clearly audible.

Russell watched the scene unfold through his single scope. Captain Barclay next to him was doing likewise through his binoculars. Winston Barclay, the son of a wealthy landowner, was the estate manager on his father's land before the war, but had been swept up with the patriotism like the rest and now found himself managing a different set of problems. He tugged on his beard anxiously weighing up the options.

"Should we counter-attack sergeant major?"

"I wouldn't recommend it sir," Russell replied without looking away from the scope. "Jerry guns will cut us to pieces if we cross the ground in front and if we try and move men up the support lines now they will just foul up with the men coming back and be sitting ducks. Besides Jerry will be in our trench brewing up before we get there. Best to stick to the plan and regroup here and go back under controlled shell fire with a full battalion if we can, once the gas has cleared."

Barclay nodded, bowing to the experience of the man next to him despite the lower rank. He was a good organiser but he was no soldier like the sergeant major, that's for sure. He summoned a runner and told him to update HQ on the plan, and request orders once they had regrouped. He wanted to cover his back in case anything went wrong.

"Jerry's in the trench sir." Russell's words made him jump back forward and continue his observations. They could see indiscriminate firing now and some hand to hand fighting as the men still tried to get away down the connecting trenches. It looked like some bizarre Burlesque play, as men in weird shaped masks struggled with each other, their faces and shapes distorted. One or two of their own men here started firing. Russell reacted without waiting for orders.

"Hold your fire unless told otherwise. Pass it on. We still have men in those front trenches. Sergeants get some fighting parties to the comms trenches at our end, in case Jerry gets bold and chases our lads up them." As men were dispatched to cover the retreat, Russell looked at Will. "And snipers, if you see any of those pointy hats and you have a clear sight, knock their blocks off."

Will had made the dash without his rifle but Ced as ever was there to back him up, and produced it as if by magic.

"Thought you might need this."

"Thanks mate. Did Franko find the sergeant?"

"No idea Will. I had to pull back before he returned."

Will nodded and immediately set about checking his rifle and cleaning the sight. A man came round handing out spare masks now and Will and Ced put them on and laughed at each other inside them.

Russell continued to watch their forward line and spotted Captain Wittering still in the trench, directing men away. As he looked he saw something catch the captain's attention who spun round, revolver in hand. Russell didn't hear the shots in all the noise but clearly saw the pistol jerk several times and a German helmet suddenly appeared and fell forward again. Then the Captain nodded and calmly turned and waved the last of the men down the nearest connecting trench.

"Ballsy bastard," Russell murmured, admiring his officer.

But not everyone was so calm and as the Germans began to drop into the trench in numbers, some of the remaining men panicked and climbed over the back of the trench to run across the open ground. Not only did it prevent their own troops from covering their retreat but it made them sitting ducks. Men were shouting at them to get down before any of the sergeants and officers needed to. But it was no good. The shells continued to rain down and now the masked German attackers were adding their own fire to the retreating men.

Sergeant Davis was spotted shouting at the men to get back in the trenches, his face completely uncovered. But as Russell went to scream at him to get out, the watching group saw him suddenly convulse wildly and fall back. Masked German soldiers appeared where he had just been standing and Will knew it wouldn't matter now whether Franko had found him or not.

"Oh God its Castle," Ced suddenly announced, nudging Will and pointing to one of the fleeing men. "I know because he tied his green scarf from his Mum round his neck before I left." Will looked through his sight to where Ced had pointed and sure enough could see a green-necked soldier running arms out wide, his rifle gone. Seconds later his arms went right up above his head and he fell down, and didn't rise again.

The wind continued to push the gas forward across the German filled trench that only an hour before they had occupied themselves, and with the morning fog still refusing to lift, it began to obscure the ground in front so the German firing became more wild; although the shells continued to fall unabated without a care for who they hit. Miraculously one or two of the soldiers who had made the mad dash across the open ground made it to the trench. Though they were not safe from the wrath of their sergeant major of course, but that could wait.

More of the British troops now appeared from the front line through the communications trenches and it would appear the Germans had known better than to follow. *Consolidating their initial success before planning a further attack of their own no doubt*, Russell thought.

The initial action appeared to be reverting to shelling from both sides, and the men were ordered to keep their heads down in case the German barrage moved forward. But right at that moment the sound of high pitched shouting came to them from the ground in front.

"Good God, one of our officers is still out there!" Barclay called out, watching the scene through his binoculars. Will panned his sight round and saw a British officer running across the ground half obscured, screaming for help.

"It's Dunn," he said without emotion.

Ced looked over now and the man was unmistakable. Russell saw it too and shook his head.

"Must have been hiding in the dugout the whole time and now made a dash for it," Ced stated, "the bloody coward." Then he lowered his voice, "Just shoot him Will and be done with it. We can blame the Hun."

"Hardly Ced when no one else is firing and the officers are watching. Much as I'm tempted."

Just then a shell landed just a few feet to his left and Dunn was lifted through the air and landed in a smoking shell hole from the previous salvo. The trench went silent watching the scene unfold.

"Christ," said Barclay.

"Thank you Christ, he means," muttered Ced under his breath.

But as they watched Dunn appeared again crawling out of the hole. His gas mask had been ripped off and he was clearly wounded. He tried to stand and collapsed with a scream. It alerted the Germans, who despite the fog started shooting in the direction of the noise.

"His legs are broken I think sir," said Russell noting how the officer couldn't stand and now crawled, moaning pitifully.

"He's a goner either way," someone said from behind Will. "If Jerry doesn't get him the gas will. His mask's gone and it's still blowing forward."

Will glanced back at the anonymous voice in the ranks of men transfixed by the scene in front. Whoever it was, he was right.

"Can we get to him sergeant major?"

"Not without losing half a dozen men or more so, and perhaps for nothing," Russell replied.

"Hold fast all of you. Nothing we can do now. I'm not losing anyone else today."

The voice of Captain Wittering made all those closest turn round and the men snapped to attention instinctively. Russell saluted his captain, proud to have him back amongst them and reassured by the presence of a confident officer. The groans of the lieutenant continued as he clawed his way forward, and the earth around him spat up occasionally as bullets missed their target.

Wittering observed the wounded lieutenant for some moments, dismayed at the failure of Dunn to tolerate the pain, as much as his awful predicament. With a sigh he leaned in to his colleague.

"Might be best if we do it. He won't evade the gas unless the wind changes and if the fog lifts the Germans will just make a pin cushion out of him anyway. Might be dying as it is for all we know."

"What are you saying captain?" Barclay asked, astounded by what his peer had suggested.

"I'm saying it's a mercy killing and if it was me out there I'd rather have a swift bullet in the head than die an agonising death in gas and dirt." He turned now and saw Will. "Company sniper can you make that shot?"

Will didn't answer. Suddenly his mind was awash with conflicting emotions. He felt nothing for the lieutenant. Dunn had caused the death of some of his comrades without doubt and he blamed him entirely for the loss of Albert. Then there was the business with the firing squad to boot, covering up for his own mistakes. But to shoot a man in cold blood, and one of their own, was a terrible thing to contemplate. He knew his dad might understand but he also knew what his mother would say were she here now. His mum had brought them up with Christian philosophies, and even out here where God seemed absent, it still felt wrong. She brought her boys up to know right from wrong even under provocation. He was saved from answering this moral dilemma, as the two captains began a heated exchange about what to do.

As the men around them looked on astonished, Ced leaned in.

"Now's your chance Will. Payback time. And you have orders from the captain. Do it before he changes his mind."

Will nodded listening, his head thumping with the pressure of the decision. He saw the sergeant major look at him, but couldn't read his thoughts and then Russell stepped in between the captains, and Will was left alone unsure what to do. Not for the first time he wished he was anywhere but here. He looked through his sights again and saw Dunn had stopped crawling now and was just lying there shouting out, over and over. It was a truly pitiful sight and he closed his eyes for a moment...

Once, back home on the farm, one of their prize cows had wandered too far over the East bank in search of tastier grass and she had slipped and got entangled in the wire fence below. The more she struggled the worse she had become stuck, her own weight and the gravity of the bank dragging her down into the wire's biting grip. By the time his dad found her it had been impossible to get to her and cut her free and he had called the vet. The gun had been the only merciful thing to do. She was too badly wounded and had lost a lot of blood. He saw Dunn now and thought about that cow lying there crying for help, and lifted up his rifle.

*

On Mill farm Agnes shivered as she set the table for breakfast. It was as if someone had walked over her grave and she crossed herself, plates in hand. She felt a knot in her chest and for some reason thought of Will. She put the plates down on the table and paused, picturing him in her mind, and said out loud, "God keep him safe. Give him strength to always follow in your shadow and guide him home to us."

"You praying Aggie love?" Harold said, coming into the warmth of the kitchen and rubbing his arms in front of the fire, the early morning chores complete once more. "Any chance you can rustle up some porridge once you've done chatting with the Almighty?" he said, without looking round.

She looked at her husband then, standing large in front of the fire. And then wistfully at the empty chairs around their table.

"Of course love," she replied snapping back into her 'mum mode' to cope. Life must go on she knew.

*

In that moment Will knew what he had to do as well. He blew some dust off the bolt action workings of his rifle and checked the firing parts once more. He loaded a bullet in and checked the sight, gauging the distance between him and Dunn and then looked at the fog beyond, checking the speed of the wind from its movement. As Ced looked on expectantly, he handed him his rifle.

"Here," he said, and moved to the nearest ladder. "Cover me."

Chapter 30 – In the box

The heat was stifling. Will awoke to the sound of buzzing flies and a loud rattling noise, and felt a steady bumping every few seconds that must have jolted him awake. He was lying down but his body seemed to be trembling uncontrollably. The constant shaking made him cough and the pain returned in his chest to remind him all was not well. He looked around fearful in that moment, and found himself in a dark box that rattled and screamed. But it hurt to open his eyes and the memory of the gas returned now and he could feel the panic rising within him. He became aware of the sound of groaning men and realised as his eyes adjusted that there were other men lying near him. He turned to look the other way and hit his head on something hard. He felt at it in the gloom and it was wooden like a coffin. 'Was he dead?' There was a smell of smoke too now that enveloped and choked his senses and made him cough again. The pain was unbearable and he cried out involuntarily.

The box shook again and the noise grew louder – cries in the dark mingling with rattles and bangs. His eyes were running from the smoke, and as he tried to move he found himself strapped down and he began to feel claustrophobic, panic gripping his limbs as he believed the box to be on fire. *'Oh god he was being cremated alive!'* "I'm not dead," he shouted. "I'm alive!"

Suddenly there was a loud whistle from somewhere outside and he flinched at the sound, and a man screamed out. *'No not cremated. He was in a trench still? An attack on its way? Was he buried alive?'* Will suddenly recalled the explosion in the communications trench and wondered if he had in fact been buried there and his spirit had run away. His mind struggled to make sense of the nightmare, trying to remember, and then a face appeared by him and he screamed.

"It's ok Corporal try and lie still. Not long to go now." It was a female voice and though the features were hard to make out Will felt

303

some comfort in it.

"Am I dreaming?" he said, scared to ask if he was in fact dead.

"No you are on the hospital train back to the coast. A couple more hours and we will be at the port. We were followed by a German plane earlier and the driver is worried we might be bombed I think, so he's sped up. But the doctor has gone to see him to make him slow down. Just try and rest. The straps are to stop you being thrown off by that lunatic French driver. Here."

She raised his head and brought some cool water to his lips.

"Just a sip now. Your throat is still burned."

The water felt like pure heaven in this nightmarish world and he collapsed back exhausted. The sun was rising once more on this world of smoke and ruin, and light arrived quickly on this summer day to peer in through the wooden walls around him. But sleep did not come and he stared for ages at the ceiling. A car horn somewhere made him turn and Will noticed a small hole in the wall next to him and found air was being pushed through it and he pressed his face against it and breathed slowly with his eyes closed. Every now and then though more smoke came in through the wooden slats from the engine's exertions, and he found himself coughing once more and winced with the pain.

He turned his head away and looked about, the dawn light now unveiling the grim scene. He was shocked to see how many men were in this carriage. They were stacked up in triple bunks with what looked like the more seriously injured on the bottom ones. He realised he must be right on the top as he only had the ceiling a few inches above him and could see other men at his level with two more men beneath each of them. He tried to count but could only move his head a little to see part of the train. Even then he worked out at least seven bunks of three on the opposite side. He made his head do the Maths guessing they would be mirrored on his side. *Twenty one times two. Forty two men, and more behind his head no doubt. God.'*

The train slowed and he turned to look out of the hole once more. They were passing buildings now, perhaps coming into a town. He could see shapes and colours, and flashes of fences and brick built structures. A white wooden porch and a garden full of trees.

Then a mother and child were waving as the train chugged past. He thought then of his grandparent's house and watching the trains going past, carrying people or goods. He recalled the sheep on the train, their faces pressed against the gaps as his was now. Lambs to the slaughter. And he cried. Unable to wipe the tears away they rolled onto his pillow and merged with the grime and sweat. He wanted to go home, to see his family again. He wanted to feel safe once more and sleep without fear. He wondered through his sobs if he would ever feel safe again, and as if to answer the burning pain came again in his chest.

*

At some point sleep must have come to him mercifully for when he awoke next he had the sensation of floating and for one awful moment thought the carriage was filling with water and they would all drown. Will wondered if he was in fact dreaming, but looked to the side and could see lamps now and people moving about. Nurses it seemed like, and soldiers too. His eyes stung and instinctively he went to wipe them and found his arms were free and joyously he rubbed at his face but it just made his eyes burn more and so he squinted in the half light. Looking down he was clearly on a makeshift bed of some kind and with fumbling hands felt for the straps that were no longer there. He went to sit up but lurched forward and felt sick, and so lay down again. The room span, and he gripped the sanctuary of his bed for safety.

"Hello Corporal Davison. Feeling any better?"

The same voice came again but behind his head this time. He turned and looked round, eyes adjusting to the new surroundings, but afraid to move too far for fear of falling. He saw the nurse more clearly now. She was kneeling by a man behind him, gently checking a bandage round his head, and she smiled when she saw him. The same spinning feeling returned as there was another sudden lurch, but he saw her lose her balance momentarily and wondered if that was his eyes or something else. Her blond hair tied back in a ponytail under a nurse's hat fluttered like the dune grass by the sea and then regained its composure.

"The sea," she answered to the unspoken questioning in his eyes. "We are on a hospital ship back to England. Well it's a cargo ship actually but they have converted it to transport men instead. You can move around on board the ship but I'd wait there until I check you first as you're bound to be unsteady. Besides I made a deal to keep an eye on you until you were safely back in England so don't want you to fall and hurt yourself now." She smiled again, her whole face radiating calm. "I'll be over soon."

Will looked over the side of the bed and found he was only a few inches from the floor. He became aware of the roll of the ship now and took comfort in it. He lay back on his bed and stared above him where large blackened pipes crisscrossed a ceiling to disappear into metal boxes and walls in the dark corners up high. He pulled the loose sheet up to his chest and felt the familiar pain return to his ribs. Somewhere far away a ship's horn blasted out twice. His mind pondered for a moment how she knew his name and then he closed his eyes and slept once more.

*

Will next awoke to an intense bright light. He blinked and found his eyes were less sore than he remembered, though his left eye still barely opened. He saw a large oval window ahead of him with wooden frames breaking up its glass into a number of squares that looked like a noughts and crosses board. As he adjusted to the sudden burst of light a Robin appeared at the window with a flourish of its wings. It tapped twice at some unseen object of interest on the sill before glancing round. Then with a flash of red it was gone and a stern face replaced it in his vision.

"Good Morning Corporal. I am Sister Dent. Back with us I see. How are you feeling today?"

Will focused on the woman in front of him and noticed several other nurses in attendance behind her, some of them with notepaper and pencils poised to capture his response. She was a vision of cleanliness, her dark blue uniform and white apron spotless and shining like the lights around her. Her hair was curly but close cropped and guarded fiercely by her hat that framed a face that was hard to age. His dad would have called it "lived in," he thought to himself. Her accent he noticed was not a Sussex one, more like the twang of the Yorkshire Light Infantry men they had played cards with on the boat to France that Archie had imitated more than once after that. It made him smile unexpectedly.

"Where am I?" he asked, after studying her absent mindedly for a few moments.

"Well I'm pleased you're smiling but that doesn't answer my question. You are in Brighton Royal Infirmary and I would appreciate it if you address me as Sister."

"I'm sorry Sister," he mumbled, and then blushed as he saw one or two of the young nurses giggle at his predicament. They stopped instantly with just a swift backward glance from Sister Dent.

"Well Corporal? We haven't got all day?"

"My eyes still hurt," he said, and then dutifully added "Sister."

"I see. Nurse Jennings, take his pulse. Can you see out of both eyes or only one?"

"Both, just about," squinting at the barrage of activity around his bed. The nurse muttered something to the Sister and she nodded briefly.

"Well write that down all of you," Dent said impatiently. "Take a breath for me Corporal."

Will did as he was told and the pain returned then and he winced and began to cough. He saw the Sister's lined face soften for a moment and then she turned round.

"Ok. Get him some water when he's able and make a note for the doctor to have an x-ray done and see what else is going on inside."

The pain thumped away now in his chest and Will felt the panic rising again as to what was the matter. He pulled on the sleeve of the nurse nearest him and she jumped. The Sister saw this and turned to Will again.

"What do you think you are doing? You do not manhandle nurses on my ward. If you have something to say then..."

"Have I been shot?" Will asked cutting her off mid-sentence.

There was a pause amongst the whole group and then the Sister stepped forward.

"No Corporal or I dare say we wouldn't be chatting. You are suffering from the effects of gas. There is damage to your throat and lungs and also one of your eyes from the look of you. But you were dealt with extremely well at the front which is surprising, and are in good hands now. As long as you behave yourself," she added with a raise of her eyes, dark eyebrows arching skywards. "Now rest."

"Did you say this is Brighton?" Will asked suddenly remembering her words.

"Yes why," Dent asked, impatient to move on.

"Is Archie Bunden here?"

She looked at Will then, and he saw two of the nurses look at each other briefly. Will wasn't sure if a brief moment of emotion flitted across her face, before the formal persona returned.

"We have no patient here of that name. Now we must move on."

As they walked away Will wondered if he had been confused about where Archie went, and then began to worry if his friend was okay. He lay there breathing slowly so as not to exacerbate the pain, and as he did so he drifted in and out of the edges of sleep, voices coming back to him in a memory…

"We are not sure yet of the extent of the damage inside him. It's not good."

It was Teresa's voice and she was talking somewhere behind him. He was aware of noise, a mixture of voices, metal clattering on metal close by, and something else. Thunder that was it. As if to support this the area lit up with a momentary lightning flash and then went back to the haze of lamplights again.

"His eyes are bad but the doctors think he may be okay. Colonel Hamilton has worked wonders with burns but this is different. We need to get him specialist care immediately. There's an X-ray unit at Béthune for the troops and we could do with seeing inside. But it's only one of five at the front and much in demand, and he could be waiting for ages."

Will could hear Teresa's words were cracked with emotion and he was scared. There was more discussion but the words were lost in the noise or his memories. Then he remembered another voice.

"You leave this to me. I'll get us to the front of the queue on an officer's

ticket." It was the captain he had met once before. He would recognise his voice anywhere. Harry Johnson.

"But he's not an officer."

"Don't you worry about that. Can he travel?"

"We shouldn't move him yet but I can soften the blow if you can get him there."

"Get him ready. I'll get the car now and call in a favour with old Bluffers."

He strode off, passing in and out of Will's vision and he heard Teresa whisper, "I'm scared for him."

"Not as much as me," Will heard himself say through strained tones. It felt as if he was looking down on himself and panic invaded his mind he might already be dead.

"Hey you. We didn't know you were awake," Teresa said forcing a smile and immediately mopped his head with a cool cloth. Then another face appeared smiling by him. It was James.

"Hello little brother. This is a fine mess and no mistake. Just as well we came over to visit. Trust you not to listen to orders. What will I tell the folks?"

He was being upbeat but Will could see the concern in his face. Then he realised he looked different.

"You have a beard James."

"Yes do you like it? Jonners says it makes me look dashing like a Musketeer of old!"

James laughed a deep booming laugh now, as if to release the pressure of the moment; but as Will went to laugh too, the pain in his chest exploded as if he had been struck by lightning himself. He began to cough uncontrollably and James leaned in to hug him.

"You daft sod. Risking all for some bloody useless officer. Who does that?"

"You would," Will answered, and managed a half smile.

"Jonners is here let's get him ready to move." Will smiled at how Teresa had slipped into their nicknames, something else that endeared her to the men. "I've done his notes and if we can get him looked at quickly I've recommended transfer back to England as soon as he's stable. It's a risk on the journey but he needs to be home."

"We'll get him there if I have to take him all the way myself." James replied.

"Here take this for the pain," Teresa said and lifted his head to drink something. She repeated it again which was odd, "Here take this…"

309

Then he was looking at the face of Nurse Jenkins and realised he was awake once more. "You were shouting out in your sleep corporal. Here take this. It will help."

It had gone dark now. The noughts and crosses window covered by dark purple curtains, and the lamps were on once more. It was always dark these days it seemed to him, and Will regretted having slept through the daytime. Had he slept for one day or two? It was hard to say.

"Take this please it's for the throat, to ease the soreness."

As he accepted a glass of some sour smelling pink liquid he observed his carer. Nurse Jenkins looked so young to him, strands of red hair curling rebelliously away from her hat, to race down the sides of her innocent face. Compared to the Sister, compared to the men he had fought and served with, even compared to the beautiful Teresa, this nurse seemed like a child.

It occurred to him in that moment that Teresa was indeed beautiful. Such a contrast in that terrible landscape. He sighed and the nurse frowned. Will had no doubt the fresh faced nurse looking at him patiently, was probably a similar age to him, and yet she spoke to him politely as if he was much older. *How old did he look?* he wondered.

"Is James a friend of yours?" she asked, taking the empty glass back from him and placing it on a trolley.

"My brother," he replied. "He's in the Guards. An officer," he added, though he did not know why, as he wasn't trying to impress this girl.

"You are all very brave, I know that much," she said unexpectedly, then puffed up his pillows and gently helped him lie back. As she tucked in his sheets around him she glanced round conspiratorially and then leaned in closer.

"That man you mentioned earlier…Archibald Bunden."

"Yes?" said Will, suddenly quite awake.

"He was here. Was here for a long time. They sent him home less than a month ago, to his Mum's I think. Thought you should know. Sister was quite affected by him."

"Really?" said Will, astonished that anything or anyone could affect the woman who had been so brusque with him earlier.

"Yes he had quite an impact on everyone here. Probably why Sister was short with you about it. She's not so bad once you get to know her you know." Seeing Will's unconvinced expression she added, "The place hasn't been the same since he left."

"I know exactly what you mean," said Will.

Chapter 31 – Silencing the opposition

Walter Miller cycled up Mill Road towards the farm. He was deep in thought about the war and more so about the reaction to come. He didn't enjoy this task anymore, and even less having the enormous pressure of having to read such devastating news about people first in the telegram office. It seemed like a constant invasion of privacy, and above all else he was now seen as a harbinger of doom; like some horseman of the apocalypse riding about on his malevolent steed to bring death and suffering to the innocent. Except his steed was an old bicycle that squeaked unhelpfully as he pedalled along despite his best efforts to move about in silence.

At least today the news was not so grim and as he leaned his bike by the gate and walked in, he comforted himself with that thought. Sally barked immediately from her outside kennel where she was resting 'off duty,' and launched the full length of the lead, falling just short of his right trouser leg. She sensed the unease in this man despite having seen him before and it put her on edge. Walter knew the distance of the rope by now but nearly misjudged it being lost in thought, and Sally's sudden rush made him flinch. He stepped around the barking dog and walked on. The Davisons had been very kind to him in recent weeks, and he was determined to ensure they were put at ease immediately.

Harold came out of the barn where he was half-heartedly trying to fix one of the door hinges that had worked loose yet again. He shouted at Sally and then saw the familiar form of Walter Miller. He took a step forward to welcome him, raising an arm in greeting but his voice trailed off as he saw the paper Walter was holding. The door swung against his arm but he hardly noticed as he watched the station master's progress up the drive, and glanced immediately to the kitchen.

As Walter approached he heard him saying, "It's okay, it's okay, it's from James and there's a letter too." For a moment Harold thought it was just some other news. Then Walter came in front of him and added "He's not dead Harold," and time stopped still. He grabbed the telegram now and read it anxiously. Walter was saying how unusual it was for a letter and telegram to arrive together and there must have been delays, speaking to fill the silence. But Harold was only half listening.

Agnes came out of the kitchen, saw Walter and her husband looking at the paper. She sagged against the door frame and had to steady herself.

"Who is it Hal? Which one," she called out, her voice seeming far off and frantic in her head despite trying to stay calm. Harold looked up and walked over.

"It's from James. Our William's been hurt. Gassed it seems. There's a letter. Might explain more. He's coming back."

She grabbed at him now, snatching the mail. The letter falling to the floor in her haste. "Give it to me. Give it me!" she shouted, the tears in her eyes. "Where is he? Where?" she shouted at Walter Miller, who didn't answer but stood there awkwardly, looking at the floor. "How bad Hal?" she said grabbing her husband's arm fiercely.

"We don't know love. We need to read the letter too. Let's get inside."

Agnes read the words on the telegram and cried out, sobbing "Will" over and over now. Harold eased her inside and turned to Walter.

"Thank you for coming. I'd offer tea but..."

"No. No Need. I'm sure he will be okay. He's a fighter that lad. I'll pray for him."

He walked back down the drive hearing the crying behind him, as he had heard more than once before. Sally wagged her tail now, assuming he was fine to be on the property, and he stopped to pat her, as much for his own comfort as hers. Then he carried on to where his bike waited, the smell of doom swirling about the oily chain on his dark wheeled stallion, as he mounted up once more.

*

313

Will felt the grass cool and refreshing beneath his bare feet as he continued to walk forwards, the strands flicking beneath his toes as he brushed them this way and that. The sun was still not clear of the building behind him and he walked in a cold shadow, the early morning moisture adding a chilling exuberance to the sensations shooting up his legs. A firm breeze blew hard against his face now, forcing him to bow his head slightly, but Will felt a great sense of relief to be out in the open air once more after days spent cooped up in the hospital. The cold air made his chest constrict however, and his breathing became harder so he paused for a moment before continuing his journey. He reflected on the letter and then knew he had to clear his head and pressed on.

Two pigeons broke from feeding on the grass nearby as he carried on his way. They flapped hard to take refuge in the nearby trees where they landed awkwardly, dislodged feathers swirling about in their wake. A line of swallows preparing to head south for warmer climes looked disdainfully at the new arrivals that had caused their perch to sway so violently, chirping at them angrily.

*

Polly Jenkins was heading home to the nurses' lodgings after another long night shift. Fastening her coat, she walked along the corridor to the main door, checking the weather as she did so. She wrinkled her nose as the trees bent against the aerial bombardment. *Definitely gloves and hat weather this morning Polly*, she thought to herself.

As she walked on, footsteps echoing off the highly polished floors, Polly reached in the side pockets of her coat to pull out the gloves. Then abruptly she stopped. Her casual glance from the window had triggered an alarm at the back of her mind. Something was different about the windswept scene on the main lawn. Oddly the image of striped pyjamas now pushed its way forward into her thoughts. As she went to put on her second glove Polly looked out of the next window more carefully. Her heart flipped over.

"Oh my god…" she said out loud, the pretty blue glove, a present from her favourite Aunt on her last birthday, dropping unnoticed to the floor where it would lie for some time thereafter. She ran for the main office, knowing Sister Dent would be in an hour early before her shift as she always was. She found it empty, Dent having already been and gone to do a hand over with the night team. *Blast her for being so efficient!* she cursed, and then ran for the main doors, shouting as she did so to a ward nurse to fetch Sister and the doctor urgently. *Now was not the time for calm.*

*

Though deep in thought, Will heard a woman shouting for him to come back, forcing its sound into his subconscious. That's odd he frowned, but continued forward bent double regardless. The female voice was soon drowned out by those of his friends, and his captain especially, ordering him to return. He knew if he looked back he would waiver so he broke into a run now, the lush grass worn away months ago to be replaced by this endless black mud that sucked at his every stride. As the first shell landed on the lawn he zig zagged away from it knowing it was his best chance of survival and dropped into a previous shell's crater to get his bearings.

Dunn was no more than thirty yards in front of him but he was not moving at all now, and the fog crept ever closer like a spider moving in on a wounded prey. There was no hurry for the predator and it toyed with its victim, swirling this way and that close to the lieutenant's stricken form. Will shot off again but this time diagonally away from the officer causing even more shouts from behind him.

"Where's he going?"

"Can't he see him for God's sake?"

"He'll never make it now."

Will knew exactly what he was doing and sure enough a few yards further on he spied the fluttering green memorial of Private Castle. He ran up to his former section man and turned him over. It was a grisly sight with a number of bullet holes across his middle that had blown holes in his flesh, exposing bones and parts of his insides. He had to fight not to vomit and rolled him back over, patting him once on the shoulder as a final parting. He reached down and pulled the mask off his former comrade's face and looked inside. There was blood on the front, probably from his mouth, and he wiped it quickly with his sleeve and then checked it to see it still worked. Satisfied he sprinted back the way he had come towards the fallen officer.

Dunn was in a bad way and had passed out with the pain. Both his legs were clearly broken and his clothes were tattered and bloody. Will lay down near him checking for signs of life and keen not to make an obvious target of himself. He looked back into the fog, relieved that he couldn't see their forward trench from here, which he hoped meant they couldn't see him either, but the gas had not gone and the wind now blew it forward once more. As he fitted Castle's mask onto Dunn, the officer jolted awake with a scream and Will put his hand over his mouth to silence him.

"Be quiet sir or you'll have us both killed."

But the lieutenant was delirious and struggled with him violently, pulling at his clothes and his mask.

"Stop it sir. I'm here to rescue you," he said, pulling the mask on firmly, "it's Corporal Davison."

It was no good. Dunn either couldn't hear or didn't comprehend anymore, the reaction to having something pulled over his head clearly making him panic, and then with one last effort the lieutenant ripped Will's air tube from the mask rendering it useless.

"Oh Jesus. You bloody idiot," Will shouted, not caring about protocol anymore, and in his frustration he lashed out at Dunn and knocked him back unconscious.

"Did you see that?" Captain Barclay asked, looking round from his binoculars.

"See what Barclay?" Wittering replied, without taking his eyes off the scene out in front of them.

"It looked like he struck the officer!"

"He's trying to lift him from what I can make out, though the lieutenant appears to be panicking. Impossible to see exactly from here wouldn't you say sergeant major?"

"Can't see anything clearly in this damned smoke Sir."

"Quite."

Barclay went to protest again but was cut off by a shout from one of the sergeants down the line.

"He's taken his mask off!"

"What?" Russell and Wittering now looked on anxiously, observing every detail despite their lies to the contrary only moments ago.

Will had no option but to rip off his useless mask and throw it aside. As he was the one that was going to be doing the lifting and carrying he thought for one moment about taking the unconscious lieutenant's mask for himself, but decided against it. He looked round to see if there were any more bodies nearby with masks on, but his luck was out. He had no choice but to make a dash for it once again, and despite his legs now aching with the exertions in getting here, he hauled the lieutenant onto his shoulders and with some effort stood up once more.

Will was surprised to feel how heavy Dunn was. Even heavier than Albert as he recalled. "Well you're too fat to be a footballer that's for sure," he said to no one in particular, and staggered forward. A zip like a bee flying past made him jump and almost fall over, and he realised the Germans were still taking pot shots into the smoke and increased his pace. He was only one hundred yards from the trench and safety now, and he could hear the men shouting him on. Another zip and this one hit the bloodied left leg of the lieutenant with a sucking sound.

"Jesus that's close."

He turned, and to his dismay saw the mist thinning in one part along the trench line and a German soldier had spotted him. With improving visibility the masked assailant climbed out of the trench to get a clear shot at Will, and egged on by his comrades was taking careful aim at the fleeing British soldier. Will knew if he lay flat he might never get up again, as they would just target him where he was, so he decided to just press on and crouched low.

The German settled the rifle into his shoulder carefully this time, fixing his sight on the struggling British soldier. He wanted to make sure he hit the right one this time, to make them both fall. He squeezed on the trigger and a shot rang out.

His cheering friends fell silent as he collapsed back dead amongst them. The previously manicured moustache of their sergeant rendered in two where the bullet had smashed through the top part of his mouth and exploded out of the back of his head. As if to herald a dramatic end to a play the smoke closed in again on the scene in front, like a curtain call, obscuring the fleeing figure of Will.

"That shut them up. Not the only bloke who can shoot well with one of these," Ced announced proudly, reloading Will's rifle. "That's a shilling I think we said Franko."

"Well done Longworthy," Russell said with the briefest of smiles, as Franko looked on sullenly despite the fact his friend had been saved.

But the British cheers quickly turned to shouts of horror as a fresh gust of wind swept the gas on and past the lumbering pair. Will suddenly realised he was in the green carpet of death and took a deep breath and broke into a run, trying to squint in the mist. Less than twenty yards from the trench, he stumbled and fell, the weight of the lieutenant knocking the air from him momentarily, and he took a deep breath in and instantly regretted it. The searing pain exploded through his lungs as the noxious gases seeped into every pore in his body, making him automatically open his eyes with the shock, and he couldn't help screaming with the effect. As his eyes began to burn as well, watering wildly against the unseen enemy, Will stumbled forward grabbing Dunn by the shoulders and half dragging, half pulling him, forced himself on.

Despite his best efforts he was unable not to breathe, the combination of the pain and the physical effort making his chest heave in short bursts. He felt himself succumbing to this swirling toxic terror. With one last cry out he hurled himself forward into the trench...

...and fell into the arms of his father.

"Easy lad, I've got you," Harold said, his wife running to catch up from behind across the brightening lawn, as their son cried out in despair.

Polly caught up with Will just as Harold had appeared across the lawn from the opposite direction. She had run flat out to catch him, and appeared dishevelled and gasping for breath with the sudden exertion. Her blue woollen bonnet had flown off as she ran and she arrived wearing only one glove, her coat flapping in the breeze, and the untied hair now blowing wildly about her face. But in that moment she cared little about the *'Rules of proper behaviour for a nurse'* leaflet they were made to read over and over, as she stared anxiously at the Davisons.

Behind them, Sister Dent was striding out across the lawn, a nurse in close attendance pushing a wooden framed wheelchair loaded with thick blankets. Dr Harrison stood, hands on hips, in the main doorway with the nurse that had raised the alarm. There would be questions asked.

Harold hugged his sobbing son in close to his chest, and felt the thin taught frame of the soldier, and not the boy who had left home. There was strength in the muscles still, but the loss of weight was noticeable. Agnes recovered from her initial shock of seeing her boy

318

stumbling across the lawn, and moved in and placed her hands on his head. They stood like that for a while as Polly lingered awkwardly nearby and began to apologise profusely and ask if Will was alright. It was a daft question under the circumstances but she had to say something.

Sister Dent came up with the wheelchair and moved in to Will immediately.

"We have to get him back inside at once. The cold will affect his lungs badly."

"And you are?" Harold said, the handsome blue eyes now ice cold in their stare.

"Sister Dent. I am the duty Sister and Corporal Davison is on my ward."

"Well Corporal Davison is our son, and we did not expect to find him walking around outside in his pyjamas unaccompanied."

The tone and words stopped the Sister in her tracks and she looked at the triangle of people and took a deep breath, in danger of losing her normal composure. Her heart was unusually racing, and she was suddenly flushed which didn't go unnoticed by Polly either, though in the moment the junior nurse was too terrified of the repercussions to care. Dent adjusted her headpiece and her approach in one smooth manner, and resumed her mantle as Senior Sister.

"You're right of course Mr Davison. And I am terribly sorry about this. Mrs Davison...my apologies Ma'am. Please let us get back inside so we can check Corporal..." The parents looked at her as one. "I mean William. So we can check your son over and then find out what happened here. This is not common practice I assure you, but I take full responsibility for this incident." She stood nervously in that moment waiting for the expected outburst but none came.

"Well let's get him back inside then." As Harold helped Will into the chair, Agnes never let go of his hand the whole time, the emotional strain evident in her face. Harold looked at the Sister and said, "No harm done I'm sure," in a tone that would have put the most distressed person at ease. It reminded her of Dr Harrison's bedside manner, even with terminally ill patients. It was a calm voice that could not be taught.

Harold eased the nurse with the wheelchair aside and pushed Will himself. The nurse, still holding the blankets, looked at Dent who shook her head quickly and resuming her working persona moved in on the other side of Will. She felt his head as they walked slowly back, before picking up his free wrist to check his pulse. Taking a blanket she passed it to Agnes to cover her son herself, who smiled at the gesture, and wrapped it round him.

"I am sorry we weren't expecting you," Dent now said to break the ice. "We never know who will come to visit our patients, as the post is so disrupted and the news from the front is always unreliable back home. Do you live locally?"

"We live in Steyning," Harold replied, "on a farm. We got a telegram from his eldest brother James about him, who helped get him back here."

"James is an officer in the guards," Agnes interjected.

"We came as soon as we heard," Harold continued as he pushed Will back over the bumpy grass. "Our youngest is with his grandparents and we have help looking after the farm. We checked into a small guesthouse down the road last night but couldn't sleep so came up here. It's no bother. We are early risers anyway."

In truth the Davisons had not been away from the farm more than half a dozen times in the twenty five years since they were married, and so this was very much out of character for anyone who knew them well. And with the exception of their honeymoon to Torquay, where they had stayed with her Uncle and Aunt for part of it, only one other occasion had not been farming related; when they had taken a weekend away to Littlehampton to celebrate their twenty year wedding anniversary. It had been a marvellous weekend with seaside walks and ice creams and a dinner dance on the Saturday, but mostly they had stayed in their room; and Agnes still chided him that they saw far less of the town than she planned, though she often smiled warmly at the memory of it.

"Well you are very welcome both of you," Dent continued, "and once we have young William settled again we will get you both a nice cup of tea."

As the unusual procession headed back across the dew laden

lawn, now sparkling in the breaking sun like a carpet of gems, the pigeons returned to their previous patch, a final barrage of insults hurled behind them by the departing swallows.

Will had been silent except for his tears, but now suddenly spoke up.

"Dad, I shot the referee."

"What? What was that son?" Harold said, leaning over the back of the chair to hear better.

"Edward Triffit. Our referee. I had to shoot him. They made me."

Harold slowed his pace but didn't stop. He looked at Agnes who shook her head, eyes full of sorrow, as Will's head slumped forward once more.

"It's alright lad. Let's get you back inside where it's warm and then we can have a proper chat." He didn't know what to make of his son's outburst in that moment and had no words to make it right. He didn't know what to make of anything about the war these days, nor was he able to discuss it and inside the anger grew again. He wanted his boys home where he could look after them. The pain returned to his back, as he felt himself tensing up, and he lengthened his stride and pushed on.

Polly moved up alongside Sister Dent who had paused near the entrance to the hospital, and offered to stay on for a while until this was sorted out.

"That's okay Nurse Jenkins, we will be fine to manage. Go to your room and get some rest."

"Thank you Sister," and apologising quietly again, she turned to go and then suddenly paused, remembering something, and pulled a scrunched up piece of paper out of her pocket.

"I found this last night, by his bedside on the floor," she said, nodding towards the wheelchair bound Will, moving back up the drive to the main doors now.

"I think it may have caused this reaction. I only read it briefly but it's from a girl..." she tailed off, looking for an answer from her senior colleague.

Dent looked at it and straightened the letter out, and nodded.

"I remember now he had several letters in his jacket we put in the locker by his bed when he first arrived," Polly continued. "It's a *Dear John*' rejection basically" she added, with a sympathetic smile. Then added, "Oh my god, sorry Sister. That was so insensitive of me."

"Thankyou nurse, its fine," Dent replied with the briefest of frowns, "off you go now."

Elsie Dent pulled out the tattered pages and glanced briefly at the note, paraphrasing the letter;

'don't know how to say this....wasn't expecting it to happen....swept off my feet....family friends for a long time.....sorry Will.....never really serious between us...always be friends though.......still my farm boy.... wish me well.....stay safe.....'

She looked away, a flash of anger in her eyes, the memory of a church and another hastily written note trying to force itself back into her thoughts from where it had been locked away. She dismissed the thought and looked up at the huddled form entering the Hospital where the doctor was shaking hands with the Davisons. She saw Mr Davison then hang back and turn to light a cigarette. He noticed her, and walked back down the main steps to the gardens away from the building, and then lit up. He was clearly upset.

Shaking her head she pushed the note back in the well-travelled envelope and noticed someone had written something diagonally across the back.

'We kept this from Easter. Read it again when you're better perhaps...'

The start of the next sentence had been smudged and was illegible but ended - *'...have to make peace with it and let it go lad. Plenty more trout in the stream! Still got your mates. Be well. C.'*

Trout indeed, she muttered to herself. Then shivered with the morning cold and pushed the envelope back in her pocket. She walked over to where Harold was smoking, picking at a loose stone on the wall overlooking the main grounds.

"You should go inside with your son, Mr Davison. I will get the nurses to get you a cup of tea."

"Do you think everything can be sorted out with a cup of tea," he said angrily, rounding on her as if startled by an intruder. She took a step back but didn't flinch, used to outbursts from angry patients and visitors alike.

"No. I don't. I think it will take us a long time to sort all of this out, even after the war finishes. There will be a lot of emotional healing required, long after the physical scars are gone. And we will have to be strong for them when they come home. Boys and girls."

Harold looked at the nurse now, his anger always momentary, dispersing already. It was hard to age her but probably looked older than she was, and he blamed the work for that.

"I'm sorry, I just…I didn't mean…"

"I know," she said. "It's the war. We are all saying and doing things we wouldn't normally. I didn't mean to be flippant. I just thought a drink and a biscuit might bring you some comfort. It can't hurt."

"No. You were being kind. That would be lovely, thank you." He stubbed out the cigarette and went to flick it away with his boot, and then sheepishly picked it up. "Sorry," he shrugged. She held out a hand and took it off him, placing it in her pocket. She smiled then, and watched him walk off back inside and then turned again to look out over the grounds, where the sun was now lighting a golden path to the main gates.

As Dent smoothed down her apron she noticed something on the hospital steps. It was Polly's blue bonnet and she picked it up, shaking it out to dislodge a small determined leaf off the top. She watched the shrinking figure of Polly walking slowly away towards the nurses' lodgings and sighed. *You're right though 'C', whoever you are, there will be plenty of us left alone after this is all over.*

Then she took a deep breath and marching up the stairs strode purposefully back inside, tossing the bonnet on the hall table as she did so. Normal service was resumed.

Chapter 32 – Chasing shadows

Physically Will was healing well, better than expected, and the medical team had been pleased with his progress. His mind however was a complete mess, and didn't share the hidden determination to get better like his body. What conversations his parents did manage to have, became increasingly darker as the memories returned again and again. Harold and Agnes soon realised this was not going to be resolved anytime soon and ended up renting some rooms nearby and left his parents looking after Fred and the farm. Harold knew his dad would be okay with local help, but found himself going back often to get away from the sterile surroundings and immerse himself in normality.

It was with some relief therefore when Dr Harrison said he was happy to release Will back into the care of his local GP, and allow him to go home. They had been visited once by an army doctor to assess a number of the patients there, and with no little input from Sister Dent, Will was signed off until Christmas for an assessment in the New Year. It was now late November, and when the time came for him to leave, he had been there nearly two months.

Tony Bassett sat on the hospital drive in his farm lorry, the engine turning over noisily. He had insisted on coming to fetch them when he got word Will was to come home saying, "It was no less than his star player deserved." As the Davisons packed up their son's things in the truck outside, Sister Dent took her moment to sit down with Will.

"I'm pleased you are on the mend William. I am sorry it has been such a difficult time for you. I am sure once you are home things will improve quickly. Amongst familiar surroundings the nightmares should lessen with the joys of some home comforts."

Will nodded, looking at the brightly polished floor to distract his mind from the terrors that still came at night, as Dent continued.

"I do owe you an apology. I was short with you when you first arrived about your friend. I know now you were very close and I can assure you he was well on the way to recovery when he left here. We did write to his mother as you asked, and posted your notes, and I am sorry you have had nothing back. But like you, I think time is a great healer and I am sure he will be in touch once you are home."

Will still didn't speak but smiled a weak smile at her. Uncharacteristically she held out her hand. "I'm Elsie. If you need anything come and see me. If you write to us here we will reply I promise William."

He looked directly at her now. Eyes lost in the shadows of his mind but took her hand and shook it.

"Thank you Sister."

His parents came in and she stood up quickly and checked everything had been collected. She handed them the notes and offered the loan of a wheelchair once more but Will shook his head.

"Stubborn like his father," Agnes said apologetically, and then they walked slowly out with far less noise and fanfare than had accompanied the departing Archie. As they got in Tony's truck, Polly Jenkins waved a little handkerchief from inside the sun room window, and Dr Harrison nodded from the stairs. Sister Dent smiled at Agnes as the truck roared into life and Tony urged it down the new tarmacked drive.

"Goodbye corporal," she called above the noise of the old engine, "and good luck."

*

Agnes watched the doctor walk away down the farm drive. The shadow clouds racing as ever across the Downs seemed to her the embodiment of her own mind. She shivered and pulled her shawl more tightly around her.

George Corbett, their family doctor, had been incredibly attentive and come out three times that week alone to check on Will and his prescribed medicines, and to offer advice. He had helped Agnes deliver Will and Fred at home, and known them all their short lives, but even his cool character had been tested by the sight of Will. As he left today he told them their son was in a very dark place, and that his mental state was particularly fragile given what he had been through at such a young age, never mind his physical injuries. Despite their constant care and attention he was barely eating or drinking anything making him weaker day by day. Agnes' mothering instincts knew she was failing despite her best efforts, and she began to feel desperate.

She watched her husband make his way head bowed towards the sheep huddled together against the top wall. She didn't know in that moment if he stooped against the weather or with the weight of emotion bearing down on them both. Even here by the house, the wind harassed her face with icy blasts, a reminder despite the autumn sunshine, that winter was hard on its heels.

The parting words of Doctor Corbett flew around her mind in similar fashion.

"…something drastic needs to happen to stop this steady decline. I don't know what else I can do…"

Agnes pondered the suggestion of the trip therefore and whether they could, or indeed should, try and get Will out of the house. Joan had suggested it a few days ago over Sunday lunch when they found it impossible to discuss anything other than the war…

"How about we go out for the day to Horsham to see the Christmas market that opened this week. All of us? It is always spectacular and might do Will the world of good to get out and be distracted? We spoke to that Nightingale woman, the organist last Sunday at church about it and she said it's bigger than ever this year with stalls and entertainers and a Father Christmas of course. Arthur and I could head home from there afterwards?"

"He was a bit old for Father Christmas before the war. I dare say he will be even less inclined now," Harold replied, mulling over the idea.

"Well a little bit of magic doesn't do any of us any harm Harold," his mum responded refusing to be put off, "least of all the children."

The words rebounded off her aching limbs. *Perhaps I do need someone to wave a magic wand* Agnes sighed, and the tears came again.

*

Despite Will's initial reluctance and noticeable nerves when the station platform at Steyning was quite crowded, they journeyed to Horsham without incident. Fred was very excited, and chatted and bounced around in the carriage the whole time drawing more than one stern look from the more elderly passengers trying to read or enjoy a quiet smoke. Agnes smiled politely and apologised more than once, but it was the icy stares returned from Harold that made them stop tutting.

Will was anything but exuberant. For some ridiculous reason he had half believed he might still see Alice at the station waiting for him, and replayed that day over and over in his mind. Then he thought of a different train journey, strapped to a bed in the dark and the smoke, the sounds of wounded and dying men relentless in the choking interior. He saw the houses and people whirring past and he remembered a hole in a wooden wall, and a child waving at them as they passed.

The winter sun illuminated the smoke from the train somewhere above the carriage, the shadows of its form flying free along the ground by the tracks as he watched. The thought of smoke made his chest ache and Will pressed his head against the glass and closed his eyes. Agnes moved and sat next to him and took his hand in hers stroking it lightly, though he never opened his eyes.

Fred stopped chatting to his grandparents for a moment and looked at them. His mum seemed sad all the time these days, and his dad never play fought with them like he used to. *Things are just not fun anymore,* he thought frowning. Harold noticed his lad had gone quiet. So he smiled wondering what Freddie was frowning about, and told him not to take any notice of the other passengers. Fred smiled back and then looked out of the window. He didn't care about the other people here. He just wished this stupid war would end soon so they could all carry on as before.

It was not a Christmas wish that would come true for a long time.

*

327

Despite the war, Horsham was alive with the spirit of Christmas. The streets were decorated and with the sun so low, lights sparkled magically along the way in houses and hedgerows, as the Davisons moved towards the town. The hard frost still clung to the rooves and pavements that remained in shadow which only added to the feeling of Christmas. In the distance the sound of a band playing drifted towards them from the direction of the park, and more excitingly for Fred, the chimes and bells of the fair called the shoppers towards it. As Fred ran on ahead, his mum striding out to keep up with him, the family group turned into the market place in the centre of the town. They stopped in amazement at the noise and aromas that now bombarded their senses to entice them in.

The fair was off to the left with a beautifully decorated carousel the focal point where families queued and cheered as it span round and round, the horses racing relentlessly up and down for their smiling riders. In the main centre, stall holders and shop keepers had been hard at it since the crack of dawn to make their wares as attractive as possible and take advantage of the people coming into town to forget their troubles. Some were genuinely sympathetic to the soldiers and were making donations for every item sold or tasted. Others were trying to tap into the swell of national pride to make a quick profit. Inevitably as the taverns opened their doors the scuffles broke out here and there, with accusations from old soldiers and wounded veterans about cowardice and profiteering at the centre of them. Harold skilfully steered his family away from any altercations or potential trouble spots and they soon immersed themselves in the sights and smells of the fabulous market.

They walked around together for an hour, looking at the various wares on offer and just enjoying the delights of the occasion as a family. Harold bought some hot chestnuts from a brazier for them to try, and they paused for a while watching a juggler perform more and more testing feats to coordinated clapping from the gathering crowd. But when he started to 'swallow' knives Agnes felt queasy and moved them on.

It was inevitable in the end that they wanted to split up with so many different things vying for their attention. Arthur was dragged away by Joan from the pie stalls to look at quilts for their bed where some particularly lovely holly patterns had caught her eye. Harold was chatting to some of the local farmers he knew and eyeing up a home brew stall when Freddie came up shouting about the fair. He was excited enough today without the boost from some newly acquired liquorice sticks that Agnes had clearly succumbed to in order to keep the peace.

"He wants to go on the Carousel but I want to look at the fish stalls first and maybe pick up some cheeses for our larder. Can you take him Hal, and then we can all meet by the fair and have a hot drink."

Harold's face fell more at the mention of a hot drink, as opposed to a cold beer, than the prospect of the fair but he nodded and said, "Half an hour?"

As he turned to go, Freddie holding his arm and jumping about, he asked, "What about the lad?"

Agnes looked at Will who was staring across the road to a bric-a-brac shop that had a very festive display in its window and seemed to sell everything from kitchen utensils to clothing. There was a particularly fetching blue coat in the window and it had caught his eye.

"Will can stay with me. Is that okay Will?"

He nodded. Seeing where he was looking Agnes said, "Why don't you go and browse in the shop and I will come and find you there. That coat matches your eyes, go and have a look at it up close if you like it."

She watched him walk off, and then gave Harold a quick peck on the cheek and waved at Freddie as he shot off towards the fair. Harold trudged off behind with a raise of the eyes to his fellow farmers.

Will crossed over to the shop and stood for a while looking at the display. There was a mixture of Christmas baubles and traditional figures in the window. A nativity scene in the centre gave its blessing in front of some shiny pots and pans, and to the right wooden painted soldiers marched gaily past some gardening implements bedecked with festive paperchains. A steam iron fought for space with an ornately decorated tea set, overlooked by a smiling Father Christmas, his sack bulging with presents for the boys and girls of Horsham. On the left a form of cotton wool had been used to make pretend snow surrounding the stands that carried men's hats and cravats, and behind a row of ladies scarves hung the dark blue coat. As Will looked at it in the glow of so many objects, he was transported for a moment back to his innocent childhood.

Without realising it, Will found himself inside the shop of '*WM Lucking and Sons,*' its shelves bulging even more with an Aladdin's cave of goods. He browsed for a moment and then moved back to the window, noticing his mum was now laughing with a stall holder pointing out a large round cheese. He smiled seeing her happy.

"Can I help you Sir?" a polite greying shopkeeper enquired, his white shirt and maroon tie covered neatly by a similarly coloured maroon apron that reached to his knees.

"Oh, I was just looking really," Will said, feeling conspicuous.

"Well there is plenty to look at that's for certain. We pride ourselves on our display every year. If I can help at all just ask."

As the man turned to go with a warm smile, Will pointed hesitantly to the coat hanging just in front of him, framed under a blue, red and gold paper chain that criss crossed the ceiling above the display.

"I like this," he muttered.

"Oh the gentleman's sporting coat. A beautiful choice sir and perfect for this cold snap. Shall I get it down for you?"

"Oh I didn't want to cause any bother. My Mum just said…"

"No bother sir; it is why I am here." And without waiting for a reply from Will, he stepped forward and began to deftly move some items to remove the coat safely.

Being called 'sir' made Will feel odd being so young, and especially after months of saying it to officers and non-commissioned officers. He was neither old nor an officer but quite liked the attention and was more than happy to be taken to the rear of the shop to try the coat on where an ornate full length mirror stood waiting patiently to flatter the next user. He admired the coat and it's seemingly endless supply of pockets, and loved the colour and texture even more up close. As he stood admiring himself in the mirror he heard the shop bell ring again as its door opened, and felt the cold breeze rush along the floor as someone entered.

Will was concerned about the cost and was steeling himself to ask how much it was, when the kindly shopkeeper excused himself for a moment and went to serve the new customer. He left Will basking in the warmth and comfort of such a gorgeous coat and he decided it could make a great Christmas gift for him if it wasn't too expensive and he would ask for nothing else. At that moment he caught an exchange between the shopkeeper and the customer and noticed it was a lady's voice, and excitedly realised his mum had entered and walked to the counter to show her the coat.

"What do you think?" he said, as he rounded a shelf neatly stacked with colanders of varying sizes, realising as he spoke that the lady in the grey fur lined coat and black boots facing away from him, was clearly not his mother. As the grey matching fur lined hat turned to face the source of the question, he found himself face to face with Alice.

She looked stunned and Will felt a wave of shock and emotion roll over him like a mill stone crushing his insides.

"I...thought you were...someone else..." was all he could mutter.

"Will..."she said, her beautiful face betraying no discomfort under the meticulous make up, that enhanced her looks even more. Except perhaps for her eyes he thought, which just for a split second flashed wide, as an animals' are when cornered by a hunter. And just a trace of a tremor in the voice, her carefully trained poise thrown for a moment. Details his military mind captured subconsciously while his conscious mind fell apart.

"I didn't know...sorry..." he said.

"It's fine. How are you Will? Enjoying the little Christmas market?" she asked, the smile covering up the surprise in a golden flash as the elegant charm returned. He felt her voice was even more cultured than before, but no less disarming.

"I'm Ok," was all he could say and he began to remove the coat, his mind struggling to form sentences or find words to ask so many questions and seek answers that had bothered him for months.

"Are you home on leave?"

"I…well…yes, back for a while," he found himself saying, not knowing where to start.

"I bet your mother is thrilled to have you home for Christmas." She put a purse back in her black leather hand bag and spoke without looking at him as she did. "And how are the family and the farm. All ticking along nicely I hope?"

"Yes good thanks and yours?" Will replied, almost in a trance.

"Very well thank you," she answered glancing at him again. "Terribly busy of course, what with Father's war efforts and all that. No end of people coming and going and constant socialising, drumming up support for the battalions. I'm helping with the paperwork. It can be quite tiresome at times."

Alice looked away out of the front windows, as if looking for something or someone. "How is your brother, the one who became an officer? Is he safe?" she continued, turning back now to smile at Will once more.

"James? He is doing very well thank you Alice. I have only seen him once while I was in France."

"I'm pleased he's okay. Very difficult times for all the men over there I'm sure, without the pressures of leadership."

"Yes," Will said, not knowing quite what to make of that remark, and he became unable to think of anything to say next and there was an awkward pause.

"I'll leave these today," he heard her say, laying two shawls on the counter and picking up the black leather bag again. Mr Lucking nodded politely from where he was discreetly rearranging items on a shelf, waiting to be spoken to. "I need to go Will. It was nice to see you again. Enjoy your time at home. My regards to the family."

He heard the words but felt now as if he was floating above the boy swaying by the counter, looking down on the awkward scene and all he could do was nod again and smile, feeling incredibly self-conscious. Will's mind was filled with instant regrets. He thought he should have asked about her brother too, and where he was, now his schooling had undoubtedly finished. He wished he had shaken her hand or made some effort to greet her better, and above all he wished he had mentioned the letter and told her why he was home, rather than just stand there staring stupidly no doubt. The door bell's clang made him snap out of his internal interrogations, and he saw Alice walk a few yards into the street and greet a tall frowning man in uniform who seemed surprised she had come out empty handed. The officer looked towards the window and Will ducked back behind the unwanted colanders, his heart thumping in his mouth. As he risked a glance back towards the windows he saw them walk off arm in arm into the market. As once before in Steyning fields, she never looked back.

Agnes entered the shop and found Mr Lucking senior behind the counter, brushing down the blue coat with a firm clothes brush.

"Good morning Madam."

"I'm looking for my son. He came in to look at that coat actually. Is he here?"

"The young gentleman is just browsing at the back Madam," he replied, "if I can be of any service please don't hesitate to ask."

Agnes walked back to where the mirror waited as ever in silent anticipation, the brooms and shovels of the 'outdoor' section standing sentry along the walls where Will now stood swaying.

"Hello Will. I've got some tasty cheese for our supper later. What did you think of the coat then love?" She was chatting away to him not realising he was miles away now in his head. She squeezed his shoulder, and as he turned round she continued her cheery dialogue without pause, "Are you listening to me William? Hey you'll never guess who I spotted outside on my way here…" and then she saw the sorrowful eyes in his crushed face, and realised he had seen her too.

"Oh Will," was all she could say, the anguished look of her son triggering her own emotive reaction and she pulled him in close.

They walked outside and saw Fred running with some boys through the stalls, Harold momentarily distracted 'testing' an ale at the home brew stall. As he saw his wife approach he quickly swigged it down, nodding to the man and then his eyes narrowed seeing his wife cuddling Will in public without a care for his image.

"Alice is here," Agnes said, her face strained with worry.

Harold glanced around the stalls automatically, and then looked down at Will; the dark shadows encamped on his face once more. He ruffled his son's hair with a deep affection and then looked at Agnes. They had planned to be here for the day, and even eat in one of the better Inns by the river that they had been to once before as a family treat, but Harold could bring common sense to any situation.

"Well we're pretty much done here anyway; I'll go and round up the others."

Chapter 33 – Lost

The bells rang out as ever across the roof tops of Steyning on this damp grey Sunday morning. The storm clouds were gathering in the east for a fresh assault, and would be upon them before lunchtime bringing further heavy rain to swell the already fast flowing Adur river nearby. For the fourth Sunday in a row since their return home however, it looked like the orchestrated peel of the bells would be ignored by the Davisons once more. But at the last minute as the single bell fell silent, Agnes slipped into the church through the heavy oak door, and took a seat in their usual pew at the back. She did not want to sing today. She wasn't even sure she wanted to be here, but she needed to speak to the Vicar and felt she couldn't do that without coming to a service again first.

The church was beautifully decorated for Christmas with a large tree at the back illuminating the gloomy corners of the high arched ceilings above. There were tasteful garlands and bouquets everywhere along the walls and the backs of the pews, and pride of place near the font was the Nativity scene. Its figurines smiled calmly once more in that moment of elation, despite the troubled politics of the time that waited outside the doors of the stable, as they did now for the people of Steyning.

Harry Best, the church warden, stepped quietly over to Agnes as the first song commenced and slipped her a hymn book with a reassuring smile.

"Page 52, *'Dear Lord and Father of Mankind,'*" he whispered, and with a squeeze of her arm, he turned and walked back to the door to check no one else was outside.

The Reverend Arthur Congreve-Pridgeon B.A., had served the parish of St Andrew and St Cuthman faithfully for some years now, and was not the sort of priest to count how many weeks it was since someone attended his church. Tall, slightly portly but energetic still despite his years, and with a kind handsome face, he instead noted when things were out of place and made it his duty to enquire discreetly as to why. He was aware of the issues at Mill Farm and was pleased to see Agnes appear this morning, as he observed the dwindling congregation over the top of his lectern. The war lay heavily on the town these days with more and more families affected, and not all of them felt the pull of the bells every Sunday as they once did. Much of his time was spent travelling the parish to listen, and pray, and to be the buffer for the anger and grief that was being thrown up, as patriotism waned and faith was shaken.

Arthur had agonised himself regularly about whether to join up to serve the Lord in the battlefields of France. His recent visit from the Bishop had advised him against it; that as such an influential vicar he was better placed to help here, but it was a struggle he prayed for assistance with every night. He was indeed seen as a focal point for the town however, and people still looked to him for answers as Agnes did now, drawing on his inner strength.

As the service ended and the last of the congregation filed out, with the usual polite remarks and reminders for the week ahead, he saw Agnes Davison had not moved from the pew. Asking Harry and his fellow wardens to do the usual round of checks, he moved over and asked if she would like to come to the vicarage for a spot of tea.

They walked round the side of the church and set off along the path towards the splendid Tudor home that still had traces of an even older occupancy within the grounds. Agnes felt as if she was fighting a losing battle herself. The neatness of the house that she entered seemed to just compound the uncertainty that now invaded her once ordered life. She was unable to get through to Will, and with two more boys away, Agnes could feel herself unravelling inside, and prayed for a miracle.

With desperate eyes she asked the Reverend if he truly believed in miracles and the power of prayer. He didn't answer directly but talked about his own personal challenges and struggles with his faith in the light of this global conflict, but said that without it he could find no sense or order in the world. Somewhere in the house a family member or pupil struggled to learn a new piece on the piano, and the disjointed notes seemed only to accentuate the conflict in her mind.

The housekeeper, Mrs Battersby, left a tray of fresh leaf tea and warm crumpets on the side board, whose steam intertwined deliciously above the two of them, as they paused in their emotive discussions for a short prayer. The Reverend then stood up and moving to the sideboard declared, "The Lord moves in mysterious ways Agnes, I know that to be true, and sometimes we just need to put our faith in him to deliver. Now to even more pressing matters, can I tempt you to a crumpet with your cup of tea?"

*

It was raining harder now. The drops beat on the attic window with an increasing desperation to be let in. Will lay on the top bunk and stared aimlessly at the ceiling. His mind blank, his spirit ebbing away into the knitted quilt his grandma had given him three Christmases ago, its fading patterns crumpled under his weight. Fred had learnt some time ago not to loiter in the room or engage his brother in conversation, after more than one object had been thrown at him to underline his demands for solitude.

Will felt the guilt of his behaviour merge with so many other memories, like the smoke from the fires his dad often lit on the farm when it drifted away into the evening fog. He felt the pain of leaving friends and comrades behind in France most acutely of all, but couldn't stop his steady decline into the darkness.

His mum had come up to see him when she got home from church, her words about her time with the Vicar and his ideas just more background noise to Will. The cake lay untouched where it had been left on the butterfly tray; the spiritual suggestions for his rehabilitation as cold to him as the mug of tea, standing idly by the Victoria sponge. It was all pointless he felt, and he may as well be back in France where at least no one expected him to do anything except follow orders.

A loud thump on the kitchen door below reverberated in his brain and made him stir for a moment. He heard his mum call "Harold" from the kitchen, and the repeated shouts made him kneel up and peer through the window, where the rain still hammered down in wave after wave of fresh attacks. Will watched with idle eyes as Harold jogged over from the barn, his coat held above his head in protection, though the wind betrayed him swirling the coat all over the place so that the rain found a way through regardless.

As he aimlessly pondered why his dad was not wearing his cap for once, he looked down and saw the frame of a man standing by the back door covered by a long dark jacket; who by coincidence was wearing a cap, and what looked like large boots. It was hard to see much more looking directly down, but he was not in uniform Will noted with relief. The visitor carried a thick stick with him, the sort his dad used to shepherd the animals, and brace against the steeper climbs on the top field. As they disappeared inside he collapsed back on the bed, his interest spent.

Will spotted a small woodlouse walking across the ceiling near his head and watched it's seemingly directionless progress with bored eyes. He felt it looked as lost as he was, drifting about without any purpose. He was aware of the voices downstairs but didn't care about visitors. Doctor Corbett was not due back for another four days and he was not expected to report to the military doctor in Horsham until he was assessed again at the end of the month. He briefly considered just taking off back to France and finding his way back to his old regiment, but the logistics of the whole process was too much for him to focus on and he just shut his eyes now, and hoped for sleep.

His hope was broken by the sound of loud footsteps coming up the stairs and then his door reverberated to several firm knocks. He sat up and swung his legs round over the edge of the bunk, his body reacting to the unexpected intrusion on behalf of his absent mind. Not more tests surely.

"Come in," he heard himself saying almost automatically.

The door flew open and Will stared at a gaunt tall man with an enormous beard and moustache. He was wearing a plain white shirt and brown worn waistcoat and dark trousers and what looked like old army boots. Although he must have left his coat and cap downstairs, the rain still dripped from his arms and legs, and unusually he had retained his stick which up close seemed dwarfed by the frame of the man.

Will jumped down and caught sight of himself now in the mirror which hung over their oaken chest of drawers, and was shocked at the stranger who stared back at him. He hadn't looked in a mirror for some time, and the sudden realisation of how much weight he had lost since he went to France snapped inside his brain. He looked back at the man swaying awkwardly in the door, his bulk filling the doorframe, the head slightly bowed to look in. The two men were held by the emotion of the moment, the memories hurtling round the room as if the wind had followed the visitor inside.

Then the bearded apparition broke into a huge grin with a shout of "Stand by your beds! Inspection!" Archie strode the half dozen steps across the room and scooped Will up in a huge bear hug, and the friends laughed and cried as they stood in that embrace for what seemed like eternity. Will felt something pop in his head in that moment and the darkness began to roll away like the storm clouds outside which chased by the easterly wind, broke up and fled across the Downs, the sun rising triumphantly to sparkle on the rain drenched roofs.

At the bottom of the stairs Harold stood with one hand on the bannister, his foot poised on the first step ready to climb to his son's rescue if things had gone badly. When he heard the shouts and cries he nodded, dabbing his eyes with his sleeve, and turned to walk out of the kitchen back to work. He saw his wife standing over the sink looking out of the window on the battered garden outside. He noticed her hand trembling as she held the side and immediately changed tack and walked up to her. He rested his hands on her shoulders and pulled her to him. She leant back into him, feeling his strength and warmth, and grabbed one of his hands with hers. Her hair smelt of baking, a buffet of sensory ingredients to his nose, and he kissed her tenderly on the head.

"It's alright Aggie lass," he said, "He'll be fine now, mark my words."

"I know Hal," she said and turned to kiss him properly, her tears cold on his cheeks. "I just want him to stay home for ever and I'm worried when he's well he will go back."

"Hey let's not talk about that now. That's for the future. Let him find himself again first."

She nodded knowing he was right but the worry never left her eyes. As he pulled away to carry on he touched a tear on her cheek. "Put that smile back on my lovely girl. He'll be wanting a bath and clean clothes mark my words and the way that Archie Bunden ate two of your rock cakes before he even went upstairs, I reckon a big lunch might be needed too!"

She smiled now to please him but also because she could focus on being a mum too and she loved that. As Harold pulled his boots on at the door he paused, "You know I never stop believing that our boys will always find a way home somehow. There's always been something special about this place. The war won't go on for ever."

He went out closing the door behind him, some of the recent storm water spilling from the frame to the kitchen floor. As she watched him stride up the path, Sally joining him from her outside kennel and let free to roam, there was a loud shout from upstairs and she smiled without pressure now.

Fred came in and looked enquiringly up at the ceiling.

"Your brother's friend has called to see him. I think he's going to be alright now Freddie," she said.

"Oh great. Does this mean you will make a cake to celebrate?"

She laughed and pulled him in close to hug him while he wriggled to get free.

"Probably, cheeky," she replied and then turned to carry on. "So wash those hands," she shouted as an afterthought. But Fred had already run off down the corridor. He grabbed Will's football and bounded upstairs with it, two at a time.

Harold stopped to light a cigarette. The sun was out again now, and despite being very low, its rays shone across the top pasture. The trip to Warnham had been worth it now, he thought to himself. *Trust the bloody army to have the wrong address for Archie's mother. No wonder he never replied. Never knew our lad was home.* He let out a deep sigh as a shout of "Wey hey, let's have it then," came from the upstairs window to greet Freddie's intrusion. Harold looked back and smiled,

Sally looking loyally at her master for her instructions.

"Standing stone I think girl," he said with a wave of his cigarette, and she shot off ahead in a widening arc understanding the words, her pace taking her effortlessly across the field. She ran, feeling the joy of the moment, while never ceasing to lose sight of her master striding up the meadow.

It was a feeling Harold felt too, from head to toe, and his back felt good as new.

Chapter 34 – Captain's armband

The pounding of the rain on the roof only heightened the claustrophobic sensation brought on by the incessant shelling that shook the very foundations of the dug-out to the core. It seemed to James that when one stopped another started and made for long restless nights in the trenches. The stifling heat of the summer was replaced by the bitter chills in winter and he gave up trying to sleep anymore on the hard low bunk, as another shell dislodged more dust and soil into the shelter.

The cold and the noise combined, and the fact his nerves were on edge permanently in here, made him always feel somehow safer outside in the trenches, as bizarre as that seemed. James always loved being outdoors back home anyway, and hated these rat infested holes they attempted to call 'home.' He slept in his clothes as they all did, always ready for anything the night might throw at them, and putting on his boots and jacket he was soon ready to take on the day once more and stood up.

He stepped over to a small stack of wooden crates serving as a table and noticed that the bowl of water left there by their 'batman' had a layer of ice over it. James paused, wondering whether he could steel himself for the experience to come, the bowl throwing up an image of a frozen cattle trough on the farm back home and breaking it with his boot. Then with an intake of breath he took a knife lying on the crate and broke it up, and splashed the freezing water on his face shaking his head to clear his mind. He noticed a maggot crawling around a small piece of stale bread near the bowl that had clearly been dislodged when he picked up the knife and flicked it away in disgust, wondering how on earth it was alive in winter. Shivering as much with the thought it had probably hatched on some warm part of one of their bodies, as much as with the effects of the water, he dried his face with his scarf.

The blanket to the door was thrown open and Captain Johnson stepped in, his own scarf wrapped tightly round his frost lined face, and he began stamping his feet and flapping his arms to get some circulation in.

"Still alive old boy?"

"Just about Jonners. How are the men?"

"Frozen like statues poor buggers, like their officers too, though I daresay the Hun aren't exactly sitting around in deckchairs drinking Martinis either."

James smiled and reached for his great coat and gloves.

"Heading out lieutenant?"

"Need to warm up Harry. Can't sleep here and besides if I'm to follow your orders I need to send a message to Béthune."

"Ah yes the debt of gratitude. Not sure why you are bothering, she more than likely won't show up." He smiled and then frowned at the black remains of the cold brazier. "No fire?"

"No wood! Wordsworth has gone off to look for some but he left us some lovely fresh water to wash in."

Harry saw the bowl of dark water on the crates, the broken ice pieces floating about like bergs in the sea, and wrinkled his nose.

"Think I'll pass. You didn't fancy burning our table then," he added as he finally removed his coat and sat on his bunk, lighting a cigarette and pointing at the old vegetable crates.

"Certainly not Harry," James said in mock indignation. "It might be bad here but if we have to start burning the furniture then we definitely are in trouble!"

They laughed together and shared a smoke.

"Any news from home?"

"Nothing more since the note saying he was back from the hospital and not faring too well."

Harry took a long drag on his cigarette and frowned again, deep in thought.

"I'm sure he'll be all right Jim," he said, blowing smoke into the dusty air. "Seemed to be of the same stubborn stock when I saw him that once. Stick to the plan. It will all be alright mark my words. And I'll get the place redecorated for you in the meantime."

"Good luck with that! I don't plan to be away that long but if you could spruce the place up a bit, pictures on the wall that sort of thing, and perhaps get some chairs to go with the table that would be lovely."

Harry threw a cup at his friend now, and James caught it and threw it back in one smooth movement.

"See what did I tell you James old fruit, slip fielder for sure! We'll set another game up when you get back."

James turned up the collar on his great coat now about his ears and braced himself to step out into the trench once more. Suddenly the uneven cramped bunk became more appealing but he wanted to be out and had things to do.

"Oh I nearly forgot. Dispatches came down from HQ. Old Bluffers has come through with my requests."

"Are they going to put you in charge of the whole Brigade?" James laughed.

"Not quite old boy. Just the 2nd Support Battalion."

James stopped, his hand still on the curtain. "But battalions are commanded by majors?"

"Indeed they are, and old Bluffers has gone and got himself a colonelcy so he has, and the Brigade commander has told him to nominate a successor."

"Good God. Major Harry Johnson?"

"At your service." He stood up now and James let the curtain fall again, and took his friend's hand warmly in a firm embrace before they hugged.

"But surely that's an order not a request? You can't demand promotion can you?" James added, smiling as they pulled apart.

"Quite so old boy. It's all been in the pipe for some time, I just didn't say anything until it was all confirmed. Not least until the request for my successor for number three company was approved. Here."

He tossed him an envelope and James opened it and found the epaulettes and documents announcing his promotion to captain. He collapsed back against the fruit crates in shock. "Good Lord."

"Good old Bluffers more like!"

"But I've just settled into my lieutenant's role."

"Well you can just settle into this too now. There's a war on old boy. Things happen pretty fast around here when we are not sat on our freezing backsides trading insults with the Hun that is. It's pretty much the same job anyway except the buck stops with you now. So when you go out there just remember it's all yours." He laughed loudly while James continued to stare in disbelief at the pips on the shoulder flashes.

"But this means you will be off to HQ?" he said at length.

"Oh yes but I will be back and forth. Can't keep me away. Besides I can't practice my spin bowling in this mud. Need a firmer track what? And you can approve your own bloody leave from now on without me holding your hand all the time. Now off you trot *captain* and I'll cover for you until you get back."

James stood up and shook Harry's hand again. Harry took the epaulettes and placed them on his shoulder covers, removing the old lieutenant ones.

"Thanks Jonners," James said, looking at his friend with a deep affection.

"Good luck Jim."

*

He walked down the trench to the communications dugout and ducked inside where another young lieutenant, fresh from England, and two corporals were working on the signals. One was on the phone to someone behind the lines while the other was tapping away at the wireless and writing down messages for the lieutenant to read. James watched the wireless tap away, lost in thought for a moment, the repetitive sound of tapping soothing in some strange way. He decided for once a hand written message might be better and went to carry on.

"Anything we can help with Davison?" the new officer asked.

"Fancy a brew up sir?" one of the corporals said, used to James' easy nature with the men.

James shook his head.

"No lads I'm good thank you."

He paused then, understanding the changes ahead. "Oh but one thing you might need to pass on."

"Sir?"

"It's Captain Davison now. I'm the new company CO."

The young lieutenant joined the men in standing up, a stool falling over backwards. The three soldiers stood transfixed, a mixture of surprise and dread on their faces for what would come next. The corporal who had offered tea was red, his mind racing as to the potential consequences of his informality; while the lieutenant who had used his surname because of their seemingly equal status could only say "Sir" once more.

James eyed them up and let the moment hang in the air. Then with a nod he stated "At ease gentlemen," and walked out, about a foot taller.

*

Despite the grey drizzle of the day the two friends chatted and laughed continually as the train huffed on towards Brighton, and Will began to reconnect with his former self. Archie saw it too, and smiled inwardly, happy to live in the moment once more.

They left the station and walked towards the beach as the sun broke through the glistening rain clouds to further lift the gloom. The two friends sat on a bench along the promenade near the pier and stretched out, allowing its warmth to caress them. Will could have stayed like that for some time but Archie was never one for sitting still, and reached into the pockets of his army great coat.

"Ta dah."

He had bought a couple of hard rock cakes in the platform café "to keep them going," feeling slightly guilty for eating most of their packed lunch before eleven in the morning. He did love Mrs Davison's sandwiches though. Will smiled at his friend, shaking his head, and wondered where he put it all. He enjoyed a good meal too but he had never seen anyone eat as much as Archie and not put on loads of weight. He certainly had a very physical job even before he joined the army, so maybe that was it and he could just burn it off being so active. *Even so it was crazy*, Will thought to himself.

But in truth he was pleased to see his friend eating again because it made him feel reassured that normality was being resumed, especially seeing how his friend had changed after being injured. Behind the bravado and the continuous fountain of rock cake crumbs cascading forth onto the floor, he knew Archie had stared into the abyss just like he had. Just like many of them had, and some like poor Ernie had stepped off into the eternal darkness too.

Archie stopped eating as Will stood up suddenly without speaking and stepped onto the shingle beach front. He watched him move off, the stones moving and crunching under the uncertain stride of his young friend's boots. A seagull circling overhead had swooped down for a moment spotting the easy pickings around the bench but veered away as Will got to his feet, and made another circle around the windswept promenade.

Will made for the waterline, though it was tricky making progress on the wet stones and he walked diagonally towards the sea. He found the remains of an old wooden jetty long since broken up, a little way from the main pier but with several planks still intact for him to perch on. He sat down here and allowed his mind to drift in and out with the waves, the stones being swept back and forth as the early morning tide turned to trudge its weary way back out once more. Further out the sea crashed repeatedly in wild steaming waves across the sand banks, twisting and turning in an endless rage across the horizon.

Will watched the foaming sea sweeping repeatedly up the beach and could not shake the image of the men doing likewise in France. In his mind he saw the Germans in the woods near Estaires pouring forward, line after line, and for some reason pictured Guptha of the 39th Rifles smiling at him before charging up the hill with a roar.

The waves came on taking huge sections of the beach and pushing the stones this way and that, before falling back and having to regroup to do it all again. *God what a waste*, he thought to himself, watching the drama unfold around his wooden throne and hugged his knees to his chest, the cold suddenly making itself known to him through his clothes. As he pulled his body into a ball for warmth, his coat crinkled with the sound of paper being crunched, and he reached into his pocket and pulled out Alice's last letter to him. He had forgotten it was in his coat. The dark stain on the outside a bloody reminder of the men whose care it had passed through.

Ced had taken it from Albert's jacket before they buried him, and not wanting to add to Will's grief had kept it again, as he had done the first time Albert gave it to him at Easter. Ced managed to push it in Will's things before he was evacuated to England after being gassed. His hastily written words on the outside a vain attempt to soften the emotional blows of the message within.

Will had read Alice's final words to him several times now, and knew most of it off by heart. He pictured her the last time he saw her, at the station hanging to the train door, as beautiful as a summer's day; and that kiss…another time completely. He decided that was how he would remember her. That was the Alice he loved. He read the letter once more, and then looked at Ced's note on the envelope. In the midst of this global madness the message finally found a home.

He sighed deeply and put the letter back in the envelope and then slowly tore it into sections and let it go into the sea. For a moment the fresh morning breeze caught the pieces and took them up into the air, dancing and spinning as Alice loved to do. Then they fell across the retreating tide and were taken out. He knew it was right to let her go. He knew it was right for her to marry someone else, someone more suited to her lifestyle, though it still pained him to think of it. He knew Ced was right for saying it, though he vowed never to tell him as much, or there'd be no living with him. He smiled. *Stay safe you cantankerous old sod.*

Will stood up and watched one of the pieces rush in for a moment and then be taken away again. The seagull had followed his progress from its spiralling flights high up above, and now swooped down expectantly to check out the unusual addition to the surface of its feeding grounds. It was used to the scraps and leftovers of these two legged creatures that came in large numbers during the summer months, but it swung away again disappointedly with a cry of disgust at the tasteless morsels floating away.

Somewhere inside Will his own pieces started to come back together again and as he listened to the gull's disdainful cry he nodded, understanding. "Take care Alice," he said out loud, his voice drowned out by the next crashing wave. "I hope you find the happiness you are looking for."

The thunder of the guns rumbled again now as their dawn chorus began afresh, the deadly percussion refusing to be ignored above the sound of the sea, and he looked out to the far horizon. Will felt its pull inside him, making his lungs ache once more.

"I hope we all can," he added, rubbing his chest. He jumped down on the shale and strode back up to the bench with a renewed purpose. The stones didn't hinder him now. He nodded to Archie who stood up. He had heard the guns too and nodded back and their eyes met saying all that needed to be said. It was time to move on.

Chapter 35 – A new season

As Will and Archie walked back to the station, the sight of troops moving in great numbers through the town in Brighton only served to underline the feeling that their stay here was all too temporary. As they alighted at Steyning station however, the familiarity of home caressed their worries, and brought a sense of safety back into their troubled minds, and they talked cheerfully as they walked up the high street once again.

The sun was setting as the friends strolled up the drive to the farm. It had only been half interested in the day anyway, and was happy to slink away to bed and let the dark take over. Will could hear voices coming from the kitchen as they approached the house, and raised his eyes at his bearded companion.

"Visitors," he said surprised.

Sally let out one bark as they passed her kennel. She had smelt Will some time ago but was too busy with her bone to come and greet him now. She could do that later anyway when she was finished. But the other one wasn't from her pack and she gave one warning bark to let him know she was there. He could get his own bone.

"Bit late now Sal," Will said, and they walked on.

They opened the door and went in and the smell of something delicious cooking in the oven made both their stomachs growl with delightful anticipation.

"See what did I tell you? I said if you put a pie in, they'd be home for supper. I knew he wouldn't disappear." Harold spoke to his wife who was sitting chatting to a strange lady at the table. Another man was by the larder getting some beer but Agnes jumped up in front of him and blocked the view.

"Oh Will I was worried, you could have told us you would be out all day."

"We couldn't Mum," he responded, embarrassed by her fussing

him in front of strangers, "we were fine honest."

"Blame's all mine Mrs D," Archie chipped in on behalf of his friend, "trains were held up with all the war traffic," he lied. "Took longer than I thought to get there, and time ran away."

"I said Archie could stay Mum."

"Well yes, of course he can. Have you eaten properly?"

"Yes..." Will began, thinking of the fish and chips Archie had insisted they have on the way back, but then his friend jumped in.

"Not that much Mrs Davison. Just what you gave us..." He sniffed and looked away.

"Just as well I put an extra pie in then." She smiled, and Archie beamed with delight.

"Yes I warned them if you were coming home tonight we'd need a pie just for you." It was the man from the back of the kitchen who spoke now, and as they all turned to look at the new voice, Will and Archie found themselves looking at the face of their sergeant major.

"Evening lads," Russell said with a grin.

"Bloody Nora, it's the CSM" Archie said quite stunned, and the pair straightened up as one.

Russell stepped forward and shook their disbelieving hands now.

"Judging by that animal attached to your face I can see you haven't been well Bunden. How are the lungs Davison?"

"Much better Sergeant Major, sir, though it can still hurt to breathe sometimes."

"And what about you, they manage to put you together again Humpty Dumpty?"

Will and Archie were in shock not just from finding their CSM standing in the kitchen and not in France, but also seeing him in civilian clothes and being jovial.

"I still have this stick," Archie replied, waving it about "but they did a proper job on me so they did sir."

"I see. Well first things first, let me introduce my wife. Ginny, this is Corporal Davison and Lance Corporal Bunden."

"Are we dreaming?" Archie whispered to Will, as the lady got up from the table and came round to see them. "Maybe we are still on the train asleep."

351

"I hope not," said Will, remembering Archie snoring with his face plastered against one of the windows, leading to the other passengers moving on to a different carriage. "You were the only one sleeping and that was a nightmare."

"A pleasure to meet you both," Ginny said with a lovely smile, her lush black hair falling in ringlets about her face.

"And you miss," said Will.

"Ma'am," was all Archie could manage, suddenly bashful in the presence of this lady.

Ginny took Will's hand then and stared at him with piercing green eyes. *A real beauty. How did the CSM bag this one?* Will thought to himself.

"I wanted to come in person and thank you. I'm so pleased you are here." She turned then still holding his hand, looking at Agnes. "Your boy saved my husband's life. I will never forget that. He allowed my Geoffrey to come home to us. To our boys." Looking back at Will she said "Thank you" very tenderly, and squeezed his hands. "Thank you Corporal."

"He did more than that," Russell added, coming over to his wife. "He saved half the company with his actions that day. Not to mention what he did for his officer when he was wounded. Proper hero this one."

Harold felt the emotion swell in his neck, and he stepped over to his wife, and they squeezed hands smiling. Will just nodded, embarrassed as ever, and then laughed when Archie whispered in his ear, "Geoffrey likes you."

At that moment Fred ran past the kitchen window being chased by two smaller boys waving sticks and Will was able to look out of the window and control his laugh.

"Our boys, Stanley and John," Ginny said, as they pushed Fred back towards the barn, sticks clashing in the latest sword fight as the assembled adults watched them for a moment.

"Anyway we are not just here on a social visit," Russell continued, "as lovely as it is to see you all and our thanks once again for your hospitality." He nodded then at Agnes. "I'm here officially to check on you Will, and it's good to kill two birds with one stone seeing you

Bunden; but I'm also here to discuss a new venture as it were."

"Shall we go out into the garden for some air and let the men talk?" Agnes said, knowing this was going to be a talk she was dreading, but realising her presence probably wouldn't help.

"That would be lovely," Ginny replied, knowing the army way, and they moved towards the door and with smiles, stepped out to leave the men in peace.

"How is Lieutenant Dunn?" Will asked then, unable to avoid the past anymore.

"He's dead son, despite your best efforts," Russell replied matter of factly. "Died from his wounds two days later, and no doubt will get a hero's requiem somewhere back home. What you did was an incredibly brave thing to do, and I'm sorry you weren't able to save the man, whatever people thought of him. But it hasn't gone unnoticed and that's why I'm here."

Will was numb at the news. As Russell continued to speak, imparting details about what happened after Will rescued Dunn and they were taken off to the hospital, his mind drifted away to the fog and choking gas, and the shouts and screams of the front. At some point the sergeant major must have stopped speaking because he was suddenly aware of his dad standing in front of him and helping him onto a chair.

"He's much better than he was, trust me, but he's still weak and I think it will be a while before he's fully recovered, so we need to go easy on my lad," his dad was saying.

Will looked up and all eyes were on him; concerned friendly eyes.

"I'm alright, just very tired," he said.

"Well this might perk you up a bit. They are giving you the Distinguished Conduct Medal lad, for conspicuous gallantry in the face of the enemy. Captain Wittering recommended you after he saw your actions at Neuve-Chappelle and a new captain, Goodman if I recall, seconded it as a character reference. So Major D'Arcy sealed it and its official."

"Good grief, the DCM, what a day this is turning out to be," Archie said. "It will look great on the kit for the new season," he added with a smile.

"I don't know what to say sir," Will stuttered, "I was just doing my duty."

"I think we all know what you have done over there has gone above and beyond, on more than one occasion. Well done lad." As Russell shook his hand for the second time that evening, his dad moved round and unashamedly gave him a hug. He whispered some words into his son's ear for him alone, and then announced "This calls for a celebration."

Harold handed out the beers they had been opening earlier when the two friends arrived, and then asked his son, "Is this Captain Goodman any relation to Celia in the church?"

"Yes. It's her husband, Dad," Will replied, "Squire Goodman is her brother-in-law."

"Well I'll be. That's a turn up for the books and no mistake. You wait to your mother hears about this."

They chinked glasses then, and Archie noticed Russell was shuffling about, as if he had something on his mind.

"Everything alright sergeant major?" he asked.

"Well speaking of new seasons and all that, there is something else…"

As they listened attentively he went on to tell them that he had been pulled out of the front line to help with the recruitment drive in England, and that part of that involved spending some time with the Southdown Battalions that Lord Lowther had raised who were now stationed at Witley camp near Godalming in Surrey.

"That's where David is," Harold chipped in as Archie looked at Will, understanding better the link to him of Lord Lowther, or more specifically Lord Pevensey.

Russell continued saying he had a friend who was a sergeant major there, called Carter, and that he was going to help him with the training, and wanted Will to go too. It would be a huge boost to the men to have one of their own back there who had already seen action, and was highly decorated to boot. More importantly, he continued, it would mean a promotion to sergeant, and as they were out of the front line currently, it wouldn't take much to move Archie as well and get him a promotion to full corporal while they were at it.

"In fact I can almost guarantee they would pay to have you transferred Bunden," he said with a grin, "though the monstrosity you call a beard would have to go."

Will had an unexpected moment of hesitation, and something like bitterness he had not expected to feel, hesitant to help with anything remotely connected to the Pevenseys. But it passed as quickly as it arose, and regardless of Alice's connections, this was a chance to have a fresh start, and more than that, to see his brother again. Of course he felt some guilt for the friends he had left behind, especially Ced, but he was sure he would see them again one way or another. *Perhaps it would be cathartic and help him move on properly from his attachment to Alice*, he thought.

So he simply said "Why not," and his dad let out the deep breath he had been holding in. Archie grinned, pleased at the promotion but inside pleased to be able to stay in England, and who knows perhaps the war would be over before they had to go back.

"That's settled then," Russell declared with a broad smile. "Now we best be on our way back to the quarters. You boys enjoy your Christmas here and get well. The army will send for you soon enough once you are signed fit in the New Year. Quicker probably as you are not going straight back over there."

They shook hands again now, and finishing his beer with a long swig, Russell picked up his coat and moved to the door. Outside they met the ladies chatting near the vegetable garden, watching the three boys charge through the barn once more, sending the half broken door clattering away.

"Time to go Genevieve old girl," Russell announced with mock formality. Then with a tone that was well known to Archie and Will bellowed, "Fall in boys!" and the two lads reluctantly trotted over.

As the Davisons watched them go, Archie said "I nearly fell in myself. Old habits and all that."

"You will stay for the night Archie?" Agnes said, "James' bed is always made up."

"Well if you insist Mrs D, it is getting late."

"Just don't get too comfortable," Harold added with a mock frown, "we need some food left for the rest of us!"

"Oh don't worry Mr Davison," Archie replied, "I'm away back to Brighton in the morning."

"Brighton?" Will repeated, surprised at this comment. "But we only came through there today."

"Yes I know but I want to go back to the hospital and pay my respects."

"Why didn't you say when we were at the station. You could have gone then?" Will continued.

"I did think about it, but your dad made me promise I'd look after you so I wanted to get you home first. You can come with me if you want."

Harold looked away at this comment, pretending to notice a problem with the wall nearby.

As Will thought about what to do, Freddie sneaked up behind Archie and whacked him with a stick and then ran off.

"Ahh got me!" Archie cried, pretending to be stabbed.

"I'll leave it for now," Will said wanting to enjoy the comforts of home, Sister Dent's parting words suddenly in his thoughts. "You can tell them I said hello. I am sure you will be well received, and you certainly don't need me to hold your hand I know that."

"True enough," Archie replied, "but I will tell them about you in between lunch and tea!"

He grinned and then picked up one of the dropped sticks and chased Fred into the house.

Harold looked at Will.

"We can be very proud of this one Mother. A real Davison that's for sure."

Agnes smiled, unsure of what that meant exactly and now asked the question that had been on her mind since the Russells arrived.

"Is he to go away again?"

"Not for a while Aggie love. He's transferring to the 'Southdowns', as an instructor. Based here in England. He will be with David can you believe."

"And Archie too," Will added.

The relief came in a rush then to Agnes, and she pulled Will in close and kissed the top of his head as they moved back towards the house, from where the shouting of the two mismatched adversaries clearly continued. Harold joined his wife and son, the three of them walking side by side with Will in the middle, the emotions of the last few weeks locking them together.

Sally finished her bone and looked up. She guessed despite the evening chill it was not time to go into the house yet, and so circled twice in her kennel ready for sleep. The sun was sliding away quickly now, its warmth long since spent, but in that moment the world felt a whole lot brighter to the Davisons.

Chapter 36 - Full Time

The truck ambled slowly up one of the larger streets in Béthune towards the main intersection at Place Saint-Eloi. It was moving carefully to try and avoid the various dips and potholes that seemed to line many of the streets here, and with good reason, for it seemed to any onlooker as if one more serious jolt and the lorry would fall apart at the seams. *Rue Ernest Renan* was no different, and what the great philosopher and historian Renan would have made of the street named after him, one could only imagine. No doubt he would curse it in several of the languages he could speak fluently, as Rose did now, sitting in a café on the side of the Square Beuvry, as the truck clunked past spraying several of the tables with stagnant water from the overnight rain. The curse from the driver was matched by Rose's previously quiet occupancy being dispelled as the water splashed her best stockings.

"Damnation," she exclaimed, attempting to pad down the water drops with her napkin with one hand, while keeping her cigarette out of harm's reach above her in the other. She then looked nervously about to ensure her expected date had not appeared yet, and satisfied, she regained her previous composure. Rose glowered at a fat Frenchman opposite her who was trying to smile sympathetically, his red beret comically perched on an oversized head, and he went back to focusing on his meagre meal and large glass of wine. *Which reminds me*, she thought, and reached out and lifted her own glass of *'vin rouge Maison,'* which she was sure was watered down, but didn't care as she had most definitely earnt it. More importantly she would most definitely *not* be paying!

Rose Kellett had been a librarian back in England when war broke out, working at Kings College University in London, which enabled her to continue her own studies on French philosophy. She wondered why she was in France, and especially as a nurse considering she felt regularly queasy at the sight of blood, and did not enjoy the mud and muck of the front one bit, not to mention the hideous rats and other unmentionable things. She recalled some dreamy ideal that she would be able to study her passion first hand while over here - a point which had drawn her to this café today as a meeting point - and then after a boozy night out with friends they had all joined up together.

Now a year on she found herself far removed from the silence and sanctity of her former life, with plenty of time to reflect on her rash act. She took another large swig of wine to fortify herself against the memories and beckoned to the waiter. The opportunity to get away from it all from time to time was therefore very welcome and was one of the reasons she had volunteered to work on the ambulance trains, if nothing else than for the change of scenery, literally.

She also took the role to test herself in some perverse way, for she was certainly no quitter; something her family ancestry would attest to, being of Norse origin and more recently living and working in the harsh landscape of the Lake District. However, as she studied her long blond locks in the bottom of the small silver side dish, she also knew that when you had a chance for some relaxation time, you should grab it with both hands.

So despite some misgivings, Rose had looked forward to today for some time now, since she met the dashing Guards' officer at the train depot and was made to promise to keep an eye on his younger brother. She wondered why she had made yet another impulsive decision, but had gone along with it none-the-less and ensured she looked as good as possible given the circumstances, which included the stockings.

'More than likely fall flat on your face Rose as on your back, you mad fool,' she thought to herself, as a small boy made his way over to her, zig zagging expertly through the tables.

She didn't need her astute intellect to work out the boy in ill-fitting trousers and a fading blue shirt was clearly not the waiter.

Here it comes Rose, she thought to herself, and sure enough the little freckled faced errand boy stopped at her table.

"Mademoiselle Keleet," he said in high pitched French that destroyed the grand heritage of her ancestral surname in one shrill moment.

"Oui," she replied a little self-consciously hoping the whole conversation would not be in French.

"Une lettre pour vous," he announced with a small bow.

"Merci," Rose replied taking the note, and then noticing him staring unashamedly straight at her, took a small coin from her purse and passed it to him.

"Au revoir," he announced through gap fronted teeth, and scurried back the way he had come.

Rose turned the letter over in her hand. She was surprised to receive a hand written note, and not a telegram, and she looked round the square for a moment to see if the author was skulking in the shadows anywhere nearby observing her reaction. She knew what it probably said given the military stamp on the envelope, and was tempted mischievously for a moment to set fire to it with a match and toss is disdainfully away without reading it. Just in case she was being watched. But she was nothing if not curious, and opened the note to see what this particular man could come up with to add to her succession of disappointments. To her surprise it was probably the one reason she would have accepted, and she wrinkled her nose unknowingly in frustration in a way that somehow made her more attractive.

"Oh dam and blast," she muttered under her breath, "now I have to pay for the wine after all."

She tapped the envelope on the side of the table as a way of thinking, as the waiter came up with the bottle of house red, keen to refill the glass of the pretty blond nurse who had drawn several admiring glances since arriving. But Rose was not the shy jilted lady he hoped she might be, when he combed his hair and checked his teeth for left over salad in the kitchen mirror having seen the boy approach her with the note.

"L'addition, Monsieur," she said in a strong tone looking through him, without the hint of a smile, or indeed a *'s'il vous plait'* to go with it, and he retreated with his ego dented but not destroyed. There would be other more grateful Mademoiselles for sure, as the war went on.

Rose got up and strode quickly back down the road of one of her 19th Century heroes. She turned over the apology in her mind, against the time wasted and the disappointment she felt. She was disappointed because she had genuinely wanted to see him again.

He would make it up to her next time for sure, he had written, or were they just more empty words, and another promise to be broken. *Perhaps…* But this one did seem genuine and he had taken the time to write to her, and express his own regret at not keeping his promise. He had even included his company details so she could find him if she wanted. *Why do that if you just wanted to cut and run?* she mused. Besides Staff Sergeant Halliday had told her this family was of good stock and that she knew his younger brother quite well too. Halliday had assured her she wouldn't be disappointed. *So much for that 'eh Staff,* she thought to herself with a raise of her eyes.

"Bloody war," she said out loud now, and paused on the corner to light another cigarette, reminding herself how to get back to the camp on the outskirts of town. It was not a short walk. *Well the exercise will do you good Kellett,* she thought to herself, *"or kelleeeet I should say,"* impersonating the young boy and making herself laugh.

Rose stood leaning against the side of a patisserie shop wall, watching the people mill about their daily lives as she smoked, as if she needed to make a decision before she could set off. Despite the cheap cigarette fumes the smell of the cakes made her stomach rumble and she regretted the missed lunch even more.

"Alright Captain James Davison," she pronounced formally, "one more chance, and it better be good wine next time!" With that she stepped off the pavement to cross the potted road, oblivious to the mud that splashed up her left calf as she did, and settled into her quick stride once more.

*

At that moment on Mill farm Harold and Will were striding up the top field towards the Downs. They reached the slate steps in the high wall and went over the top together, and pushed on in silence towards the standing stones, their breath coming in hard blasts now that blew the steam from their lungs into the late afternoon air. They stopped at the stones and turned to view the farm, Sally jumping onto one of the smaller pieces of rock that she favoured which had broken away from the main group many years ago and now lay flat amongst the cobwebbed bracken. She sat here panting, waiting for an order, or the next movement from her master. Down below smoke billowed from the two chimneys on the main house and though the sun was yet to set, the lights were already on in the farm, candles burning steadily in the windows; and even up here the tree could be seen sparkling in the bay window of the sitting room in anticipation of the magic of the coming day.

It was Christmas Eve, 1915.

Fred always insisted the lights were on early as Christmas approached, and helped his mum light the candles every year, with some concern always on his mother's part. In truth Harold was just as proud of his electric tree lights, and stood admiring the distant window for a few moments, even though the detail was just a blurry glow in reality from way up here. They could both hear Fred shouting though, and for a moment Harold thought he caught the shadow of his youngest son skitter past one of the glowing windows.

This really is a beautiful spot, Will thought to himself, and after the lifeless hell of the trenches where dark mud and stagnant pools robbed man and nature of all colour, it seemed to him like a dream at times to be back. His dad handed him a small pack of chocolate now, and Will beamed in gratitude.

"I said there would be more for you when you returned Will, remember?" Will nodded, as he chewed and passed a piece back to his dad. "I never forget what I promise lad."

They sat in silence for a moment, perched on the ancient cold rock that had witnessed so many changes through the ages. The emotion was there between them, although neither of them voiced it. Somewhere across the town a whistle blew for full time in a game of football or rugby, a Christmas Eve fixture to try and raise spirits no doubt. Harold glanced at his son, staring away into the gathering gloom, and noticed him flinch at the sound.

"It's great to have you here Will," his dad went on trying to read his thoughts, "even if the manner in which you came home wasn't a happy one. We can't wait to see David either. Wonderful for them to have time off from training at Christmas."

"Yes it is," Will replied, coming back into the moment and ignoring the mention of his injury. "It will be great to see him again and catch up."

There was a rumble of thunder then to the south towards the sea, but there were no clouds anywhere and they both knew what the noise probably meant on this crisp clear winter's eve. Will rubbed at his chest automatically and imagined the scene, the smells and the sounds rushing back to him now...

...men running for cover as the evening barrage dropped in and their own guns replied; the ground shaking and the ceilings spitting earth, trembling ready to burst; the anxious looks and black humour amongst the men cowering in the dug-outs; and sometimes the screams and cries in the dark as a bomb found a victim...

"Your Mum's worried they'll send you back," his dad said, cutting into the nightmares that encircled Will in that moment.

"I know," Will replied, returning to the here and now. His dad was puffing on a cigarette he must have lit while his mind was elsewhere, amongst the dark shadows. "I might not have to though. Might not be a need next year," he lied unconvincingly. Harold could see through it at once, but simply said, "Let's hope so eh?"

Just then a Heron appeared on the lower fields flapping effortlessly along towards the far houses, despite its awkward size and shape. They watched it cruise above the houses for a moment before it dipped down out of sight.

"He'll be after Mrs Bennett's pond again no doubt. I told her to put a net on her prize fish. If she's ignored me then Christmas will come early for that one and he'll empty the lot."

Will popped the last piece of chocolate in his mouth and savoured the luxury, nodding to his dad as he did so. His chest pain eased as he closed his eyes to enjoy the melting moment even more. In that moment they both became aware of an engine noise, not on the roads below but above them, and they looked up for the source of the interruption, shielding their eyes against the dipping sun.

A double winged fighter plane came into view trailing the route the heron had flown moments before, but much higher and with far more noise and effort it seemed to Harold.

"One of ours lad?"

"Yes Dad. At least I certainly hope so," he added, but certain he could see the British circular markings on the side. As it came right over them Harold stood up and waved his cap a few times towards it.

"He can't see you Dad, he's much too high."

"That may be, but I like to cheer him on his way."

Will smiled looking at his dad's awe of this amazing piece of technology, and went over spontaneously and gave him a hug. Harold was momentarily thrown by this, but patted his son on the shoulder a couple of times, and said "Alright lad."

As they watched, the plane circled slowly round and came back behind them to their left before circling again, lower this time following its original path. As it came overhead once more they both waved now, Will shouting "Merry Christmas," enjoying the moment of togetherness that dispelled his previous torment. Amazingly the plane suddenly dipped its wings from side to side twice, a universal recognition sign. The pilot had clearly seen them and was saying "Hello" back. They cheered then and waved furiously some more, delighted by the experience.

As they watched the plane fly over Steyning, its engine fading into a distant hum, they became aware of more noise from below and looked to see Agnes and Fred shouting by the kitchen door. Sally responded with several barks, and Harold went to pat her as he strained his eyes down the fields.

"Easy girl," he said, stubbing out his cigarette and then taking a couple of steps forward towards the wall. Sally mirrored him, crouched low, her head moving back and forth between her master's hand and the noise. When the signals came she would be ready, and her body trembled with the possible excitement of work.

Will stood up too now from the stone he had been leaning against, his young eyes that had served him so well at the front, now homing in on the scene below. He could see his mum was practically jumping up and down on the spot, and Fred suddenly rushed forward towards something or someone that was hidden from them by the old barn on this side of the drive.

"Not seen her this excited since I asked her to marry me," Harold said to no one in particular, both of them temporarily transfixed by the scene. At that point a man appeared, his arm round Fred and walked forward to be enveloped by Agnes.

"David is home," Will said with a smile, and Harold looked round smiling too and said, "Best be off then."

But as his dad started forward Will noticed his mum had left the two boys and was walking forward, and then another man came into view, and now it was Will's turn to be excited.

"There's someone else there, look," he said, and Harold paused by the wall as Will joined him. Sally leapt up onto the top as effortlessly as you would stride over a front doorstep, and hesitated then, frustrated that they were not moving.

"Who is it?" said Harold, the light drawing down quickly now, making it impossible to make out the shapes below, but the shouts from his wife continued and he frowned.

"It's James. James is home," Will answered quietly, and Harold jumped now, his body jolted by the sudden emotion of the moment.

"James...?" he repeated, his voice trailing off, "but he's in France?" Will just shrugged, his face a broad smile.

"All my lads home," Harold muttered to himself, tears in his eyes, and then with a loud cry he shouted "James!" at the top of his voice and virtually vaulted the wall.

*

As he stumbled down the top field, Harold saw Sally in a fast trot alongside him and threw his arm forward. "Away girl to the house," and she went like a stone from a sling, barely visible in the high grass, across half the field before he had even turned back to look at Will

365

still propped on the wall top. "Come on Will, let's go," he called and strode forward downhill not waiting for a reply.

Will watched his dad go, and swung his legs over the wall. He could see the little group by the house were still all hugging together, and he nodded contentedly. Then the thunder called to him again from across the sea and for a moment he felt guilty that he was not there, with his friends, and he pondered on his decision to transfer to the Southdown battalions. His mind was a jumble of thoughts and emotions so much having happened since he left home, that he could scarcely make sense of it all. The pull to be with his family was very strong, which he felt now more than ever knowing they were all just a couple of fields away at this special time of year.

Whatever he said to his dad though, and despite his new training posting, he also knew that he had unfinished business in France and that wouldn't go away. His chest ached again, right on cue, and he held it automatically. He would never be able to explain it in a way they understood, he just knew that sooner or later he must return.

"Once more unto the breach 'eh Albert old friend," he murmured out loud with a sad smile.

Will stared down the field at his dad who was half running, half walking to stop himself tumbling forward but still trying to rush back to the house. Sally was leaping the second wall already close to the farm, way ahead now, but still glancing back in case she was needed elsewhere. His dad paused momentarily and his voice carried up the hillside to him.

"Hey slow coach. I thought you were famous for your speed? Come on Will! Race you!"

Like a gun going off, those words cut through all the gloom in an instant, triggering instincts learned years ago. With a shake of his head and a laugh Will launched off the wall in pursuit of his dad. He never could resist a challenge.

Acknowledgements

So many people and places have led me on my journey that as this is the first of a series of books, (one hopes), I should start at the beginning.

Sincere thanks therefore to English teacher, David Margett at Thirsk school who encouraged me to write more, not less. Also the extremely talented Anne Carrick and Graham Finch at Ripon Grammar school who took that premise and gave it a hearty shove, through English and Drama. Demetrius came through in the end and I did indeed take *the path less trod* (albeit via a very arduous and circuitous route).

And on the subject of RGS (and never start a sentence with 'and'), thanks to a current sixth former there- Natasha Lovel- who had a YA view on the early chapters to guide me, when they were very raw, and even put her phone down for a short while which I took as a huge compliment. I hope the finished product does the same. To her parents also, who are dear friends and supporters. *Now give me that horizon.*

For history who can look further than the late, great and supremely funny Dr Marcus Merriman at Lancaster University, who taught me to look *beneath the facts and behind the lines.* I hope they allow cigars in heaven. Lancaster remains a very special place.

To numerous contributors for this particular work, a lot of which may yet be used on subsequent novels, who have all given kindly of their time, knowledge and permissions, especially the following: The National Farmers Union; the Women's Institute of Sussex; the Royal Sussex Regiment Association (in relation to the Southdown Battalions particularly); Simon Jones, Battlefield guide and WW1 expert author; Andrew Mackay, History teacher and author of the excellent Young Lions series; Steyning Football Club; the brilliant staff at Steyning Museum; the Reverend Mark Heather of St Andrew and St Cuthman church in Steyning (got there in the end Mark); The very talented editor and writer Ros Whistance, and the Star Inn, Steyning.

The support: My unbelievable design team of Lilly Louise Allen and Kumiko Chesworth, more of whom are found elsewhere in this book, and Professor Martin and Dr Karen Gill, for their patience, loyalty, humour and above all belief in the magic.

But for magic there is no other place to go than the inspirational, heart-warming and life changing writing centre of Moniack Mhor in Scotland. Half of me wants to keep it a secret and half to shout it from the Glens and Mòrs. To my brilliant tutors Cynthia Rogerson and Ross Raisin, who taught me emotion over rules; and for the class of 05/17 - thankyou is not enough. The group that have nagged, cajoled, edited and smiled at me along this road – I (we) did it. To which I should add my recent tutors at MM of Mavis Cheek and Helen Lederer, who also took time to review this work, despite it being a comedy course, (or perhaps because of it!); and for the very humbling and gracious feedback once more. *For we have seen the chimes at midnight.*

Last but not least – my family. For a writer I find it hard to express in words the emotions I hold for them, for their unswerving love and support, not just in this book, but in the journey to get here and all that that entailed, in which my wife had the starring role. Reading to my children has given me much joy over the years, and I hope that my books can bring that joy to other families too. JS

Lilly Louise Allen is a Watercolour Artist and Illustrator based on the Isle of Wight in England.

Lilly specialises in editorial food illustration and art for food establishments and events. However her portfolio extends far beyond these interests and she is a highly talented artist that I have been fortunate enough to work with on my novel. She has captured my imagination through her work in a brilliantly emotive design.

Kumiko Chesworth is a Japanese designer with a background in film, living in the UK. She has set up Amadori design with a focus on designing things which are simple and beautiful with a little bit of fun.

She is held in high esteem amongst her peers and it is a privilege to have her support me with this book.